Praise

THE HUNGRY GHOSTS

Finalist for the Governor General's Literary Award

"Selvadurai's work reminds me that the contemporary novel doesn't necessarily have to resort to thrills or highjinks in order to find its usefulness. Here, it unforgettably explores the interplay between individual intention and the tragedy of a nation's history." —*The Globe and Mail*

"This young romance, like something out of an Edmund White novel, is beautifully and powerfully imagined. . . . Calling to mind the work of Indo-American writer Jhumpa Lahiri, Selvadurai does an excellent job contrasting Sri Lanka and Canada." —*Winnipeg Free Press*

"*The Hungry Ghosts* is an accomplished, resonant novel. The solid characters and diverse events, the Sri Lankan and Torontonian flavours, and the poetic conclusion will leave readers feeling as though they've lived a thousand and one stories, and lacked for little." —*Quill & Quire*

"Selvadurai deftly navigates his home country's complex politics and evokes its culture and terrain in ways that dazzle all the senses. And Shivan's grandmother is a superb character—self-serving yet sympathetic. . . . It's taken the Sri Lankan-Canadian author ten years to deliver this, his fourth novel. It was definitely worth the wait." —*NOW Magazine* (NNNN)

"From his debut novel, 1994's *Funny Boy*, to his latest, *The Hungry Ghosts*, he's meditated on his birth country's fraught mélange of history, politics and religion while developing a style that's anything but bare bones and laconic." —*National Post*

"*The Hungry Ghosts* [is] a haunting story of longing, family ties and forgiveness. . . . honest, touching work." —*Calgary Herald*

"[The grandmother is] a character to rival Dickens' Miss Havisham. . . . Selvadurai has wonderful talent." —*Toronto Star*

"An epic novel . . . [that] adds a new maturity of tone, scope, language and character." —*The Gazette* (Montreal)

"This story feels epic for the ground it covers, temporally and geographically, and also for revealing how legacies are handed down through generations." —*Maclean's*

"Triumphant and heartbreaking. . . . As the book closes, a new truth is revealed: we are still hungry for more Selvadurai." —*Xtra!*

"*The Hungry Ghosts* is lustrous in its depictions of duty, dislocation, and the ways love and relationships haunt the human heart." —*Georgia Straight*

"*The Hungry Ghosts* is Shyam Selvadurai's fourth novel, and almost certainly his best. The themes are familiar, from the personal strife caused by the narrator's sexuality and ethnicity, to the political backdrop of Sri Lanka's civil war, but the whole narrative is handled with an accomplishment and quiet authority that marks a real step up in Selvadurai's prose. . . . [The book] feels like an author's coming of age, and a work of considerable stature." —*The Republic Square*

""Unflinchingly insightful, Shyam Selvadurai's new novel evokes the clashing manifestations of human desire and longing in two continents." —Pankaj Mishra, author of *From the Ruins of Empire*

"Shyam Selvadurai's long-awaited novel is an unsettling and moving account of a family—and a nation—at war with their own selves." —Tan Twan Eng, author of *The Garden of Evening Mists*, winner of the Man Asian Literary Prize

"A sprawling yet intimate story of identity and loss, *The Hungry Ghosts* is full of the love and terror of families, and of the difficulties of finding one's place in the world—a ravishing portrait not just of one man but an entire country's search for a resting place." —Tash Aw, author of *The Harmony Silk Factory*, winner of the Whitbread Book Award

THE
HUNGRY GHOSTS

ALSO BY SHYAM SELVADURAI

ADULT FICTION

Funny Boy

Cinnamon Gardens

Story-Wallah! A Celebration of South Asian Fiction (editor)

FICTION FOR YOUNG ADULTS

Swimming in the Monsoon Sea

THE HUNGRY GHOSTS

SHYAM SELVADURAI

ANCHOR CANADA

Anchor Canada edition published 2014

ISBN 978-0-385-67068-5

Cover image: Richard Bryan/Arcaid/Corbis

Printed and bound in the USA

Published in Canada by Anchor Canada,
a division of Random House of Canada Limited
a Penguin Random House Company

www.randomhouse.ca

10 9 8 7 6 5 4 3 2 1

For Andrew,
who is, to me, “like rain soaking a parched land.”

"Destiny is fixed; all doors open onto the future."

Kalidasa, *Shakuntala*

PART ONE

I

On the day I turned thirteen, my grandmother, with whom my mother, my sister and I lived by then, invited me to go for a drive after school. I came into the living room after changing out of my uniform, to find my grandmother standing by the grand piano, frowning with impatience, as our ayah, Rosalind, knelt before her and dabbed prickly-heat powder in the crooks of her mistress's arms, careful not to leave white marks. When my grandmother saw me, a sparkle of anticipation lit her eyes. Then her frown deepened to mask this delight.

As we got into the old Bentley, I felt my own anticipation, which had been building through the school day, reach a new peak. Her silence about my present made me certain that the gift was going to be generous—and I had already dropped many hints about an imported Raleigh ten-speed bicycle. I noticed she did not direct our driver, Soma, as she usually did. He already knew the destination, which was certainly the Fort, where the cycle shops were.

That drive through Colombo comes back to me now, the image of my grandmother as she was then, chin jutted as if holding her own in an argument, back settled confidently into the base of her spine, hands clasped around a lace-edged handkerchief with which she would periodically dab her forehead and chin, releasing a swell of Yardley's English Lavender perfume. She wore a butter-yellow cotton sari, its pleats starched to a knife edge, a string of pearls around her neck, forearms garrotted in gold bangles. Unlike most women in Sri Lanka, she did not carry a handbag but toted around a small purse woven out of coconut fronds. My grandmother was a woman who had others carry things for her.

I can picture myself, too, on that ride, thin arms and bony wrists brushed with newly sprouted fuzz, hair cut and styled in the latest feathered fashion, dressed in imported jeans and red short-sleeved polo shirt, my neck straining forward, clavicles shimmering with the effort, nostrils daintily flared as if to some subtle danger, my long eyelashes casting a shadow over my high cheekbones—well aware of the advantages my beauty brought me with my grandmother.

As we went through the city that day, however, the car did not veer towards the Fort but instead took another route, and we were soon in the wealthy neighbourhood of Colombo 7. I turned to my grandmother, but she would not meet my gaze. After a few detours down elegantly treed streets, the car came to a stop in front of a large two-storey house, much grander than the one we lived in and set in a vast garden. "Come, Puthey," my grandmother said, referring to me by the affectionate extension of *putha*, "son," that she always used with me.

I opened the door, but did not get out. She nudged me out, then led me up to the gate, her hand on my shoulder, and when we were before it, she waved at the house with its generous pillared verandah at the end of the long driveway. "This is yours, Puthey."

She smiled at my astonishment. "When I die, this house and all my other properties will come to you." She giggled, delighted to have caught me out in this way, but confident I would be pleased with the largesse of the inheritance she intended to give me. She told me that an American couple who worked in the embassy were renting it at a very high cost. "Of course, I'm no fool." She tossed her head. "They don't pay me in our useless rupees. That would be like pouring honey into a pot of feces," she added, using one of those pithy sayings that enlivened the Sinhala language. "No, these suddhas pay their rent in dollars, into a secret account I have in England." She squeezed my elbow, her breath like mildewed bread as she leaned in to me. "You must never tell anyone that, Puthey, not even your mother."

My grandmother began to point out various features of the house, her tone suddenly businesslike, looking keenly at me to make sure I was paying attention. I nodded, but my mind was already in recoil.

I knew my grandmother owned numerous rental properties, as she was a woman of great restlessness, frequently going out to inspect her houses, get repairs done, evict tenants or see her lawyer about deeds and land transfers. But this was the first time I was seeing them. She was showing me the future mapped out for me.

Our next stop was her "Pettah property." As we drove towards that older part of the city, I glanced occasionally at my grandmother, wanting to protest, to beg for release from this future. My apprehension only grew when we arrived.

The walls of this dilapidated row house were smudged with black and green fungus, its roof patched with rusted takaran where the red tiles had fallen off. The wooden verandah sagged, and its pillars were cracked and leaned precariously.

My grandmother strode up the front steps, across the creaking floor boards of the verandah and rapped on the front door.

A child called out from the other side, asking who it was. "Tell your mother the Ariyasinghe Nona is here," my grandmother replied.

After a moment the child said, "Amma is not home."

My grandmother made a contemptuous sound. "Of course she is. Where would she go, ah? Siriyawathy, let us in."

Bolts grated back and the door opened. A woman stood before us, eyes bewildered. Strands of her uncombed hair had sprung into a halo about her face and the red flowers on her dress had bled into the white background. The child, peeking from behind his mother's legs, was dressed only in a pair of shorts, belly distended from malnutrition.

"What is this, hiding-hiding from me, ah?" my grandmother said, grimly amused.

She pushed past the woman and led me down a narrow corridor, rooms on either side like dark groves on a forested path, paint peeling like bark, floors rutted with cracks. All the while, my grandmother complained about how much more money she could make if she rented this property as a chummery for factory girls, which she was thinking of doing. When we finally left, she called out, before shutting the door, "Siriyawathy, you can come out of hiding now," then gave me another bemused smile.

As we went down the verandah steps, she took my arm for support. "That Siriyawathy must have done something very bad in her past life, Puthey. Otherwise, look at her, recently widowed with a small child to raise. It's a terrible thing to be living out the effects of a bad karma, nah?" She sighed and shook her head. "But what is to be done? No one can escape their past actions, not even our Lord Buddha could."

That day, my grandmother took me around all her properties in Colombo. There were fifteen, and they varied from the grand house in Colombo 7, to middle-class bungalows, to row houses that were barely more than slum dwellings.

When we finally arrived back at our house, I left the car, not holding the door open for my grandmother, and hurried up the front steps. I went to my room and sat on the bed, staring at my hands.

After a moment, my grandmother stood in the doorway, eyes wide with concern. "What is it, Puthey, are you unwell?"

"I . . . I'm just tired, Aacho. You know, it's this heat. It is so hot now, and the walk home from school is difficult in this heat, trudging through the dry pola grounds is awful. And it is frightening, too, because there are stray dogs, and some of them I am sure are rabid, and—"

My grandmother let out a peal of girlish laughter. She came over to me and tugged teasingly on my earlobe. "This boy, he is so sweet and thoughtful, can't even ask for something directly, ah. You were in such a big-big hurry to come to your room, didn't you see what was right there, leaning up against the side of the verandah?"

I pulled back from her touch, and she nodded to confirm my guess. I leapt up and rushed out to see my new Raleigh bicycle. My grandmother followed, saying to Rosalind, who was waiting for her, "This boy is so funny, but so sweet, too."

My birthday gift was the exact red and purple colour I had hinted at, and my grandmother had been even more generous than expected. The bicycle was outfitted with an imported headlamp and pedals that glowed in the dark. I cried out in delight and embraced my grandmother. She patted my arms in a pleased, pushing-away gesture. Knowing just how to make her melt, I knelt and touched her feet in the traditional gesture of veneration. "Ah-ah, Puthey, no need for that, no need," she murmured in the ritual protest an elder made at such an action, then lifted me by the shoulders.

A few days after that visit to her properties, my grandmother summoned me to the front verandah. I found her seated in a planter's chair, feet up on the wooden planks that swivelled out from under the arms. Her cousin, Sunil Maama, who always smelt of mothballs and dusty books, was in attendance, seated in a lower cane chair. He was our family lawyer, a gentle man with a sheepish smile and a nervous habit of pushing greying strands of hair over the bald spot on his head. He was not a great lawyer, but was competent enough, and my grandmother stuck with him because he was family and because she could bend him to her dictates.

He was passing her documents, which she examined, holding them some distance away, as she was too vain to wear glasses except in the privacy of her bedroom. She signalled me to come and sit at her right on a stool. Sunil Maama gave me an abashed smile, eyes blinking like some night creature caught in daylight.

My grandmother rustled a document and held it out to Sunil Maama. "Tell them I will not pay more than fifty thousand for the entire property." The "them" she used was the derogatory "*oong*."

Sunil Maama pressed his hands together. "But Daya, these people are fallen on hard times, nah? We should not exploit them."

"Sunil, don't talk nonsense. Are they going to get a better price than mine?"

He looked down, stroking his battered briefcase.

"No," she continued. "And at least I am honest. I will actually pay them the money up front. Some mudalali will promise-promise and only give half, then take possession and never pay the rest." She flicked the paper at him. "They are better off with me and they know it. Why, these people are ridiculous in their expectations, like farmers who do not cultivate their fields but then weep because they have no harvest."

He took the paper and muttered, "It's bad karma, very bad karma."

My grandmother gave me a wry look, as if we were in cahoots against this weak, pathetic person.

"Now, on to the Pettah property." My grandmother waited as Rosalind brought out two cups of tea and some Marie biscuits and put the tray on a table in front of her. She helped herself, but did not offer Sunil Maama anything, though he was eyeing the tea. Her revenge for his comment about karma. "The rent is three months in arrears. We have to evict them."

Again Sunil Maama looked pained.

"What else do you want me to do? How can I keep losing-losing money?" She turned to me. "I have been more generous with that Siriyawathy than the elephant Paraliya was with our Lord Buddha."

"But give her a little time more, Daya. After all, she has been your tenant for years now, and the rent is only in arrears because of the husband's death, nah? I have talked to Siriyawathy, and she tells me her brother is coming from the village with a cousin to stay. They will help her meet the rent when they get jobs. She might even take in a university student."

"Look at her, will you!" My grandmother slammed her cup on the saucer, and tea slopped over the edge. "Now she is trying to run a rental business in my property, making it into a chummery and no doubt keeping a tidy-tidy profit." She shook her head and fiercely nibbled on a biscuit. "That's it. She must go. Today itself, I must deal with this."

Sunil Maama gave her careful look. "You know the laws, Daya, you cannot easily evict a tenant in this country. It will take a decade at least in court."

"Court? The laws?" My grandmother appealed to the skies. "Whoever said anything about going to court?"

"Then what?"

But I saw that Sunil Maama already knew what my grandmother had in mind.

She snorted. "The courts and the law are for bloody fools who want to pay out their fortunes to that band of blood-sucking leeches known as lawyers."

She gestured to the remaining cup of tea, which was now quite cold. "Come," she said to Sunil Maama, "drink, drink."

Later that afternoon, when I was in bed reading, my grandmother pushed her way through the curtained doorway. "Come, Puthey, we must go somewhere." She straightened her sari palu, then bustled out. When we were in the car, she ordered the driver to take us to Kotahena.

Kotahena abutted the Colombo harbour and was the uglier, mundane side that all port cities have beyond the more scenic areas. The road that took us to Kotahena passed alongside the harbour, but its dirty waters were blocked from our view by unpainted, crumbling buildings, jetties and massive cargo containers. There was a smell of tar and lorry grease in the air. Once our car left the main road and turned down one of the narrow side streets, we were in a slum of shacks that were like stalls in some grotesque carnival, constructed from different hued bricks, cement block and billboards for things like Marmite, Kandos chocolates and Milo. From these rust-flecked signboards, smug middle-class parents and their plump children in starched white school uniforms beamed at us. An open sewer, green with algae, bubbled along under the raised front steps of the houses. My grandmother's sari rustled like dry grass as she shifted in her seat. She darted a glance at me, then frowned out the window.

We made our way through a sharply winding ribbon of a road, so narrow I could have reached out and touched the dwellings on either side. Finally the car came to a stop in front of a well-kept brick bungalow, set back from the street. In the centre of the cemented front garden was a mottled pink marble fountain, plastic flamingos and penguins standing around it like guests at a cocktail party. The bungalow's windows had heavy bars across them, and the front door was secured by an iron grille with a design of strangled vines.

My grandmother ordered our driver to blare his horn. A woman stuck her head out of the window. She nodded, smiled, and soon a man rushed out of the house, buttoning up his orange paisley nylon shirt as he hurried down to the gate, his green polyester trousers flapping to the slap-slap of his rubber slippers.

When he got to the car, he leaned in at the window. "Ah, nona, you bless us with a visit."

Up close, I could see that his nose was pitted with acne scars. A folded line of flesh down his right cheek gave that side of his face a sucked-in, disapproving look, which contrasted oddly with his merry expression.

"How is the business, Chandralal?"

"Thanks to your generosity, doing very well, nona."

"I'm always pleased to hear that, Chandralal. I know how to back a good man."

"I would be nothing without your patronage, nona."

"Chandralal, I want you to meet my grandson."

He had of course seen me, but now that the introduction was made his face lit up as if he had just noticed I was there. "Why, nona, he looks just like you."

"No, no, he is much better looking. But really, you think he does look like me? I suppose people say he has my forehead."

"I would be honoured if you both came into my home and had a cup of tea. My wife and daughters would be delighted."

My grandmother's silence was eloquent. She opened her purse, drew out a piece of paper as if it were soiled and handed it to him. "Something I need taken care of."

"You don't have to say another word, nona."

My grandmother counted out a number of fifty-rupee bills and handed the notes to him with the prim smile of a society hostess proffering refreshments. "I gave you a little extra for doing it so promptly. After all," she smiled coquettishly, "you're becoming a big mudalali and everything. Soon I won't be able to afford you."

He blushed as he counted the money, his lips moving as he flipped through the notes. When he was done, he gave her a boyish grin. "Thank you, nona."

I had been observing their interaction and the exchange of money, unsure what it was all about. As the car pulled away, my grandmother, aware of my unasked questions, said, "Chandralal is a good man. He works hard to better himself, unlike a lot of our people, who sit in the shade of trees and hope rice will fall from heaven. Yes-yes, he is a good man. Always remember that, Puthey. You can depend on Chandralal. He will always be ready to help you."

And just from the way she said this, I finally understood. Our eyes met. My grandmother sighed, fiddled around in her purse, drew out a scented handkerchief and mopped her face. "This heat, when will it let up? Is the monsoon never to arrive?"

I leaned back against the leather seat, the image of Siriyawathy with me, her bewildered eyes in their deep sockets, her son's distended belly. Then there was Chandralal, with that knife scar on his face.

And yet I was not truly surprised at what my grandmother had just set in motion. For by now I knew her well, and this latest action of hers, though more extreme, was like others I had witnessed in the past.

The next day, after I had returned from school and eaten lunch, my grandmother invited me to come out again with her. I did not want to go, but I could not resist her.

When we arrived at the Pettah property, Chandralal was waiting astride his scooter, back erect, arms extended to clutch the handlebars as if he were riding a horse. Clustered around him were three men in sarongs, their naked upper bodies brawny and matted with hair, their eyes drug-reddened. As my grandmother got out of the car, Chandralal grinned and saluted, index finger tipping the middle of his forehead. He hopped off his motorcycle and with a bowing gesture ushered us towards the house, grinning like a boy at a cricket match. Furniture was piled in one corner of the verandah, the cracked-open arms and legs revealing the whiteness of the wood under the dark stain, like bone jutting through flesh. The door had been kicked in, a starburst of splinters around the lock. Chandralal had secured it again with a latch and a large padlock. He presented the key to my grandmother gravely.

The house was bare, yet there were remnants of the life that had been lived here, and as we went from room to room, my grandmother complaining about all the supposed damage Siriyawathy and her family had done, I noticed a few broken toys that had belonged to the son, a woman's comb lying on the bathroom sink, its middle teeth missing. Later I saw, on the living room floor, the shattered photograph of a man who must have been Siriyawathy's dead husband, judging from the faded garland of flowers around the frame.

My grandmother stepped over the photograph as if she had not even noticed it, and I understood that she was so confident of her dominance she did not fear my judgment. Yet she had miscalculated her power over me. For that was the moment, as I now recall it, when my betrayal of her began.

Tonight, those years of childhood and adolescence with my grandmother are even more on my mind than usual. For tomorrow my mother and I will take a plane to Sri Lanka, then bring my ailing grandmother back here to Toronto; and the life we knew there, the life that has haunted and misshaped us all, will come to a close.

This finished part of the basement, where I stand looking out at the back garden through the barred window, used to be my bedroom before I moved out of my mother's home to Vancouver. There have been great changes since I lived here, seven years ago. Gone are the mirrored squares pasted to the far wall—remnants of the previous owner's bar. Some of the squares were missing, and when I used to get dressed before them, I would see myself in fragments. Gone, too, is my box-spring mattress on the floor and the scratchy, synthetic brown-and-white comforter I sweated under so many nights. In its place is a futon covered in a purple duvet with a pattern of white stars and quarter moons; gone, also, is my rickety table teetering with university textbooks and papers half written. A second-hand sofa with a nice design of lavender flowers has replaced the two tub chairs left by the previous owner (mossy-green monstrosities pocked with cigarette burns). But the biggest change is the odour of the basement. When I lived here, the lime-green carpet would get wet at a certain place whenever the washing machine was on, due to faulty plumbing. Now, grey and white flecked industrial carpeting stretches tight from wall to wall, neatly cut and hammered into place at the baseboards. The smell in the room is no longer musty and waterlogged, but parched, like dust.

The only item left from my previous life here is the chest of drawers, still full of my old clothes from the mid-1980s, hopelessly out of fashion now, a decade later.

When my mother led me down here earlier today and I had surveyed all the changes, I said, teasing her, "I see that your friend David has been very busy with his toolbox fixing things up for you." My mother is shy about this man in her life. Although they have been together for six years, she still refers to him as her friend.

"David?" my mother replied, face scrunched with mock mystification. "Why would I need David to do this? After all, aren't I my mother's daughter?" Then she added in a good imitation of my grandmother, switching to the Sinhala my grandmother always spoke, "I will not let any mason-baas or carpenter-karaya take advantage of me. No, no, I am one step ahead of all those jackals."

I nodded, lips pressed together in amusement. But then a silence came between us and my mother went to look with great interest at a book on the shelf.

Later, before she left to spend the night at David's, my mother insisted on dishing out the various curries she had bought me at the local Sri Lankan takeout. She rushed back and forth from the kitchen to the dining table, thrusting the plate at me to confirm there was enough of each dish before she put it in the microwave, saying, "I hardly know what you eat anymore, what your likes and dislikes are." Even though the meal came with rice, she made some more, saying nothing tasted as bland as reheated rice. Once she had put the plate in front of me, she brought down a makeup case from her bedroom and proceeded to do her face in the powder room mirror, an eccentricity she justifies by saying it has the best light. As she put her makeup on, she watched me in the mirror and I could feel the weight of what she wanted to discuss.

When she was done, she came out of the powder room and declared petulantly, as she had many times in the last hour, "Why on earth doesn't your sister call us? I can't stay around forever. Surely to goodness, she must be out of her classes by now?"

"She'll call," I murmured. "You know Renu, she probably got involved in some discussion with her students, or in helping one of them with their essay."

Usually, comments like this make my mother smile at the thought of her fierce scholarship-winning daughter, who has just completed her Ph.D. at Cornell. But this time she did not appear to hear me and went to glance out of the back patio doors as if expecting someone.

"And yes," she began, as if we were already in the middle of a conversation, "this is a depressing time for us to visit Sri Lanka, it really is."

I nodded in agreement. The three-month-old ceasefire between the new government and the separatist Tamil Tigers had just collapsed, with the Tigers bombing two Sri Lankan navy ships and plunging the country back into the brutal civil war that had been raging for the past twelve years between the Sinhalese majority and Tamil minority.

"It's all so sad, so depressing, I must say," my mother continued. "We all had such hope for our beloved Sri Lanka."

I too had shared her hopes. The new president, Chandrika Kumaratunga, had come into power only a few months ago on a platform of peace, promising the country a new beginning. Sri Lanka had been through what was probably the most savagely violent time in its recent history, with many of the leaders, and the movements, vanishing as if they had not existed. Even the new president had lost her husband to this violence, a much-beloved actor turned politician. She shared his belief in granting the Tamil minority some self-determination, a belief for which he had been assassinated by Sinhala extremists. People trusted she would heal the wounds of war and usher in a new era for Sri Lanka. They had given her an overwhelming majority to do so, and even the Tigers canvassed for her in the Tamil areas. But, last week, the Tigers had declared the president was not really serious about peace talks and commenced hostilities, forcing her into a military offensive which she was now calling a "war for peace."

The true bleakness, for me, was seeing a leader with an enlightened vision trapped in a vortex of hatred that was so all-consuming she had no choice but to participate in it. Her situation and the recommencement of the war in this new phase reminded me of those Buddhist tales my grandmother often told, in which a karmic crime travels with characters into their next reincarnations, the same enmities playing out in a new phase, the characters helpless to escape the fruits of their karma.

"Poor Sri Lanka." My mother sighed and twitched the sheers closed.

"I don't know when we will ever see peace," I replied to provoke further discussion, wanting to forestall whatever she was preparing herself to say about me or my life.

"I don't expect I will see peace in my lifetime." My mother now fussed with ornaments on the wall unit, still not meeting my eyes.

"I hope one side wins and ends all this, for the sake of the poor people caught in between," I declared.

My mother did not appear to hear me, examining a little ceramic teapot shaped like an elephant as if it were not hers. Then she put it down abruptly and came to stand across the table from me. "Shivan, I'm afraid for you." She leaned in, palms pressed on the table, near tears. "Your expectations are too high. This trip will not fix your problems." She nodded at my surprise, "Yes-yes, I know about your problems in Vancouver. Your sister finally broke her silence and told me everything." She raised her eyebrows to communicate how concerned Renu must have been about this trip to reveal my secrets. "Then, there is this . . . this saying goodbye to our old house and being back in Colombo, where, you know, all that happened. It will be too much, Shivan. You have been away too long. Seven years since you were last there, for goodness sake."

"You're wrong. I am ready. It will be good for me to do it. I have to make this trip, Amma," I pleaded, as if she had the power to deny me. "Coming to terms with what happened will help me sort out my life."

"I don't know, I don't know. I should have said something before you left Vancouver. But you're so hard to talk to sometimes, son. Everything always ends up in a fight with you and I don't have the energy to take you on, what with preparing for Aachi's arrival."

Before I could respond, the phone rang and my mother rushed into the kitchen. It was my sister, and my mother spoke to her for a while in a low voice before she signalled me to take the phone.

"Ah-ah, what's this I hear?" Renu said trying to affect amusement. "Amma is worried you might fall apart on the trip."

"Yes," I said acidly, "I plan to go stark raving mad, tear off my clothes and run around Colombo. You can come and visit me in Angoda when they put me in there with all the other lunatics."

"But Shivan, seriously, I am worried that Sri Lanka will disappoint. You have such high hopes pinned on this visit."

"And you choose to tell me this now? All the time I was in Vancouver, you didn't mention it. Instead you go behind my back and talk to Amma. I will never trust you again."

"I'm sorry but I was so worried and—"

"Well, what do you want me to do about it now?" I exclaimed. "Why have you both held off on this until I am here?"

My sister was silent and my mother watched me with a grimace of pity, sensing the fear behind my anger.

"Shivan, I'm really sorry I didn't say any of this before," Renu replied at last.

I handed the phone to my mother.

After the call, she rushed around getting her coat and scarf, checking her hair in the mirror, wretched with failure. To hide my fear I glowered at her. We kissed goodbye tersely, not meeting each other's eyes.

"Remember, your task," she said, pressing my arm.

I nodded.

My mother is having problems with cockroaches. In her absence, David will get the house fumigated. All foodstuffs in the kitchen have to be thrown out before we leave, the fridge emptied of anything that will rot.

Here in Toronto, the melting April snow brings a sense of the world wrung out and parched. It is impossible to believe that, across the country in Vancouver, daffodils bloom and the grass is a summer green. I long for the moist greenness of the city, the jewelled moss on rocks, like gems on a dowager's gnarled hand. And I am filled with longing for Michael with his tousle of black curls, his way of standing, hands jammed in pockets, neck tilted as if looking over a fence, smiling like he is watching children at play. I long for the metallic smell of him in bed; miss, with a tightening at the base of my throat, our apartment on Harwood Street, its minuscule balcony perched like a sparrow's nest on a corner of the twentieth floor, our morning coffee at the little table there, gazing at the familiar view of English Bay and Stanley Park, the ships ambling along the horizon. I miss our bus ride to the university where we both work, miss how, as the bus crosses the Burrard Bridge, the sea glitters below, sunlight trembling on passing sails.

That life feels like a distant thing, as if it was not just last night that Michael and I, after dinner, walked down to English Bay as we used to in the early days of our romance. Finding a log to shelter us from the wind, we huddled together under a blanket and sipped brandy from a flask as we talked about our day, Michael chuckling at my sarcastic comments on the people passing by.

Yet after a while, a silence fell between us, and in the silence I knew we could both feel all the goodness draining away, as it so often does these days. Michael took a swig of brandy and offered the flask to me, but I shook my head and stared out at the sea.

"You won't leave me, promise me you won't, Michael. I know it's ridiculous but I am so worried, so frightened about this."

Our knees were tight together and he ran his hand up and down my shin. "No, I will not leave you," he said, weary from being asked the same thing so many times in the past weeks.

"You say that, you say that," I said, close to tears, "but I feel you will leave me. I deserve to be left."

"Shivan," he said, and forced me to take a long gulp of the brandy.

I glance at my watch and count back the hours. It is 5 p.m. in Vancouver. Michael has just finished work and will be heading across campus to get the bus into town. He will soon return to our apartment, stopping off at Safeway on Davie Street to get groceries. His kitten, Miss Murasaki, will be waiting for him, paw fluttering under the door, sensing from his footsteps down the corridor that it is him. Then, as he prepares dinner, he will be in the quiet centre of himself after a day of department politics and negotiating the entitlement of students and professors. The sounds and smells from the other apartments around him—the scrape of a chair or hum of a vacuum cleaner above, the muted conversation of the French couple next door, the tight vehemence of their language, as if bickering in public, the dog in the apartment on the other side who greets his mistress with a mournful baying—all this will be a cocoon around Michael. And I feel that he will be relieved I am not there by his side, assisting with dinner; relieved that he is finally at peace.

I stride over to my chest of drawers, open the top one and stare at the clothes within. A faint smell of the old basement damp rises up. After a moment's hesitation, I fling garishly patterned sweaters, frayed shorts, acid-washed jeans, worn underpants and skinned-at-the-heel socks onto the floor, emptying drawer after drawer. When I am done, I go into the unfinished part of the basement, take two garbage bags from the shelf above the washing machine and gather the clothes into them.

I stumble upstairs, leave the bags by the front door, then pour myself a quarter-glass of Scotch from the kitchen cupboard and drift into the living room. On the wall unit, there is a framed photograph of my grandmother. It was taken on the front verandah of our old house, and my grandmother is seated in a wheelchair with my mother standing behind her. I hold the photograph closer to the light and peer at my grandmother's useless left hand, twisted upwards in her lap like a taxidermied claw, her mouth puckered, the skin on her left cheek stretched. All this is the result of a series of strokes, each one taking a bit of her away. The doctors tell us that she will continue to have these strokes, losing various mental faculties and physical abilities, until finally a great stroke takes her from us.

The furnace has stopped, and the muted roar of air through the vents slows to a ticking. The ceiling creaks and shifts, as if someone is moving around on the second floor. Right above me is the room prepared for my grandmother. Earlier, when my mother took me around the house to show me all the improvements, she slipped ahead and shut the door to that room, as if worried what the sight of its new furniture might do to me. I have not been in there yet.

I go into the kitchen and pour myself more Scotch, taking a swift gulp. The rush of heat in my blood has little effect on my mind. I take a second swift gulp, emptying the glass.

2

My grandmother, despite her sternness, had a girlish love of Buddhist stories and would clap her hands and chortle when she heard a good one. She also enjoyed narrating them, her face radiant with intrigue like a traditional storyteller, voice hushed with delight. When I was a child, she would always tell me one of her stories at the end of the long afternoon vigil I kept in her bedroom while she slept. It was a reward for having done my homework quietly, sitting on the coconut-frond mat by her bed. She would wait until our ayah, Rosalind, had brought her cup of tea. "Ah-ah, now Rosalind," she would declare to this woman who had been her servant and companion since childhood, "now what is that tale I love so?" And before Rosalind could respond, my grandmother would add, "Yes-yes," then name a particular story.

"So it is," the old ayah would say with a flicker of a wink at me, "it surely is one of your favourites, Loku Nona. Now, how does it go?" Which was my grandmother's cue to launch into the tale.

Sometimes she told a story she'd narrated before, but brought a different angle to it, filling out a scene until it became a subplot, giving a minor character greater presence on stage, or sometimes simply retelling a scene as the full tale—these variations so numerous, I am not sure today what the original story is, and where my own interpretation veers off from hers.

Tonight I am thinking of one story in particular, a story where a narrative moment became its own tale, which she named "The Thieving Hawk." In it, a hawk steals a piece of meat from a butcher and rises triumphant into the sky. Soon, however, other hawks surround him and try to pluck the meat away, tearing at the thieving hawk with their beaks and claws. He tries to escape them, refusing to give the meat up, even though he is bloodied and wounded. Finally, however, his agony is unbearable and he lets the meat fall. The other birds swoop down to grab it, tearing and clawing at each other now. The thieving hawk flaps away, injured and starving, but free of the thing that caused him such suffering.

That is how I think of my mother in the days after my father died, sprawled out in a plastic chair, head tilted towards the morning sun, exhausted but at peace, her waist-length hair, which she had let down over the chair back, flickering with sunlight. When my sister and I spoke to her, she was mild and gentle, touching our faces and arms with her fingertips, no longer cruel and shooing us away. She began to do things she had never done before, such as bathe us, feed us with her own hands and read to us in the evenings. In the middle of the night, I would often feel my bed give as she climbed in and held me close, gently pressing up and down my limbs, as if checking for fractures. Then she would get up to repeat this affection with my sister.

When my father was alive, there was hardly a night my sister and I fell asleep without the sound of our parents' fierce whispering in the living room or outside on the verandah, my mother crying, my father pleading. Sometimes, my mother would not be able to contain her anger and she would yell at my father, calling him a ponnaya, a faggot, railing at his weakness and incompetence.

When they first met, my father had been a junior executive in a prestigious shipping company, but soon his ineptitude began to affect the company, and when he lost a major Japanese client he was fired. Over the next few years, my parents, my sister and I moved continually as my father's bungling cost him job after job. With each sacking, he fell to a lower level of employment, until finally, by the time I was six years old and my sister eight, he had sunk to manager of a little guest house in Wellawaya. Its hospital-green walls were dusty with collapsed cobwebs and the furniture smelled of mould. The seven bedrooms had toilets with cracked cisterns and leaking rusty taps, a collage of fungi on the walls. An open drain carried water and sewage from the toilets to an underground cesspit.

The rooms, when they were occupied, were usually taken by travelling salesmen and low-level civil servants on circuit. From our manager's bungalow at a far corner of the compound, we would hear their drunken bawling, the same tired baila songs with their lewd lyrics. In typical Sri Lankan form, the men would not eat until they were tight, and so the staff was kept up well past midnight before dinner was served. My father would return to our quarters in the small hours of the morning, bleached with fatigue.

Not long after we moved to the guest house, a kindly stranger, whom we would later know as Sunil Maama, my grandmother's cousin, started to visit us, coming once a month and always bringing my sister and me a box of Kandos chocolates. My mother was imperious, speaking crossly as if she were doing him a favour tolerating his visit. At the end, he would always give her an envelope of money, and each time my mother sneered, "Is this her money?"

"No, no, Hema," Sunil Maama would say with an anxious smile. "It is mine."

"Well," my mother would declare, even as she opened the envelope and counted the notes, "if it is hers, I don't want it."

After Sunil Maama's third visit, my sister and I wanted to know who "her" was. "Your grandmother, who else?" my mother snorted.

"We have an aachi?" Renu tucked in her chin, incredulous.

"Yes, of course, did you think I was born in a rubbish bin?"

"But why haven't we met this aachi?" I asked.

"Because," my mother paused for emphasis, "she hates you."

We stared at her dumbfounded. "Why?" Renu finally demanded.

"Because you are half Tamil. Your grandmother did not want me to marry your father because he was Tamil. And now that you are half Tamil, she hates you." My mother said this in a way that would not tolerate further questions.

We were not really surprised that someone hated us for being Tamil. For by the early 1970s, the tension between the majority Sinhalese and the minority Tamils was escalating, particularly around the latter's desire for a separate state. My father was resented by the waiters and other workers in the guest house, who were all Sinhalese, and he had a hard time maintaining discipline. Though the staff were kind to us, they felt no compunction referring to him as a "Tamil dog" in our earshot.

My sister—whom my parents' discord had made caustic, and who looked like a midget spinster with her sharp, dark-skinned face and hair cut in rigid lines—would often taunt me, saying I could never escape being a Tamil but that she would marry a Sinhalese one day, change her last name and no longer be Tamil. Then she would be rich and never allow me in her house, whereas I would end up a beggar man. This threat would send me howling to my mother, who would cry, "Stop being such a baby," and bat my arms off her.

Our father died of a heart attack, keeling over with a surprised shout one morning while doing the accounts in his office. We barely knew him, and so his death had little impact on us. He would be gone from the manager's bungalow in the morning before we woke up, and come back when we were asleep, spending all day at his office to avoid my mother. Occasionally, he had tried to do something fatherly, such as take us into town to see a visiting circus troupe, but he was so awkward, begging for our affection with chastened glances, that we felt stifled by him and were always glad to return to the rudeness of our mother. We saw that by losing our father we had this new, gentle mother, and we gladly traded him to death in exchange for the person she had become.

That first time we visited my grandmother's house, we walked along the length of its high perimeter wall, jagged blue and green glass glinting along the top, and came to a stop before the gate with spiked iron bars. Renu and I stared up the curved driveway at the grand whitewashed bungalow, its red-tiled roofs adorned with a melody of wooden fretwork along the eaves. The front verandah had carved pillars, linked to each other by lattice panels, all painted white, and a turquoise-and-grey mosaic floor. A polished silver four-door Bentley T sat before the verandah under a carport. My mother, dressed in the white sari of a widow, did not ring the bell, but stood at the gate waiting. Soon a plump old woman wearing a sarong and blouse ambled around from the back of the house and peered down the driveway as she wiped her hands on a dishtowel. My sister and I knew this had to be the legendary ayah Rosalind, about whom my mother had spoken so lovingly in preparing us for this journey. My mother raised her arm and the ayah was still for a moment. She began to hurry down the driveway, the dishtowel, which she had tucked into her waist, flapping like some tired sorrow. When she got to the gate, she let out a choked sob and struggled with the latch. "Aney, baba," she cried as she stepped out, "the gods have been good to grant me this sight of you." She began to weep, touching my mother's face, her hair, her shoulders, her arms, saying, "Aiyo, baba, look at you, so young and already a widow."

Soon my mother was crying too. "I never thought I would see you again, Rosalind, I never did."

The ayah held my mother's head against her spice-stained bosom. "You are home now, baba, you are safe."

She noticed us, and letting go of my mother knelt on the ground, the sweetness of roasted cumin powder coming off her. Rosalind gently took my hands in hers. "He is beautiful," she whispered to my mother, "just like you were as a child."

"Don't tell him that," my mother said with a laugh and a sob. "He's already spoilt enough."

Rosalind patted Renu on the head and said she had heard that my sister was very good in school, just like our mother had been.

"I suppose I should go in and face her," my mother said, tightening the sari palu around her waist, then blotting her tears with a handkerchief.

"I told Loku Nona you were coming, baba, I thought it was best."

My mother sucked in her lower lip. "And?"

"She acted like she hadn't heard, but then she yelled at me that the rice was not cooked enough." Rosalind grimaced. "Just keep your temper."

The old ayah ushered us to the kitchen in the back courtyard, which, like most Sri Lankan kitchens, was a tin-roofed shed, its half-walls blackened with soot. "Shivan, Renu, you stay here with Rosalind." My mother patted the bun at the nape of her neck, pushed her handbag over her shoulder and went into the house.

The old ayah beckoned my sister and me to sit on low stools, then she gestured to the plates set out on a long, scarred table that had a kerosene stove and a coconut scraper attached at one end. "Banana fritters. I made these especially for you." The ayah covered the fritters with kithul treacle before placing our plates before us.

As we tucked into them, she sat on another low stool across from us and watched with great satisfaction, every so often stroking our arms or pushing the hair from our foreheads.

After what seemed a long time, my mother came back, her eyes red and cheeks grimy. "She will provide an allowance, but she wants us to leave."

Rosalind drew in her breath. "No, no, baba, you cannot give in so easily." The ayah's eyes narrowed as she looked me over. "She needs to see her grandson." Rosalind took away my plate of fritters, raised me to my feet, smoothed down my hair and straightened my collar. "Yes-yes, let her see him."

"There's no point, Rosalind."

The ayah grabbed my hand. I pulled away, terrified now, but she held on and bustled me into the pantry, with its spice safe and ancient refrigerator, and from there into the main part of the house, which was built in the old Sinhalese style, with a vast high-ceilinged saleya, that was both living and dining room. Curtained doorways led into bedrooms from the saleya, the unused rooms with their doors closed to keep out the dust. Rosalind strode to one of the curtained doorways and slipped me through.

A tall, thin woman in a long nightgown and housecoat was seated elegantly upright in bed, polishing a tiny silver teapot, the coverlet scattered with porcelain ornaments and silver objects.

My grandmother snorted like a startled horse and dropped the teapot, which clinked and bounced on the mattress. I began to whimper under her stare, sneaking frightened glances at this stranger with knotty arms, rope-like tendons in her neck, long greying hair in stringy strands about her shoulders.

She finally looked about as if searching for some escape, then picked up the silver teapot and began to rub it vigorously, her gaze sliding towards me, then darting away. "Rosa-lind, Rosa-lind!" she suddenly yelled, her voice shrill. "Come here! Immediately."

When the old ayah presented herself, my grandmother cried, "Have you given the boy something to eat?"

Rosalind sucked in her breath, dismayed. "I never thought to, Loku Nona."

"Why not?" my grandmother shrieked, flinging her polishing cloth on the bed. "Is there only cow dung between your ears?" She fluttered an arm in my direction. "This poor little boy has probably not had a meal since breakfast. Can't you see the way he is crying from hunger? Aiyo! Take him away, take him away. Feed the poor thing, for goodness sake." With that she grabbed her cloth and began to rub another ornament, muttering under her breath.

Rosalind took my hand and we left. My legs were trembling from witnessing my grandmother's anger, but Rosalind looked well pleased with herself and nodded to my mother, who was in the saleya with my sister. The ayah set me up at the dining table with another plate of fritters, which I greedily consumed, being ravenously hungry in that way one is after a fright.

As I ate, my mother sat at the table watching me with a wry defeated smile, my sister glaring at this second helping of fritters she had not been offered.

There was much activity going on in my grandmother's bedroom, and after some time she bustled out wearing a white Kandyan sari, hair knotted at the nape of her neck. She glanced past my mother and sister to me, then she flapped towards the front door, chin tilted as if I had slighted her in some way. "Rosalind," she said, crooking her finger for the ayah to follow, "I am going for my evening pooja. Tomorrow, when you go to Sathiya Stores, buy two plastic school lunch boxes. One blue and one pink."

"Yes, Loku Nona." Rosalind shot my mother a triumphant look.

My grandmother saw the look. She rummaged through her coconut frond purse, then let it fall to the ground, coins spattering over the polished red floor.

Rosalind made to go forward, but my mother lifted her hand. She rose from her chair. Getting down on her knees, she crawled over to take the purse from my stony-faced grandmother, then, still on her knees, scrambled around to retrieve the coins, all the while keeping her luminous gaze on my sister and me. When every coin was picked, she crawled back to my grandmother and handed the change purse to her. My grandmother took it and continued towards the verandah, her car starting up as she went out to it. My mother stayed on her knees looking after her. She was twenty-nine years old and her life was over.

My mother recently told me that she still dreams of her husband, the same dream she has had since his death. In it, she encounters him at my grandmother's gate or standing by a pillar on the verandah or sometimes outside the market. He is reborn as a peréthaya, a hungry ghost, with stork-like limbs and an enormous belly that he must prop up with his hands. The yellowed flesh of his face is seared to the skull, his mouth no larger than the eye of a needle, so he can never satisfy his hunger. He just stands, staring at her, caught between worlds. For years, the anguish of that dream would continue into her day, because my mother believed she had caused his death by her anger and there was no way to beg his forgiveness, or at least reach some companionable peace with him.

In Sri Lankan myth, a person is reborn a peréthaya because, during his human life, he desired too much—hence the large stomach that can never be filled through the tiny mouth. The peréthayas that appear to us are always our ancestors, and it is our duty to free them from their suffering by feeding Buddhist monks and transferring the merit of that deed to our dead relatives.

My grandmother had her peréthaya stories too. In one of them, a king, Nandaka, has been away at war and is riding back to the capital with his troops, victorious. He reaches a crossroads, and seeing that one of the avenues is smoothly paved and shaded with trees, he takes it, not realizing it leads to the haunt of peréthayas. Soon his men grow fearful, as an odour of rotting flesh blooms around them and wailing shimmers the air. Looking back, they see that the road they travelled has disappeared. "In front of us the way is seen," they cry, "but behind us the road is gone." King Nandaka spies a great banyan tree ahead, and when he reaches it he finds a feast spread out by the roots. A man, who has the luminescent beauty of a deva, bedecked in jewels and gold-threaded silks, appears and welcomes the king, inviting him and his followers to eat and drink. Once they are sated, the king asks the man if he is indeed a deva. "I am not, your majesty," the man replies, "I am a peréthaya." The king is shocked and demands to know by what virtuous deeds he, a peréthaya, has acquired such splendour. The man explains that he was miserly in his past life, but he left behind a daughter who delighted in doing good deeds and being generous. A few months after her father's death, when a monk, famed for his piety, came to her village, she invited him to her house, fed him and offered him a saffron robe, asking him to transfer the merit of these actions to her dead father. "It is thus that I live in such splendour, your majesty," the peréthaya concludes, "through the fruit of my daughter's good deeds."

In front of us the way is seen, but behind us the road is gone.

Soon that house of my childhood will be no more. Once we have left Sri Lanka and brought my grandmother back here to Canada, it will be torn down to build a block of flats. For a moment, an image arises in my mind of the bulldozers crashing into the verandah, those carved teak pillars and lattice panels splintering, the turquoise-and-grey mosaic on the floor shattered, the intricately wrought antique doors, with their images of lotuses and peacocks, smashed to smithereens. A sigh that is almost a cry rises out of me.

3

LIKE RAIN SOAKING A PARCHED LAND. That was how my grandmother described our first encounter when she told me her life story years later. "I looked up from my unhappy life, Puthey, and there you were. And my heart broke then, broke with happiness." There are many times when I have raged inside at that phrase of hers, at that malformed thing she calls love. Yet I know, more than anyone else, that love always comes with its dark twin—the spectre of loss, which drives us to do such terrible things.

In those first few days, we hardly saw my grandmother, as she was always out on errands. When she was home, she stayed in her bedroom and ran the household from there. Though she had taken us in, she remained obdurate towards her daughter and refused to have meals with us. Yet I had noticed that whenever our paths crossed, my grandmother gazed at me as if I were something fragile she was frightened to touch. One afternoon, returning from an errand, she stopped in front of my sister and me as we sat cross-legged on the verandah floor playing cards. A squall of emotions passed over her face before she flapped on to her bedroom with a little "humph." Renu giggled. She gripped my arm and hissed, "The grandson is the most important. So you better be nice to Aachi, otherwise we will get thrown into the street. If that happens, I will always hate you."

I shook my arm free and glared down the driveway. I could not deny I was the favoured one.

Renu, either to punish me for being preferred or to secure our place in this house, decided to make our grandmother a bouquet from the garden. When she was done, she thrust it into my hand and declared, "Shivan, you must take it to Aachi."

"No!" I dropped the flowers on the ground and folded my arms over my chest. "No, I won't."

"Yes, you will."

I was no match for Renu. She grasped me by the arm, marched me into the saleya and pushed me through the curtained doorway. My grandmother was seated in her bed reading a newspaper, and she lowered it, startled.

"Thank you very much for allowing us to be in your house," I said, my throat dry. "For . . . for you, Aachi."

I held out the bouquet. My grandmother frowned at it and then at me. A tremor slackened the corners of her mouth. I put the flowers on her bed and bolted.

Renu and I crept around the side of the house to our grandmother's bedroom window. We carefully lifted the bottom edge of the half-curtain and peered in. She had picked up the bouquet and was smelling it, the look on her face like someone convalescing after a long illness.

We grinned at each other. I was delighted with myself, as if I alone had thought up and executed this feat of daring.

The next morning, my grandmother paid Renu and me a visit. We were seated at a table on the back verandah, writing out some exercises our mother had set to prepare us for entrance into one of the more prestigious Colombo schools, exercises also intended to keep us out of trouble while she was visiting principals, begging to have us taken on as charity students. She was also looking up old school friends who might help her find employment through their fathers or husbands.

Though it was a short walk from her room, my grandmother was panting slightly when she came out onto the verandah. I grinned at her and kicked my foot against the chair leg, feeling that I had won a new status with her. She gave me a frosty stare and I hurriedly returned to my work.

After a moment, I felt her standing behind me and her shadow wavered across the page. My mother had instructed me to copy out sentences from the Grade One *Radiant Way* primer. My writing was ill-formed and I had made numerous errors. With my grandmother looming over me, my hand began to shake and my scrawl grew worse. She clamped her fingers on my shoulder, nails digging into my flesh. "Erase that. Start again."

I rubbed out the words I had written. In doing so, I erased the line above, which was correct.

My grandmother sucked her tongue against her teeth in a prolonged "*ttttch.*" "Look at this child," she declared to no one in particular, "cow dung in his head."

I glanced at my sister, but she hunched over her work, dreading she might be next. Rosalind glanced over as she grated a coconut in the kitchen. The coconut flesh rasping and tearing on the scraper was like a warning from her. I began to write my line again, but this time, in my nervousness, I pressed too hard and the pencil point broke.

"You did that on purpose, nah?" my grandmother cried, as if it was a personal insult to her. "Think you can make a fool of me?" She slapped the side of my head.

I whimpered and rubbed my nose, a heat swelling up under my scalp.

My grandmother snatched my pencil away. "Where is the cutter?"

Renu held it out to her, keeping her head bent. My grandmother grabbed it and sharpened the pencil. Her grinding fractured the silence. She thrust the pencil at me and flung the sharpener on the table.

I began to write the line again. My grandmother had over-sharpened the pencil and the point was wobbly. I wrote cautiously, but there was only so far I could go before the tip broke again.

My grandmother drew in her breath. I put down my pencil and clasped my hands tightly in my lap. "You are deliberately trying to mock an old woman and make a fool of her, aren't you?" Her breath was hot on the top of my head.

Renu slid the sharpener over. My grandmother snatched it and flung it into the backyard. "You think that because I'm an old woman you can hoodwink me?" she shrilled. "You think you can make a laughingstock out of me?" She dragged me up, my chair squealing along the floor.

"No, Aachi, no," I pleaded. "I'm sorry. I promise I won't do it again."

My grandmother grabbed my ear and pulled me into the saleya and through to her room. She shoved me away, went to an almirah in a corner and slid her foot under, feeling around until she kicked out a dusty old leather slipper. She brushed it against the side of her housecoat. My grandmother crooked a shaking finger and pointed for me to bend over the bed. I stayed where I was, gawping at the slipper. "Come," my grandmother ordered, using the pejorative "*vareng.*"

"No, I won't. You're not my ammi. I hate you, you old woman."

I had used "*gaani*," the rudest form of "woman," and my grandmother's face flushed. "You wicked boy," she wailed, and rushed at me, slipper raised. I made to dart away, but she gripped my elbow. I writhed and twisted, my arm burning from her grip, but she held on. I could smell the scorched odour of her sweat under the rose talcum powder. The noise outside of crows cawing, traffic rumbling by and vendors calling seemed magnified in the room as we grappled to gain mastery in desperate silence. Finally, my grandmother felt me weaken. She let out a cry and brought the slipper hissing through the air against my arm. I yelled at the hot sting and broke from her, stumbling sideways just as my grandmother brought the slipper down again. She was aiming for my back, but instead the slipper hit me across the face. I screamed and cradled my cheek. For a moment we were still, then my grandmother sat down on her bed, head in her hands, and I turned and rushed out the door.

Rosalind and my sister had been listening outside, too afraid to intervene, and they followed me to my room. The ayah led me through into my bathroom and made me sit on the closed toilet teat. She took a bottle of gentian violet from the medicine cabinet, knelt in front of me and, pouring some of the liquid on cotton wool, dabbed my bruises, which were bleeding where the nailheads on the slipper sole had punctured my skin. I yelped at the smart.

Rosalind tucked me in and knelt by the bed, stroking my hair. As I lay under the coverlet, the shock of what had happened wore off, and I began to stutter hiccupping sobs. Renu paced the room, her face stern.

Once I was sufficiently calmed down, Rosalind sat back on her haunches and looked at us gravely. "Your amma must never find out about this."

"But why?" Renu cried, then added, "I'm definitely telling Ammi."

Rosalind sighed. "Your amma has enough hardships. I don't think she could bear anything else." She took my hand in hers. "This is difficult for you to understand, but what your grandmother did to you, she did out of love. She has singled you out, her grandson.

"Yes," she nodded, to our glares of disbelief. "She is just a woman who life has made different. This is her strange way of trying to love you. So," she raised her eyebrows, "can we make a pact not to tell your mother?"

After a moment my sister half nodded, but I ducked my head.

I lay in bed for the rest of the day, and in the late afternoon I heard my mother come into the house, calling to us. My sister rushed into the saleya to greet her, Rosalind following.

"Ammi," I bawled, "Amm-i!"

"What's going on?" my mother asked Rosalind.

"Oh, nothing, baba, he just fell and hurt himself."

My mother's heels clicked. She pulled aside the curtain and came into my room.

I thrust out my arm, offering up my bruises, and tilted my cheek so she could see the purple welt. She dropped her handbag on a table. "What happened, son, what did you do?" She held my wrist and examined the bruise.

My sister and Rosalind were also in the room now.

I began to sniffle. I suddenly wanted justice. "Aachi did this to me. With a slipper."

My mother became very still. Her grip tightened on my wrist, then she let go of my arm and straightened up.

"It's nothing, baba," Rosalind began. "You know how your mother is, she—"

"Aah, that wretched witch," my mother whispered. She strode out of the room, and we all followed. I, in particular, wanted to see my grandmother worsted.

The pistol shots of my mother's high heels echoed across the cavernous saleya. When she got to my grandmother's doorway, she ripped back the curtain and went in. "How dare you touch my child!"

My grandmother was getting dressed for temple. She turned from the mirror and examined my mother. "Get out of my room." Then she went back to pinning the sari palu to the shoulder of her blouse.

The slipper was lying on a side table. My mother grabbed it and flung it in the wastepaper basket, much to my delight. "You will not ruin my children's life like you did mine."

My grandmother had finished pinning her palu. She wound it around her waist in preparation for the battle, then turned to my mother. "Remember your place. This is my house. I have allowed you to stay. You are lucky."

"You allow me to stay because you don't want to lose face with your friends and our relatives."

"You're wrong. I let you stay because I shudder to think what disgrace you would bring on our family name if I allowed you to live on your own. What horrible mistakes you would make."

"I don't know what you mean." My mother crossed her arms over her chest.

My grandmother let out a bark of a laugh. She leaned towards my mother. "Look at where your mistakes have brought your children. Look at them! Tamil, poor and undereducated! You're a disgraceful mother. A failure!"

My mother gripped her chest tighter, eyes filling with tears.

Renu glared at me. I was the one who had brought this humiliation on our mother.

"I wish you were not my daughter." My grandmother's voice was melodious with longing. "Every day I wish it was so. But I accept that this is my karma, that I must have done something terrible in my previous life to deserve you. Through meritorious deeds at the temple, I am trying hard to work off the ill effects of that karma." She pushed past my mother and left.

My mother began to weep.

"See what you have done," Renu hissed. She rapped a tokka on my head. "Now we will be forced to leave and live on the road because of you. We will become beggars."

I rushed out of the room. My grandmother was hurrying across the saleya. When I caught up with her on the verandah, she quickly scoured her cheeks with the heel of her palm then glared at me. "Go away, you wretched child."

"Aachi, I . . . I promise I will be a good boy." My voice was husky with fear. "Please don't put us out on the road, please don't let us become beggars."

Her lips thinned in astonishment. Then a change came over her face, a readjustment. "All I want is your welfare," she declared in a tone both haughty and injured. "That is all I want. The very best for you."

"Yes, I know, I know."

"Is it right for you to call me a gaani like I am some woman selling bananas at the corner? Is it right to say you hate me when I have shown you nothing but love?"

"No, no."

"If you had done your homework well, if you hadn't played around with your pencil, breaking that point on purpose, none of this would have happened."

"Yes, I was wrong, Aachi, I am sorry." I massaged my right elbow as if it were tender.

"And what is a few strokes with a slipper? You had better get used to it, because in the school you are going to, there will be a lot more of those. And not from a frail old woman like me."

I nodded vigorously, as if agreeing the punishment had been light.

"Hmm, anyway, you seem to have learnt your lesson. Which is a good thing. It shows you are an intelligent boy underneath this wildness you have brought with you." She turned and went down to her waiting Bentley T in the carport.

I crept back to my room and curled up in bed.

My window opened onto the back verandah, and I could hear my mother seated at the opposite end, still crying. Rosalind clicked her tongue soothingly, as if she were feeding hens.

"I was wrong to return, Rosalind," my mother said when she had quieted down. "This is a mistake. I must take the children away."

"And live on what, baba? Loku Nona will not give you an allowance now. She has chosen him."

"But it's unbearable, Shivan being in this position."

"Whatever punishment the poor child has to endure, his future is secure. Think carefully, Hema-baba. After all . . . ," the ayah was silent for a long moment, "she is not entirely to blame."

"Rosalind! How can you say that?" My mother's voice trilled with insincerity.

"There are children involved now. You cannot afford to make another mistake."

"He's a boy," my mother pleaded, "a little boy."

And so I understood that my mother would not defend me anymore. She was no longer in control of our destiny. I was.

That night, as we ate dinner on the back verandah under a dim naked bulb that cast a pallid glow, I found myself observing my mother and thinking for the first time about how she must look to an outside eye, cheekbones stretching her skin, lips dry and chapped, blackish-purple hollows at her temples. She had always been thin, but now I saw that she had grown even more so since my father's death.

The next morning, instead of sitting with my sister, I took my copybook and *The Radiant Way* to my grandmother's bedroom. She lowered the bank statement she was reading and her eyes followed me as I went to sit on the mat by her bed and begin my work. Even though she frowned sternly as she went back to the statement, I could tell she was glad I had come to her.

After some time had passed, my grandmother folded up her glasses, gathered her bills and accounts and put them on the side table. She glared to warn me against any mischief, but there was no real rancour in her gaze now. She lay back and closed her eyes. The laundry basket was not far from where I sat. The smell of lavender perfume and rose talcum powder seemed to deepen the sweat and damp of unwashed clothing. The fan whirled sluggish air about. I could feel the perspiration gathering in the crook of my arms and knees.

When I was sure my grandmother was asleep, I crept to the window and looked out through its thick bars. Renu was playing batta. She stopped, her feet planted on two squares, the batta stone in her hand, then continued with the game as if she had not seen me.

Two days later, my mother came home with a box from Perera and Sons. She gathered us together around the back verandah table, and once Rosalind had brought cake plates and a knife, she announced she had been offered a job as an apprentice editor at the *Lanka News*, a paper owned by a friend's father. My sister and I had also been accepted into the schools she wanted.

The ribbon cake had hard vanilla icing and sugar flowers, the sort we only ever had at birthdays. My mother beamed at us. "Happy?"

We nodded, but there was a troubling new vivacity to her manner, a harsh glitter in her eyes. As she began to cut slices, she said, not looking at us, "Children, how was your day, what did you do?"

"I had a tea party," Renu replied.

"Alone?" My mother passed the first slice of cake to Rosalind, who was standing behind her. "You know, you must look after your brother. He is, after all, the youngest. You should include him in your games."

"He couldn't play," Renu started to say, "he had to—" I kicked her in the shin.

My mother continued to pass out slices as if she had not heard, the knife sighing as it cut through the hard icing. She kept my piece beside her, and once she was seated she beckoned me forward and hoisted me into her lap. She kissed the back of my neck, her teeth grating briefly against my flesh. "But you are still my baby boy, my best, darling boy, aren't you?" Her arms were tight around me.

"Yes, Amma," I whispered. Sitting there in her hot embrace, breathing in her cheap perfume that smelt vaguely of chlorine, I glanced down at the slice of cake and was repelled. Yet when she held out the first forkful, I forced myself to take it, the crumbs prickling my throat.

"Yes, children," she said, "a bright future is before us. Indeed it is."

Another of my grandmother's favourite stories begins with the line, *Like a leopard stalking its prey through tall grass, a man's past life pursues him, waiting for the right moment to pounce*. It is the tale of a monk named Chakkupala, who, at the moment of achieving enlightenment, becomes blind. The other monks are puzzled by this and they appeal to the Lord Buddha for an explanation. The Tathagata, who can see both into the future and past, narrates an earlier life of Chakkupala's, when he was an eye doctor. During that time, a poor woman asked him to cure her eye disease. In return, she said, she would put herself in bondage to him. Once cured, however, the woman pretended she was still afflicted to avoid becoming his slave. Angered, the doctor gave the woman another potion which permanently blinded her. Her blindness, the Tathagata tells his monks, was the result of bad karma from her past lives. But the laws of karma are such that, once the negative effect of a bad karma is played out, it drops from a person. The doctor by his evil deed took on the burden of that bad karma, which was coming to fruition now in the monk Chakkupala.

This is how I think now of that long-ago moment when my mother held me tight and fed me cake, the weight of her own history pressing down on me, passing over.

4

A WEEK AFTER I BEGAN MY VIGIL IN HER ROOM, my grandmother waited until my mother had departed for work one morning, then kept me back from school and took me to the row of toyshops on Front Street in Pettah. The arcade running the length of the shops was crammed with large toys, such as tricycles, dolls houses and scooters, and the passageway reverberated with the cacophony of wound-up dolls, the hooting and chugging of trains, the looped repetition of the Woody Woodpecker Song. With a tip-tap on my skull, my grandmother murmured, "Go ahead, Puthey, choose one thing. Whatever you like."

In my excitement I couldn't fix on what I wanted, something new always taking my fancy. Finally one of the store owners, who was a better salesman than the rest, convinced me to settle on his blue-and-green imported scooter. He had chosen one of the most expensive toys, but my grandmother paid for it with the snap of a hundred-rupee note. When I thanked her, I called her by the affectionate appellation for grandmother, "Aacho."

For the rest of the morning, I trundled my scooter up and down the driveway. Soon I had learnt how to give myself a good push and glide with both feet on the platform, not falling.

Renu arrived home in the early afternoon, and when she saw the scooter her face tightened. She gobbled down her lunch and came out to assert her claim. Lifting the scooter out of my grasp, she set it behind her, rested back against the handlebar and declared, "You're too young for a scooter. Let me show you how to use this. And, anyway, it's a girl's toy."

"No, it isn't," I cried, and tried to get around her. "Blue and green are boys' colours not girls'."

"What do you know?" She struggled to pry my sweaty hands from the handlebar. "You are just a Grade One baby. I am in Grade Three and I am telling you that scooters are for girls."

But I would not let go, and after we had struggled for a while, Renu got impatient and gave me a shove. I staggered back and fell, shards of gravel scraping my elbow and forearms. I wailed as she set off down the driveway. Soon Rosalind and my grandmother came running.

"What is it, Puthey?" my grandmother cried, as she and the ayah helped me to my feet and dusted me off.

"Look, Aacho, look at that girl." I flung my arm in the direction of the driveway. Renu had reached the gate. She turned around to come back but, seeing the two women, stood still.

"You. Come over here," my grandmother cried, using the insulting "*vareng*." She gestured frantically to my sister.

Renu stayed where she was. My grandmother hitched up the edge of her ankle-length housecoat and set off down the driveway. Renu still did not move, and when my grandmother reached her, she glared up at her elder without flinching.

"Give that scooter to your brother. Who told you to use it? Did I buy this for you?" My grandmother referred to my sister as "*oomba*," the "you" used for the lowest castes.

Renu threw the scooter on the gravel, scratching its paint. She began to stalk away, but our grandmother grabbed her by the plait, drew her face close and said with bitter contempt, "Yes, I see where you will end up. Like mother, like daughter." Then she shoved Renu away, wrinkling her nose.

I am not sure what our mother heard from Renu that evening, but she came looking for me. I was around the side of the house, washing my scooter at the garden tap.

My mother stood over me, breathing hard. "Your sister is all you have in the world, after I am gone. You had better learn now to share with her. I insist you let her take turns on the scooter."

"No," I cried, "it is mine. Aacho gave it to me, not her. She can get her own scooter."

"The problem is you are being spoilt by that woman. You need some discipline. You are turning into a selfish, arrogant child. Yes-yes, this spoiling has to stop. You will share your scooter with your sister or not ride it at all."

"I don't have to do anything you say. This is not your house. This is Aacho's house, and she says this scooter is mine and I don't have to share it."

My mother grabbed me by the front of my shirt and hauled me to her. "I am your mother. You will always listen to me first."

She shoved me away and ran her hand over the top of her head. Then, with no warning, she began to cry loudly in a helpless way. She hurried towards the verandah.

I rushed after her. "I am sorry, Ammi. I will do as you want. I promise I will share my scooter with Renu, I promise I will."

When we reached the front steps, my mother turned to me, her face grim. "The reason that Renu cannot have her own scooter is because I cannot afford to get her one. Do you understand that, Shivan? I cannot afford it."

"I'm sorry, Ammi, I'm sorry."

She nodded to accept my apology, then entered the house.

After that, I rode the scooter only when my mother was away. When she was home I loaned it to Renu so that my mother would see I was obedient.

From then on, all my grandmother's gifts felt to me like a betrayal of my mother, an affront to her poverty. I loved to read, and my grandmother, knowing this, took me once a month to the K.V.G. de silva Bookshop so that I could pick what I wanted from the latest arrivals. My choice always included a few new editions from my favourite writer, Enid Blyton. I made sure that my mother never saw me reading the books. When I was done with them, I stored them under my bed. Finally, however, Rosalind got worried that the piles would encourage cockroaches and spiders. She hauled out an old bookshelf from the garage, and I came home from school one day to find all my books on display. I stood in the curtained doorway, my neck prickling as if some secret vice of mine had been exposed. I wanted to return the books to their hiding place, but knew this would only raise questions.

Later that day, my mother came searching for me and saw the shelf. Her face took on a look of pain.

"What are you staring at?" I demanded. "Have you not seen books before?"

My mother gave me a long stare, her head shaking slightly.

After the episode with the bookshelf, my mother insisted I go with her once a week to the Thimbirigasyaya market. Every Saturday we trudged the fifteen minutes to the market, vehicles bellowing dust and diesel fumes as they sped by. My mother ignored my sullenness and chattered on about her work or asked about my studies, all the while holding an umbrella to protect us from the sun. I replied tersely, furious. When we were done, I had to carry our shopping bags home.

"I cannot do it all," she would explain. "You children are so pampered and cosseted. How you will last in the real world, I don't know."

As time passed, I developed a seething anger towards my mother and sister. By my early teens, this anger had grown so powerful, I could barely bring myself to speak to them. Even the slightest reproof from my mother or jibe from my sister would send me into a rage. Their lives, despite drawbacks, were free of my grandmother; their lives were actually better for us being here. And this happiness, I saw, had been won at my cost.

My mother loved her work. She enjoyed dealing with journalists, the excitement of deadlines, the commissioning of pieces, and she soon rose to run the newspaper's women's section. She made female friends at work who were single, divorced or widowed like her, and they often went to see films or plays at the Lionel Wendt Theatre. She also renewed ties with old school chums. All this compensated for the anguish of living with a mother who would not even speak to her unless absolutely necessary. When she had to discuss something with my grandmother, she would stand before her curtained doorway and ask humbly to enter. During their terse conversations, my grandmother kept her face averted.

Renu complained she had to tolerate the snobbery of classmates, but I felt she greatly exaggerated her suffering. She was very popular with the teachers because of her intelligence, and being a charity student did not affect her status. She had also quickly learnt to draw the mantle of her poverty about her haughtily and stare down with martyred disdain at any classmate who dared speak of her charity status. Very early, Renu positioned herself as a champion of the downtrodden. By the force of her character, she attracted a circle of girls who shared her convictions about the oppressed and, even though they came from some of the wealthiest families, took up her attitude of denigrating wealth. My sister was often busy on weekends doing work in slums or visiting the elderly, anything to stay away from my grandmother's home. She always had a crush on some teacher, whom she worshipped with lambent-eyed adoration, carrying the woman's books and manoeuvring to sit near her on school trips.

After that fateful thirteenth birthday, I no longer kept vigil in my grandmother's room while she slept. Instead, I accompanied her on errands having to do with the properties, learning the trade of my patrimony. As part of my new duties I also had to sit in on Sunil Maama's weekly visits to my grandmother, ostensibly so I would grow familiar with legal terms. My grandmother would often ask me if I had spotted anything irregular or needing improvement in one of the documents under discussion, one eye on Sunil Maama, who patted his bald spot to make sure the strands of hair were in place. I hated having to respond, and even though, in time, I was able to spot mistakes, I would always shake my head. She would then pounce on the problem and jab at the paper before flinging the deed or tenant agreement at poor Sunil Maama.

One of my grandmother's tenants was a Tamil couple, the Thurairajahs. They became her tenants soon after they lost their house and livelihood during civil riots between the Sinhalese and Tamils in 1977. They had been professors at a southern university, he in mathematics and she in English literature. The husband now taught science at an international school. When my grandmother and I came over to collect the rent or attend to a repair, Mrs. Thurairajah was often asleep, and she answered the door with her waist-length plait half unwound, sweaty wisps pasted to her forehead and cheeks. Despite this disregard for her appearance, Mrs. Thurairajah walked as if she effortlessly balanced a water pot on her head, and she spoke in a low, cultured tone. There was often a vacant look in her eyes, as if she were lost deep in herself. My grandmother, who was polite to her middle-class tenants, had no special like or dislike for this couple, and in fact respected their education and refined demeanour.

A few months after they became our tenants, we visited the property, and I saw that in the living room—which had so far been sparsely furnished with Galle antiques, no doubt saved from the mob—there were shelves filled with books from boxes that had been stacked against a wall. While my grandmother took the rent from Mrs. Thurairajah and inquired about the condition of the house, I casually drifted towards the shelves, hands in pockets, not wanting to seem intrusive. What I gleaned right away was that most of the books, though in English, were translations of works by Spanish, French and Latin American writers, or novels by Indian, African, and Chinese writers. It had never crossed my mind that anyone but British and American people wrote novels. Mrs. Thurairajah had seen me gawking. After she had paid the rent to my grandmother, she came over with an indulgent smile.

"I think you might like this book," she murmured in her elegant contralto. Reaching into the shelf, she drew out R.K. Narayan's *The Guide* and offered it to me.

I blushed at having been caught peering at her things. "No, no," I protested. But she pressed the book on me and finally I took it.

I was so keen to read the front and back flaps, particularly the author's biography, that I did not notice my grandmother's reaction to this exchange. When we were in the car and I was bent over, gorging myself on the first chapter, she declared, "You know, I am not a Tamil-hater like a lot of our Sinhalese people, but I believe the Thurairajahs got what was coming to them."

I glanced sideways at her. She was angry and trying to hide it, fiddling with the catch of her purse.

"Yes-yes," she nodded at my surprise. "They must have been very bad and cruel teachers. After all, it was some of their own students who came looking to kill them, who burnt their house." She pretended to look through her purse, frowning.

I put *The Guide* down on the car seat between us. The giving of books was her right.

The next time we visited Mrs. Thurairajah asked me what I had thought of her gift. I blushed and stammered that it was not for me, that I did not enjoy such novels.

By the time we returned that afternoon from our errands, I was ripe for mischief and went looking for my sister to torment her.

I crept into her room and found Renu looking out the window, giggling on the phone, which she had brought by its long cord from the saleya. "Don't be silly, he is not interested in me at all," she exclaimed, then added coyly, "Eee, what do I want with some fellow trying to cop a feel at the back of a cinema."

She saw me and hurriedly got off the phone. "What do you want?" she cried. "Have you never heard of knocking? I could have been naked."

"Help." I made a gagging sound. "That would have ruined me forever." I held out my hands, proclaiming a headline: "Brother Drops Dead at Sight of Sister's Hideous Nakedness." I went on, "Brother Levelled to Ground by View of Sister's Grotesque Backside. Brother Has Fits, Froths at Mouth, Bites off His Tongue and Goes into Coma at Sight of Sister's Monstrous Mammary Glands."

I had by now developed what I considered to be a scathing wit, more out of loneliness than anger—the need for a second voice that would help me build a barrier against the world.

"Get out." Renu flung a pillow at me.

I ducked it. "So who is this local Lothario panting after you? Clearly some chap without a modicum of good taste." I sauntered further into the bedroom, hands in pockets. "Must be a graduate from the Sisters of Charity Home for Mongoloids or the Rajagiriya Home for the Blind.

"So, tell-tell," I continued, as Renu picked up a book and pretended to read, "who is this deaf, blind mute who has developed a penchant for the abhorrent?"

"It's none of your business. Leave me alone."

"Ah, but I must be acquainted with this rare species of fellow who has a predilection for breasts the size of limes and a backside like the rear of a double-decker bus. Hmm, I wonder how he'll ever find you in the dark, given you are blacker than the night?"

"Get out, get out." Renu flung her book down.

I grinned lazily and then, holding her gaze, opened her top dresser drawer. "Heavens!" I gasped, hands to cheeks. "What is this?"

I seized two Kotex pads, slung the loops around my ears and began to waltz about.

"Shivan!" Renu rushed at me and snatched at the sanitary napkins, but I slipped out of her reach. She punched my arm, and the next thing I knew I had hit her in the face, the wet slap of my palm cracking the air. She cried out in shock and stumbled towards the bed, clutching her cheek. For a moment we were still, my sister regarding me as if I were a stranger. My hand tingled from the impact with her cheekbone.

"That will teach you to never touch me again. Never touch me." I left the room, chin high to hide my dismay at what I had done.

By the time my mother got home that evening, there was a purple bruise on Renu's face. My mother called me to her room. I strolled in, hands behind my back. My mother was standing on the far side of her bed as if she needed a protective barrier. She peered at me. "Shivan, how could you hit a girl? I am so ashamed of you."

"Shame is for the unwashed proletariat, so I don't deign to—"

"Don't talk to me in that ridiculous way. You're not on a stage."

"Ah, I see that Mother Dearest, Mother Fairest, is offended."

"Shivan, shut up."

"Or perhaps I should say Mother Unfairest."

"I know she hit you first, but you were annoying her. Anyway, it doesn't matter, you can't hit your sister back. A man must act in a chivalrous manner towards his women folk. No matter how much they provoke him, a man must never touch his women folk. He can scold them or even berate them, but—"

"Yes, yes," I yelled, "take her side the way you always do against me. You always do."

"No, Shivan, that is not true."

"It is, it is, you love her more than you love me."

"Ah, Shivan, how could you even say that." My mother stepped back.

"How can I say that? You ask me? You dare to ask me that?"

I ran to my room, flung myself on the bed and beat the pillow, letting out a muffled howl of rage.

5

WHEN THE MIND BURNS WITH ANGER, immediately cast aside those angry thoughts or they will spread like an unchecked fire travels from house to house. Those were words my mother repeated, from a book called *Guide to the Bodhisattva's Way of Life*, when she told me the story of her life many years later.

For my mother, too, the pivotal moment of her childhood was her father's death when she was eight years old. He was a distant but kindly presence, a man who was often away on circuit as a judge. He would sometimes bring her toys from his travels around the island. Depending where he had been, the gift would be brightly painted clay cooking chatties from the south, or a woven palmyra elephant from Jaffna. He seemed unaware that he often brought home the same gifts. My mother never pointed this out, shy around him because he, too, was shy. When he talked to her, he would periodically suck in his breath through gritted teeth, as if he had a toothache. At fifty-five, he was less like a husband to my grandmother than one of those self-effacing elderly bachelor uncles who live on a niece's charity. He had married when he was forty-six and my grandmother just seventeen. They had separate bedrooms because my grandmother claimed he stayed up too late at night working and disturbed her when he came to bed. The room she assigned him was at one end of the front verandah, a room typically allotted to a relative living on charity.

By the time my grandmother was twenty-four, she had already amassed many properties, and my grandfather regarded his wife with the befuddled look of someone who had just noticed some object that had been there all along. He was particularly awed by her tantrums, the way she would yell at Sunil Maama for some incompetence, Sunil wringing his hands and gasping, "Sorry, Daya, sorry." She would also rant at tradesmen who tried to sell her bad goods, and at carpenters or pipe-baases who had done a shoddy job. When she began one of her tirades, my grandfather would creep away to his room. Occasionally, he gently protested at dinner, particularly after she had humiliated Sunil. She would hear him through and then say mildly but firmly (for she was often tranquil after a tirade), "But I am right about this, nah? I am always fair-thinking."

He was never able to deny that she had lost her temper for good reason. "But, dearest, is it necessary to be so fierce about it?"

"Otherwise?" My grandmother would indicate for Rosalind to refill her husband's plate. "I am, after all, a woman. Men, by their very nature, will always try to take advantage of me. If I am not strong with them, they will rob me. And," a steeliness would enter her voice, "no one is going to shame me by taking advantage and then laugh behind my back, telling everyone I am some gullible, pathetic fool."

This always shut her husband up, and my mother would be aware, in that way of children, that something heavy and unspoken muffled the clink of her parents' cutlery against their plates.

When my grandmother passed my mother on the verandah while she was doing her homework, she would sometimes stop to say a few stiff words like, "Ah-ah, very good, doing your school work," or, "Now, have you eaten properly today?" or, "That uniform is looking a bit worn. Ask Rosalind to take you to Mrs. Deutram's to get some new ones made." All this was said in a distant but pleasant tone, as if my mother was a servant's child or a cousin's daughter sent to board so she could go to a good Colombo school. And my mother was grateful for this lack of interest. She did not want to be noticed. All the love she needed, she got from Rosalind.

What my mother remembered most about her father's funeral was the novelty of my grandmother's dry hand in hers as they stood watching the coffin slide into the roaring red of the crematorium furnace. The moment the doors closed behind it, my grandmother dropped her daughter's hand as if unaware she had been holding it and walked away to greet important guests. Among those present, my mother had noticed a group of unknown women, some of them ancient. They were country folk in puffed-sleeve blouses and sarongs that were out of fashion in the city, where Colombo ladies wore the sari. She had thought they were servants because of their clothes, but also because her mother ignored them. Yet soon after these women had appeared at the cremation grounds, Sunil Maama and his wife had touched the older women's feet as a sign of respect. One of the oldest, who was massive and square, had taken Sunil Maama's arm for support as they stood watching the smoke whirl from the chimney.

Rosalind led my mother away to sit on the marble steps of a nearby mausoleum and poured her some iced lime juice from a flask. "Who are those women?" my mother demanded.

The ayah took her time replacing the lid on the flask. "They are your amma's aunts and cousins."

My mother already knew that her grandparents were dead, but the news that she had other relatives on her mother's side, not just Sunil Maama, was a shock. She turned to gawk at them, but Rosalind pulled her gently around by the chin. "The old lady who is leaning on Sunil Maama's arm is his mother. Now drink your lime juice."

Back at the house, these relatives were sent to sit in the garden with the peons, lowly clerks and old servants who had come to pay their respects. My mother hid in a nearby araliya tree and watched how they leant over to whisper urgently about this insult, their faces prim with outrage. The older women chewed bulath leaves, their teeth and lips discoloured red, the wad like some living thing scurrying about in their cheeks. They wore elaborately carved circular brass chunam containers, like fob watches, attached to their hips by chains. The women would flip the lids open, scoop the white paste onto a bulath leaf then cram it into their mouths to augment their wads. My mother was intrigued by the dexterity with which they spat out red streams of bulath juice into the garden, never dribbling on their chins or staining their white blouses.

The women kept their voices to a discreet murmur, except for Sunil Maama's mother, whom the others addressed as Thushara Nanda, and who seemed to be the matriarch of the clan. She was quite deaf, leaning into the conversation, ear cupped. "Yes-yes," my mother heard her say in a loud nasal tone, "that is in the past now. Why is Daya still holding a grudge against us? After all, she was the one who got herself into that position, nah? She is the one who made a vesi of herself with that man." The others tried to hush the old woman, but either because she did not notice or did not care, she continued, "And who had to face the consequence of her lasciviousness? We did. After she went off to live in Colombo High Style, it was our young girls that bore her shame and had difficulty getting proposals."

My mother was stunned to hear her own mother, who seemed so indomitable, called a "vesi," a term she did not understand but knew was the ultimate insult to a woman.

When these women were ready to leave, my grandmother came out to them. "Ah-ah," she said with a rictus of a smile, "you are going."

Sunil Maama had come along behind her, having been detained earlier by fellow lawyers in the house. He went around now, giving the women envelopes of money while my grandmother stood, clasped hands pressed to navel. The women took the envelopes stonily, but my mother sensed their need. Vindication flickered at the corners of my grandmother's mouth. Yet once the women had left, her face buckled into an ancient tiredness and sorrow as she gazed after them.

And so my mother Hema saw for the first time that her mother had weaknesses, too.

When she was fifteen, my mother sat for the Senior School Certificate. Exam results in those days were published in the papers, with students who had done best at the top of the list, failures at the bottom. My grandmother was vaguely aware that her daughter had sat for the certificate. The day the results were published, my mother rose before dawn to wait with Rosalind for the paper, so she already knew how she had fared when, at breakfast, Rosalind, hand fluttering with excitement, laid the paper in front of her mistress, folded to the results page.

"But what is this?" my grandmother snapped at the improperly arranged paper. Then, seeing what was on the page, she gave her daughter a keen glance before bending to run her finger along the list from the bottom up.

"At the top, Loku Nona," Rosalind cried. "At the very top!"

My mother had won distinctions in all eight subjects, one of only twelve students to do so island-wide, and one of only two girls. My grandmother stared at her daughter, then turned to Rosalind, who beamed and nodded. My grandmother scratched her cheek as if she did not know what to do with this piece of news. Then she nodded at my mother. "Ah, very good. Yes-yes, very good."

The phone soon began to ring: first Sunil Maama and his wife, calling to congratulate my mother; then my mother's principal, various friends, the mothers of these friends, her father's relatives. Soon my grandmother was getting phone calls, too, from business associates and bank managers, colleagues of her late husband in the Ministry of Justice. As my grandmother answered the calls, my mother noticed that her tone grew more and more proud and proprietary. Soon she was saying things like, "Yes-yes, I had no doubt she would get eight distinctions. It was no surprise at all. Hema has always been a very bright student." Or, "She is my daughter, after all, why are you acting so surprised, ah?" Or, "From the time she was a little girl, she was smart-smart." Or, "Yes, indeed, I have very big plans for her. No marrying at seventeen or anything like that. My daughter is a modern woman."

Sitting on the verandah listening, my mother felt strangely deflated.

A few days later, my grandmother took her daughter to lunch at the Grand Oriental Hotel's Imperial Room, which overlooked the harbour. She invited Sunil Maama, too, because she felt it was unseemly for women to dine out alone; also, she really did not have anything to say to her daughter. During the meal, she spoke only to Sunil Maama, but gave sidelong glances at my mother, saying, "How wonderful it is for young women these days, nah, Sunil? All the advantages. Why, you can become a doctor or a lawyer now. Who knows? One day a woman might rule the country."

Later, when they were alone in the car going home, my grandmother, face averted, slid a royal-blue velvet box across the seat to my mother. It contained a Ceylon Stones jewellery set—a matching necklace, earrings, bracelet, ring and brooch.

When my mother thanked her hesitantly, my grandmother declared with relief, "Ah, you like it? Well done, duva, well done." She reached out, hesitated for a moment, then patted my mother's hand. "Take out the necklace. Try it on."

My mother drew out the necklace and rested the cold stones against her clavicles.

My mother's success at school had wrapped itself around her shoulders like a gossamer shawl. She had loved her classes, loved the validation from teachers and schoolmates. She had felt a happy lightness, studying in the library after school, the sun slanting in through the window, mynahs chirping outside, a breeze coming to her, smelling of salt from the distant murmuring sea. Then there had been the week before the exams when she, along with other girls hand-picked to succeed and bring prestige to the school, were kept back for afternoon tutoring in the staff room. This was a hallowed place, forbidden to students, and my mother had felt grown up to be invited in. The teachers had treated the girls like equals, with a relaxed merriness. My mother enjoyed how they had turned girlish recalling their own school days, teasing each other and the girls, divulging their college nicknames, letting their hair out of rigid buns to lie in coils about their shoulders. A peon had been sent to get treats such as mango or pineapple achcharu, freshly fried vadais or mutton kotthu roti from the nearby Muslim restaurant. As they sat around spooning the food into their mouths, the girls, grown bold, would ask the teachers about their lives and marvel at who these women had been before they came to work here, at who they were outside the institution. The teachers had painted an irresistible picture of university life, seducing the girls into trying even harder.

My mother had scored distinctions in the sciences, but also in the arts and humanities. She had not made up her mind which path she wished to pursue for the Higher School Certificate. My grandmother, however, soon decided on sciences in preparation for medical school. She informed my mother of this decision matter-of-factly. Opposition was useless.

One afternoon, on a day when my mother usually had tennis practice, the family car arrived early at her school and the driver told her she was wanted at home. She came back to find four men lined up in chairs on the verandah, faces twitching with nervousness, my grandmother standing over them, beaming among the sniffles, frayed cuffs, shrunken trouser legs and oil-soaked hair. The tutors were to prepare her daughter for distinctions in physics, chemistry, zoology and botany.

My mother enjoyed her extracurricular activities and excelled in sports, drama and debating. Now, however, she was expected to come home right after school and spend each afternoon and early evening in the gloomy study, fan swirling the dusty air above while she tried to pay attention to the droning of these tutors. She felt suffocated by their odour of sweat mixed with chalk; it was the odour of quiet defeat.

My mother began to pretend she had forgotten her tutorials, returning late, then acting surprised if she found a tutor waiting. The men soon complained to their employer, and one evening my mother arrived home to find my grandmother seated on the verandah, eyes large with rage and fear. She paused on the top step, frightened but also exalted at the possibility of freedom. My grandmother, with the swiftness of a snake, leapt from her chair, strode towards my mother, and grabbed her plait. "You think you can fool around and ruin your life? I'll show you, yes I will." She yanked the plait so hard that my mother yelled and clutched her head to keep the hair from ripping out of her scalp.

Rosalind came running, but all she could do was stand there wringing her hands, afraid to do anything that might increase her mistress's wrath. My grandmother dragged my mother by the hair to her bedroom, slapping her all the way. She shoved the curtain aside, pushed my mother inside, drew the seldom closed door shut, locked it and pocketed the key.

"Let her starve in there tonight," she panted to Rosalind. "She must be broken now, otherwise there is no hope. That girl is trying to make a laughing-stock out of me. After all this praise from everyone, she wants to fail and humiliate me? No, no! Hema must succeed."

Groping for escape, my mother visited her father's sister. These in-laws had been barely tolerated by my grandmother during her husband's life, and since his death she had cut them off. The level of her animosity suggested to my mother that there was some dark knowledge to be gleaned from these relatives. Her aunt was glad to see Hema, and it wasn't long before the conversation turned to my grandmother. "Yes-yes," the aunt declared, "Daya is lucky our brother married her." My mother had heard this many times before, but now she asked, "Why was my mother lucky?"

Her aunt's back arched with pleasure and she sat back in her chair, arms outstretched, a cat sunning on a warm rock.

It seemed that when my grandmother was sixteen, an older cousin named Charles had come to stay in the family compound. He had grown up in England and was a very handsome man, the aunt said, speaking as if she actually knew him. Far too elegant and sophisticated for Daya. In the weeks that followed, Daya had fallen violently for this man. She had thrown herself at him, following him down to the beach at night, where he went to swim. He was a decent man, according to the aunt, a gentleman. He had ignored Daya's declarations, gently advised her to be more prudent, told her with honesty that he did not love her back. But she persisted, and he, being a man after all, gave in. They were caught in a compromising position. News of this swept through the village, and Daya was shunned, even by her extended family. Whenever she had to visit town, people would turn away at the sight of her, and sometimes boys would throw pebbles, whistling lewdly and singing out, "Vesi, vesi." According to the aunt, it had been an act of great charity on the part of her brother to marry such a fallen woman. An act of kindness that had never been appreciated by my grandmother, who now spat on the memory of her own husband by cutting out his family. By which the aunt meant they were entitled to some of the wealth he had left his wife.

This story and what my mother knew of her own mother did not seem to match—and if she had really wanted the truth, or at least a version closer to the truth, she could have asked Rosalind. But the account was good enough for her, a first step towards freedom.

What my mother had in mind as an escape, she could not yet tell. Perhaps she sensed already what she would do and it was so awful that she turned from it, unable to contemplate where such an action would leave her. So my mother continued to sit patiently through her tutorials every afternoon, and her tutors soon reported to my grandmother that Hema was both docile and quick at her work. The next three years passed in this way, and when she was eighteen my mother sat for her Higher School Certificate.

She went to the first exam intending to do her very best. Yet once she was seated in the classroom and the exam bell had rung, she found herself observing a gecko crawling after a fly on the ceiling, the spinning, humming fans, the girls crouched over their desks, the invigilators standing in the doorways and murmuring to each other across the hall. All this created a hazy shimmer across my mother's mind. She watched the minutes pass on the clock, then studied the other girls busily working around her, noting their school ties and the barrettes and ribbons in their hair, the styles of their shoes, their various tics and twitches of nervousness, how some girls clutched rosaries and other religious totems on their laps. At the halfway point, an invigilator made a tour of the room, and when she saw my mother's blank examination book she nudged her and whispered, "Are you ill? Do you need a Disprin or something?"

"No, no," my mother whispered back. Seeing the woman's concern, my mother began to answer the questions frantically. But too much time had passed, and when the bell rang she let out a burble of despair and kept working until, finally, the invigilator had to pry the booklet from her.

As my mother left the classroom, she knew that even though she would not fail, she could not expect anything more than a credit. She felt frightened and cornered by this saboteur within, helpless in her grip. During each of the remaining three exams, her mind drifted from the questions and she would find herself, as before, looking about the room, observing the other students. Then a voice inside her would cry, "What are you doing! You are eating yourself!" and she would frantically try to answer a question, only to soon lose interest again.

My mother, when she told me about those examinations, said she could not make sense of her actions, even to this day. It was as if some element of karma was at play, just like in those old Buddhist stories, some bad effect from a previous life realizing itself in this one. My mother laughed as she said this, yet I sensed she half believed it, as I, too, have come to half believe that we sometimes make choices inexplicable to us.

The results came out a couple of months later. This time, my grandmother rose at dawn to wait. She and Rosalind spread the newspaper out under the dining-table lamp and craned over the columns. My mother watched as my grandmother ran her finger down, beginning at the top; watched the frown crease her forehead, the furrows growing deeper. After she had reached the end of the first page, my grandmother declared, "But there must be some mistake, they must have forgotten to print Hema's name." She glanced at Rosalind and then at her daughter. Perhaps she saw something in my mother's face, because she quickly turned the page and ran a shaking finger down the columns that now listed only credits and passes. When she was halfway down she let out a throttled cry. My mother had received credits in physics and biology and a mere pass in botany and zoology. "But, how can this be, it's not . . ." My grandmother stopped, seeing the mixture of emotions on her daughter's face.

In the silence the women could hear the Milk Board van outside the gate, the clink of bottles, a lone scooter passing, its puttering like the call of a lost bird. My mother pressed her folded arms into her stomach, ready for a beating.

"Why?" my grandmother said. She sank into a dining chair and covered her face with trembling hands. "Oh, God, I am cursed. Rosalind, I am cursed," she whispered. "Here it is again. My happiness denied. The naked peréthi, I *am* the naked peréthi."

My mother looked at her, not understanding.

Rosalind, who appeared to get the reference, forgot decorum and rested a hand on her mistress's shoulder. After a moment, my grandmother pushed her chair back and stood up. She stumbled away, then turned to her daughter. "You don't know what you've destroyed. You don't know how lucky you were to have this chance to not end up like me."

"Don't worry," my mother cried, anguished. "Don't worry, I'll never end up like you. Because I am not some vesi who throws herself at a man and ruts around with him on a beach, like a bitch in heat."

My grandmother stared at her daughter in disbelief, then her face hardened. She drew herself up and walked away, steadying herself on the edges of the furniture as she went.

For a week my grandmother stayed in her darkened room. Occasionally, my mother caught glimpses of her through the curtained doorway, lying with arm across forehead as if she had a migraine. Then one evening my grandmother got out of bed with great energy. She put on a white sari and left for evening pooja at the nearby temple, a place she had only ever visited at important times like Vesak or the New Year or my grandfather's death-anniversary dana. This marked the beginning of my grandmother's religiosity. She had accepted that she would find no happiness in this life and must bear her karma. She would perform many acts of merit to ensure a better future life, doing good deeds for the monks and the temple, which was the highest form of merit. And she instructed Rosalind that her daughter was to eat all her meals on the back verandah.

In the months that passed, my mother watched her less-intelligent friends get into university. She could have sat the exams again, but she did not dare approach my grandmother for another year of school fees. Other friends started to take cooking classes with the famous Anita Dickman and go to needlepoint and ballroom-dancing classes in preparation for becoming society wives. Some of them, by nineteen, were already engaged or married. No one came forward to find my mother a husband. She began to sever contact with her school friends, unable to bear the pity and concern in their eyes; unable to bear their splendidly appointed new homes, their doting husbands and plump babies; unable particularly, if they were in university, to bear their talk of medical or law school or be introduced to their student friends. Sometimes, when no one was looking, she would open a friend's medical text and read a page. Then a cry would rise in her: "How have I come to this place? How?" And her throat would swell with rage at her mother. She hated her home, but was trapped by it. Her life would be lived out as a spinster with a mother who never spoke to her. When she thought about this future, often in the middle of the night, she would moan aloud.

My mother was twenty when she met my father. She was a typist by then at the shipping firm where he worked. He had none of the smart briskness, the arrogance, of the other young executives, and he walked with a slight drag, as if wearing shoes too large for him, his shoulders stooped, his bulbous nose scarred by old acne. He had a nervous crack of a laugh, and instead of flirting with the typists in the entitled manner of the others, he stuttered when asking for anything. My mother sensed that he liked her, and, being desperate for affection, signalled him over when he appeared at the door of the steno pool. They were soon having lunch together and going to films at the Regal Cinema in the evening, or for sunset walks along the Galle Face Green esplanade, or to cheap dinners at Tamil cafés. He proposed to her two months after they met.

When my mother told my grandmother she was getting married, she replied, "A Tamil and a Christian," as if such foolishness was exactly what she expected from her daughter. "Are you blind to what is going on in our country? Have you forgotten the 1958 riots, how Tamil people lost their homes and businesses? How Tamil women were raped, the gold earrings ripped from their ears? By marrying this man, you will become one of those women, mistaken for Tamil because of your surname."

She said all this with disdain, as if speaking about a servant girl on their street who had got pregnant out of wedlock.

"I am a fair person," my grandmother told her. "I will give you a dowry. You can have that house of mine in Nugegoda."

"I don't want a cent from you," my mother cried, her voice ragged. For she understood my grandmother's offer came from relief at being finally free of her daughter.

6

To TRULY IMAGINE FREEDOM, one must understand how one might escape. My understanding occurred when I was seventeen. By then, out of sheer loneliness, I had become an even more voracious reader and was the favoured client of a book-man who turned up at our gate once a week, an old wooden tea chest filled with books roped to the rear carrier of his bicycle. He would spread a pink tarpaulin on the verandah floor, then lay out his recent findings, each sun-bleached, monsoon-curled tome handled as if it were the finest glass, that raw-rice odour of pages in the tropics rising up to me as I knelt on the other side of the tarp. I chose what I wanted, then gave back the volumes I had bought the last time. He credited me a certain amount for these returns and I paid the difference. I devoured practically anything. Georgette Heyer, Victoria Holt, Dickens, Thackeray, Austen, Agatha Christie, P.G. Wodehouse, Leon Uris, Tolstoy were all swallowed in great gulps. I also favoured the biographies of old Hollywood stars, whose movies I would never see, there being no market for them in Sri Lanka. I read about the torrid sex lives, the ghastly childhoods, the ruinous marriages, the alcoholism and drug abuse, the sheer madness of the likes of Joan Crawford, Vivien Leigh, Judy Garland and Jean Harlow as if they were spicy potboilers.

Then one day I chose the biography of Montgomery Clift, moved without fully realizing it by the star's beauty on the cover. Over the next few days, I read with growing wonder about his love of men; read about where such desire led—the soliciting of sex in dark streets and the backrooms of seedy bars, his body pawed over by rough sailors. The star despaired over his homosexuality (a word I had not encountered before) and became addicted to alcohol and pills, finally crashing his car into a telephone pole and ruining his once-famous beauty. In the last photograph taken before he died of a heart attack, Clift, at forty-six, looked shrivelled and haunted.

I was repelled by the actor's life. Yet this aversion was surmounted by the momentous discovery that I, too, was a homosexual. And with this realization, vague sexual desires, dreams and furtive masturbation coalesced around that word. The sheer surge of my suppressed adolescent lust swept away shame or guilt or fear, along with the warnings, revealed by the biography, that my life would be miserable.

At school, now, I allowed myself to contemplate how beautiful boys' necks were when they were thrown back in a laugh, the aching, vulnerable knob of their Adam's apples; the way beads of sweat trembled in the indentation between their noses and lips, the way thin white cotton trousers pulled tight across thighs when they sat. That easy contact with them caused a constant spilling over of warmth within me—brushing against a classmate's hips when entering a class, the boy with whom I was sharing a textbook unconsciously pressing his leg against mine, his heady smell of sweat and Lifebuoy soap.

During the interval, I took to standing on the open second-floor corridor watching a rugger game in the quadrangle below, observing the flecks of grass and dried mud on stringy thighs, the glimpse of white underpants when boys were tackled, the sweat that glistened on their collar bones, hair so charmingly slicked across foreheads. I had always been repelled by sports, but now I longed to be down there among my classmates, to grab a boy by the waist and bring him down in a tackle, to lie on top of him, crotch pressed against his crotch or stomach or buttocks; to embrace a boy who had scored a goal, to stand with my arm around the sweaty hot shoulder of a team mate. I'd lean against the balustrade to hide my erection and my head would grow light with desire. Finally, to distract myself, I would tear my eyes away to the sky or the rooftop or the crows along the gutter.

Most of the boys in my school were wealthy and would be going abroad for higher education; most of them had chosen America. During the interval they constantly talked about how America, besides offering a superior education, was a Mecca for sexual adventure, the place where women were for the picking.

The idea of sexual freedom began to take root in me, too. If America offered such opportunity for sex with women, did it not offer similar opportunity for people like me? I was provided with the answer in that random way one often finds answers—in my dentist's waiting room, where I read a *Time* magazine article on the gay movement in San Francisco and New York. I smuggled the magazine home and hid it under my mattress, taking it out many nights to read the article again and study the photographs of men holding hands and kissing right there in the street.

I became a member of the American Center Library, housed in a mansion on Flower Road. The library's ground floor contained a room largely devoted to periodicals and prospectuses for American universities, along with well-thumbed copies of SAT and TOEFL study books. I often ran into boys from my class there, leafing through booklets and taking down information on where to send applications and what scholarships were being offered. As I looked through the prospectuses, I would pause at pictures of students lying in the grass, sun glinting in their hair, or hunched around a cafeteria table in earnest talk, or walking arm in arm down a corridor. I would gaze particularly at the men. Once in America, I told myself, I would become the person I really knew myself to be. In America, I would be popular, I would be gregarious, I would be witty, I would be handsome. In America, the sun would glint in my hair as I lay on manicured university lawns or strode across campus with my new friends. And I would never return to Sri Lanka. The glistening blond wood of the library floor, the faintly chlorinated smell of air conditioning—always a smell of privilege in the tropics—confirmed this promise.

Yet when I left the American Center Library—often having hung around until it closed—and cycled home through the rapidly descending dusk, a clogging misery would spread through me. I was not smart enough to get a scholarship, and my grandmother would never allow me to go abroad to study, even though she could afford the fees. My future had already been decided.

It was at the American Center Library that I first got to know Mili Jayasinghe. I see him, for a moment now, not as the person I would come to know so well, but as the icon he was at that time: captain of the first eleven cricket team, head prefect, son of Tudor Jayasinghe, one of the richest men in Sri Lanka. I see him walking along school corridors with his easy loose-limbed grace, hands in pockets, white shirt and long pants crisply ironed; I see his long, elegant features and his glistening black hair, falling over his forehead to obscure his burnt-caramel eyes, his skin, from his Burgher mother, the tan of unglazed pots. A coterie of boys was always around him, their worship unstinting, because Mili was easy with his friendship. He did not withhold it, like other popular boys, as a privilege to be earned.

That afternoon at the American Center I was bent over a prospectus for a San Francisco university when I felt someone's gaze on me. I looked up and saw Mili watching me from across the room. He signalled with two fingers to his lips that he was going outside to smoke and that I should come with him. I gaped, then looked down at the prospectus, sure he must be gesturing to someone else. Though we had been in the same class for years, I had never spoken to him beyond an occasional mumbled greeting. After a moment, his shadow fell across my page. "What, Shivan, are you blind or something? Let's go out and have a fag." He smiled with amiable amusement to show he understood my surprise at being selected but thought it silly. I got up and hurried to keep pace with his loping stride, close enough to notice for the first time his scent like sea water.

Mili led me to the shade of an araliya tree. As he leaned back against the trunk, his arched torso strained the gap between his shirt buttons, revealing his navel and the fanning of hairs around it. He drew out a cigarette, lit it, then offered the pack to me. I shook my head. For a while he was quiet, enjoying his cigarette, eyes hooded as he gazed into the mid-distance and exhaled smoke. I stood before him, right arm rigid across my stomach, hand clutching my left elbow.

"How is Renu, by the way?"

"My sister?"

"Yes, Renu. Don't you know I volunteer with her?"

"Volunteer?"

He grinned at my bewilderment. "At Kantha. You know, the women's organization."

Kantha was headed by Sriyani Karunaratne, Renu's history professor at the University of Colombo, which she had entered that year. Karunaratne was a feminist, and Renu's feelings about men and the power they enjoyed over women—the condition of her own mother; the male students who harassed her because she was more intelligent than they were—had found expression through feminism. My sister approached everything with fervour, and she had soon become embroiled in fighting for the rights of women employed in the garment factories in the recently opened up free trade zone.

"But why on earth do you volunteer for this organization?" I asked, surprise making me bold.

"Because I want to make a difference in the world. I want Sri Lanka to be a better place."

I nodded, but was still baffled at Mili Jayasinghe undertaking such work, which was the province of unpopular, sanctimonious, weak, often religious boys in our school.

"What are you planning to take in America?" he asked.

"Um, English literature." I blushed, caught unawares by his question.

"I'm going to study international development." He gave me a long but timid look from under his lashes. "Unlike a lot of buggers who are planning to get the hell out of this country and never return, I want to come back and put something into Sri Lanka. I want to make things better for people who are poor and suffering here. I love Sri Lanka, and I'm not going to desert it. And I'm certainly not taking over my pater's bloody garment factories and exploiting poor women."

I understood he had asked me what I was going to study so he could tell me about his own plans and hear how his ideas sounded out loud. I was probably the first boy in our school he had confessed them to, and no doubt he'd singled me out because he counted me among the poor and downtrodden, being a charity student. I sensed his vulnerability, his shyness about his ambitions.

"Gosh," I said, "if you keep this up, you'll be the Mother Teresa of Sri Lanka."

He laughed. "That's good, machan. The Mother Teresa of Sri Lanka." He tilted his head to one side. "I didn't know you were such a wit."

"Yes, yes," I continued, thrilled at this compliment, "when you come off the plane, freshly returned from America, multitudes will line up to garland you and touch your feet." He laughed again. "Our very own Sri Lankan Gandhi. You will ride in a bullock cart, to show you are a humble man of the people. Women will let down their hair and swoon when you pass."

"What else?" He grinned, body tilted back, eyes slightly narrowed, as if appraising an object for purchase.

"Oh, there will be no stopping you." I was sweating from my desire to impress him. "Soon your teeth will be stained red from chewing bulath. You will smoke foul-smelling beedies instead of American cigarettes, you will stop using deodorant and be rank with the true odour of Lanka."

"And what will I wear?"

"Hmm, I was going to say the national costume, but realistically that is no longer the outfit of the common man. You certainly don't want to go about looking like a politician. No, you will wear a loin cloth and walk around with a scythe over your shoulder to show solidarity with the workers."

"A loin cloth! But my arse will be on display for everyone to see."

"Yes, that is why I said women will let down their hair and swoon. At the sight of your hairy backside. And of course chief among your admirers will be my dear sister. Our very own goddess Kali, She Who Is Blacker Than the Night," I said, shamelessly offering up Renu to get another laugh.

"That is too much, machan," Mili tittered. He drew on his cigarette and exhaled, dark purple lips parting and pulling down slightly at the corners. He cocked one leg against the tree trunk and his grey jeans pulled tight. I looked away.

"So, are you finished at the library, Shivan?"

"I don't know."

"Why don't you come back to my house? It's not far from here. Do you have a bike?"

I nodded.

Mili led the way towards Cinnamon Gardens. The Jayasinghes lived on Horton Place in a three-storey Georgian mansion with a long driveway that curved around an oval of lawn. There were square turrets at either end of the house. When we reached the gate, Mili pointed to one of the turrets. "My room is up there. You'll like the view, machan." He grinned. "With binoculars, you won't believe the Cinnamon Gardens titties I have seen."

"Ah, the Sex Fiend of Cinnamon Gardens," I declared, wanting to prevent any serious discussion of women and sex. "The Daring Deviant of the Propertied Classes."

He nodded to egg me on as we wheeled our bicycles up the driveway.

"Read all about it." I held up my hand to declaim a headline. "Scion of Noble Family Reveals All about Damsels of Cinnamon Gardens. Find Out Who Has One Tit, Who Has No Tits at All, Who Is Three-titted."

We were almost at the house now, and I noticed a Mercedes-Benz was parked in the porte cochère, a driver lounging beside it. When he saw the car, Mili halted, frowning. Then he continued up the driveway at a quicker pace, as if he had forgotten I was with him. I followed. Once we reached the house, Mili shoved his bicycle against a wall and said to the driver, "Are they already home from the club?"

The driver nodded. Some silent exchange sent a twitch of alarm over Mili's face.

He turned to me. "Machan, the pater and mater are home, so maybe another time, ah?"

"Yes, of course," I said. Yet before I could turn my bicycle around, there was a gabble of voices within and footsteps clattered towards the verandah.

Tudor Jayasinghe strode out of a French door, his bald head bent as if about to charge, Mili's mother following. Some of the loops in her elaborate hairstyle had come undone and lay in coils about her shoulders. "That's right, leave, you bloody bastard," she shrieked. "Run to your bloody whore." She took off one of her high-heeled shoes and flung it, hitting her husband in the back.

He spun around and moved towards her, fists raised in a boxer's stance.

"Don't touch her, you bloody shit." Mili rushed up to the verandah. He shoved his father away and stood with arms outstretched to protect his mother.

Mr. Jayasinghe looked like he was going to hit Mili, but then his fists fell by his sides. He turned towards the car, rubbing his forehead with the heel of his palm. Mili's mother collapsed into a chair and began to cry with great choking sobs.

"Amma, Amma, don't." Mili knelt to embrace her. "What's the point in crying?"

She clung to him, still sobbing.

I had already seen more than was decent. Turning my bicycle, I rode down the driveway, wincing at how loudly my tires ground the gravel.

Even if Mili's mother had not mentioned the "bloody whore," I would have guessed the cause of the quarrel, for the Jayasinghes were a prominent family and the gossip about them was well known. Mili's father had a mistress, a famous film star, and the two of them were frequently seen about town at various hotels and clubs. He had even brought the mistress to Nuwara

Eliya for the racing season and set her up in a suite at the Grand Hotel. He would spend days, and sometimes nights, with her, abandoning his wife and son at their holiday chalet. Mrs. Jayasinghe and Mili had become virtual prisoners, unable to attend the races or go into town for fear of meeting the couple in public. I was sure, now, that the real reason Mili had joined Kantha was to rebel against his father. The organization protested against conditions in the very garment factories Tudor Jayasinghe owned. I knew from Renu that people from Kantha frequently went out to the free trade zones to educate women workers about their rights and offer practical help with housing and birth control. By participating, Mili was shaming his father.

The next day, during the school interval, Mili sat, as he often did, on the teacher's table surrounded by his admirers. I read at my desk, watching him. He had avoided me the whole day, and now, aware of my gaze, he glanced at me helplessly before looking away.

7

Since childhood, I had been aware of an escalating tension between the Sinhalese and Tamils. In 1977, riots flared in parts of the island, though Colombo remained unaffected. The loss of Tamil lives, homes and businesses only gave strength to the Tamil Tiger rebels and their fight for an independent homeland. As I grew into my teens, the rebels began to bomb state institutions, rob banks and kill policemen. In retaliation, the government passed the Prevention of Terrorism Act, which allowed them to make arrests without warrants, hold a person indefinitely without laying a charge, use confessions made under duress as admissible evidence and dispose of bodies without an inquest. The torture and disappearance of Tamils only invigorated the independence movement. By 1981, parts of Sri Lanka were again in the grip of communal riots, sparked by a clash between Sinhala and Tamil students at a sports event. And once again, Colombo was spared, apart from a few days of curfew.

How lightly all this registered on my consciousness. I don't even remember much talk about these incidents. Perhaps we Sri Lankans could not bear to look directly at the increasing tension; perhaps, also, we could not imagine our country sinking to the level it ultimately did, could not imagine we were capable of such degradation. It was inflation that I most remember people complaining about. The government, under pressure from the World Bank and the IMF, had opened up the economy and devalued the rupee. A pound of chilies quadrupled in price while salaries remained the same.

Then, during June and early July of 1983, when I was eighteen and about to take my A-level exams, the violence speeded up. Tamil Tigers frequently attacked soldiers and policemen; in return, more Tamil civilians were tortured and disappeared. Sinhalese thugs and some soldiers destroyed Tamil shops in the eastern town of Trincomalee; in retaliation, Tamil Tigers burnt a Jaffna train. This allowed the railway authorities to cancel all trains to Jaffna, the Tamil capital, effectively cutting off the food supply.

On July 25, my sister and I were having breakfast in the saleya with my mother, when the doorbell rang. Rosalind went to answer it and returned with my grandmother's thug, Chandralal. Rosalind's pursed lips and large eyes told us something terrible had happened. My grandmother was having breakfast in her bedroom, and Chandralal went to talk with her. The ayah now told us what she had learnt: thirteen soldiers murdered by the Tamil Tigers had been buried the previous evening at the Kanaththa Cemetery in Colombo. A mob had gathered at the funeral and then fanned out through the neighbourhood, burning Tamil houses and killing Tamil people.

We were only a ten-minute car ride from the cemetery. Sunlight slanted in through the windows across our tablecloth, babblers chirped and squabbled among the hibiscus bushes, music from a radio next door drifted in. It was impossible to believe this news was true.

My grandmother emerged from her room, followed by Chandralal. She was gripping the yoke of her housecoat, a fleck of jam on her chin.

"So, you've heard?" she said to my mother, addressing her in a civil tone for the first time since we had moved into her house.

"Well, perhaps last night has seen the end of it," my mother replied, also forgetting her usual curt tone with my grandmother. "Surely the government will act to stop it?"

My grandmother gestured for Chandralal to speak.

He cleared his throat. "I've heard rumours that certain members of government are behind the rioting. The funeral mob, it seems, was armed with electoral lists telling them which houses were Tamil." I had been mechanically eating but now lay down my cutlery, the clang of my fork loud in the silence. "These members of government say they are sick of the Tigers and wanted to teach Tamils a lesson." He winced as if apologizing for them.

"So, what shall we do?" my mother whispered.

"Well, we are registered as a Sinhalese house," my grandmother replied. "But just to be on the safe side, Chandralal is sending two of his golayas to keep guard."

"I must leave soon, nona," Chandralal said. "You never know when curfew will be declared."

A look passed between them. "Yes-yes, you must indeed go," my grandmother cried as if she were delaying him from some pleasant event.

She followed Chandralal out to the verandah and they talked in low tones for a while. Once he had left, she returned with an odd glint of excitement in her eyes, which she tried to hide with a stern frown as she bustled towards her room.

"How can you trust that man, Amma," my mother called out after her. "He's just a common thug."

My grandmother increased her pace. "*Chandralal* is loyal to me."

"Yes, yes, that is all very well, but I don't trust him."

"Well, what choice do you have?" my grandmother shot back as she disappeared into her room.

And so for that week we stayed at home while the waves of violence crashed around us, then withdrew, only to surge forward again. We could not go out, and even avoided standing at the gate, fearing unfriendly neighbours or their servants might recall we were Tamil and inform the mobs. The only comfort we had was the presence of Chandralal's golayas, who played cards and carom in the shade of the front garden, and who, despite their burly appearance, were friendly and deferential, calling my sister and me "baba," as if they had been long-time servants of our household. When we had our lunch on the back verandah, they ate turned away from us in the kitchen on low stools, as if not wanting to give offence. I spent most of my time reading. Hours passed slowly, my fear so constantly present I was not even aware of it until rumour that a mob might be coming down our street would send a clang of terror through me.

One day, the Tamil houses on the roads around ours went up in flames. For a few hours in the afternoon, we could hear the roar and crackle of fire, the crashing of furniture being destroyed. Once, a woman screamed, a gargled sound so chilling it haunts me to this day. The air was rancid with smoke and we walked around with handkerchiefs pressed to our noses, coughing and gagging when it was at its worst. In the evening, bits of ash floated into my grandmother's garden, settling on her flowers.

Our street escaped the violence, and it was only later that we found out we owed that to Chandralal. Not only had he posted two henchmen at our house, he had spoken to the local gang lord and reached a deal with him that left our street inviolate. We didn't question why Chandralal had gone to such lengths to save us, or what deal he had made. Perhaps we didn't want to know.

After the riots, like everyone else, we had no choice but to pick up our lives and continue with work, school and, in my case, examinations. But Sri Lanka and Colombo were not the same. There was a sizzle of fear in the air, and a car backfiring would cause pedestrians to turn quickly towards the sound, bodies tensed. Then there were the burnt Tamil shops on Galle Road, the blackened interiors like gaping maws. We never went, like others, to ogle the destroyed houses on neighbouring streets, but little messengers of the destruction would periodically arrive in our garden—birds feathering their nests with crisped book pages, squirrels carrying cupboard knobs and buttons to bury in our flower beds, or an occasional bone whose provenance we did not want to guess. We made sure to be home before dark; Colombo became a ghost city after sunset.

Many Tamil students in our school were destitute, and I avoided looking at these boys when I passed them in the corridor. Because I was only half Tamil, my mother had been able to choose what language stream she put me in, and she had chosen Sinhala, the language of Colombo and government. Now I was frightened that my classmates, who had often baited Tamil boys, would recall I was part Tamil too.

Those students unaffected by the riots were asked to bring in uniforms, exercise books, pens and pencils to aid Tamil students. Mili Jayasinghe took the lead in collecting these items, soliciting money from students to help teachers who had lost their homes, raising funds for the funeral of an A-level commerce master who was murdered with his family. Mili exhorted his classmates during the interval to donate clothes and canned goods, to offer up their allowances. The language streams normally kept to themselves, but now Mili visited Tamil classes and asked boys to come out for a game of cricket or rugger.

All this earnest effort lowered Mili's reputation among the very boys who had worshipped him before. His charitable exertions were seen as unmanly and excessive. I watched his admirers withdrawing, as if his diminishing status was contagious. But Mili seemed unaware of this withdrawal—either that, or he did not care.

It is odd now to think that Mili was the one who handed me my freedom.

One morning a few weeks after the riots ended, he cornered me in the corridor. "I say, Shivan, how is your family coping with all this? I was so happy to learn you weren't affected."

"I . . . I, we're fine." I glanced around, hoping no one was listening.

"Ah, I'm very glad to hear that," Mili said with great enthusiasm, as if he had known my family well for a long time. "Are you all planning to emigrate, too?"

"Emigrate?"

"Yes, don't you know? The Canadian and Australian embassies are offering to fast-track immigration for Tamils who want to leave Sri Lanka. You have to meet certain criteria, like fluency in English and things like that." He sighed and pushed the hair back from his forehead. "What a brain drain. The country will lose so many of our doctors, lawyers and engineers, not to mention school teachers. We damn Sinhalese deserve this."

The recent upheavals had shaken loose some desperate courage in me, for after school that afternoon I cycled to the Canadian High Commission on Gregory's Road. There was a high wall around the building with rolls of barbed wire along the top. The massive takaran-covered gates were closed, but people were being let in through a smaller gate by the guard's room. I lined up, too. The applicants ahead were being asked to hand over their identity cards in order to enter. I took mine out. When I got to the guard, he looked me over and asked what I wanted. "I . . . I'm here to pick up an immigration form." He squinted skeptically, so I added, "Yes, my mother, Mrs. Rassiah, called ahead and spoke to a lady, a Mrs. . . . Peiris?"

"You mean Mrs. Perera," he said with a grim little smile. I had been fingering my school tie all the while, and I noticed a change in the guard's demeanour when he glanced at the colours of my premier school. "Here is my ID." I held the card out to him in a lordly manner, hoping he would not observe my trembling hand.

After that I easily obtained the form, mentioning to the receptionist that my mother had called Mrs. Perera.

When I got home, I spread the form out on my bed and stood gazing at it. The familiar household sounds—Rosalind pounding roasted chilies in the mortar, the hiss of the gardener's sheers as he trimmed the croton bushes outside my window, the grinding piano scales of our neighbour's daughter—came to me as if from a distance. It seemed unbelievable that these few sheets of paper could be the beginning of a great change.

When my mother returned from work, I went to see her. She was unravelling her sari, part of it snaking along the floor. She looked up from unpinning the pleats and her eyes narrowed in surprise. I seldom came in to talk these days.

"Amma." I held out the form.

My mother took it with a little frown, then her brow rippled in astonishment. "Why are you giving this to me, Shivan?"

"Why do you think?" I replied rudely, hands in pockets, trying to appear nonchalant.

My mother threw the form on the bed and finished unravelling her sari. She stepped out of its puddle around her feet, twitched the neckline of her blouse into place, then sat on the bed and picked up the form. Outside her window, I could hear the *hush-hush* of the gardener watering the flowers beds with a hose.

"It seems that Canada and Australia are offering expedited immigration for Tamils who want to get out and—"

"Yes, I am aware of it, Shivan."

"You are?"

"Of course. Tamil people at work are applying."

"Then why didn't you think of us?" I cried.

She plucked at the chain around her neck, then shrugged. "I was thinking of changing my name back to Ariyasinghe, and changing yours and Renu's as well."

I was surprised by this, and troubled that my mother felt things were this bad.

"But immigration, Shivan. It is a large move." She sighed deeply.

"I know," I whispered. I came to sit by her. "But think of the life we could have there, Amma. Renu and I could go to a foreign university. Think," I held her gaze, "of the freedom for me."

Her eyes widened. Then she knelt on the floor and began to fold her sari, head bent. I was desperate to escape her misery but forced myself to sit there, fearing that if I left I would lose this precious chance at freedom.

It took my mother a couple of days to make her decision. One evening after my grandmother had gone for pooja, she summoned my sister and me to her room. She was sitting at her dressing table, the form laid out on it, all filled in. She looked at us for a long moment. "What would you think about immigrating to Canada?"

She spoke as if it was her idea; she had taken the burden off me.

"Canada?" Renu said. She grabbed the form and scowled at it. "Why?"

"What do you mean *why*, Renu?" my mother cried. "Are you not aware of what has happened in this country?"

"But I'm in university. I like it here."

"Sri Lanka is finished. It's time to get out. If so much rioting was caused by the death of thirteen soldiers, what is going to happen when twenty are killed?" My mother moved a ring up and down her finger. "And many more will be killed. This riot has only made the Tigers more powerful, more determined to get what they want. There is going to be a lot more violence. And Colombo Tamils are sitting ducks." She caressed my sister's arm. "Just think, Renu, you can go to a better university. One that isn't constantly shutting down because of student hartals."

My sister glared at the form and left the room.

Yet by the next evening, Renu had come around to the idea of immigration. Sriyani Karunaratne, her history professor, had told her that there were programs on feminism in the West called "women's studies." My sister could pursue this interest with greater focus in Canada and Professor Karunaratne had urged her to seize this opportunity.

The man who interviewed us at the Canadian embassy was plump and spoke with a wheeze. His bald crown was sun-reddened and peeling, and he had gathered his remaining hair into a thin ponytail that hung wetly down his back. Despite the office air-conditioning, he constantly rubbed his face and neck with a handkerchief, great bruises of perspiration in the armpits of his shirt. As he looked over our papers, I studied the posters of snow-capped mountains and sparkling rivers running through mint-green valleys. In odd contrast to these images were other posters of children and adults from the nations of the earth, decked out in their exotic national costumes and posed before the same gothic building, which I would later learn housed the Parliament of Canada. These immigrants seemed to smile down at us prospective applicants in a smug and distancing way, as if we had to prove ourselves worthy before their smiles would become genuine.

The official asked my mother a few questions about her work and looked at her qualifications. When he found out my sister and I planned to attend university, he inquired about what we wished to study and recommended some colleges. He kept saying, "When you are in Canada," until finally my mother leaned forward, fingers knitted. "Sir, you keep saying *when* we are in Canada. Have we . . . already passed?"

"Oh, yes," the man said, as if surprised we did not know. Then he smiled. "This is just a formality. Of course, you have to get through your medicals and security checks." He peered at us over the top of his glasses. "I may safely assume that none of you have TB or have engaged in criminal activity?"

"Oh, no, of course not." My mother let out a bark of amusement at his lame joke and my sister and I tittered, faces locked in grins.

The official asked where we wanted to settle, and my mother said Toronto, because that was where other Tamils were planning to go. He half-heartedly suggested Winnipeg, Saskatoon or Calgary, as if he knew we would never go there but considered it his duty to push other parts of Canada.

We were soon done. The official walked us to the door and shook our hands, his palm cushiony and damp.

The moment we were outside the gates of the High Commission, my mother let out a shout of happiness and hugged us. Seeing the pleasure on my mother's and sister's faces, I felt that the thing I had set in motion was real. It became even more real when our taxi pulled up to the house and I saw my grandmother sitting on the front verandah, reading a newspaper. We glanced at our mother, knowing that because we were in our good clothes our grandmother might ask where we had been.

"Children," our mother murmured. There was a new twitch of energy to her. She stepped out of the taxi first and held the door open for us. As I climbed out, I glanced at my grandmother. She had lowered her paper and was studying us, eyes unblinking, face inscrutable.

My mother led the way up the front steps, head raised, handbag tucked under her arm, high heels castanets against the floor. As we followed her, I jerked at my collar to loosen my tie, frowning with concentration.

"Shivan," my grandmother snapped, "come. I want to go and look at a property."

"No, Amma, Shivan has just been out," my mother called over her shoulder as she bustled into the saleya. "I want him to take off his good clothes, have a shower and do his homework."

"Come, Shivan, come." My grandmother gripped my wrist as I made to go by her.

"Shivan, I want you to come inside and do as I say." My mother's voice punched out each word.

I looked from one to the other, then gently freed myself and continued into the house.

When I got to my room, I slumped down on my bed, pulse throbbing at the base of my throat. Then, before I knew it, I was clutching my head, whispering, "What have I done? What have I done?"

My grandmother did not ask where we had been that afternoon. She did not comment on the contest with her daughter and the decision I had made. She acted as if nothing had changed. Over the next days and weeks, as I looked at leaking cisterns and holes in roofs and rotting floors, or sat with her and Sunil Maama going through documents on the verandah, I felt a constant terror. I wanted, for a reason I could not explain, to stop what I had begun.

Three months later, we received our landed papers. It was my mother who led the way across the saleya to impart the news, eyes sparkling with triumph. My sister and I followed, not looking at each other but our shoulders touching for comfort. My mother, as always, stood before the curtain and called out, "Amma?"

"Yes? What is it?" my grandmother replied.

We found her in bed, bolstered by pillows, going through a bank statement. She glared at my mother over her spectacles, rustling the statement to indicate she wished this meeting to be brief. Then she saw my sister and me hovering in the doorway and a stitch plucked its way across her forehead. She sat up a little straighter, hands folded in lap, her face emptied of any emotion. Sweat prickled the back of my neck.

"Amma," my mother said, her voice resonant with gloating. "I have some news for you. I want you to know that we, the children and I, have been passed for immigration. To Canada."

After a long moment, my grandmother picked up the bank statement again and examined it.

"We will be leaving in a few weeks, Amma." My grandmother still did not respond. "Is that alright?"

"Why do you ask me?" The statement fluttered as if my grandmother had palsy. "It seems I have nothing to do with your decision at all."

"Very well." My mother walked towards the doorway, then stopped, remembering something. "If you wish for us to leave your house, Amma, I have arranged—"

My grandmother flung down her paper and cried, as if pleading with an invisible person, "Look at the way she talks to me? All these years I have allowed her to live under my roof, all these years I have been a good mother, and see, just see, the way she repays me. Aiyo! What did I do in my past life, to deserve this . . . this wild bitch of a daughter?"

My mother's face flushed. "Eleven years I have lived under your roof, and in all that time you have never sat at the table and had a meal with me." Her right hand sliced out a rhythm on her left palm. "You call that being a good mother? I have hated every minute in this house and so have my children. Never mind your past life, you will pay for this cruelty in your future life. And no amount of bana and danas and donations for bells and robes at the temple will make up for what you have done."

"Get out," my grandmother whispered through gritted teeth. "Get out."

"Are you saying you want me to take the children and leave your house? You only need say the word."

My grandmother yelped. She looked around, picked up a paperweight from her side table and flung it at my mother. We cried out as my mother ducked. The paperweight crashed into the wall and shards of glass spattered across the floor.

Renu rushed to protect our mother, putting an arm around her shoulder, glaring at our grandmother. My mother let out a shuddering breath, and allowed herself be led out by my sister. I made to follow.

"Stay."

My grandmother beckoned me forward and I went to stand by her bed.

"Ah, Puthey," she said, her voice sad, "I know you had nothing to do with your mother's actions." She held out her hand. I took it, and she pulled me down on the bed beside her. "This must have been so hard to keep to yourself."

I gritted my teeth to hold in gulping sobs, but they came.

"Ah, Puthey, Puthey." She held my head against her bony chest and I clung to her, crying freely. Soon I felt her chest heaving as she sobbed too. "I am cursed by my karma," she whispered more to herself than me. "I *am* that Naked Peréthi. Am I to have no happiness in this life? Is everything I love to be taken from me?"

Finally, I tore myself away, ran into the saleya, past my mother and sister who stared at me, stricken, and into my room. I went into the bathroom, slammed the door, closed the commode lid and sat on it, sobbing into my hands, unable to stop, unable to understand why I was crying when everything had worked out as I desired.

My mother and sister did not speak to me about my outburst, but over the next few weeks I caught them observing me, frightened. I spent long hours reading in my bedroom or going for solitary bicycle rides. I was bloated with a new exhaustion and would sleep in the afternoon only to awaken heavy-headed and groggy.

My grandmother never mentioned our imminent departure and carried on as if nothing had happened. Yet her face was gaunt and empty. I could sense my mother begin to doubt what she had done. When we visited friends or my late grandfather's relatives to say goodbye, she would insist, as if they had contradicted her, that this was the best decision she had ever made in her life, that she could not wait to wipe her feet of this "godforsaken shipwreck of a country." Renu and I would often find her in the kitchen, seated on a stool beside Rosalind, peeling onions and garlic or sorting through kankong leaves. Every night, now, Rosalind lay her mat on the floor by my mother's bed in the way ayahs do with their charges. The murmur of their voices through the wall prevented me from falling asleep.

When my mother purchased our tickets, she informed my grandmother of our date of departure. That evening, while we were having dinner, my grandmother came out and sat at the table. Rosalind made to bring a plate, but she waved her away. "I have reached a decision. I am going to buy a house in Canada." She smiled wryly at our stunned faces.

"But how will you get the money to Canada," my mother asked, "what with currency restrictions and everything?"

My grandmother rubbed her forehead. "I have been putting away money over the years, quietly-quietly, in a London account." She sighed lightly. "Yes, I will buy this house."

"I don't need your house," my mother said.

"I'm not buying the house for you. This house is for Shivan." She looked at me with numb longing. "I need to know my grandson will have something in his new life that will help him." She grimaced at my mother. "I know that I cannot trust you to take care of my grandson. I shudder to think what ruination you will come to, left to your own devices in a foreign land."

My mother flushed and was about to retort, but Renu spoke up. "Take her damn house, Amma. It's the least the woman owes you, after the terrible way she has treated us. Who cares if it's in Shivan's name."

My mother turned to me. "Son?"

I did not know if I wanted this reminder of my grandmother in my new life. Yet, placed on the spot, I found myself nodding to say we would take her gift.

"Very well," my mother said. "When I am in Canada, I will open an account and you can transfer the money there."

After that, my grandmother contrived to spend as much time with me as possible, and we were frequently out on errands. As I looked at the various problems with her houses or visited banks or sat with her and Sunil Maama, going through documents on the verandah, my life seemed to pass before me as if I were watching it through a train window.

A few days before our departure, Sriyani Karunaratne, whose husband owned various hotels, invited all the people involved with Kantha to spend the day at a beach resort and bid farewell to Renu. My sister was flattered by the honour and delighted to have this last chance to be with her heroine. She usually did not take much trouble with her appearance, wearing skirts that reached down to her shins, hair tugged back in a plait. Yet that morning of the farewell party she was in a great flurry about what to wear and even borrowed my blow-dryer to tease her hair in a new fashion.

Renu was not ready when her friends arrived, and much to my annoyance I was sent to tell them she would be a few more minutes. There was a convoy of vehicles waiting outside the gate, and when I stepped out, shielding my eyes against the glare, someone called my name. I peered towards a packed car. In the driver's seat was a foreign man in his mid-twenties with pale skin reddened by the sun and whitish blond hair so fine his scalp was visible. Mili Jayasinghe sat beside him in the front passenger seat. He waved at me, yanked the door open and got out.

"Machan," he cried, as he came up to me. He clapped me on the back. "So, you're leaving our beloved island."

I heard a slight accusation in his tone, and I was suddenly furious at him, standing there so handsome, so confident. "Well, I am sure we Tamils will be missed. After all, who are the Sinhalese going to kill now?" I said "the Sinhalese," but it was clear I meant "*you* Sinhalese."

Mili was startled. "Yes, of course, Shivan, what choice do most Tamils have?"

"If we are abandoning Sri Lanka, it's because Sri Lanka abandoned us first."

"Definitely, machan, definitely," he said, bewildered by my rising voice.

Before we could say anything further, Renu rushed out, crying, "Aiyo, so sorry, men." There was a general calling out of greetings and chatter about which car they could squeeze her into.

"Well, Shivan," Mili said gently, and held out his hand to me. "I wish you the very best of luck. I wish you much happiness in Canada."

"Thank you," I mumbled and shook his hand, ashamed at my outburst and not meeting his gaze.

The evening before we left, my grandmother took me to the Wellawatte Kovil for a Ganesh pooja. My grandmother, like all Buddhists, turned to the Hindu gods for intervention with life's daily problems, these being beneath the Lord Buddha, who had transcended all desire. Ganesh, the remover of obstacles, was appealed to in times of crisis and change. The evening Ganesh pooja was always crowded. We took our place at the back, but soon a temple worker beckoned my grandmother forward. She always paid for this privilege, and when the priests opened the inner sanctum doors we were the first to surge forward, pushed by the crowd behind us.

The prime position was by a series of bells suspended from the ceiling in front of Ganesh. A rope dangled down from each clapper, and my grandmother, as she always did, held on to the upper part of one rope and indicated for me to take the lower end. Soon the windowless chamber was thick with incense, and on a cue from the priests we began to ring the bells. The clanging seemed to bulge the black stone walls outward. As I swayed back and forth with my grandmother, sweat trickling down my face, the boundaries of my body dissolved and melded into the *gong* of the bells, the reek of incense, the chanting of priests. My grandmother's hand had slid down over mine. I glanced at her, but she pretended not to notice. Together our hands moved in unison, ringing that bell.

We were to leave for the airport in the late afternoon, and throughout that last morning my grandmother stayed in her room. My mother, sister and I were acutely aware of her silent presence. I was possessed by the conviction she would make some surprising move that would stop us from going—some plot she would launch at the last minute to prevent my escape. But the morning passed busily, with a stream of visitors coming to say goodbye as we packed.

My mother had suggested that in anticipation of the long journey we should rest for an hour in the early afternoon. A sudden lull descended on our house, made all the more pronounced by the frantic bustle earlier. Rosalind, who had kept close to us, lay her mat by my mother's bed, and I could hear their voices and our ayah crying.

Suddenly there was much activity in my grandmother's room, followed by the slap of her slippers as she scuttled out into the saleya. "Rosalind," she called, but without waiting as she usually did for the ayah to appear, she continued on towards the front door. "I'm going out for a few hours. I'll be home for dinner."

I sat up in bed and listened to my grandmother's footsteps diminish into the distance. The car door slammed and the vehicle trundled down the driveway.

I could hear the grating call of a crow, the neighbour's child ringing out the choked sound of her broken tricycle bell.

"Thank God," I whispered to myself, "thank God, thank God."

And I vowed that I would never return to this house or this country again.

ঌ

In the story of the naked peréthi, a poor woman comes upon three drunken men who have fallen into an alcoholic stupor. She steals their clothes and money. A few days later, a monk is passing by her abode and she invites him to stop for a meal. She holds a sunshade above him as he eats, her heart filled with gladness. Because of this meritorious deed, she is reborn in a golden mansion on an island in the middle of the ocean. Yet because she stole from the drunken men, she is naked and hungry. Her wardrobes are full of fine clothes, but if she tries to put them on, they burn her skin like sheets of hot metal and she flings them from her, screaming. Her banquet table is set every day with the most sumptuous meals, but if she tries to eat, the food turns to urine and feces or swarms with maggots.

One day a storm blows a ship to the shores of her island. The captain and his passengers, upon seeing the naked peréthi, are terrified. But once they hear her story, they are filled with pity and offer any help they can. Among the passengers is a lay disciple of the Lord Buddha, and the peréthi says to the captain, "Nothing you can offer will free me. Instead, feed and clothe this lay disciple and transfer the merit to me." When the captain clothes the lay disciple in golden-threaded garments, the peréthi is immediately adorned in the finest Benares silk; when he feeds the lay disciple, a feast appears before the peréthi and she finds she can eat.

Many years would pass before I understood that my grandmother saw herself as that naked peréthi, marooned on an island, surrounded by so much that is good in life but unable to enjoy it. Everything she touched, everything she loved, disintegrated in her hands.

PART TWO

8

My mother's back garden has mounds of melting snow in corners, punctured with holes, as if machine-gunned. The cold is bearable because there is no wind. I take a swig from the mickey of Scotch I have brought with me. I can hear our neighbours, despite their tightly sealed doors and windows—the wail of a child, scolded by its mother in some clipped Chinese language, a ribbon of Hindi film music, the sizzle of a late-night dinner, a dog's staccato bark. Water gurgles and glops in the culvert beyond these back gardens, a steady counterpoint to this human activity. I open our gate and step out onto a narrow strip of grass from which the land slopes down to the channel. The black water is like oil, glinting with shards of light from the surrounding houses and a cluster of apartment buildings on the other side of the culvert. Looking up at these looming towers filled with immigrants, a line from one of my grandmother's stories comes to me. "They stand at crossroads or even outside the walls of their homes, these silent peréthayas. They are standing at their own gates, wanting to be let in." I murmur these lines as I begin to clamber down the slope, the water now a roar.

The maudlin sentimentality of my thoughts makes me realize I am quite drunk; and my drunkenness has given me the courage to come down to the culvert, something I have never done before. The descent is too slippery in winter, and in summer jagged voices of young men rise to our house, accompanied by the occasional shattering of a beer bottle. After I've made my way to the bottom, my shoes squelching in the muddy slope, I take another gulp of Scotch. As I begin to waver along the culvert's edge, I recall the first time I saw Canada from the plane—how, despite knowing we were arriving in summer, I was surprised at the green grass and trees between the stretches of grey highway, tarmac and squat rectangular buildings. In my imagination, I had been expecting snow.

❦

An old schoolmate of my mother's named Shireen Subramaniam was to meet us at the airport. My mother had written to her asking if she could suggest a cheap hotel we might live in until we found more permanent accommodation. Much to my mother's surprise, this woman, more acquaintance than friend, had replied that she and her husband, Bhavan, would be delighted to offer us hospitality until we got on our feet. My mother, while grateful, was uneasy about this generosity, as if she suspected something was amiss. There was a stridency in her voice when she told friends and relatives about this invitation, saying things like, "Yes-yes, we were good friends. I knew her very well."

As my mother, my sister and I dragged our bags off the luggage carousel and loaded them onto carts, we avoided looking at each other. The distractions of immigration formalities and negotiating this foreign airport had kept our anxiety at bay. But now, as we cleared Customs and made our way to the automatic doors, our apprehension swelled, turning to panic as we came out onto a low platform and found the arrivals lounge before us packed with people pressed up against the ramps that led down on either side into the chaos. We stopped, not knowing which way to go, bewildered by the muddle of foreign faces below, white, Asian, black, the babble of so many languages as people shrieked out greetings and instructions to their relatives and friends, the blurred stridency of PA announcements. Travellers, brought up short by our indecision, bumped into us and shoved past. We were gaping at my mother, waiting for her to identify this friend. What if Shireen and her husband had not come? What if they had forgotten the day? What if they had changed their minds? As if she had read our fears, my mother said, "I . . . I have their phone number, just in case."

She gripped her luggage cart, set her lips grimly and strode down one of the ramps. We scanned the crowd for a Sri Lankan face, and soon we saw a woman holding a placard with my mother's name on it.

"Shireen?" my mother cried, her voice fracturing with relief.

"Hema?" she cried back, her eyes popping behind gilt-edged glasses.

We hurried together towards the end of the ramp, separated from Shireen by the rail.

When we reached her, this woman threw her arms around my mother as if they were long-lost best friends. Startled, my mother submitted to the embrace.

"My, how grown up these children are!" she cried, as if she had known us when we were little. She embraced Renu and me in turn, pressing us against her bony form, gold bangles and necklace cold against our skin. "Welcome, welcome to Canada! Now, you children must call me Aunty Shireen." She beamed at us.

Aunty Shireen was angular like a faceted jewel, her carefully back-combed hair gleaming with lacquer. Her grey pinstriped suit had sharp creases, her pink silk shirt shimmered. She seemed genuinely pleased to see us, and our anxiety began to ease a little. She slipped her hand into the crook of my mother's arm and said, as she led us towards the elevator, "So, tell-tell, child, how are things back home?"

My mother, because she had nothing else in common with her, informed Shireen about their school friends. I had the impression from Aunty Shireen's slightly exaggerated reactions that she really did not remember these people.

Soon we were on the highway, and I gazed out at large billboards, taking in the plump gleaming food of fast food chains, models in department store clothing, the hard, gleaming bodies of men in an underwear ad. The sheer size of the billboards seemed a promise of affluence and happiness. Then there were the cars, so new and clean, not belching diesel smoke as they did in Sri Lanka. The speed at which everyone drove was terrifying, the foreignness of a seat belt constricting.

As she drove along, Aunty Shireen informed us that her husband had gone on a week-long golfing trip with some of his fellow real-estate agents. "Oh, he was so disappointed he couldn't be around to welcome you," she said, her voice resonant with some emotion I couldn't identify.

In Colombo, a fifteen-minute trip was considered long, and this drive, which took an hour, seemed to go on forever. Soon the streets all began to look alike. I wondered if Aunty Shireen had made a mistake and we were looping back; the billboards we passed had the same images as the ones we had driven by earlier.

The Subramaniams lived in the upscale suburb of Unionville. Once we pulled into their subdivision we were in the midst of large detached houses with three-door garages and sloping manicured lawns, rock-lined flower beds prim with rows of colourful portulacas. I felt I had been in a place like this before, and it took me a moment to realize I had seen versions of it in numerous American made-for-TV films. I felt a thrill of satisfaction; I had arrived in the middle of my dreams.

Aunty Shireen's house reinforced this sense of arrival, with its shiny hardwood floors, oriental carpets, grand piano and gilded Chinese furniture upholstered in red silk. Everything about the interior gleamed and sparkled, especially her kitchen. We took in its smooth white cupboards, marble counters, deep black stove and dishwasher, and when Aunty Shireen opened her refrigerator, we gawped as brilliant lights came on to illuminate a glossy white interior, spotless glass shelves, an array of bottles filled with things we had never tasted, like corn relish and capers. "Ah," Aunty Shireen said as she turned to Renu and me with the smile of a magician about to pull off a final dazzling trick, "I know just what these young people want." She drew out a massive plastic bottle of Coca-Cola with a flourish and began to pour us tall glasses. Coca-Cola was still a luxury in Sri Lanka. As I took my first long draft, the bubbles pleasantly tickled my throat and I blushed with delight.

After our drinks, Aunty Shireen took us down to our apartment, oddly brusque now. Though she called the flat a basement, it was really above ground, with patio doors leading out to the back garden. It ran the length of the house, with a sitting area, galley kitchen, two bedrooms and a bathroom. The carpet was an immaculate white shag, my sock-clad feet stroked by its silky pile as I followed our host. She led us solemnly from room to room, pointing out the light switches, opening and shutting the glinting taps to display the water pressure as we stood on fluffy bath mats that released the smell of dryer sheets. In my allotted room, the wallpaper was bottle green and purple stripes, like a Victorian gentleman's study.

When we were done the tour, Aunty Shireen became her jolly self again and cried, "Now, you all get changed and showered, then we will have dinner." She winked at Renu and me. "I know exactly what you will be wanting." She paused for dramatic effect. "Kentucky Fried Chicken!"

The morning after we arrived, I went out for a jog. I had told myself that when I arrived in Canada I would take up this sport I had seen so many Americans do in films. I had even got myself an outfit—a blue track suit with double white stripes down the outside seams, a matching head band. I made my way along the sidewalk with the lumbering gait of a first-time runner, fists clenched, elbows pressed to my sides. Some of the neighbours were up getting papers, watering lawns, walking dogs, gardening. I was acutely conscious they were white, but they did not seem aware of my difference, and a few even raised a hand and called out, "Morning," as I passed. Soon another jogger bounded towards me, a tall blond young man. He was wearing shorts and a singlet, and I felt caught out in my full track suit, now sweat-slickened inside. He passed me with a military nod, leaving me diminished by the hairy whiteness of his muscular limbs.

How rife with clichés our arrival was: the Coca-Cola, the KFC, the billboards, the white shag carpet, the resplendent fridge, that passing jogger. By the time I came out, a year later, I understood that abject awe at Coca-Cola and shag carpet was not cool. I would pretend to the other young gay men I met at groups or bars that I had not been awed at all by Canada. I said I felt no culture shock, acting like I had slipped into this world as if it were my natural element.

A week after we arrived, Bhavan, or Uncle Bhavan, as we soon called him, returned from his golfing trip. Aunty Shireen had taken us for lunch at McDonald's and we came back to find a sleek silver Jaguar in the driveway. "Ah, Bhavan is back!" Aunty Shireen shrilled, her voice snagging on his name. My family glanced at each other uneasily.

When we entered the house we saw Bhavan in the kitchen, flipping through his mail on the counter. He was squarely built, with the round stomach of a mudalali. Aunty Shireen sang out his name as we took off our shoes in the foyer, but he did not acknowledge our presence. Once we had removed our coats, she led us in to meet him. "Bhavan," she said anxiously, "are you deaf or something?"

He slit open an envelope with the careless flick of a silver knife, his pink moist lips a stern line, his luxuriant moustache prickled tight. We stood in awkward silence as he scanned the letter. His beige safari shirt was open at the top, thick gold chain and medallion nestled in his matted chest hair. Bhavan threw the letter on the counter and turned to us. A brilliant grin split his face. He held out his arms and declared in a deep rich voice, "Welcome, welcome!"

In turn, he took each of our hands in both of his, gazing at us with fervent goodwill, inquiring how we were liking Canada and what we had done so far.

We took the first opportunity to go downstairs to our apartment. Shireen followed. As we unloaded our shopping bags, she went about plumping cushions on the sofa, tugging the curtains into place. We watched her, feeling something awful was coming. Finally, she turned to my mother. "The thing is, Hema, we . . . we usually charge for this apartment."

My mother struggled to hide her surprise, then cried with relief, "But Shireen, why didn't you say anything before. I would be so happy to offer you rent."

Aunty Shireen's eyes brimmed with gratitude.

"Now, come, come." My mother pressed Aunty Shireen's arm. "You have been most generous. Tell me how much you would like."

Aunty Shireen said they usually charged twelve hundred dollars, but because she and my mother were such "dear old friends," she was only going to ask for a thousand.

"Yes, yes, of course," my mother replied, then declared, "Oh, you children are putting the groceries away all wrong," and rushed to sort out our alleged mistakes so Shireen would not see her disquiet at the high rent.

Once Aunty Shireen had left, my mother turned to us and said with false cheer, "Well, that is settled. I suppose we should be grateful, nah, to have such a nice place." She added, to reassure us and herself, "Anyway, it's only temporary. Tomorrow itself I will ask Bhavan to start looking for a house."

Yet when my mother approached Bhavan, now so warm and friendly, he looked dismayed and said, "But what is the hurry?" and Aunty Shireen added, "You just got here."

"You don't like being with us?" Bhavan pouted.

"No, no, Bhavan," my mother assured him, flushing, "it's just that my mother wants this house bought soon."

"Our home is so cheery with these children. Stay, stay."

Aunty Shireen murmured in agreement.

Bhavan leaned close to my mother and frowned. "A word of advice, Hema. Don't be in a rush. That is the biggest mistake new immigrants make. Live with us for at least six months to a year, and slowly-slowly we will look around until you find the area you want to be in. Always pick your area first, I tell my clients. Then set your price and don't budge from it. I never let my clients rush into things."

It was the first moment we realized how alone, how helpless, we were in this country.

In the weeks that followed, Uncle Bhavan showed my mother how to prepare a resumé, something she'd never had to do in Sri Lanka. Aunty Shireen took her to buy office outfits and then to temp agencies. Soon my mother was going out on assignments.

The Subramaniams had no Sri Lankan friends. Mingling within the Sri Lanka community, they told us, was not the way to get on in this country. "What is the point of coming here and remaining in a ghetto," Uncle Bhavan would thunder after he'd had a few drinks in the evening. "Our bloody people are so closed-minded. And Canadians resent this racial exclusivity, this spitting on their hospitality. After all, they have been so kind, allowing all our bloody buggers into their country."

It was clear that they would not look fondly on us making connections with the growing Sri Lankan community in Toronto, and we were cowed enough to comply.

The Subramaniams never cooked Sri Lankan food in their house, and this was one of the rules Aunty Shireen informed us of soon after we arrived. Both husband and wife said that the lingering odour of curries smelt like cow dung, that "our people" didn't know how they shamed themselves going out in public with their coats stinking of spices; that they pitied the poor Canadians who had to sit next to them on the subway or bus. They didn't want their "very dear friends" coming over and thinking they were a couple of "pakis," these dear friends being Canadians they fraternized with at the Buttonville Golf and Country Club.

Yet I quickly saw that there was something defensive behind their contempt for the growing Sri Lankan population. They had become out of touch with Sri Lanka and did not fit into the new community. And the community's indifference to perceived white expectations—cooking Sri Lankan food, forming their own social groups—made a mockery of the sacrifices the Subramaniams had endured to integrate, sacrifices that were increasingly unnecessary. Though my family never talked about it, we were desperate for an excuse to leave.

Our escape presented itself soon after Renu got a job at a mall. Uncle Bhavan offered to drive her to work and back, as the mall was far from where we lived and there was little public transport. I had also got a job at a nearby doughnut shop, and I arrived home one evening to find Uncle Bhavan in the family room, sprawled out in an easy chair, feet on a stool, watching television. Aunty Shireen, who worked as a chartered accountant downtown, had not come home yet. "Ah, son." He raised his hand. "How are you?" He had never called me "son" before. His voice and smile were weighted with regret.

I came downstairs to find Renu seated on the sofa, eyes red, my mother holding her hands. One glance from them told me what had happened.

My mother was truly upset at Bhavan, but she also gloated with triumph. Within a week he had helped her buy a tiny row house in the suburb of Scarborough, closer to downtown.

In our poor ward of L'Amoreaux there were only cheap identical houses and multi-laned grey roads on which traffic roared. The only recreational activity was shopping at the Bridlewood Mall. Our short dead-end street, Melsetter Boulevard, had two lines of row houses facing each other—flimsy board structures surfaced with anaemic-pink concrete bricks with brown asphalt roof shingles continuing a third of the way down the front facades. The tiny lawns were parched, the spindly trees gnarled, some limbs producing no flowers or leaves. Tall apartment towers beyond the back gardens spread their long shadows over our street.

Still, it was our first home in Canada and represented life on our own terms. The day we moved in, my mother called all the Indian stores in the Yellow Pages until she found Sadroos, which sold Sri Lankan products. That first night, she splurged and ordered in a pizza. We had no furniture and sat on the worn rust-red carpet, as if at a picnic. "How lucky we are to have this house," my mother said as she held up a slice of pizza in salute. "A new future is before us, children."

"A new future," we echoed.

Yet as we ate our pizza, a gloom came over me, and I could see this despondency in my mother's and sister's faces too. This luck my mother had toasted was not luck at all, but my grandmother's gift to us.

A few days after we moved in, we noticed that the lime-green carpet in the basement became damp in the centre whenever we used the washing machine. We called in a plumber to look at the problem. He would need to dig up the floor to find the leak. The job could cost thousands of dollars. We told him we couldn't afford it and he grimaced in sympathy. "You're new here, aren't you?" He shook his head. "Looks like you've been had. Whoever sold you the house knew about this."

He explained to us that the odour, which we had thought was just how basements smelt, was actually the smell of damp. Anyone who had lived in this country, particularly a real-estate agent, would have recognized it.

9

THE CULVERT NEAR MY MOTHER'S HOUSE PASSES under a bridge that spans the main road and continues between steep banks rising to back fences on either side. As I make my way beyond the bridge along the edge of this open drain—past the clumps of filthy snow on the banks, which, as they melt, reveal nibbled Styrofoam cups, yellowed globules of Kleenex, condoms, straws, dog shit, cigarette packs, tattered mittens and scarves—I think again of that moment when we saluted our new future.

A few months after we arrived in Canada, I started my first year at York University, studying English literature. The university had been built in the 1960s and '70s, and its structures were relics of the era's worst architectural excesses—massive, starkly functional, a paucity of windows, a predominance of concrete. They were scattered about a windswept landscape and reminded me of grey boulders abandoned by a glacier. The considerable distances between buildings had necessitated a labyrinth of underground tunnels along which students could travel when the weather got too miserable. The tunnel walls were covered with images of fierce bearded men vomiting blood, snakes coiled to strike, fangs bared, poems that rhymed badly, elaborate graffiti tags of the artists. Parts of the wall were white where the university had come along and painted over the graffiti, but it was a losing battle.

York had been established during a period of great student unrest, and the campus was designed to keep us on the move with very few places to congregate—lots of corridors and hallways, few common rooms and courtyards.

The centre of the university, if there was a centre to this haphazard scattering of edifices, was the Ross Building, a lumbering mass built in the brutalist style, its inner and outer walls exposed concrete. With its tiny slits of windows, it resembled the secret service department in some fascist country, where unspeakable things were done to people.

Most of the first-year classes were held in vast lecture halls, tiers of orange plastic seats rising in a vertiginous slant from the strip of floor where the professor lectured. I felt like a cork bobbing in the whorl of students coming and going around me. As I sat in those classes, twisting pen between fingers, I would watch other students talking and laughing with each other, sharing a bar of chocolate or a bag of chips. Eavesdropping on conversations, I came to realize that most of them were either in residence together or, if they were day students, had known each other in high school. When a class broke into tutorials for its second half, the more intimate atmosphere provided a chance to make friends. Yet despite my willingness to take on a difficult or long novel other students balked at, to share pens or paper, to initiate discussions, no classmate seemed interested in any interaction outside the course. The more I tried to force friendships, the more awkward I became. When I attempted to strike up a conversation, I was aware of a new creaking to my voice, my gestures too big, my laugh a bark. I was sure the other students sensed my desperation. It hung about me like body odour.

After an evening class on Thursdays, I passed a student residence on my way to the bus. A party would often be in progress, rooms jammed with bodies, students shrieking out lyrics and stomping to the beat of a song by Annie Lennox or the Pet Shop Boys. Someone would lean out the window and bellow "Paaarty!" or "Fuck the world!" or some obscene political curse about Mulroney, Thatcher or Reagan. I would draw my jacket about me and keep my eyes on the ground, afraid someone might see my craving to be one of them, and mock me.

Their merriment would linger with me on the hour-long bus ride home. Often the bus would be crowded and I'd be unable to find a seat, because in addition to regular students there were the adult learners, all of us disgorged by the university after its last class. I would hold on to a bar with one hand, my arm wrenching from its socket as the bus swayed or abruptly stopped. In the winter, melted snow sloshed in the ridges of the floor and left salty rims on my boots.

I became aware that the two places downtown students considered cool were Kensington Market and Queen Street. I called the TTC information line and the young woman I spoke to was very helpful, especially after I pretended to be a tourist. She gave me directions for Kensington Market, but when I mentioned Queen Street, she said, "Sir, which part did you have in mind? It's a very long street."

"The . . . the part that has lots of fashionable cafés and bookshops and other nice stores."

"Ah, sir, you mean Queen West."

She then gave me alternate directions to Kensington Market which would take me through "Queen West."

After I boarded the westbound Queen streetcar and it set off, I was sure I had written the instructions down wrong, because we were travelling through a corridor of tall buildings. Once the streetcar passed University Avenue, however, the buildings suddenly became two- and three-storey, with quirky window displays, the dummies often naked or wearing just hats and gloves and contorted into humanly impossible positions, some even dismembered. I sat back in my seat, arms folded tightly, an excitement humming in me. I tried to appear casual, indifferent, as I gazed out at the second-hand bookstores with wooden floors and large bay windows, a shoe shop with a display of fairies fluttering upwards in a diagonal, as if towards some luminosity, each bearing a shoe in her hands as an offering. A man dressed as Wonder Woman stood by the entrance to a comic store, handing out leaflets to pedestrians, who teemed the sidewalks of Queen West. We soon passed a huddle of pavement stalls—something I had never expected to find in Canada—and I turned to gaze at the chunky silver jewellery, knitted gloves, scarves and hats from Peru, strange foreign clothes, incense and shawls from India, tie-dye shirts. Two black men with dreadlocks and red-yellow-and-green tams were playing a drum and a guitar in front of the stalls, pedestrians dancing to their reggae music.

Kensington Market was like the bazaars of Colombo's Pettah, shoppers crowding the roadway because the stores had taken up the pavements with their wares. Vans and delivery trucks beeped their horns, trying to edge through the throng, but the shoppers largely ignored them, stopping to examine vegetables, buy bread and cheese. I drifted further into the market, nudging my way through the crowd. The metallic odour of raw beef and chicken in the butchers' shops, the tang of salted fish hanging on hooks outside a Chinese store, the loamish smell of rice in large gunny sacks, the familiar stink of durian like a clogged drain, were the smells of a Colombo market, and I felt heady with homesickness. I could not help stopping to touch the thin, long eggplants (unlike the fat, round Italian ones we tolerated from the Bridlewood Mall), the okra, bitter gourd, snake gourd, yams, and, to my joy, rambutans and mangosteens. Even though the rambutans were expensive I bought a few, and as I continued through the market I sucked on each fruit until all the sweet pulp was gone from the seed.

I ended up on a quieter street and saw ahead of me a café with soiled checkered floors, its dark walls chaotic with posters and notices. The front patio was crowded with young Canadians who leaned over the cracked tabletops in animated discussion or tipped backwards on the legs of their faded painted chairs. My footsteps slowed as I passed the patio, but I did not have the courage to go in. Instead, I stood at a store window a few shops down and gazed sideways at the colourful hats and jackets these Canadians wore, some of them dressed only in black, faces painted white. Their voices drifted to me like the raucous cries of parrots.

After turning a corner, I found myself on a street that sold second-hand clothes. One of the shops had set out racks of clothing on the pavement, unattended. I strode to a rack and began to scuttle through the jackets and vests, expecting the store clerk to rush out any moment to make sure I wasn't stealing something. Soon a young woman with a thick hoop through her nose ambled out. Her smile was shy and kind, her voice lilting and splintered like an adolescent boy's as she called out a "huloo." I nodded stiffly and moved to another rack that had hats pegged on hangers, ready for her to inquire what specifically I wanted. Instead, she came and stood with her arm resting on the rack, one booted foot cocked over the other, watching me with a smile. When I unpegged a hat to show I was serious about buying something, she clapped her hands lightly and laughed, "That is the exact one I was going to suggest to you!" She pointed excitedly to a mirror and I went and tried it on, grinning sheepishly. "That's very Duran Duran," she said with approval.

I bought the hat. She suggested I wear it, but I shook my head dumbly. I did not have the guts to sport it on the street until I had practised in front of the mirrored squares on my basement wall.

Only later, when I had left the market behind me, did I realize the young woman might have been attracted to me.

On that hour-and-a-half ride back home, the numbing tedium of the journey scraped all the pleasure and excitement out of me. It had started to drizzle, streaks of grime leaking down the bus window. The rows of grey-brick houses, stretches of wasteland, a field with a circle of overturned white lawn chairs in the middle of it, were familiar sites I passed every day, barely registering them. But now they were unbearable.

That initial visit downtown released me from a fear I had not even been conscious of: a fear that white people, the natural inheritors of the life I craved, would share looks of dismay when I entered a café or store. I would be rebuffed with curt service, ignored by waiters and clerks. But everyone on that visit downtown had seemed indifferent to my presence. The famous Toronto coldness had proved to be a blessing.

I began to haunt Queen West, going down on weekends, meandering up and down the strip, stopping to gaze at window displays. I spent hours in used bookstores, reading the first chapters of books as the sun slanted in, a thousand dust motes whirling in the beams. If the book appealed to me, I would put it in a growing pile on some shelf or window ledge, then choose what I could afford at the end of my visit. I learnt that, for the price of a coffee, neighbourhood cafés tolerated students spending entire mornings or afternoons reading at a table. The smell of old books in Canada was different from the raw-rice odour of books in Sri Lanka. Back in Scarborough on a Sunday evening, I would often pick up one of my purchases and sniff its greenish, crushed leaf scent—a promise that my life would not be confined to this suburb, that pleasure awaited me the following weekend too.

I was in a used bookstore one afternoon, looking through the fiction section, when I saw, lying among the numerous pamphlets on a windowsill, a bright pink one which asked, in bold white letters, "Are You Gay?" Just the word *gay*, out there in the open, sent a frizzle of coldness through me. I glanced around to see if anybody had noticed the pamphlet or my attention to it, then slipped the pamphlet into the book I'd been inspecting, paid for the novel and hurried out.

When my family was asleep and I could be sure they wouldn't barge into the basement to do laundry or get something from a cupboard in the unfinished section, I took the pamphlet from my bag. *If you think you might be Gay, and need help coming to terms with your sexual orientation or just connecting with the community, this pamphlet is for you.*

I read the booklet over and over again, and finally turned the light off and lay on my bed, hands behind my head. Here it was, the information I needed to search out a community in my city. And yet I could not do it; could not perform the simple task of calling the help line listed at the end of the pamphlet. It was an action beyond me, like trying to rise and do a chore when delirious with fever.

Since our arrival in Canada, my grandmother had written to me fortnightly. Soon after I found that pamphlet, one of her letters arrived. It began with a familiar worry that felt to me like an accusation.

> My dearest Puthey,
> I have not heard from you in more than a month and I am very concerned that your letters to me have been thrown away by the postal office. Do you remember not to lick the flap of the envelope, but fold it inside? That way the rogues who work in our postal service will not think you are trying to send me money, open the envelope to steal and then have to throw the letter away. If you leave the flap tucked in, they can look for money and still send the letter on to me. Also, you must remember not to put your name on the return address as those devils might not deliver it because you are Tamil.

I skimmed through the rest of the letter, which was not so dissimilar from the earlier ones, telling me about the conflict between the Tamil Tigers and the government, the killing of soldiers, the further devaluing of the rupee, which had doubled the price of rice, the rising rate of crime and how, no matter what Sunil Maama or Chandralal advised, my grandmother was not getting a watcher; not going to pay someone to sleep the night on her verandah. The letter ended as they often did.

> How is the house? Is everything in working order? If you need money for repairs please let me know and I will have a deposit made from my London account. How are your studies? I would like to know, as I have not heard a word for so long.
>
> If I don't have a response to this letter, I will be truly worried.
>
> Your loving Aacho

I had not written to my grandmother in six weeks and she had written me three times, always saying the same thing about tucking in the flap of the envelope.

Irritated and guilty, I ripped a sheet of paper out of one of my spiral notebooks and sat at my desk.

> Dear Aacho,
>
> I am in shock that you have not heard from me. Have you really not received my past three letters? I too have not received your letters. In fact this is the first one I have got in a long while. What is going on? Did you get the address right on the letters? Do you trust our postman? Oh, Aacho, I hope you have not been fighting with the postman.

I put down the pen, unable to go on with the lies that always filled my letters. I went to stand at my basement window and looked through the bars at the dirty snow in the backyard. There was no way I could bring myself to write about my new part-time job in housekeeping at a motel in the suburb of Richmond Hill—the hour-long commute past used-car dealerships and long, low windowless malls like penitentiaries. Then there was the New Richmond Motel itself, with its fake wood-panelled lobby, the grubby orange-and-rust shag carpet smelling of stale cigarettes and old beer.

Later that night when the house was quiet, I took out the pamphlet from beneath my mattress and studied the whole thing over, as if I had never read it before. When I got to the telephone number at the bottom, I glanced at the clock. It was almost eleven. No one would answer the phone, but still, I would call from the extension in my basement. The very act of calling, even if only to get an answering machine, might give me the courage to try back tomorrow.

The phone rang for a long time, and the more it rang the calmer I became. Then, just when I felt I had collected the necessary courage to call again and was about to hang up, someone picked up the receiver.

"Hello?" a man gasped. "Hold on a sec."

He put down the receiver, then inhaled and exhaled deeply to control his breath. It took all my will to stay on the line, as if I were straining under something impossibly heavy.

Finally he came back on the phone, and with a laugh that was both merry and easy, said, "Sorry about that. I'd left the office and was halfway down the hall when the phone rang."

"It's . . . that's quite alright."

"Are you from India?"

"No, no."

"Sorry, I shouldn't have asked. You don't have to tell me anything about yourself."

"No, no, it's really alright you asked."

"It's just that I used to visit India quite a bit, particularly Goa. Although now I go to Thailand on my holidays."

After he told me this, I felt it was rude not to tell him I was from Sri Lanka.

"How wonderful. I've always longed to visit there."

"You should go. It's very pretty."

He asked me about the Tamil Tigers' chances of getting an independent country and if I thought there would be a solution soon. I was taken aback at how much he knew about the country, even the names of the president and prime minister. Most Canadians I met thought Sri Lanka was part of the Caribbean.

"Are you a refugee?" he asked, after I had answered his questions about the political situation.

"No, I came here with my family. We're immigrants."

"I live near this area called St. James Town, where there's a lot of Tamil refugees. I feel so sorry for them. Actually, I used to have a friend who was

Tamil, from Jaffna. A man named Cheran Muttuswamy. His family is from the village of Point Pedro. Do you, by any chance, know him?"

"Um, no, I . . . I don't, unfortunately."

He must have read my mind, because he laughed. "Of course. Why should you know him? There are millions of Sri Lankans."

By now I trusted him. He told me he was a social worker with troubled youth, and soon I found myself telling him I went to York University and what I was studying there. All this time, we had not mentioned a word about my reason for calling.

Finally he said in a businesslike tone, "So, what can I help you with?" After my silence became prolonged, he added, "Please, take your time telling me."

"I found this pamphlet, your pamphlet, in a bookstore, and I read it and . . ." I fell silent again.

"And you're gay, and you've never said this to anyone before, right?" he said gently.

"Yes. Yes, I have never said this to anyone. And yes, I am gay."

It felt so strange, those words coming out of my mouth, and the next moment I was crying. As I sobbed, he talked to me in a soothing tone about how it was alright to be gay and how one could find a lot of happiness in coming out, a lot of support, that I did not need to be lonely anymore, that he knew exactly what I was feeling because he had spent his teens in a small town in the 1960s and knew as well as anyone what it was to feel different and alone. His voice, with its depth and quiet authority, calmed me. When I was no longer sniffling, he said, "Look, it's sort of late and I must get home. Would you like to meet in person?"

"Yes, yes, I would like that a lot."

He gave me directions to a café at Bloor and Spadina. "By the way, my name is Ronald. And you don't have to tell me your name. Some people feel more comfortable making up a name."

"No," I replied, "I want to, I really do. It's Shivan."

"Well, Shivan, I'll see you in a couple of days."

Once I had put down the phone, I lay on my bed, limbs heavy with fatigue.

I arrived at the café early, and after darting a look around to see if anyone was trying to catch my eye, I sat near the door, hands clutched under the table. After a while, worried I might be evicted, I bought a coffee from the counter and returned to my seat. In my nervousness, I sloshed some on the table as I sat down and was patting the mess with paper napkins when someone said, "Shivan?"

A man in his thirties stood before me.

I struggled to my feet and thrust out my hand, dumbly. He held it in both of his, head cocked to one side, blue-grey eyes twinkling to say it was okay for me to be nervous and he was glad to see me. I got a whiff of his cologne, a sweet lime fragrance.

"Let me get a coffee too." He patted my shoulder and went to the counter.

I sat down, and after a few moments allowed myself to examine him as he stood in line.

For an older man, he was quite handsome, with tanned skin, broad cheekbones and square jaw. I liked how, when he smiled, furrows cut through his full cheeks and the pink bags under his eyes grew more pronounced and shiny, little lines radiating out from them like eyelashes. The top buttons of his white shirt were open to reveal a turquoise tank top underneath, short sleeves rolled up to draw attention to his biceps. I could not tell if his stockiness was muscle or fat, as his shirt was loose. He might have been aware of my scrutiny, for he casually looked everywhere but at me.

When Ronald came back, he declared, "So," and sat down, swinging his leg over the chair as if mounting a horse, "tell me how you are doing in Canada."

"Fine, fine," I replied, grateful he had started with a neutral subject. "It's such a great country," I continued, lying like I always did to Canadians. "I can't tell you how happy I am to be here. Everything is so ordered, so clean. The people so nice and welcoming. Yes, it's wonderful."

"Wonderful?" His blue-grey eyes twinkled, those attractive little pouches appearing under them. "That is not a word I would use to describe this place."

"No?" I asked, surprised.

"I find most of my fellow Canadians pinched and Protestant. Until about fifteen years ago, you couldn't get a drink on a Sunday. Even sidewalk cafés were illegal. I hate how unnatural and artificial and snobbish people are. And how it's always about outer appearances. Canadians are so uptight physically; we never touch and embrace in the casual way people do in other cultures."

As he spoke, he struggled to keep the merriment in his eyes, but he sounded wounded, as if he had been hurt by the coldness of Canadians, as if he, too, was an outsider.

"Take Goa or Thailand, for instance," Ronald continued. "People there are so warm and gentle and accepting of others. They live closer to nature and are more true to their real selves. I mean, men in Thailand and India who are just friends often put their arms around each other and embrace and hold hands. You would never find that here."

He stopped himself with a laugh and wiped his lips on a napkin. "Sorry to go on. It's my favourite pet peeve. Now, tell me more about yourself. Do you have a job at the moment?"

I told him about the motel and he shook his head. "Sounds dreary. You should get another job."

"But I lack Canadian experience."

"That shouldn't be an issue, Shivan. You don't know the system, being new here. I'll bring you some job-searching information the next time we meet. I help my young clients get on their feet all the time."

"Thank you." I blushed, grateful for this, but also grateful he was already willing to see me another time.

"Now, on to business," he said with a wink and a grin. He produced some pamphlets from his bag on being gay and also on AIDS and how to avoid getting it. After he had explained the AIDS pamphlet, he said, "And have you had sex with a man yet?"

I flushed under his steady gaze.

"That's okay, that's good actually. Don't be in a rush, Shivan. Before taking that step, you should make sure it's the right time and place, and with the right person. Someone you know and trust. Someone who has your very best interests at heart. Promise me you'll do that. Promise me you won't rush."

"I . . . I promise," I replied, blushing again.

"God, you men from the East are so beautiful!"

He laughed at my astonishment. "Sorry, I hope you don't mind my saying that. Do you? Do you mind?"

"No, no, not at all," I blurted. "It's a compliment. Thank you."

Ronald smiled as if I had given him a gift, then, seeing I was uneasy, changed the subject. He drew me out with questions, and soon I found myself telling him about my life in Canada, the words pouring out.

When we left the café, he walked me to the subway, and gave me a small salute when we reached it. "Until the next time?"

I grinned and nodded.

He stepped forward and hugged me. I was stiff with surprise, but recalling what he had said about hating Canadian uptightness, I put my arms around him. After a moment he pulled back, gave me a pat on the arm and declared, "Well, Shivan, I look forward to seeing you soon," then gave me his business card.

Over the next few days, I called Ronald late at night when my mother and sister were in bed, or from a pay phone at York when I had my evening class. He was always warm and friendly, and soon I was so easy with him that my wit, buried for so long, surfaced. I enjoyed making him laugh at my sarcasm, relished being able to speak without that creaking in my voice, or my bark of a laugh.

One thing that surprised me was how negative Ronald was about the gay community. He told me that the "ghetto" was very "cruisey," a word he explained meant men constantly searching for sex with other men. "You can't go to buy a damn carton of milk or do your laundry without some queen trying to pick you up." He also hated the other people he worked with at the phone line: "A bunch of sour, vain, shallow queens." This was why he worked the late shift, so he could avoid "that gaggle of nattering ladies." He spoke about the community and his fellow volunteers in the same wounded way he had talked about Canadians, as if personally hurt by them.

We had known each other a week when Ronald asked me to his home. He lived in upscale Cabbagetown in a renovated three-storey house. When he opened the door he was beaming. He pulled me in and hugged me as if we were old friends who had not seen each other for a long time. Then he gestured to the Persian carpets, white couches, glass-topped tables, chrome-legged chairs and declared, "Welcome to my humble abode."

As I followed him into his living room, I gazed at all the sculptures and artwork from India and Thailand. Seeing this, he smiled. "I am an honest person, so I will tell you, Shivan, I couldn't afford this place on my social worker's salary.

My father used to run a factory in our home town. I inherited some money."

He got me a glass of wine, and then, when I was seated on a couch, he picked up a photo album from the table and scooted close. He let the album fall open across our knees. We had to press them together to keep the pages balanced. "I've been dying to show you my Bangkok photos," he said. As he turned the pages he pointed out the temples and palaces and floating flower markets. There were also a lot of photos of him with his Thai friends, all of them young men. "They are very poor," he said, "I do what I can to help them, given I am blessed with so much."

As Ronald continued to talk about each friend there was such warmth and happiness in his face that I could not help thinking how lucky I was to have met such a good person. On the last page of the album was a letter from one of his friends, thanking him in broken English for the money he'd sent for his mother's eye operation.

Once he had put away the album, Ronald said solemnly, "There is something else I want to show you." He opened a drawer in a side table, took out a framed photo and held it out to me with both hands, as if it were a sacred object. The photograph showed Ronald at Niagara Falls with a handsome man of about my age, who looked Sri Lankan.

"Cheran Muttuswamy?" I asked and gave him a long look to say I surmised they had been lovers.

He nodded, lips pressed together.

"Where is your friend now?" I handed back the photograph.

"Married and in Scarborough," Ronald said with a sigh as he slipped the photograph into the drawer.

"So," he said, turning to me and rubbing his hands together, as if wishing to put away his sorrow, "what would you like to do this evening? Anything you want."

I was silent, because the thing I wished to do most with him was something I knew he would dislike.

He nudged me in the ribs and grinned. "Come on, Shivan, be honest."

My grin was more of a grimace, and I looked at my hands before I said, "I know you hate it, but could you please take me to see the gay community?"

"Shivan, you know how I feel about that."

I nodded, feeling bad at the pained look on Ronald's face.

"It's a cesspit," he said gently, taking my hands. "You will fall easy prey to those vultures and make your life a piece of trash. Promise me you won't do that."

"Yes, yes, I promise, Ronald."

"You must think I'm crazy, don't you?" he whispered.

"No, no." Then, feeling I had to make recompense for my slip-up, I added, "I don't think you're crazy at all, Ronald. In fact, I think you're a very kind person. You're so good to me. You really are. Other people wouldn't have bothered with someone like me."

"Ah, no, Shivan, don't say that." He put his arm around my shoulder. "You have so much to offer the world, you do. You're so charming."

"Really?"

He chuckled at my plea for validation and took my face in his hands. "So fucking handsome, and you don't even know it."

I grinned happily, but when he did not let go of my face and his look became searching, my grin pulled tight. He leaned forward and kissed me on the lips. "So, beautiful," he murmured. His lips felt cold and wet against mine. He moved his hands down to my shoulders. "Do you mind that I did that?" I was surprised at how vulnerable he looked, as if he was going to cry.

"It's alright, Ronald, it's alright." By which I meant it was alright he had forgotten himself.

But he took my words for permission, and he leaned forward and kissed me again. His tongue nudged my lips and I opened them. He slid his tongue in, moving it about languorously. I felt myself growing hard. I began to kiss back desperately, pushing myself into him. I pushed so hard, we nearly lost our balance. "Whoa!" Ronald grinned. "Shall we go upstairs?"

I nodded, yet I couldn't move from where I was. Ronald took my hand in both of his and led me up the stairs, his smile gentle.

The bedroom was done all in white. Its king-size bed was higher than my waist. I had lost my erection and now had an overwhelming desire to urinate. Ronald pointed out the washroom, which was massive, with both a Jacuzzi and a glass shower stall. "Take your time," he said as I went in.

When I came out, I stopped, disoriented, in the beam of the washroom light. The room was dark, the heavy curtains drawn.

"Over here."

Ronald was under the bed covers, his head and naked shoulders visible.

"You can leave the washroom light on if you like."

I nodded and made my way cautiously across the room. When I got to the bed, I reached out to pull the covers back and Ronald laughed good-naturedly. "Aren't you gonna get undressed?"

"Um . . . yes . . . sure." I turned away and began to take off my clothes.

I did not know how naked Ronald was under the covers, if I should keep my underpants on or not. Would I seem too eager if I took them off?

He was propped up on his elbow, a small smile on his face, watching me, waiting. I took my time slipping under the covers so he could tell me to remove my underwear, if that was the way things were done. But he said nothing. He settled down on his side to face me.

Ronald put an arm around my shoulders. I did the same to him.

He breathed out. "Wow, your hands are freezing."

"Um . . . are they?"

He laughed to say he understood it was just my nervousness. Then he shifted into me, his hand slipping down my back, drawing me close. We began to kiss. I slid my hand down Ronald's spine. He did not have his underwear on. But by now it did not matter, for he was pulling mine down to my knees. He drew himself in even closer and held our erections together.

After we were done, Ronald asked if I wanted something to eat or drink before we went to sleep. He put on the bedside lamp and I saw he had a hairy paunch and his chest was flabby, his nipples pointed.

"I . . . I have an early class tomorrow, I must go." Something was crashing within me.

"Do you?" he fondled my ear and looked at me quizzically.

"Yes," I declared, my voice cracking with the desire to escape. "I have left my books at home. So I must get them."

After a moment, he nodded and his lips set in a thin line. He gestured for me to get out of the bed.

As I got dressed, I could feel his cold stare on me. When I was done, I turned to him. Ronald was seated, bolstered by pillows, arms folded. "Shivan, have I been a good friend to you or not?"

"You have, Ronald, of course you have. I am so grateful for everything you have done for me."

"Funny way you have of showing me your gratitude."

"But what have I done?" I pleaded. "I have no choice but to go home."

"You don't have a class tomorrow." He said it with such certainty that I couldn't contradict him. "You return my friendship with lies. Is that how you show your gratitude?"

"Please, Ronald." I came and sat on the bed. "I . . . I must go home."

He picked at a nub on the duvet. Outside, I could hear a couple passing in the street, the raucous joshing of the man, the woman's sexually charged laugh.

I stood up and began to fumble with my shirt buttons. Then I took off my trousers and underwear. When I was in bed again, he slid down on his side and tugged at my shoulders for me to turn towards him. He slipped one arm under my ribs and stroked my hip with his other hand. "I know exactly how you're feeling," he whispered. "It's okay to be frightened, to even be repulsed by what you have done. But you need to recognize that they are your feelings and not transfer them to me. Okay?"

I nodded. "What about my family?" I asked as a last appeal. "They will wonder why I have not come home."

He picked up the phone from the bedside table and set it between us.

Fortunately, no one answered, and I left a message saying I was staying over at a friend's house. Ronald watched me with grave approval.

I had to work the next afternoon, and I got home to find that Ronald had called and left a message. I did not call him back. Over the next few days he telephoned often and left messages, but I never returned them. By now my mother and sister were starting to look at me oddly, wondering who this person was. To allay their suspicions, I called Ronald from a pay phone at York. I begged him never to call me again.

"You are a sly, calculating person who uses people," he shouted down the phone at me. "You didn't even have the decency to call and dump me until I had humiliated myself by calling so many times."

I was so frightened that I hung up.

One of the bookstores I frequented had a help-wanted sign in its window. I went in to apply and got two shifts on the weekend and one during the week.

When I left the bookstore, a warm autumn breeze was blowing up from Lake Ontario. Gauzy clouds scuttled by at a tremendous speed, casting a lively play of light and shadow onto the busyness and colour of Queen Street. As I stood there in the crush of pedestrians, my shirt flapping against my skin, a busker played a catchy tune on a harmonica close by and the smell of roasted coffee beans wafted out from a nearby café.

It had been a month since that final phone call with Ronald and I felt recovered from the encounter, sure that good changes were coming.

The following Friday evening, I went down to Isabella Street. I had by now discovered the gay newspaper *Xtra!* and found out that there were a couple of bars here. Komrads was on the second floor and there was a line to go upstairs to the dance floor. As I stood in the queue I listened to patrons talking around me and realized I was one of the few men who had come alone. I kept glancing over to the group in front of me, the one behind, hoping to be included in their conversation, a polite, willing smile on my face. But they ignored me, and when I happened to catch the eye of one of the men, he returned my tentative smile with a haughty glare. He whispered something to his friends and they glanced over and giggled.

When I was finally in the bar, I stood in a corner for what seemed an interminable amount of time, looking at the passing men, watching a drag queen twirl fans on the dance floor. Finally a man stood by me and introduced himself. He was about fifty, with grey hair and a lean, sharp face. I was so grateful for his attention that, even though I did not find him attractive, I went to his apartment and had sex with him.

It did not take me long to realize that in a community so devoted to the worship of beauty, I was generally not considered good looking because of the colour of my skin. In the meat market of 1980s gay bars, I was not prime steak. I did not, however, lack for attention. I attracted the old and the ugly, and because I had come to the bars looking desperately for love and companionship, I took what was offered to me, though none of these liaisons lasted very long, some barely a night. My foreignness was often my appeal, and these white men ascribed both a submissiveness and feral sexuality to me, one man begging me to put on a loincloth and turban that he had in his closet.

There was a smattering of other non-white men at the bars, but I avoided them as if fearing contagion. Occasionally, an Indian man, and even once a Sri Lankan, would strike up a conversation with me, mainly to share his problems. I always kept these conversations short and moved on, not wanting to see in their haunted faces a reflection of my condition. We did not belong in the gay world because of our skin colour, yet spurned by our own people, we had no choice but to linger on its fringes.

For a while I stopped going to the bars, but soon my loneliness became too acute and I decided to attend a coming-out group.

The very intimacy of the gathering, the fact that we were supposed to share our lives, only made me feel more lonely. These men knew nothing of Sri Lanka, and their earnest interjections of "cool" and "neat" when I found myself having to explain the world I had come from grew tedious and produced a bleakness in me. I tried initially to be witty, hoping this would win some admiration. The rest of the group responded with dutiful laughter, but I could tell that Sri Lankan humour was different from theirs in some way I could not name and they were merely being polite. Or perhaps I truly failed to be witty, because when I spoke in the group I was very conscious of my accent, hearing my voice as if in a lagging echo.

Dating was forbidden. The group leaders, who were older social workers, wanted to create an atmosphere that was different from the bars. Yet under the guise of all this earnest sharing, the same hierarchy of the bars existed. The person everyone wanted to know, to be paired with during one-on-one discussions, was a blond boy who, with his plaid shirts and straight-acting manner, looked like he had stepped right off a farm.

There was a black man from Trinidad in the group. I sensed, in that way we well-bred post-colonials from the old British Empire recognize each other's social markers, that his family back home was rich. But here he had moulded himself to fit white expectations, become more street black, more ghetto. He was immensely popular in the group and everything he said was hailed with great good cheer or serious attention.

The group was only for eight weeks. At its final meeting, we learnt that this black man and this blond boy had been carrying on an affair all the while. I received the news with a sickening lurch in my stomach that went beyond mere jealousy. The black man had slipped through the tight fence into the world of the charmed, the happy. I did not know how he had done it; I did not know what he had that I lacked, and I felt anguished at my ignorance. Without knowing what was wrong with me, how could I change or fix myself?

10

The culvert has come to an end at a field, where it disappears underground through a concrete tunnel. I scramble up the slope of the gully and find that, even though it is late, there is a surprising number of people in the field: young couples with their arms around each other; parents with a child who runs in hectic circles, brought here, no doubt, to wear herself out; dog walkers patrolling the periphery. A corridor of electrical towers cuts through the centre of the field, making us all appear diminished and fragile against this row of hulking pylons that stride the field like robotic monsters, massive limbs planted in the brown mud.

In that first year, my life brushed lightly against my family's. One of the few things my mother and I did together was our weekly grocery shopping at the Bridlewood Mall—a re-creation of our chore in Sri Lanka, which I undertook with the same bad humour. I hated the bundle buggy I had to drag, its wheels skidding and throwing up mud in the cold rain, or becoming choked with blackened snow and shuddering to a halt. Then I would have to kneel, the pavement sinking its icy teeth through my jeans, and unclog them before we could continue, the wheels yelping every time they bumped over a mound of snow. Often the bundle buggy wasn't large enough and coming home I hefted shopping bags while my mother heaved the buggy along. In winter, I could not rest the bags on snow-mudded sidewalks for momentary relief. By the time I reached our front door, my legs would be bowed in a fruitless attempt to relieve the bone-ache of my shoulders.

Our long trek to the mall took us past lines of row houses in a state-subsidized complex, each unit so small it was impossible to imagine a whole family living there. Most of the front gardens were untended, though occasionally one of the tenants had planted some scraggly pansies or impatiens. The mesh on screen doors was torn and curling upon itself. There were always abandoned coats, skirts, trousers and all manner of footwear on the sidewalk as if the tenants had fled some disaster. The dumpster at the end of the complex was piled with garbage bags, flung haphazardly and split open, squirrels and sparrows scavenging among the contents.

Every time we passed the complex, my mother would declare, "What a truly blessed country this is. What kindness and compassion that even the weakest, the poorest, are taken care of."

I would glower in reply.

The white tile floors and pale-grey walls of the Bridlewood Mall reminded me of a hospital. There was a seam of skylight running the length of the ceiling, but the rays that filtered through had a curious fluorescent quality, only enhancing the sterility within.

On evenings and weekends a group of Jaffna Tamil boys in their late teens and early twenties loitered around the escalator. They flocked together tightly in whispered, snorting conversation, then flew apart in cackles of hilarity, only to return to their huddle again before flying apart once more. The boys wore cheap plastic jackets and jeans from Bargain Harold's or BiWay and sported scant moustaches as badges of their manhood. They were in Canada because their families in Jaffna had gathered all their meagre resources and sent them over as refugees, to avoid conscription by the Tamil Tigers. The young men spoke no English and some of them had never been outside their village. The boys' forced hilarity and sliding sheepish eyes suggested the heavy burden on their thin shoulders.

When we passed them, my mother always said, "I am so grateful I was spared the sacrifice their mothers made. I don't know how I could have borne not having you children around me. Yes, yes, we are lucky. This blessed country has been so good to us."

She said this fervently, as if accusing me of ingratitude. I was puzzled and irritated by this accusation and greeted her comment with defensive silence.

After we had finished shopping, my mother sometimes liked to visit an old pioneer cemetery in a corner of the mall parking lot. It was sequestered from the rush of traffic by a short wall, pine trees and bushes, and had the feel of a country graveyard, the conifers sighing in the wind. While I stood by the entrance, hand on bundle buggy to signal my impatience, she would go around and peer at the graves. Her careful inspection, as if this was the first time she was seeing them, would enrage me. Fragments of gravestones were embedded in the wall with names that meant nothing now. One fragment had the word "Farewell" below an engraving of two clasped hands. Another just said "Mother." This was the one she liked to stop and stare at longest, some emotion working through her face.

"Amma," I would call, "come on, for God's sake, it's late and I'm cold."

She would leave the graveyard reluctantly and, as we made our way across the parking lot, say, "Imagine, Shivan, all these people died here without ever seeing their loved ones back home. How lucky we are to have planes."

I would stride on in grim silence.

Renu, much to my envy, fared better socially than I. My sister's year at a Sri Lankan university had not been recognized by York and so she found herself, like me, in first year. Within a month of starting at university, however, she had formed a circle of friends in her women's studies program. My sister was constantly away volunteering at the women's centre on campus or out with her friends at pro-choice rallies, after which they would go to the Toronto Women's Bookstore downtown to pick through the latest arrivals, then end up around the corner at Future Bakery for coffee and cake, or mashed potatoes slathered in mushroom gravy. On weekends, she went straight from work to be with her friends, only returning late at night. Though we had never met these friends, Renu referred to them by their first names, as if we did indeed know them. There were four in her close circle—Jan, Pamela, Trisha and Suzanne.

Renu soon began to lord it over me, saying I should try harder to get some Canadian friends. "Be careful you don't end up confining yourself to Sri Lankans," she would warn, face puckered as if offended by some smell.

"I have no intention of doing anything of the sort. Do I have a single Sri Lankan friend?"

"There is no point coming to this country if one is going to keep in the old ways," Renu would continue as if she hadn't heard me.

"Anyway, what is so great about Canadians?" I'd demand, annoyed at her superiority, but also jealous. "They are a bunch of pasty-faced ignorant people. They know nothing of the world. Most of them couldn't even place Sri Lanka on a map."

"One of the things I can't stand about people like you, Shivan, is how you slag off Canada and Canadians." The word "slag" was new to her, and she wielded it, along with "joe job," "blockhead," "frigging," "hoser," "Jesus H. Murphy," "mother of fucking god" and other choice expressions, as if they were insignia of the exclusive club she had been let into.

"After all, Shivan, they took us into this country out of the goodness of their hearts. Are Canadians coming to kill you and burn your house because you are Tamil? Haven't Canadians paid for that grant you got this year to cover your tuition fees?"

"You sound just like Shireen and Bhavan," I'd reply. And if that didn't shut her up, "You are mentally colonized, treating white people as if they are gods" certainly did.

There were other things my sister said that should have troubled me, but I didn't register their import. She had begun to talk a lot about "internalized sexism," and how her understanding of feminism in Sri Lanka had been so tainted by living in a "sexist, misogynistic, patriarchal society."

"Sri Lanka is the most sexist and violent place for women on the earth," she would declare at dinner. When my mother contradicted her, pointing out that women were freer and better educated in Sri Lanka than in most of Asia, she would cry, "Ah, here you go, Amma. This is your internalized sexism speaking. You are so brainwashed you are now defending your oppressors."

Towards the end of the first semester, Renu declared one evening as we were clearing the table after dinner, "I want to invite my friends here next Saturday night." She said it defensively, as if we would object.

My mother shot me a surprised glance. "Yes of course, Renu."

We continued to tidy up in silence. My sister always spoke about her friends as if they were too exalted for us to meet them, let alone bring home.

When we were washing the dinner things, my mother asked delicately as she handed Renu a dried dish to put away, "And will they eat our food, or should I make something Western, like hamburgers or pizza?"

"Of course they'll eat our food," she said, and clattered the dish into a cupboard.

I paused in my washing to give her a disbelieving look.

"But what about spice?" my mother pleaded. "Should I leave out chili powder?"

"No, no, just make the food like we eat it. They want to taste the authentic thing."

My mother looked skeptical. I could also tell she was nervous. Never having cooked in Sri Lanka, her curries were often too oily, the vegetables mushy, sauces smoky from charring the bottom of the pan.

Renu worked on Saturday mornings, and she left for her shift pretending not to notice my mother was cross and anxious in the kitchen and I was sullen at having to clean up for her friends. What hung in the air unsaid, as my mother and I went about our tasks, was that we'd never had white people in our house before. We were awed at the prospect but annoyed we felt this way.

Janice, Pamela, Trisha and Suzanne arrived together. When they rang the bell, Renu, who was fierce and harried by now, rushed to the door and flung it open. "Helloo," she trilled.

Her friends shrieked greetings and flung their arms around her. Their faces were flushed, as if they expected nothing but a good time.

My mother and I were waiting by the dining table with tight smiles. Once the guests had removed their shoes, Renu brought them in. She presented us as "my lovely, charming family." We shook their hands and murmured greetings. I had expected they would all look manly, but Jan was the only one who fitted that stereotype, with her short spiky hair, black jeans and man's white shirt with epaulettes. She gripped my hand and gave me a curt nod. A flintiness momentarily stilled her features as she took in my mother's sari, then she greeted her in the same curt way.

"Mmm," one of the women said, "what is that delicious smell?"

My mother blushed at the compliment. "I do hope you like Sri Lankan food. We were willing to cook something else, but Renu said you would like to try our cuisine." Her accent had changed, as all ours did when addressing white people—an odd tightness to her vowels, talking from the front of her mouth.

"Yes, of course," "Looking forward to it," "This is so thrilling," Pamela, Trisha and Suzanne cried. Jan nodded grudgingly.

My mother ushered them into the living room and I was sent to get drinks and salted cashews.

When I came back with a tray, the four women had squashed themselves on the sofa, my mother and Renu seated on the loveseat at right angles to them. I served the guests, then perched stiffly in an armchair at the other end of the room. My mother asked them about their summer, what jobs they had and if they were from Toronto. Once this line of conversation was exhausted the room fell silent.

"I say, Renu," one of the women said, after the silence grew unbearable, "have you heard about the latest position coming up at the centre?" To address Renu, she had leaned forward past my mother. Soon the women and Renu were discussing the university women's centre, my mother pressed back in her seat so they could talk across her, smiling and nodding to stay in the conversation.

Renu had extolled the co-operative, non-hierarchical nature of the centre, but there was a definite pecking order among her friends. Jan was at the top, and the other women often turned to her for approval. My sister strained forward into the conversation, hands gripped together, her usually vivid expression subdued. She was at the bottom.

My mother's curries, despite her best efforts, were even less tasty than usual because she had underspiced them to suit white palates. Still, sweat ripened on the women's faces. After a heroic struggle, they confined themselves mostly to the plain boiled rice.

When they left that evening, Trisha, Pamela and Suzanne pumped our hands and told my mother what a fabulous meal she had made, how they would always remember it. Jan saluted us ruefully in farewell.

"They're nice girls," my mother said, after we had shut the door on them.

"*Women*, Mother, *women*," Renu cried, wretched and defeated.

The next Saturday, rather than going out straight after her morning shift at work as she usually did, Renu returned home. As my mother and I went about our tasks, we were attuned to every sound from her room, aware that my sister, who was constantly on the phone to her friends, hadn't made a call all afternoon. When she came down to get tea, we pretended to be very busy.

"I have a massive paper due."

We nodded vigorously, but she could tell we didn't believe her.

Like watching for a fever to break, we waited to see what Renu would do about her Tuesday evening shift at the women's centre. I was relieved when she went to do it. Her social success had brought me hope of similar achievement and, despite my envy, I did not want her to fail.

Renu picked up her weekend activities again, but I could tell she wasn't really enjoying them because she came home early, looking depleted. And gradually, over the winter semester, she withdrew from her friends until by April, when the year finished, she was just as alone as I was.

Later that summer I came out to my sister, desperate to share my loneliness and failures in the gay community. She was supportive, as I had expected, and urged me to tell our mother, saying, "You won't be truly free until you do so." When I balked, she didn't press me. I felt she had advised this because it was received wisdom from the centre.

In return, Renu told me what had happened with her friends.

The beginning of her break from them had taken place a few days after our dinner. She was to meet her friends at a university café, and when she came up to their table, one of the women said, "Ah, we've just been in the middle of a furious discussion. You are the only one who will have the answer."

My sister was immediately on alert. They had not been in the middle of any such heated discussion.

"We certainly don't think this, Renu, but we're curious to know if *you* think the sari is a symbol of female oppression?"

"Renu, do the women in Sri Lanka, the feminists you knew, view it as a symbol of patriarchy?"

"No," Renu answered, bewildered, "I have never heard them say that."

"See!" one of them said to Jan. "We told you!"

Jan sat back in her chair, palms flat on the table, and gazed steadily at Renu. "It's just that my former girlfriend, who is South Asian, always said it was a symbol of oppression. All those yards of material wrapped around a woman's body are intended to keep her from moving very fast. Like bound feet in China."

"Evidently, Jan's old girlfriend also felt that the nose ring South Asian women wear, as a sign they are married, was like putting a nose ring in a cow you owned."

One of them squeezed Renu's arm. "Anyway, we think the sari is a beautiful national costume."

"Yes, I wish we had a national costume like that."

"We were just dying to know what you think."

Yet before Renu could say what she did think—that women worked in construction wearing saris, that doctors performed surgery in saris—her friends moved on to discuss the executive director at the women's centre and their ongoing issues with her. Renu knew then that some judgment had been passed against her.

When my sister was finished her story, she walked about the basement, picking things up and putting them down. A letter from my grandmother lay on my desk, and before I could stop her, she picked it up and began to read aloud in a wry tone, like we were complicit in mocking my grandmother. "'My Dearest Puthey, I was so relieved and happy to get your letter today. I thought I would sit down and write to you immediately, as you seemed so worried I had not got your earlier letters. And you did not get mine again either! How very strange.'"

My sister raised her eyebrows, more to herself than me, then continued in a hushed, faster way. "'I was delighted to hear about your summer job in the lawyer's office. I am hoping this means you are thinking of law as a possibility? I am also hoping, Puthey, that the friend whose lawyer father got you that job is a boy. Females you must be careful of.'"

My sister stopped reading and put the letter on the desk. She gave me a small sympathetic smile. "I really miss all those women at Kantha, Shivan, I really do miss them." She sighed. "I wish we had never come here."

Towards the end of that summer, my sister and I were on the subway when we ran into Otara, an old classmate of Renu's in Colombo. The women had barely known each other in school, Otara being the kind of rich, snobbish, vacuous girl Renu detested. But from the way they shrieked in recognition across the carriage, rushed to meet and grappled in an embrace, I could tell they had both been looking for a friend. Otara, it turned out, was at York University too. Renu's cries of astonishment over the coincidence were high with relief.

When the new semester began, my sister joined York's Sri Lankan Students' Union. Otara was secretary, and her fiancé, Jaya, was president. There were enough such students at York by now to form a union, so great was the exodus after the 1983 riots—not just Tamils but Sinhalese and Muslims as well, who saw no future for their children in the country. There was also a Tamil Students' Society, its members Tiger supporters and believers in the independent state of Eelam. Otara and the union looked down on the society. Soon Renu, too, was chiming in with comments such as, "Eee, instead of fighting for Eelam, they should fight to promote deodorant among their members," or, "Eee, hasn't anyone told those Yalpanam types that coconut hair oil stinks."

Renu, Jaya and Otara presided at the union table on Thursdays in Central Square. I avoided the table if I was passing through the square, knowing that Renu would signal me over frantically, then give me a sisterly ribbing.

Jaya and Otara were a comical couple. He was tall and gangly with a wide floppy mouth and small close-cropped head that reminded me of a pencil eraser. Otara, barely five feet and plump, wore large hair bows, short frilly skirts, leggings and little pink boots in the girly style made fashionable by Madonna. She was convinced Jaya was having affairs, and any interaction he had with a white woman brought on a storm. Once, when the union members were at Jaya's house, she was discovered rifling through his drawers for condoms.

Jaya had a car and gave Renu and me lifts home. On one occasion I walked into our meeting place, the Vanier Common Room, to find Otara on a sofa, sobbing into her handkerchief, short plump legs, which did not reach the floor, pumping. Soon voices from the corridor drew nearer and Renu bustled in, lips thin with worry, a desperate Jaya in tow.

"Oh, Otara," Renu cried, rushing forward, arms outstretched, "forgive, forgive. He didn't mean it about leaving you. I've talked to him." These histrionics happened often between the couple, with Renu acting as mediator.

Otara sobbed with renewed vigour. She threw her chubby arms around Renu and clung to her while Jaya stood by, arms stiff, fingers splayed as if it took all his willpower not to run from the room.

Renu got Otara to promise she'd not be suspicious of her fiancé, then sent the couple to make up in the corridor.

The moment they were gone I demanded, "Why do you hang out with these ridiculous types? What do you get from all this breaking up, making up?"

"Someone has to help them," Renu replied, as if such matters were beyond my understanding.

"Why? It seems they'd be better off without each other."

"It's the Sri Lankan way to help friends in trouble. You have forgotten that?"

My anger was really at the change in my sister. She, who had once lectured me on staying away from the community, was now embroiled in friendships with Sri Lankans she wouldn't have tolerated in our country.

Our home became the rendezvous for union members, even though Jaya's parents, being doctors, had an enormous house. When I came home in the afternoon or early evening, I would often find the gang lolling about our living room or seated at the dining table playing poker for small change. On seeing me, they would call, "Shivan, come, machan, sit with us," or, "Shivan, why didn't you come with us to the film last Saturday?"

"You are so exclusive, Shivan," Renu would always say with a sisterly pout. "Even I never see you anymore. What do you do with yourself?"

This was her cue for the rest of them to cry, "Clarice!" My secret girlfriend they had invented.

"Ah-ah," they would tease me, "putting it to Clarice, were you?" "How is your lovely Clarice today?" "Ah-ah, I think I saw you in the Scott Library with your darling Clarice."

I'd storm downstairs, hoots of mirth following me. As they returned to their game, their boisterous pleasure would drift down to me, a fire at which I could not warm myself.

Later, after the gang had left, Renu would come down to talk under the pretext of doing laundry. She'd stand, dirty-clothes basket nestled on her hip, looking at me with long-faced commiseration. "What to do, Shivan? Sri Lanka is a conservative society and it is not going to improve. We must be careful for Amma's sake. If people found out she had a gay son, it would ruin her position in the community."

"You're homophobic, you're homophobic," I would cry, my voice breaking with anguish.

The mothers of union members soon became friends or good acquaintances too, through their children. My mother, like her new friends, made puddings, cutlets and patties for birthdays or weddings, went with other women to shop for fabric, helped sew curtains, bed skirts, sari borders and blouses, crocheted blankets and pillowcases for expectant mothers, took an aged parent to a doctor's appointment or tended a sick friend. She was often away on weekends, and if she needed an extra pair of hands, Renu went with her.

We were frequently invited to birthday parties, anniversaries and other social occasions. I never enjoyed these events, but despite my protests I went to all of them, drawn by the chance to at least stand at the periphery of vivid lives.

Otara's and Jaya's mothers, Aunty Poones and Aunty Vasanthi, were the leaders of this maternal coterie. Both were from Tamil Cinnamon Gardens families, and Aunty Vasanthi was a doctor. They wore large diamond mukkuthis that clung to their right nostrils like hard-carapaced parasites, golden ropes of thalis around their necks and a jumble of bangles that clattered with the weight of the best gold. They had the sartorial habit of taking their sari palu in a cowl behind their neck, trailing its end down their chest—the effect like that of the thick garlands worn by campaigning politicians.

The two women had a cloyingly sweet way of talking to people they felt beneath them, and this was the tone they used with my mother, who was humble and abashed in their presence, grateful for their patronage.

Otara and Jaya had yet to be formally betrothed. Their mothers began to plan an engagement party, with matching saris for the bridesmaids-to-be and an elaborate dinner in a banquet hall.

One Saturday when I was not working, my mother wheedled me into going with her women friends to carry bags while they shopped for saris on Gerrard Street. I agreed in my usual aggrieved way, but I didn't mind going; it was a chance to be involved in some activity, to feel warm and included, to be called "thambi" or "mahan" by these women.

When Aunty Vasanthi's minivan pulled up in our driveway, it was crowded with the women corralled into helping. They clucked and twittered, saying, "My, you have brought your boy." "How very sweet of him to give up his Saturday morning." "Now, let us squeeze over and give Shivan-thambi some room." I was put in the back seat.

As Aunty Vasanthi drove off, she said in her sugary sweet tone, "My, how good your boy is, Hema, coming along to help us old women."

"Yes," my mother replied, "I have never had a day's trouble with him."

The women turned to nod at me approvingly. "He is a very fine boy," Aunty Poones pronounced. "I am a good judge of character."

"Oh, yes," my mother agreed, forgetting her humble manner and growing boastful, "he is very obedient, Poones. Most boys these days, aiyo, you know, alcohol, drugs, loose living."

They tisked in agreement. I stared out of the window with a fixed smile, wishing my mother would stop.

"Now, what are you studying, mahan?" a woman asked. "I have forgotten."

Before I could reply, my mother declared, "English literature."

"Oh."

By this they were less impressed.

"But that is good," my mother enthused. "Why, with an English degree you can become a teacher in this country, nah? Seventy thousand you end up making."

"Really? My, how different from Sri Lanka."

I had gone back up in their esteem.

"Girlfriends and such things?" Aunty Poones demanded.

"Of course not, Poones," my mother replied, appalled. "Chee, chee, he has no time for such nonsense."

"Ah, very good, very good," they murmured, appraising me with even higher esteem.

"One has to be careful," Aunty Vasanthi said with the sigh of experience. "White women are always after our men, you know. Where will they find husbands like our boys?"

"Also excellent in his studies," my mother added. "The professors love him."

"And your mother, Hema, how is her health?" another woman asked.

"Fortunately no problem there, but she is getting old."

"And how are your attempts progressing to get her over here?"

"Aiyo, I have tried and tried," my mother said, careful to avoid my astonished stare.

"But you must not give in so easily," Aunty Vasanthi cried, and from the way the other women nodded, I could tell this was a well-travelled subject.

"Ask her to come for a holiday. Once she is here, she will like it. Particularly if she comes in the summer."

"She will not even consider a short visit," my mother sighed. "These old people, they can be so stubborn, so fixed in their ways." Another sigh. "After all, who will look after her when she is too feeble to take care of herself, nah?"

I finally caught my mother's eye and she looked trapped for a moment, her doleful expression slipping before her glance skittered away.

"Don't give in, Hema. Insist that it is your turn to look after her. A way to repay her kindness and love when your beloved husband died. My! All the affection she poured on you and your children, paying to send them to the best schools. She will be rewarded in her next life for that."

"Yes," my mother said with less enthusiasm, aware of my stare.

"Aiyo," one of them said, "widowhood is such a trial, as I well know."

"And you were widowed so young, Hema." The women clucked in sympathy and my mother looked pious.

"What a tragedy for you. To lose such a loving husband and father, such a wonderful provider."

When we were finally on Gerrard Street, my mother pressed some money into my hand and said bossily, "That Poones and Vasanthi like to look in all the shops before they decide to buy anything. Go treat yourself to samosas and faluda. We won't need you for a while."

What was commonly referred to by South Asians as Gerrard Street was in reality the few blocks of that road devoted to Indian stores. Since it was a nice fall weekend, the pavements were crowded, and odorous with the smells of frying chickpea dough, incense and fumes from cruising cars.

I squeezed by women who stood in front of sidewalk racks crammed with gaudy salwar kameezes and saris, which they held up for inspection with the contempt that was always the first step in fierce bargaining. Outside a couple of restaurants, waiters were barbequing corn marinated in lime and chili powder.

After I had found a restaurant and bought my samosas and faluda, I sat at the counter in the front window, food untouched, wretchedly surveying the large families who strolled in the sunlight—the men chewing on paan as they wheeled prams, children licking kulfi popsicles, mothers gobbling chaat from tubs, shoving spoonfuls at husbands and children. A group of Sikh teenagers, their topknots tied in colourful cloths, skimmed and ducked through the crowds on roller skates. They were followed by boys on tricycles, dressed up in waistcoats, shorts and ruffled shirts. Little girls skipped to keep up with the band, ribbons and sparkling barrettes in their hair, shiny bindis on foreheads.

In all the years we had lived in Sri Lanka my mother had borne the burden of her widowhood with dignity and never lied to friends about her marriage or the enmity that divided her and my grandmother. But here in Toronto, her life had taken on an edge of desperation. It occurred to me that it had been there for quite a while, without me noticing.

What had driven my mother to reinvent herself, she told me many years later, was a realization that came to her, not in a flash, but slowly—revealing itself the way the persistent lap of waves gradually wears down the surface of a rock to expose glittering mica beneath.

In that initial year, as my mother sat at temporary desks in temporary offices—so alike she could not tell them apart, looking down, sometimes in surprise, at the work she was doing, thinking she was still engaged in a job she had done somewhere else—first inklings of the realization began to reveal themselves. As she stuffed envelopes, photocopied, collated, filed, typed lists and letters, as she stared dazedly at other immigrant temps in their own worlds, as she looked out from upper floors at the sinister grids of suburban industrial parks with their crouched buildings on tarred lots, as she sat in lunch rooms listening to permanent workers discuss office politics, as she shambled around malls on her breaks, gazing at all the things in the window displays she could not afford to buy, the realization grew clearer until she finally understood that she had repeated her own history. She had tried to escape her mother and ended up in a worse place.

My mother began to feel a choked longing for her job at the newspaper with its excitement of deadlines, the journalists and their eccentric habits, that pleasure she always felt on Friday evening when the galleys of the women's section she edited would be spread out before her by a peon. Then, pulling her desk lamp close, she would lean forward to pore over the pages, filled with satisfaction. She missed her friends, too, the holidays in their country homes, the other single women at work with whom she saw an occasional film or play, followed by dinner at the Flower Drum Restaurant, where they'd feast on crab claws in ginger sauce, battered prawns in chunky pineapple and capsicum gravy.

When my mother lay in bed late at night, unable to sleep, she would think about how it was now morning in Sri Lanka. Her old ayah would be making kola kanda porridge or was crushing spices under the miris gala or chatting to the fish seller, who had come with his fresh catch.

Her participation in the Sri Lankan expatriate community, this reinvention, was a rope that kept her from sliding into despair.

A few days after that trip to Gerrard Street, I returned from university to find Aunty Vasanthi's minivan parked in our driveway, ponderous in the evening gloom. The front door of the house was unlocked.

She and Aunty Poones were seated at our dining table, Otara between them, her face numb with misery. My mother was at the head of the table. Her bewildered eyes hardly registered my arrival.

Seeing the anger on the aunties' faces, and Otara's desolation, I knew why they were here and was surprised I had not figured it out before.

My mother stretched her arms forward on the table, hands clasped tightly together. "If what you say is true, then my daughter is not the only one to blame. Jaya is responsible too."

"He is a man," Aunty Vasanthi declared. "My son, like most men—"

My mother tightened her lips contemptuously. She and Aunty Vasanthi locked gazes, then my mother narrowed her eyes and looked away. "Jaya is equally to blame. His being a man has nothing to do with it at all."

Aunty Vasanthi was about to retort, but Aunty Poones touched her wrist. "The thing is, Hema, you know, my daughter and Jaya are not just boyfriend-girlfriend. We are allowing them to date because we are in Canada, but it is an arrangement. The dowry has been settled. Properties in Colombo have been written in each other's names."

"They are to be engaged in a few weeks," Aunty Vasanthi cried plaintively.

After a moment, my mother turned her locked fingers, stretching her arms out. "I will talk to my daughter. She will break this off."

The women rose to their feet. Aunty Vasanthi strode to the front door as Aunty Poones took Otara by the elbow and helped her up.

"Thank you, Hema." Aunty Poones kissed my mother's cheek. "These are just youthful indiscretions. Let it not come between us, here in a foreign land, where there are so few of us." She patted Otara on the shoulder. "Everything will pass."

When they had left, my mother moved to the kitchen and continued with her cooking. I stayed in the basement as long as I could, but eventually I had to come up and begin my chore of laying the table.

Soon there was a clattering of keys outside and we heard Renu exclaim in annoyance when she locked, rather than unlocked, the door. She came into the hallway and began removing her shoes. My mother went to stand beside me at the dining table.

"Renu!"

"Yes, Amma?"

"Get in here."

My sister came slowly into the dining room. Her eyes widened when she saw us. Then her face became hard and expressionless.

"Where have you been?" my mother demanded.

"Out with Otara and Jaya."

"The thing is, Renu, Otara was just here a few minutes ago. With her mother and Aunty Vasanthi."

A look passed between Renu and me. She put her hands in her coat pockets as if searching for something. "I'm going upstairs."

My mother let out a gurgle. "Are you my daughter? The one I raised to be decent and honest? I don't recognize you."

"Renu, Renu, say you are sorry," I pleaded. "I know you didn't initiate this. That Jaya must have led you on."

"Why should I say I'm sorry?" Renu replied with a little smile. "Jaya and I love each other."

"But they are to be engaged," I said gently. "It is an arranged marriage. Did you know that?"

"Yes."

"Why, Renu, why did you do it, then?" My mother held her hands out, pleading.

"Because I'm sick of not having anything." She glared at my mother and me. "Jaya loves me, I know he does." Her voice trembled. "He loves me, he told me so."

"Don't talk to me about love," my mother cried. "You have deceived your friend and made a shameful vesi of yourself."

My sister and I both flinched.

"Yes, a vesi. That is what you have become, aided and abetted by that weak, pathetic Jaya."

"Amma—" I began to protest on behalf of Renu.

"After all I have done for you both, after all I have sacrificed, this is the reward I get?" My mother rushed into the hallway, pulled the front door open and, without a coat, went out into the cold rain in her slippers.

We didn't dare go after her.

My mother's birthday was a few days later and we were treating her to a Chinese meal.

I dressed and came upstairs to find Renu seated at the dining table examining her nails.

I yanked at my cuffs. "Where is Amma?"

"Changing. She didn't like what she was wearing." My sister's tone was flat, warning of some crisis.

I found our mother seated on her bed in a dressing gown. She was leaning forward, chin cupped, tears dripping down to puddle in her palms. A sari lay coiled on the floor.

I sat beside her. "Amma, don't cry, what is the point?"

"Everything is ruined, just ruined."

My mother wiped her face on her dressing-gown sleeve, then tugged at the bangles on her wrist. "We should never have come here, never. Look at what this country has done to Renu. Why else would she have acted this way? I made a big mistake bringing you children here."

She got up, took a tissue from a box on the dressing table and blew her nose. Then she picked up the sari and began to fold it in a measured way, as if it took all her strength to do so. "I'm dreaming about my mother all the time now. The same two dreams. In one, I see her walking in her usual brisk manner ahead of me. I call to her, but she doesn't hear me, and when I catch up she does not know who I am and apologizes pleasantly, saying she has no daughter called Hema. The other dream is worse. I'm walking past the Wellawatte market and she is seated outside the market begging, her skin covered with sores. I bend to reason with her, but she turns her head away, and I don't know if she has lost her mind or is just angry because I abandoned her."

My mother finished folding the sari and put it away in a drawer as I watched her, appalled. Hot air ticked through the pipes and the bright overhead light removed all shadows from the room, giving it a hospital sterility.

The next week, on our way to do grocery shopping at the Bridlewood Mall, my mother kept ahead, face stern, chin tilted up. Young Tamil men were hanging around the escalator, but my mother said nothing about their plight and glared at one of them who got in her way.

When we were at Price Chopper, I took a basket and waited, like I always did, for my mother to name the items I was to find. I left her with the cart by a pile of oranges and went on my search. I returned to find her still by the oranges, cart empty.

"Amma?" I put down my basket and touched her arm.

"I cannot do this." She shook my hand off. "You do it." She thrust the list at me, hurried towards the entrance, pushed past customers at the checkout, and left the store.

I stared at the list. Seeing that we needed six oranges, I began to pick mechanically through the pile for the good ones. Finally I had collected all the groceries but did not have the money to pay for them, so went looking for my mother. She was on a bench in the cemetery, staring into the distance as if at the horizon, arms folded, legs stretched out and crossed at the ankle. Gulls whirled in the wind, their cries reminding me of summer visits to Lake Ontario. When I came up to her, she gave me a long hollow look. "I wonder what these people must have felt, dying in this country. If I die in this godforsaken country, please don't scatter my ashes here. That would be unbearable."

I sat down next to her, frightened by the desolation in her face.

November days turned dark by four thirty. A perpetual wind blew in from the north and it stung tears from my eyes. I no longer looked up at the sky or at the world around me. Leaves crumbled, and when it rained clumps stuck to my feet. The crabapple tree in our front garden was bare now. Its branches seemed elongated, as if wrenched upwards by the low grey sky. The first snow fell, melted, turned black, froze into sheets of ice, became slush.

Then once again the brown grass was revealed, off-white dog droppings like bundles of wool.

Renu and Jaya's relationship did not survive long. Under pressure from his parents, their friends, relatives here and in Sri Lanka, Jaya gave in.

He came to visit late one evening, standing in the doorway, twirling his car keys, smiling sheepishly at me. Renu and my mother had hurried to their rooms and did not come down. He sat at the dining table tapping his keys on the surface, sneaking timid glances up the stairs.

Jaya was taking the winter semester off and going to Sri Lanka. Next year, he would transfer to McGill University in Montreal. He wanted to try to get into medical school and McGill had the best program. Otara would study English literature at McGill. When he finished relaying all this, he looked at me helplessly.

After he left, I went upstairs to Renu.

She was at her desk, drawing—an activity she had taken up since the affair with Jaya ended.

I sat on the edge of her bed. "It couldn't have worked out, Renu," I said gently.

My sister did not respond for a moment. "He's a bloody coward. If Amma and our father braved Aachi to get married, why couldn't he have done the same? I was willing to take on everyone for him."

"But look what happened to Amma and our father."

"We're here now. Jaya grew up in Canada, for God's sake. This is not Sri Lanka. People are allowed to change their minds, aren't they? To marry the person they love?"

I didn't respond, because what I had to say was obvious. We might be living in Canada, but we had brought Sri Lanka with us.

A few weeks before Christmas, my mother had what she later euphemistically called an accident. She swallowed ten sleeping pills and then, in a panic, woke us up to take her to hospital.

She was put in an emergency room with white, oil-painted walls that glimmered under the fluorescent lights. There was a steel supplies cupboard in one corner, and nurses came and went, indifferent to my mother's privacy or suffering. Renu and I took turns in the sole chair by the bed, holding our mother's hand and gazing at this woman whose face was scrubbed of expression, her damp hair severe against her skull; this woman who breathed in the way of an exhausted child. We could hear someone in another room ululating, a rising "oh-oh-ohh" of pain that reached a plateau, then lifted into a higher register until she was screaming. After a silence, the cry began all over again. When I wasn't holding my mother's hand, I leant against the windowsill and looked out at the flat roof beyond, littered with bottles, cans, piping from an uncompleted job.

After this, Renu began to spend all her free time at York's Scott Library. She found a full-time weekend job. When she was home, she stayed in her room.

On my mother's first day back at work, I came home to find her preparing dinner, face grim. She was still wearing her office clothes, and as she rushed around the kitchen with a new manic vigour, her narrow brown skirt hobbled her knees and her beige blouse stood out like a shell.

"Amma?" I said hesitantly.

She flicked a sidelong squint at me, then continued with the cooking.

Renu had returned moments before me and was looking through the mail on our hall table. She gave me a warning glance before sauntering upstairs.

"Are you alright?" I asked my mother, edging into the kitchen.

I reached out to touch her and she shrugged to ward off my hand. "Yes, yes, I'm fine. Just go change, Shivan." She bent over the chopping board, white scalp visible through her thinning hair.

"I'll continue the dinner, Amma. Why don't you go and put on something comfortable."

"I said I don't need help."

Fearful of leaving her alone, I began to move around the kitchen, checking the boiling potatoes, picking up a dishtowel from the floor. "What else are we having? Shall I prepare another vegetable?"

Her fingers danced at dazzling speed over the curve of an onion, the knife a hair's breadth behind. Chopped pieces fanned across the board.

"Well," I said, "we can have frozen peas." I got them out of the freezer.

My mother threw down her knife. "Shivan, get out! Get out of my bloody kitchen!"

I looked at her, my eyes wide, clutching the bag of frozen peas. She grabbed the bag and flung it in the sink. After a moment I left, walking in a stiff haughty way to hide my humiliation.

Once I had showered and changed into a sarong, I came back upstairs. My mother was now rushing between the dining table and the kitchen. Though her pace had not increased, I could see in her absolutely still face that her anger had risen. I stood helplessly by the table, getting in her way. She brought out the pork chops and banged this final dish down on the table, a bit of oily gravy trickling over the side.

"Where is that Renu?" Before I could respond, she went to the bottom of the stairs and yelled, hoarse with rage, "Renu! Come down this very instant."

My sister appeared on the landing.

"Do I have to call you for dinner? Am I your servant?"

"I was just coming down, Amma."

My mother bustled into the hall and returned with an aerogram from Sri Lanka that in my distraction I had not noticed. "What rubbish are you telling this woman?" she cried, the opened aerogram unravelling as she held it out between two fingers. "A job in a lawyer's office? A trip to Montreal with friends? Are you so ungrateful for the life I have provided that you must lie? Why don't you tell this wretched woman the brave truth of how I go out to a job where I have to put up with an ignorant, patronizing supervisor half my age? A woman who thinks Third World people live in trees, but whose grammar and spelling are appalling? You should hear the way she talks to me, as if I am a halfwit. But what can you expect in this country? A bunch of barbarians." She flung the aerogram on the table, pushed past my sister and hurried upstairs.

I went into the kitchen and Renu followed. I took two glasses and filled them with water. My sister got out the cutlery.

"Gosh, what is her problem?" Renu said in a light tone, giving me a sympathetic grimace. "She's fit to be tied."

"She's had a hard day, Renu, can't you see?" I snapped. "She's had a hard day."

These angry evenings became routine. While other women on the bus and subway after a day at work recharged themselves with a chocolate bar or bag of chips, a magazine bought for the commute, my mother worked herself into a fury over her small house with its stale cooking smell like propane gas, her bedraggled garden with its dying tree and exhausted soil, the irritation of her neighbours' lives seeping through thin walls. By the time she arrived home, she was filled with bilious vitality and tore around the kitchen, banging pots and pans, throwing spices into sizzling oil, not caring where they spattered, yelling at my sister and me if we dared come in. When she was done, she'd stand by the table, watching us as we took our places. Her food, because it had been prepared in such anger, was often unpalatable, but if we didn't finish everything she served, or avoided a dish, she would rail at us for being ungrateful, the words tripping out so fast she stammered.

When she was not angry, my mother moved with the meticulousness of someone ill or unsteady on her feet, marshalling all her energy and parcelling it out to get through a day.

On weekends, she went to malls and wandered listlessly around looking in the windows. Her other weekend activity was to read for hours at the Bridlewood Mall's public library. She would return from there at peace. Renu and I were pained and scared that our house, our company, were so distasteful our mother needed to escape to find tranquility; it was almost a relief when she slowly soured to rage again.

A ridiculous hope, fuelled by helpless fear, drove me to tell her I was gay; a belief that sharing this thing about myself would bring back the mother we had known.

One evening after dinner, I went up to her room, my sister trailing behind for support. Our mother was lying on her side facing the wall.

"Amma, I have something I wish to share that is very important, very dear to me. Something that makes me happy, and finally at peace with myself."

She continued to face the wall.

"Amma, I am gay. Homosexual."

Her back stiffened. "Why are you telling me?" she finally asked. "What do you want me to do about it?"

"I . . . I don't require you to do anything. I only want you to know, to truly understand your son."

She turned and looked me over. "Are you an idiot to choose to be gay when this plague is going on? Do you want to die young? Have I brought you into this world and sacrificed so much for you to destroy your life?"

"Amma, Amma," Renu intervened, "it's not a choice. Shivan is naturally like this."

My mother waved her hand to dismiss the idea. "If I had known you would throw away your life, I would have aborted you. Yes," she continued, nodding at us, "I would have strangled you at birth."

I leaned back against the dressing table and closed my eyes, light-headed. "I wish you had strangled me at birth," I said after a moment. "You would have done us both a service. People like you should never be allowed to have children, because look what you do to them. You're a terrible mother, a failure. What misery you have brought to our lives."

She lurched up in bed. "Why did you feel the need to tell me? Why should I have this burden? Isn't my life hard enough? Look at what you have done to me, look at how you are burdening me."

"I hate you! Why don't you just take more pills and put us all out of our misery."

"Shivan!" Renu yanked my sleeve.

"And let's not call what you did an accident," I continued, unable to stop myself, even though my mother had now pulled into herself protectively. "You took those pills on purpose so you could bring even more misery and hardship to your children's lives. You are a selfish woman, a horrible selfish woman!"

I took the stairs in large strides. When I was in the basement, I paced, declaring between gritted teeth, "How dare she, how dare she speak to me like that."

After that, we stopped eating together as a family. Once my mother had cooked, she went upstairs and lay down, returning to eat at nine o'clock, by which time my sister and I made sure to be in our bedrooms for the night.

As Renu and I ate our dinners, we watched TV in companionable silence or talked about our lives. My outburst had made Renu realize how unhappy, how fragile, I was. She asked me about the gay world and my trials in it, nodding encouragingly as I confessed my continued unhappiness.

I envied her, because she could escape. In her second year she had continued to maintain her A-plus average. Professors often invited her to their offices to discuss scholarships at Ivy League universities in America and advise her on the application process. "Yes, Canada is the shits," she would say. "I am getting the hell out of here." And she'd wave her arm to encompass not just the house and our mother, but also the country.

II

I AM PANTING LIGHTLY FROM MY EXCURSION across the field and through its corridor of electrical towers, my shoes heavy with mud. I sit for a minute on a bench to catch my breath and peer down an empty road. The growing warmth has caused a mist to bloom up from the glistening concrete, and the street lamps have trembling rainbow nimbuses around their lights. I remember how in Sinhalese there are two words for rice: "*haal*" for the hardened grain, which becomes "*buth*" when it is boiled. In speaking of our inability to reverse actions, our inability to change karma's ripening, we say that haal, once it has started to become buth, cannot revert to being haal.

After a few moments, I rise and begin the walk back to my mother's house.

In the spring of 1988, four years after we had arrived in Canada, Sunil Maama called in the early hours of the morning to tell us that my grandmother had suffered her first stroke.

The ringing phone became incorporated into my dream and I reached half awake for the basement extension, then pulled my hand back as if from fire. When I did lift the receiver, my mother, as if inquiring about a minor household repair, was saying, "How bad is it, Sunil Maama?"

There was a lag between their voices, and part of Sunil Maama's reply was cut off by the echo of her question. All we heard was, ". . . can tell . . ."

"What?" my mother exclaimed.

They were both silent, waiting for the reverberations to clear.

Sunil Maama spoke, emphasizing each word: "Nobody can tell at the moment. Daya is in intensive care."

"Does one of us need to come?" my mother asked in an equally measured way.

"Not yet. Best wait and see a few days."

Their breath across the phone line was like the distant sound of the sea. "Thank you for calling," my mother finally said.

"Hema, I'll call you tomorrow, at 7 a.m. your time."

"Yes."

"Daya asked about her house, if everything was okay with it."

"Yes, yes." My mother's voice was impatient.

"Tomorrow, then."

"Tomorrow."

She put the phone down.

When I came upstairs, my mother was standing by the patio door, looking out through the sheers at our garden, which was revealing its shapes in the dawn light. She was remote and spectral, the bones of her face sharp, hair tousled, lips greyish brown without makeup. Renu sat on the sofa, dressing gown trussed tightly, eyes narrowed with worry as she watched our mother, wondering what this news would do to her. She glanced at me to communicate her concern, but I would not meet her eye. I sat on the stairs that led to the second floor, my hands clasped, dread mounting within me.

Over the next few days, as we waited to hear if my grandmother would pull through, I could hardly swallow sometimes for the dryness in my throat. She had seemed so indomitable, so enduring a presence in my life. But now I was understanding I might never hear her voice again, never feel her touch on my arm, never have anyone call me "Puthey" in that loving tone.

One afternoon, I was working at the bookstore when it started to rain. I stood at the counter, chin on knuckles, gazing out through the mud-flecked window. The world outside—pedestrians hurrying by, half-human, half-umbrella; slowly passing vehicles sending up graceful fans of muddy water; blurred neon store signs—all appeared insubstantial.

I was at the end of my university career, with a degree in English literature. A few days before we got the call from Sunil Maama, I had visited a government employment office and seen how unqualified I was for most postings on the boards. Even the majority of summer jobs were beyond me. I did not have experience as a waiter or camp counsellor, did not have a lifeguard's certificate; and I knew better than to apply for jobs in light construction or with the Parks and Rec department, because these jobs, which paid the best, went to white men. As I looked at the other young people taking down contact information, I felt how much I was still an outsider in this country.

University had provided a rhythm to my life, and I had drifted through, reading textbook after textbook, typing paper after paper, swotting for exams at the end of each term. In the summer I would work at the bookstore and whatever other retail jobs I could scramble for. Now, beyond the summer, there was the void of fall and winter, and beyond that the void of all the years to come.

Then there was the troubling fact that since the beginning of winter, for a reason I did not understand, I was going through a sexual dry spell. Despite adding Sunday tea dances to my weekend visits to bars, I could find no one who wanted to sleep with me who wasn't completely unpalatable. Many nights I took a bus home, long after the subway closed, surrounded by immigrants coming off late shifts, smelling like dusty cardboard boxes.

I had a frequent dream about love, inspired by some story my grandmother must have told me. In the dream, I lived in a cave, my clothes suggesting medieval Sri Lanka—chest bare, a white dhoti wrapped around my lower body, hair pulled into a topknot. I had a beautiful lover, though I could never remember his face when I awoke. His dhoti was green silk with gold stars, and he had a large emerald in the middle of his topknot. My dream comprised three moments of leave-taking. In each, my lover repeated the same line with great sorrow: "My food and drink I get by the power of this jewel. You ask too much. I cannot part with it." The first time he said this, he was in my cave; the second, he was farther away from me, at the foot of the steps leading up to my grotto. In the final, and most strange moment, he stood in the middle of a flowing river. After he spoke, he dove in. There was a flash of a shimmering green snake's body, then he was gone. I would wake up from this dream filled with sexual desire and a bewildering sense of loss.

My sister was doing much better than me. In her final year, her social life had picked up again after she got a part-time job at a women's shelter that catered to an immigrant and non-white clientele. "We women of colour," was her new catchphrase, which she said with a toss of her head to encompass friends she'd made among the employees. These friends came home periodically, when it was Renu's turn to host the Ngame Reading Group, named after the African goddess who gave human beings their souls. The women were fierce and intense like Renu, and would take over my basement to have their discussions. They used terms I did not understand, like "voice appropriation," "Orientalism," "liminality" and the "subaltern." The women discussed writers I had never heard of, despite four years of English literature—bell hooks, Audre Lorde, Gayatri Spivak, and, in softer tones of pleasure, the novels of Toni Morrison, Anita Desai and Maxine Hong Kingston.

There was also much berating of "this racist, parochial country stolen from the First Nations." "Racist" and "parochial" were part of Renu's new insignia of belonging. She used them to describe everything from York University to the Toronto Transit Commission. Since I was, in her estimation, also a "victim of the patriarchal order," she would often corner me for a confidential chat. "There is so much work to be done in this racist, parochial country, Shivan," she would say. "Things have to change. These bloody whites must be forced to take their heels off our throats."

The previous fall, Renu had applied to do her master's at Cornell University, where a famous Indian feminist professor taught. So singular was her desire for this placement, she would not apply anywhere else. Even her new friends worried about this decision and pressed her to try other universities, but Renu would reply in a quiet, sad tone, "If I can't get what I want, I'll keep working at the shelter."

During the late fall and early winter, while she waited to hear from Cornell, Renu went on a diet of grapefruit and bran cereal. My untidy sister became fanatically neat, folded clothes in her closet in rigid columns, book spines aligned on shelves. After I'd sat on her bed and held a pillow while talking to her, Renu would plump the pillow to some specification and lay it carefully beside the other even as I was walking towards the door. She would rage if I borrowed a book or pencil without asking.

It was a relief when she got into Cornell in February with a full scholarship.

We had seen our mother even less than usual over the past year. She had, by now, secured permanent employment in a lawyer's office as a secretary and was adequately paid. Yet she'd taken a second job at a doughnut shop in the Bridlewood Mall, where she worked evening and weekend shifts. The franchise was owned by an Iranian woman named Azita, who was erratic and constantly changed the demands she made on employees. The only people who stayed working for her were middle-aged immigrant women. Their tyrannical boss united the employees. They would call my mother at home to tell her of Azita's latest outrageous demand. My mother called these women too, and even went out with them sometimes before or after a shift. And for the first time in her life, my mother claimed she was suffering from migraines. She would occasionally lie in bed for a day or two, curtains drawn, refusing all our offers of food.

As the weeks progressed, my grandmother remained stable but unchanging. I often took out her letters (which I could never bring myself to throw away) and flipped through them, aware now that the feeling of suffocation her advice and gossip used to evoke had faded. My mind would return again and again to a trip she and I took once to Negombo, where she had rented a bungalow on the beach. My grandmother had grown up in a coastal village and knew the lives of fisher people well. They would often come to talk with us as she sat ensconced in a planter's chair on the verandah. Using colloquial village Sinhala, she'd argue with them about weather predictions and what the sea offered at this time of year. My grandmother and I would go down at dawn to the beach and she'd haggle with the fishermen until she got prawns and seer fish cheap. In the evenings, after our dinner, we sat on the dark verandah, I on the floor beside my grandmother's chair, both of us looking out to the boat lights twinkling on the horizon. I had never seen my grandmother's face so placid with contentment.

As I went about my daily tasks of looking for a job and working in the bookstore, I savoured details of that memory—the salty sea breeze that blew through the verandah, the sweet taste of fresh prawns, the smell of my grandmother's talcum powder and lavender perfume as she sat next to me, the feel of her rough dry hand on my head.

Then after weeks of stasis, my grandmother suddenly improved and within days was moved out of intensive care and into a private room, secured by Chandralal. According to Sunil Maama, my grandmother's thug, now greatly moved up in the world, visited her daily, consulting with doctors, threatening staff if my grandmother complained of anything.

She was soon well enough to talk on the phone and requested I call her. The hospital switchboard operator was expecting my call and put me through to her room immediately.

"Puthey," my grandmother shouted down the phone, her voice slightly slurred, "Puthey, how are you?"

I could not speak for the lump in my throat. "I . . . I am fine, Aacho," I finally blurted out. "How are you?"

"How am I, Puthey? Why, I'm being robbed blind by these rascals. This hospital is run by a bunch of rogues. Last night, I am sure, somebody took my gold necklace, because I do remember bringing it with me."

I found myself smiling at her fierce tone, her familiar distrust of other people. "But are you eating well, Aacho, are you resting a lot? I worry about you."

"Well, I eat the food that isn't stolen from my tray. And what else is there to do but sleep in this place?"

She went on to praise Chandralal. "Like a son, Puthey, he has been like a son to me."

I felt jealous, and changed the subject. "Now, tell me, what do the doctors say?"

"Aiyo, Puthey, I'll never recover all my strength again. For the rest of my life I will have to use a walking stick. And my face, Puthey, the left side is partly paralyzed. That is why I am talking as if I am slurping tea at the same time."

"Ah, I am so sad for you, Aacho."

"What is to be done, Puthey? It is my karma."

We were silent. I could hear her breath across the line as we each waited for the other to put forward what we wanted.

"Aacho," I finally said, "I think I should come and visit you. My university is over and I feel—"

"Ah, yes, Puthey," she said, voice hoarse with relief, "it is a very good idea. I will have Sunil make a deposit into your mother's account for the ticket. Today itself he will do it."

"Aacho, Aacho," I said, overwhelmed by what I was committing to, "do you want to say hello to Amma or Renu?"

"No, no, don't worry. This call is already too expensive. No point wasting money and making the phone company rich."

As we said our goodbyes, my grandmother reiterated that Sunil Maama would send the money for my ticket that very day.

I put the phone down, shrugged at my family's astonishment and sauntered towards the basement stairs. My mother followed, Renu trailing behind.

"Shivan, son, you're not serious about going back, are you? Why do you want to return?" she pleaded.

"She is family. Despite everything, she has been good to us. Without her hospitality, we would have been poor. Even this house, we are living here rent-free, and—"

"I forbid it. I knew that woman would use her illness to pull something like this. There is no need to go. She is fine now. Yes, yes, I forbid it. Wasting time and money—"

"Who are you to forbid anything?" I yelled, all the pent-up rage I had felt in the last few years, all my disappointments, pouring out of me. "Why shouldn't I go back? What is there for me in this shit of a country? I hate being here. Do you know how much I hate it? Have you any idea of the misery I am living in here?"

My mother turned to Renu in appeal, but my sister was regarding her with raised eyebrows. "Are you surprised he wants to escape, given the hell hole we live in?" She drew out the word *hell* so my mother understood it referred to her. Renu walked away upstairs, her voice rising as she went, shrill and plaintive. "I don't care, it's none of my business. That woman never had a moment for me. I hope she dies, frankly. Yes, I really hope she just dies. That would put us all out of our misery. Bloody nuisance that woman is, clinging to life."

"Shivan," my mother pleaded, but I slammed the basement door and went down to my room.

I sat on the edge of my mattress and stared at my fractured image in the mirrored squares on the wall.

In the following weeks, as I prepared to go back, my mother's face became even more gaunt and deep circles appeared under her eyes. I would catch her sometimes looking at Renu and me in a haunted way, lips slightly parted, as if she wanted to say something and was waiting for us to notice her. Yet when she caught my glance, she would turn away to busily scrub the counter or do some other chore. Once, she actually had dinner with her children, but all of us were so awkward she went back to her old routine.

I was often awakened in the early hours of the morning by my mother walking the length of the house from the kitchen window to the patio doors, where she stood for a moment before retracing her steps. I would lie, arms pressed by my sides, and listen to her go back and forth, that pause at the patio doors the most unbearable thing for some reason. My basement window would change from black to cloudy dawn, this greyness seeming, to my sleep-deprived mind, like fog against the window. Once she had returned to bed, I would fall into a sleep that was full of nightmares I could never remember when I woke, a few hours later, my throat dry and aching from lack of sleep, my forehead heavy.

One evening my mother came down to the basement. I was on my knees folding laundry from a mound on the mattress. She had a copy of the Sri Lankan *Sunday Times* in her hand.

"Are you aware of what is going on in Sri Lanka?" She rustled the paper at me. "Have you any sense of the madness you are committing yourself to?"

I continued to fold my laundry. She knew I had not kept up with the news on Sri Lanka, just as she suspected my continued ignorance was wilful. I did not want anything to spoil my joy at returning.

Still, it was impossible to avoid all news, given that Renu talked regularly to her new friends about the situation on the phone or when they visited. My mother also got the *Sunday Times* every week and left it lying around, and I couldn't help but see bits of news. So I knew that, as in those Buddhist tales, the karmic crime of hatred between the Sinhalese and Tamils had taken on a new incarnation. A new actor had entered the maelstrom. India, under pressure from its massive Tamil population in the sub-continent's south, had intervened. About a year ago, Sri Lanka and India had signed an agreement which brought Indian troops to the Tamil areas to take charge of the situation there. The Tigers, who had enjoyed support from India, had agreed reluctantly to the truce. For a few months peace reigned and the country looked like it would shed its bloody past, its hatreds, and move towards a new era. However, within three months the Tigers had broken the truce, killing five Indian para-commandos by strapping burning tires around their necks. In retaliation the Indian Army launched a month-long campaign to win control of the north and their ruthlessness turned the Tamils against them.

My mother was not really concerned about this fighting between the Tigers and the Indians, which was taking place far from Colombo. Her concern was with yet another actor who had entered into the frenzy—the JVP, a Marxist group that had led a failed insurrection in the early 1970s. The JVP had taken advantage of the unemployment in the country and the massive rise in the cost of living, along with the increasing anti-Tamil, anti-Indian hostility among the Sinhalese, who by now feared that Sri Lanka was on track to become another of India's states. Soon the JVP was leading attacks on security force camps, staging daring robberies, declaring strikes no one dared disobey. They banned women from wearing Indian saris, shops from selling Indian goods and even Sri Lankan business men from importing Indian pharmaceuticals. Their power was so universally acknowledged that they were known as the Government of the Night or the Little Government.

Though Colombo had remained unaffected for a long time, the effects of the JVP's actions were beginning to be felt in the capital now. The JVP had led an unsuccessful assassination attempt on the prime minister and president within the parliamentary complex itself, killing a minister in the process. But their most notorious crime in Colombo was the recent killing of the beloved actor turned politician Vijaya Kumaratunga, whom the JVP had declared a traitor because he was sympathetic to the Tamils. Half a million mourners had turned out for his funeral and his widow, Chandrika Kumaratunga, had fled the country with her two children, fearing for their lives.

After my mother had elaborated all this, she came farther into my room and stood over me. "I suppose you are too young to remember the JVP rebellion in the early 1970s. Thank God it failed, otherwise all of us Cinnamon Gardens types would have been murdered and you children sent to labour camps for re-education." She lifted her hands, then let them fall in disgust when I didn't react. "Shivan, they are murdering people all the time in the south. When they call for a work stoppage no one dares to go out. Between them and the Tigers, not to mention the Indians, you will have to deal with curfews and blackouts and bombs and God only knows what else."

I took a pile of clothes to a drawer, brushing past her. By not responding I was daring her to command me again to stay.

To put some distance between us, I began to refer to my mother, when speaking to Renu, as "Our Lady of Angoda," and make biting comments about her madness. Renu found this funny and appalling and would say, "Chee, Shivan, how can you joke about Amma belonging in that asylum? It's a vile place."

I was certain the reason behind our mother's new anxiety was my return to Sri Lanka, but Renu disagreed, insisting it was delayed shock at our grandmother's illness. She patted my shoulder and advised me to ignore our mother's behaviour. "You are doing the right thing. You need closure with Aachi. You need to take charge of your own life, to shrug off the burden of Amma. She must learn to move forward on her own."

My sister had written to her old history professor, Sriyani Karunaratne, and asked her to please look out for me. "She's really nice, Shivan," Renu said as she gave me the professor's phone number the day before I left and made me promise to call. "Being a feminist, she's gay-positive. I'm sure you could use someone like that in homophobic old Sri Lanka."

During the bus ride to the airport, my mother looked out the window and didn't speak to Renu or me. Once I had got my boarding pass and was ready to go through Security, she held my arms and said in the tone of a prepared speech, "Shivan, your life is here now. I want you to remember that. You're only going for four weeks, and you're not to let her convince you otherwise."

"No, Amma," I said, bewildered. "Of course I'm coming back."

"She will try and persuade you, I know her. I'm frightened for you, Shivan, I am. I feel this trip is inauspicious."

"For heaven's sake, Amma," Renu said, rolling her eyes at me, "what a way to say goodbye. Inauspicious!"

I laughed uneasily, then gave my mother an angular embrace. "I must go."

After I went through Security, I looked back at my mother, with her handbag clutched under her arm, and I felt disturbed, as if what she had said was a truth I had not yet considered.

There is a tale called "The Naga King Manikantha and the Hermit" that must have inspired my unsettling dream about the lover who visited me in a cave. In the story, two brothers take up the monk's life, living as hermits far from each other in grottoes along a riverbank. The Naga king, Manikantha, is swimming by one day when he spots the younger brother and takes an immediate liking to him. He begins to visit every day, and soon the two are close friends. Manikantha takes a human shape when he visits but, before he leaves, always reassumes his serpent form and embraces the hermit, coiling himself around his body. Even though he loves Manikantha, the hermit is terrified at this transformation and grows thin and pale, the veins standing out on his skin. His older brother comes to visit and inquires about the reason for his poor condition. The brother advises the hermit to ask three times for the jewel the Naga king wears on his forehead. The hermit does so, and on the third occasion Manikantha leaves him forever. But the hermit grows even more pale and thin because he now pines for his friend. His older brother comes to visit again, and discovering the reason for his worsened state, says, "Importune not a man whose love you prize, for begging makes you hateful in his eyes."

The final lines of that strangely inconclusive tale make me think of Mili Jayasinghe the first time I saw him after my return to Sri Lanka, waiting for me outside my grandmother's gate, grinning with shy delight as he stood beside his motorcycle, the sun shining in his hair.

PART THREE

12

I HAVE FINALLY REACHED MELSETTER BOULEVARD, but when I turn onto it, I stop. My mother's car is parked in the driveway. Pushing my hands in my coat pockets, I hurry towards the house, panicked at how I left it—sliding doors unlocked, empty glass smelling of Scotch on the counter, my grandmother's photograph abandoned on the dining table.

My mother is at the kitchen window peering out, arms crossed over stomach. When she sees me hurrying up the front path, she rushes to open the door, for I have forgotten to take a key.

"I tried calling, but you did not pick up."

"Just went out for a walk." I turn away and take off my shoes.

"I finally came over because I was so worried."

Glancing at her, I am taken aback at the way she looks. I was so lost in my memories I expected to find her as she was then—hair sheared short, face sharp. Instead, her hair is now in waves to her shoulders with silver streaks enhancing the dark tan of her skin, her face full and heart-shaped. She wears a garnet brooch at the neck of her soft pink silk blouse, both gifts from David.

"Son, *where* have you been?" The question is heavy with how she found the house in my absence. I am suddenly very conscious of the whisky bottle bulging in my inner pocket.

"Why do you worry so much?" I demand. "You could have tried phoning again."

"I did," she says quietly.

I go into the kitchen and she follows me. The glass has been washed and put in the drying rack, my grandmother's photograph is back in place.

"Perhaps . . . perhaps I should stay home tonight."

"What? Why? You don't need to be here. Stay with David." The thought of her being with me is unbearable.

"But there is so much to get done." She gives me a significant look.

I regard her blankly, then turn quickly away. But she has seen that I've forgotten the task I promised to do of emptying the kitchen of all perishables, so the house can be fumigated.

My mother opens a drawer and pulls out a garbage bag.

"Amma, I will do it. I . . . I just felt like a little fresh air."

I go to take the bag and she winces at the alcohol on my breath. I step back, ashamed.

"Shivan," she says, trying to be stern but sounding helpless. After a moment I reach into my inner coat pocket and put the mickey of Scotch on the counter. When she sees how much I have drunk, her face crumples, then becomes impassive. "I will stay tonight."

"No, no," I say, louder than I intended, my nerves stretched to the breaking point.

"Oh, Shivan," she says, near tears, "I wish I had stopped you earlier from this plan to go back for your grandmother. You are so unhappy, son, so troubled. I don't think you can take anything more. And I worry about the effect of Sri Lanka on you. Then there is your aachi . . ." She gives me a miserable look to convey what I have already guessed. She has not told my grandmother about my impending arrival.

"The truth is I've been too frightened to tell her," she says quietly. She begins to remove her coat.

"I'm sorry I didn't start the kitchen before," I say. "I promise, I will do this."

I watch the struggle on her face, as if she were listening to another voice within her. She pulls her coat back on. "I suppose no one can take another person's journey. It is the hardest thing about being a mother." She glances quickly at the Scotch. I can tell she wants to take the bottle with her and has to force herself not to do so.

"Please don't go out again," she says, as if this one assurance will fix her worries.

Following her out into the hallway, I promise I won't.

She points to the garbage bags. "Why are you throwing out all these clothes?"

"They're old and out of fashion. Most of them are slightly mouldy."

She is not paying attention, frowning as she buttons her coat and searches for gloves in her pockets. "And this news from Sri Lanka. The closer I get to arriving there, the more it depresses me, this endless hatred and enmity. Why did the Tigers have to break the truce, why? And why did Chandrika respond with violence too and not try to get them back to the table? Her husband Vijaya would never have done that."

"It's not so easy, Amma. Her hands are tied. All actions are compromised, tainted, in Sri Lanka."

"War for peace. How can she describe war in this cynical way?" My mother lets out a sad laugh as she slips her gloves on. "I feel ashamed that David is reading such things. What must Canadians think of us?"

"I didn't know that David takes an interest."

She gives me a look that says I am being an idiot. "Of course he takes an *interest*, Shivan." There is a small proud smile on her face; David loves her, he will fret while she is away.

"You . . . you shouldn't keep David waiting." I am suddenly desolate.

She kisses me distractedly and leaves.

I watch her go down the driveway to the car. A few snowflakes have begun to fall, and a wind has suddenly picked up. As she opens her car door, my mother tugs her scarf into place and glances crossly at the sky. She looks small but capable, a woman in control of her life. This battered old red Honda Civic is an emblem of her accomplishments. She will not let David drive her around, a trait he finds both endearing and exasperating. After six years, she still won't move in with him. She will not give up this house.

The moment her car leaves, I shut the door and lean against it, closing my eyes for a moment. Then I begin to pull things out of the kitchen cabinets with frantic, trembling hands, throwing packets of tea and biscuits, tins of cocoa, coffee and Ovaltine, bags of raisins, peanuts, salt, pepper into the garbage bag my mother left on the counter.

My arrival in Sri Lanka that spring of 1988 came upon me suddenly. I had taken a sleeping pill to make time pass faster on the tedious plane journey and was awakened by the bustle of passengers standing up, stretching, hauling down bags to look for combs, brushes and compacts. The flight attendants were coming around clearing away the last glasses of juice and alcohol, folding up newspapers. Then the pilot announced, "Ladies and gentlemen, we can now see Sri Lanka," and there was a rustle of excitement as people craned over fellow passengers for a view.

Out my window were dense clouds. Then we were through the clouds and below us was the sea, golden pink in the dawn light, its waves seemingly frozen from up here, like scallops along the edge of some giant seashell. A sweep of beach was bordered by acres of coconut trees, the mound of a dagoba rising out of this greenery like a boulder, its whitewashed surface also pink in the dawn light. It seemed unreal to be seeing Sri Lanka after all this time. There, there it was, lying below me, yet I could not imagine landing, could not imagine looking up at those coconut trees and smelling the ocean. I felt suddenly like a foreigner about to enter a strange land, this plane the last point of familiarity from which I would be ejected into a chaotic, frightening world. I shook my head to chase away the thought, trying to take comfort, as the plane landed and hurtled along the tarmac, at how normal everything looked, the shuttle buses going to and fro, other planes coming in and taking off in an orderly way, the airport building in the distance newly painted. As we came off the plane and were ushered to the shuttle buses, I smelt that odour of Sri Lanka, like the inside of a dry clay pot, an odour I had never really noticed when I lived here, but which now, because of my long absence, my foreignness, I recognized as the smell of home.

My grandmother was sending her car, and since it was so early in the morning, I expected to find the driver waiting as I came out of Customs into the arrivals lounge. A mass of German tourists teemed confusedly beyond the exit, calling to each other like lost birds, a Sri Lankan guide trying to shepherd them to the currency exchange booths and the waiting bus outside. They finally moved on and I saw my grandmother seated at the far end of the lounge. She raised her hand briefly and I began to wheel my cart towards her.

My memories of her, I was realizing, had been from a child's point of view and I was struck by how small she was amidst the bustle of activity. When I reached her, we were still, gazing at each other. Her face was thinner and more lined, and the stroke had puckered her right cheek upwards. There was a walking stick beside her seat. My grandmother nodded to say, yes, she had changed. "Ah, Puthey." She indicated for me to bend towards her. She took my face in her hands and kissed my cheeks. "You have come back. I have so longed to see your face." Her speech was slightly slurred, the right corner of her lower lip stretched tight and glistening.

A warmth flooded through me at the love in her eyes. "Ah, it's so good to be back home, Aacho."

Our old driver, Soma, appeared with a porter in tow. "You took your time coming." She glared at her driver, who was grinning with delight at seeing me. She transferred her glare to the porter. "How much do you want? We are not foreigners."

He named his price in a wheedling tone and there was some fierce bargaining before my grandmother brought him down to half what he had asked. As he took my cart, she said to me, "Foreigners are ruining these fellows. Giving them tips-tips and everything."

She reached for her walking stick. I offered my hand, but she waved it away and, using the stick, levered herself from the chair. Now she did grip my arm, and we began to walk along an open-air corridor that led to the chaos of cars, vans and buses parked outside the building.

"How is your mother?" she asked, and then sighed. "Her error has trailed her, nah? If she had listened to me, she could have had a very different life." Seeing my discomfort, she added, "Anyway, what is to be done? We must all live out our karma."

By the time we got to the car, her breath had taken on an irregular flutter and sweat beaded her forehead. She leaned back in the seat, eyes closed as the porter loaded the trunk. When he came around to her window to collect his fee, she shoved the money at him, muttering about rogues and scoundrels.

As we drove towards Colombo, I looked out at the world we were passing. Children in starched white uniforms and ties stood at bus stops, cloth bags slung over their shoulders. Early office workers waited alongside them, the men in slacks and white shirts, the women in saris clutching handbags. The workers mopped their brows with handkerchiefs, laughing and talking with each other. Bicyclists rode by, one with a huge bunch of bananas strapped to his rear carrier, another transporting his entire family, the wife perched sidesaddle on the back rack, two little girls on the cross bar. In roadside restaurants, little more than shacks with roofs of rusting takaran, hoppers were being cooked on kerosene burners, vadais fried in vats of oil. I glimpsed people at trestle tables with banana leaves before them piled with idli, thosai, or string hoppers, onto which bare-chested little boys in soiled shorts dolloped soupy sambar out of metal buckets. Then there were the hundreds of pariah dogs in that easy cohabitation with humans, some sitting outside the restaurants, quivering for any scraps that might be thrown at them, others lying on the road, ambling out of the way as approaching vehicles blasted their horns. The garden walls, whose lower ends were stained with brownish-red dust, had bougainvillea spilling their abundance over the tops. Araliya trees were in full bloom, their fallen petals lying in the dirt; huge tamarind trees spread their canopies over the road. Everything about the landscape was familiar and strange at the same time; that odd disjunction of coming home to a place that was not home anymore.

As we drew closer to Colombo, large billboards appeared for things I had not eaten in five years, whose taste I knew so well—Lemon Puffs, Marie biscuits, Glucorasa, Kandos chocolates—and promoting these products were the same cricket players and actors and former Miss Sri Lankas. A cinema poster announced a new film starring Gamini Fonseka and Geetha Kumarasinghe, and as I read the Sinhalese lettering, I felt the delight of rediscovering that other language which had lain submerged within me for half a decade.

The car arrived at my grandmother's house, and some moments after the driver pressed his horn, Rosalind pulled back the gates, craning her neck to see me.

"Ah, yes," my grandmother said, gesturing at the ayah as we passed her, "prepare yourself for a monsoon of tears."

The house, like my grandmother, was smaller than I remembered. In honour of my visit, no doubt, she'd had it recently whitewashed, the red tiles and wooden fretwork replaced or mended.

When I stepped out of the air-conditioned car, the air was loud with the rasping of crows, the blare of traffic on the street, a koel shrilly winding up its notes in the mango tree. And now the heat, which I had not been so aware of, pressed its weight against my skin.

Rosalind was hurrying up the front path, and when she reached me she started to cry, taking my hand, touching my face, saying those same words she had spoken to my mother all those years ago. "Aiyo, baba, the gods have been good to allow me this sight of you before I die. I never thought I would see you again."

My eyes started to well up too, and I hugged her, something I had never done before.

My grandmother hobbled around the car to us. "Ah-ah, have you got the breakfast ready?" She did not approve of my show of affection and blamed Rosalind for it.

I protested that I was not hungry, but my grandmother waved her hand. "Of course you are. You don't want to disappoint our Rosalind. She has been up from four o'clock cooking. Now go and wash."

In my room, everything was exactly as I had left it—the blue curtains with green polka dots, my light-blue coverlet, its nubbles worn with age and washing, the picture above my bed of a boy in a field of poppies. The shallow slot on my white wooden table contained my old Parker fountain pen and a few yellow pencils, half used. My old sarong was hanging over the chair, worn Bata slippers beside my bed. The almirah released a swell of camphor when I opened it. My clothes were neatly folded, shirts on hangers. I went over to the bookshelf and knelt, hands on knees, staring at the Famous Fives, the Secret Sevens, various Agatha Christies, my copies of *War and Peace* and *Pride and Prejudice*, numerous Jeeves and Woosters. I drew out *The Magic Faraway Tree*, sat on the edge of my bed and read the first page, remembering what joy it was to lie in bed, the fan grating above me, lost in the world of these books. Every so often, I recalled, I would surface from the fictional realm to take a spoonful of sweetened condensed milk mixed with chopped bananas from a bowl beside my bed. Forgotten was my guilt about acquiring these books and how I had kept them hidden from my mother.

"I sometimes come in here and sit. It brings me comfort." My grandmother had been standing in the doorway, watching me. She waved her hand. "Go, go, wash quickly. Rosalind is beginning to complain the food is getting cold."

My old towel was over the rack in the bathroom. As I splashed my face and rubbed the familiar sandalwood soap into my skin, I felt as if I were washing away not just my journey but also the past five years.

In honour of my arrival Rosalind had made the auspicious breakfast of the Sinhala New Year—kiribath, ambul thiyal, katta and seeni sambol, beef curry, kavum, kokis, lavariya and ambul bananas. She stood behind my grandmother, who was seated on one side of the table. The only other place setting was to my grandmother's right, at the head. "Aacho—" I began, but she waved me to the chair, saying, "Come-come."

I sat, awkward at this elevation. Rosalind began to dish out food for me. I tried to stop her giving me too much, but she would not hear of it. "Look at you, baba, you're so thin. Chee! I thought Canadian food was supposed to be healthy."

My grandmother did not eat much and instead, like Rosalind, watched me. I ate to please them both.

After breakfast, as I sipped a cup of tea, a sudden exhaustion swelled through my limbs. My head jerked as if in protest against sleep.

"Why don't you take a nap, Puthey," my grandmother said. "We'll wake you for lunch."

I lay down on my bed. The next thing I knew, it was early evening. Despite the fan above, I was sweating. The glare of the sun hurt my eyes and there was a metallic taste in my mouth. I pushed myself up on my elbows but then fell back, putting my arm over my face to block out the light. After a few minutes, I forced myself out of bed and went to take a shower.

When I stepped out of my room, the saleya was deserted. Beams of sunlight cut across the floor, a thousand dust motes whirling in them. My grandmother had left for the temple, as she always did at this time. I walked around the saleya, picking up familiar objects and putting them back. From the kitchen I could hear the muffled thumping of pestle against mortar, but before I could go and chat with Rosalind, my grandmother's car pulled into the carport, and I went to greet her with a smile.

13

The novelty of being back in Sri Lanka soon wore off. Without the routine of school or visits to the American Center Library, without the bickering, complaining, laughing companionship of my mother and sister, time became a boggy thing that pulled me into a torpor. Because I had been so solitary when I lived here, I did not have old school friends to invite me on trips or to dinners, clubs and the theatre. My grandmother did one errand each morning and I always went with her. Afterwards, she stayed in bed to gather enough strength to attend the temple. She never had dinner with me, as the evening pooja left her exhausted, and also because she did not eat much anymore. At seven, she would have a cup of Bovril and a piece of toast in her bedroom, then fall asleep. I had forced Rosalind to give up serving me at dinner; my years in Canada had made me uncomfortable with this. I dished out my meal in the kitchen and ate alone in the darkened saleya, a book propped in front of me, rereading one of my old classics by the dim light above.

Boredom drove me to call Renu's old professor Sriyani Karunaratne.

I had met Sriyani only once, when my sister and I had gone to see a play at the Lionel Wendt Theatre. Renu knew her heroine would be attending, and as we waited for the performance to begin she kept getting up from her seat to scan the theatre. At last she cried out, "Oh," and signalled frantically to a woman with greying hair cut in a pageboy style, dressed in white slacks and an emerald-and-gold striped Barbara Sansoni shirt.

"Sriyani-akka," Renu gushed, as the woman came up to her.

"Ah-ah, you're here," Sriyani replied in an even, pleasant tone. She was short and plump, with an olive complexion and a hooked nose that had a tiny diamond mukkuthi in it. She seemed rather amused at my sister's adoration, and she nodded at me, eyes crinkled with goodwill.

My sister introduced me, and Sriyani declared, "But, my, you look just like your mother."

I blushed under her gaze and blurted, "You know my mother?"

"Of course. We were in school together. I was a few years senior, but, you know, your mother just stood out. Miris, they used to call her. Fiery, like a chili, and so extremely smart."

I liked her, though I had not expected to, imagining that she would be sharp and self-righteous like Renu. I sensed a quick mind at work beneath her serene, mildly amused manner.

When I finally telephoned Sriyani one evening after my return, a male servant answered and asked suspiciously who I was. He conveyed the information to Sriyani, who said in the distance, "Ah-ah, yes-yes."

Her footsteps approached the phone at a leisurely tip-tap. "Hello," she said, in her low, cultured voice, "is that you, Shivan?"

"Um . . . yes." I did not know what to call her. It should be Aunty Sriyani, as she was an older woman, but I knew this was not right.

"Well, well, it's nice you're here," she said evenly. "You must come and visit me."

"I would like that."

"Yes-yes, you must come," she continued, as if she had not heard me. "Why don't I send the car for you tomorrow and we can have lunch, hmm?"

"Thank you. Um . . . what time shall I be ready?"

"Oh, you know, lunch time," she said vaguely. "See you then," she added briskly and put the phone down.

I was dressed by eleven thirty and lay on my bed, reading under the fan. About half an hour later, someone rang the bell at the gate. By the time I had put away my book, fixed my flattened hair and straightened out the wrinkles in my shirt, Rosalind had answered the summons. "Someone has come for you," she said, as I passed her in the saleya. "A young mahattaya on a motorcycle."

At first, when I came out the gate, I did not recognize Mili, leaning against his motorcycle, arms folded. He had grown a moustache and beard and was dressed in jeans, a white kurta and Indian sandals. "Shivan, it's been a long time."

I stared at him closely. "Mili Jayasinghe?"

He nodded and laughed shyly. "Ah! I got you!"

The dark brown silkiness of his beard and moustache brought out the caramel of his eyes. A lock of hair had fallen over his forehead. He pushed it back, then held out his hand. "I work for Sriyani now."

"Ah," I said, as I shook his hand. "So you've done what you wanted."

He frowned questioningly.

"To work with the poor, to better Sri Lanka."

"You have a good memory, Shivan," he exclaimed, sounding grateful I had remembered. "I completely forgot I told you."

Then we had nothing to say to each other and I felt I had become again the awkward boy of my adolescence.

Mili got back on his motorcycle. He offered me the extra helmet. "Hop on. Sriyani is waiting."

I hesitated for a moment, then clumsily swung my leg over the back seat, my jeans stretching so tight I was afraid they would rip. I did not know what to do with my hands, and Mili, sensing this, said, "You better hold on to my waist, I go fast."

I put my arms lightly around him and he was off with a roar. I gasped then held on tight.

The office was not far away, and in ten minutes Mili screeched to a halt at a gate and beeped his horn. A young man in a sarong came running to let us in. When we reached the empty carport, I struggled off the motorcycle, my legs weak from the ride. "Um, thank you very much." I handed him the helmet.

"You're welcome." He appeared wounded at my polite formality. I nodded, smiled faintly, and went up the front steps, surprised at his reaction but not knowing how to remedy the accidental slight.

The office was in a converted house, living and dining rooms subdivided by partitions. There was a desk in the foyer where a receptionist sat. She sent me upstairs immediately.

When I got to the first landing, Sriyani was standing above at the top of the stairs, one hand resting on the banister, watching me with that mildly amused smile of hers. She was wearing grey slacks and another of those vividly striped designer shirts for which she seemed to have a fondness.

"So, I see you survived the ride."

I grinned and nodded, sheepish for some reason under her gaze.

"Don't worry, I'll send you back in my car. It will be much more comfortable, hmm? Come," she beckoned me up the last steps and we shook hands.

"Now, how is your sister? I get her very interesting letters. Seems she loves her studies and has made lots of friends."

I told Sriyani the good news about Renu's scholarship to Cornell. As I was speaking, Mili bounded upstairs, taking two steps at a time, panting slightly from the effort.

"Ah, Mili, are you happy now that you are reunited with your old school chum?"

Mili smiled at me diffidently.

"When I told Mili you were coming, he insisted on picking you up." She raised her eyebrows at him teasingly. "I think you have frightened our guest. Poor fellow, he's from Canada, he's not used to our wild ways on the road."

"Sorry, Shivan, I—" he began, but I cut him off with a gesture.

"No, no it was fine." Then, to break this barrier of politeness between us, I added, "I see you've become the Peter Fonda of Sri Lanka. Whizzing around on your motorcycle, and all that."

They stared at me, taken aback, as people often are when someone shy attempts to be witty. Mili threw back his head and laughed, and Sriyani made a small "humph" of amusement.

He squeezed my shoulder. "I'll take that as a great compliment. *Easy Rider* is one of my favourite films."

After Mili had excused himself and gone to his office, Sriyani gave me a tour, taking me from room to room, introducing me to workers and showing me a bookshop they ran. The focus of Kantha had expanded from women's rights to human rights in general. The organization compiled reports documenting cases of abuse, torture and killings, and these were used by groups like Amnesty International to pressure Western governments to tie the giving of aid to a good human rights record. One of the main projects at Kantha was to help organize meetings between Sinhalese, Tamil and Muslim women whose children had been tortured or killed. "We must start with the mothers," Sriyani said to me. "That is where the solution to our problem ultimately lies."

When we got to Mili's office, which he shared with a woman named Ranjini, he was standing by a cabinet, going through a file. There was something studied in the way he rested elbow on cabinet, right ankle cocked over left, frowning as he read. He had kept track of our progress towards his office. "Ah, Shivan, come, please sit." Mili gestured to the chair across from his desk.

"No, no, you cannot monopolize your old chum. Poor fellow must be starving. I must give him lunch." Yet having said that, Sriyani went off to deal with a peon, leaving me alone with Mili.

We grinned at each other awkwardly. "What do you do for Kantha?" I finally asked.

"Ah, yes." Mili began to tell me about his work, which was to compile reports and send them off to foreign organizations. He came around to where I had taken a seat, placed a report before me and leant over as he flipped through the pages, explaining. His kurta, swelled by the overhead fan, brushed lightly against my cheek, bringing with it a smell of sweat mingled with the cloves used in cupboards to freshen clothes.

"But the work I do is really nothing," he said ruefully, taking back the report. "Unfortunately, my anglophile Cinnamon Gardens upbringing has made me useless in Sinhala and Tamil." He gestured to Ranjini, who had been following our conversation with birdlike curiosity, head tilted to one side. "She is the real hero of Kantha. Was even jailed once by the Special Task Force." Ranjini giggled and gave me a droll look to say Mili was exaggerating her accomplishments. With her long traditional plait and modest ankle-length Sinhalese dress, I found it hard to imagine her as a champion of human rights.

Mili perched against the desk, so close his leg pressed against my thigh. Half glancing at me, half gazing out the window, he began to fill me in on the situation in the country. The Special Task Force (the STF, as he referred to it) was using the Prevention of Terrorism Act to arrest Tamil men without laying charges and hold them indefinitely. The victims were frequently stripped and beaten, chili powder rubbed into their eyes and genitals, their bodies burned with hot rods or cigarettes and subjected to electrical shock. Meanwhile, the Indian troops were also guilty of torture and executions. Last October, following a confrontation with the Tigers near the Jaffna Teaching Hospital, the Indians had stormed the hospital and massacred over seventy doctors, nurses and patients. The Tigers were no better and had slaughtered en masse Sinhalese people who had returned to Jaffna, where they lived.

Then there was the JVP, who were slowly crippling the country by calling for strikes and announcing the closure of various government departments. A few posters by the JVP announcing a general strike were enough to shut down a town or city in the south. Anyone who disobeyed was murdered. They targeted not just civil servants and politicians but also their families, relatives and friends. In retaliation, the government had secretly formed a Sinhalese paramilitary unit called the Green Tigers who were killing suspected JVP activists every day, leaving their bodies on the sides of roads as a warning to others.

What Mili was saying seemed so removed from the normality all about us, he could have been talking about another country. Next door was a Montessori, where the children were singing "Hickory Dickory Dock." The sound of the piano, the students' shrieks of "dock" and "clock" and their giggles drifted in to us.

I was also distracted by the heat of his leg against my thigh, the shift of his hips under the thin cotton of his white kurta. Our meeting at the American Center came back to me, that way he stood leaning against the araliya tree, one leg cocked against the trunk, neck tilting upwards. Had he been displaying himself for me all those years ago, and was he doing the same now? Mili had come to the end of his narration. In the pause he caught my eye, then looked away. A warm pulse, a small terror, really, started up at the thought that he desired me. "And so how is the tits-viewing going in Cinnamon Gardens?" I asked with a nervous laugh. "Have you written your bestseller exposing the marvellous mammary glands of the moneyed classes?"

He chuckled, gently cuffing the side of my head. "Gosh, you have an amazing memory. I forgot I even told you that."

"And?" I asked, grinning, persistent. "How is the tits-viewing going?"

A tremor crossed his face and he turned to shuffle papers on the desk. "No, no more tits-viewing."

"Taken up other forms of perversion, perhaps?" My tone was light, but I was skirting close to the edge.

He pressed his lips together and nodded, noncommittal, his eyes skittering away from mine.

Sriyani came in to our silence, saying, "Goodness, goodness, how time flies. We must have lunch."

I followed her, my eyes lingering to make sure Mili returned my smile, which he did in a shamefaced way.

Sriyani had to get her handbag and give some instructions to an assistant. When she and I were finally on our way towards the stairs, we passed Mili in the corridor, frowning at a cork board that had various postings on it.

"Mili," Sriyani said wryly, as we drew level with him, "aren't you going home for lunch?"

He blushed. He had been hanging around in the hope Sriyani would ask him along.

As I followed Sriyani downstairs, I glanced back at him. Mili had changed. He had lost the old languid poise that had made him so worshipped during our school days. There was a new restlessness to him.

A few days after I met Mili, my grandmother took me to see a new property she had acquired. She instructed our driver to take us to the "Wellawatte house." Then she sat back in her seat and fussed through her purse. This was the first time we were seeing one of her properties since my return, and as we drove through Colombo I felt as if I were falling back to the years of my adolescence, trapped under the weight of her dominance. I shook my head to dismiss this notion, but it sat huddled in a corner of my mind.

When we reached Wellawatte, my grandmother said, "Ah, yes, Chandralal is meeting us there."

She smiled at my alarm. "Don't worry, it's not that. Our Chandralal is a big mahattaya now, much richer than me. He does not need my money anymore."

I was about to ask why he was joining us, but then we turned down a street and I caught sight of the burnt and boarded-up houses on either side. Wellawatte was a Tamil area and had suffered greatly during the riots five years ago. These destroyed houses, sprayed with Sinhalese graffiti saying, "*Tamil pariahs,*" "*Tamil dogs,*" "*Rape a Tamil woman for Lanka,*" made me even more uneasy.

"Puthey, all that is past now," my grandmother said, seeing my dismay. "Riots will never happen again in this country, and do you know why? Look who has suffered the most. The Sinhalese. As people are saying, the Sinhalese have eaten themselves." She waved her hand at the ruined houses. "And all these Tamils have emigrated to Australia and Canada and are even richer than before."

"No, Aacho, that is not so. Tamils are poor in those countries, very poor."

"Rubbish, Puthey. All their children are getting free foreign educations, while our Sinhalese children cannot even go to university with all the student hartals happening here. Those Tamils will end up doctors and lawyers making dollars, not useless rupees."

"There are no free university educations over there. That's just a myth." I glared at her stubbornly.

After a moment, she let out a little laugh and patted my shoulder, smiling fondly, as if she found my views ridiculous but endearing.

I looked out the window, annoyed at her dismissal.

The car stopped in front of a grand house with a large garden, the only building on the street that was intact. A Pajero with tinted windows was parked beside the gate. My grandmother grimaced ironically towards this expensive SUV which was the vehicle of choice for politicians, drug lords and newly rich mudalalis. "See what I mean about Chandralal?"

A driver came around and opened a passenger door. Chandralal got out. He wore a white kurta and sarong and had grown so corpulent in the last five years his new crescent of a moustache looked like a pencil slash on his bloated face.

My grandmother tittered at my astonishment. "Our Chandralal is trying to be a politician, that's why the national costume. The next time there is an election he is going to run for Kotahena."

Despite his newfound wealth, Chandralal came up to our car with a humble, foolish grin and opened the door on my grandmother's side.

"Ah, here you are, madam," he declared, no longer addressing her by the feudal "nona" but using the neutral English term.

"I have brought you a surprise, Chandralal."

"But look who is here!" he cried in delight, his eyes all but disappearing into folds of fat. "It is our young sir come all the way from Canada." He reached across my grandmother and clasped my hand. The old knife wound was stretched and shiny on his fat cheek, the pores of his old acne enlarged.

I smiled back, thawing slightly at his genuine pleasure.

Chandralal assisted my grandmother out of the car and gallantly offered his elbow. She gripped it tightly as he led her in through the gate, his head bent towards her, his smile gentle, moving slowly so as not to tire her.

The house was empty, and my grandmother, aware of my silent question, said, "I bought it from a Tamil family who have emigrated to Australia. I was originally thinking of renting it out, but Chandralal, who has been like a son to me, suggested I build a block of flats here instead. The price of land in Colombo is increasing every day. So the wise thing is to build up and then sell off the flats. People are making millions that way." Though she was talking to me, she looked mostly at Chandralal, like a child parroting a lesson, and he nodded vigorously in encouragement.

"See, your Aachi is as clever as always." He grinned at me. "The stroke has barely affected her."

"Oh, no, Chandralal," my grandmother said with a small laugh that was almost coquettish, "I am now truly an old woman, approaching death."

"Ah, madam, don't say that. You are only sixty-four. You will outlive all of us."

"It's nice of you to say that, Chandralal, but you know the wheel must turn and I must pass to my next life." Her sad gaze was resting on me, as if she hoped to memorize my face and take its impression into her next reincarnation. She gave herself a little shake. "So, yes, I'm happy to hear demolition starts tomorrow."

They began to discuss the architect's blueprints Chandralal had brought, spreading them out on a windowsill. He explained to her the various stages of the building process and she expressed her amazement and praise at how fast he was getting everything done. Since I was not needed, I went through the house, looking in the rooms. The family had left nothing, not a broom or an old toy, but in the back garden three girls had crudely carved their names in the trunk of a mango tree. *Ratna, Mala, Sundari.*

I turned back to the house, heavy with questions I would not allow myself to probe, a gloominess settling on me like the salty crust of a sea mist.

Later that afternoon, while my grandmother slept, I found myself wandering around the saleya. I drifted into my mother and sister's rooms, whose doors and windows Rosalind kept shut to keep out the dust. The tomb-like quality of these rooms, the greyish light filtering in through glass panes smoky with dirt, only increased my melancholy.

14

Sriyani's assistant called some days after our lunch to invite me to a party at the Karunaratnes' home. I told my grandmother, who was lying down after our morning errand, head propped up by pillows. "Ah, yes," she said, "the communist man's daughter. Mother was Indian, distantly related to Nehru. The father met her when he was in Bengal studying at Tagore's school. He came from one of those old Cinnamon Gardens karaya families. The parents were very revolutionary in their time. I believe both were jailed for sedition by the British. Nice woman, the mother. Her Sinhala was better than a lot of real Sinhalese. And now didn't she hold a seat in parliament? Yes, I think she did."

My grandmother, a woman of her time, knew the genealogy of every important family.

"You have been bored here, haven't you, Puthey?" she said suddenly. I began to protest, but she waved her hand. "Don't say no, you are my grandson, I know you." She closed her eyes and nodded. "Yes-yes, this is good. It's very kind of Mrs. Karunaratne to take you under her wing. We have some nice papaws ripening in the garden. I'll have Rosalind send her a box."

Sriyani's husband was a successful hotelier and they lived in the wealthy enclave of Cinnamon Gardens. My grandmother had loaned me her car, and as I was driven to the party I found myself both nervous and exhilarated at the prospect of seeing Mili Jayasinghe there. Since our last meeting, I had thought about him a lot and the possibility he might be sexually interested in me. Yet I had warned myself that Mili's interest could be nothing but the cordiality of an old school acquaintance; his displaying himself, even his mild flirtation, nothing but the posing beautiful people indulged in without thinking. Yet as the car turned down Rosmead Place, where Sriyani lived, I could not subdue the warmth that spread through me, even as I told myself this hope was ridiculous.

Sriyani was on the verandah of the Karunaratnes' sprawling old colonial bungalow, wearing an avocado salwar kameez and lilac shawl, greeting the many guests who milled around her. As I went up the steps, I could hear a slightly scratchy recording of "Isle of Capri," the laughter and chatter of guests like waves breaking around the *oomph*ing of the tuba. Sriyani excused herself from the visitors and came to me, saying, "Ah-ah, you're here, I must present you around." She introduced me to her husband, Priya, who was standing by the carved teak front doors. He was well over six feet and stooped in that way of tall people who are constantly bending to those below them. He wore a batik shirt, crisp linen pants and smoked a pipe, its stem hanging from a corner of his mouth, which was twisted with wry amusement at this odd assortment of his wife's friends drawn from different social classes.

Sriyani ushered me into the living room with its antique furniture, holding on to my arm so she would not lose me in the jam of guests, the air hazy with smoke that shimmered a mother-of-pearl under the lights.

The inside of the house had been renovated to resemble the vernacular style of architecture, the back wall removed so the interior and exterior mingled. In the centre of the living room was a sunken mada midula open to the sky with large-leaved crotons and palms in pots. There were Hindu and Buddhist statues in nooks and paintings on the walls by famous Sri Lankan artists like Ivan Peries, Senaka Senanayake and George Keyt.

Sriyani guided me to the mada midula, where guests were lying on mats among the plants, bolstered by large colourful cushions. Mili Jayasinghe was laughing and chatting with Ranjini and other workers from Kantha, his lanky frame stretched out across the floor, more like the teenager I remembered. As Sriyani came down the two steps to the mada midula, the men started to rise hastily in respect. She gestured for them to stay where they were. Mili saw me and he looked flustered. "Shivan," he stood up. "How are you?"

"Oh, fine, fine." I realized I was picking at the edge of my collar and quickly dropped my hand.

"Now you are safe," Sriyani said to me with one of her inscrutable smiles. "Look after your old school chum." She wagged her finger at Mili, and went back to the front verandah.

He beckoned me to join their group, but I sat on the steps, too much a stranger to sprawl with them. Mili made to resume his earlier position, but then picked up his drink and came to sit by me. I felt a little fizz of delight.

The others asked me about the politics of the growing Jaffna Tamil community in Toronto, which numbered close to a hundred thousand. They were keen to know if I thought the community donated voluntarily to the Tigers or did so out of fear for their families in the Tiger-controlled areas. I told them I had no contact with the Jaffna Tamil community, being half Sinhalese and from Colombo. They seemed rather disappointed, as if they had hoped for an on-the-ground report.

Ranjini had come to sit on my other side. She appeared, for some reason, to have taken a fondness to me, smiling and nodding at me with great friendliness. Once they had quizzed me, Mili's friends returned to talking about the latest exploits of the JVP which included setting fire to some government-run buses and the killing of a minister in the south, along with his body guards. After some time, I asked Ranjini if she knew where the toilet was. Hearing this, Mili promptly jumped up. "Come, I will show you."

There was a modern extension, its two floors carefully concealed behind trees so as not to overwhelm the old bungalow. As he took me to the stairs that led to the second floor, he inquired about how I was finding Sri Lanka and what I had done so far. Then we both fell silent, our footsteps loud on the polished concrete steps. On the second floor, he led me along a dim corridor lit by an occasional sconce and pointed out the bathroom.

When I came out, Mili was leaning against the wall near the door. He nodded and went past me to use the toilet. Alone in the corridor, I was seized with the idea that if anything was going to happen between us, I would have to propel it, have to act now when he came out. There were various pieces of art on the walls, and as I glanced at them I noticed a framed black-and-white photograph. A young man was turned three quarters towards the camera, right hand on hip. He was naked, save for a loincloth through which his genitals were visible, his body lean and hairless, his oiled skin bringing out the play of light and shade on his muscles and ribs.

The door to the bathroom opened. Mili came towards me. I gave him a quick tense smile, then turned back to the photograph, fear tightening a band across my forehead. After a moment, I felt his presence next to me.

"That's a Lionel Wendt photograph," he said quietly. "You know, the man the theatre is named after. Did you know he was a photographer?" He smelt of rum and salty sweat and some muskiness.

"No." I looked up at him, then plunged forward. "The man, he's so beautiful, don't you think?"

He held my gaze, even though I could see, from the timid terror in his eyes, it was taking all his will. He swallowed, his Adam's apple straining against his throat.

There was a burst of guffaws from the main house and we glanced involuntarily in its direction. Then, seeing each other's consternation, we laughed.

I took Mili's hand, opened a bedroom door and pulled him inside.

The room was dark except for a lamp on a dresser. I pressed him up against a wall, my tongue pushing against his teeth, trying to force his mouth open. His hands trembled as he gripped me by the upper arms, then pushed me away.

"Shivan, Shivan," he whispered, "someone . . . someone might come in here."

He was gesturing towards the door, and I stared at it, dazed, then quickly leaned past him to lock it. "You really are a jumpy bugger," I said with a little choked laugh. I pushed my tongue against his teeth again. He opened his mouth, half smiling, half shaking his head, at my boldness. We kissed, our breath escaping in little impatient-sounding sighs. Mili ran his palm down my back and tugged at my shirt to slip his hand underneath. I reached into the waistband of his trousers, my hand sliding beneath his underwear to his buttocks. He groaned against my lips and pressed his arm between us to stroke me through my pants.

Someone was coming down the corridor towards the toilet. We pulled back from each other.

"I really think we should go downstairs," Mili whispered.

"Yes," I replied reluctantly.

We tidied our clothing, now shy to look at each other. Mili opened the door, glanced in both directions and signalled that the corridor was empty. As I passed him I rested my hand on his chest.

When we were amongst the guests, as if by some unspoken agreement we separated. I returned to the mada midula and sat next to Ranjini, and Mili went to talk with some men who had just come in.

Ranjini was very curious about my life in Canada and told me, in return, about the village she came from near Matara and how she had studied Buddhist literature in university. There was a man named Sri with the bushy beard of a poet or a revolutionary who sat next to her as we talked. He also worked at Kantha. Stocky and very dark-skinned, he had that Negroid hair and nose that some Sri Lankans have. I could not tell if they were a couple. They did not touch, but then Ranjini, with her traditional ways, might not have been comfortable doing so in public.

Dinner was soon served, and by then I had grown weary of the small talk, which I found hard to keep up with, distracted by how Mili so assiduously kept his distance from me. Once the meal was over, I made my excuses, lying that I was still having terrible jet lag. Sriyani walked me out to the front verandah and we chatted while one of her houseboys went to look for my driver among the vehicles on the street. Just as my car was pulling up the driveway, Mili came hurrying out onto the verandah. "Shivan, I didn't know you were leaving." He looked alarmed but chastened.

"You seemed so involved in your conversation. I didn't want to bother you." I offered my hand, and when he placed his in mine, I shook it formally.

"But why are you going so soon?" He gave me a pleading look.

Sriyani was watching our interaction, smiling in that subtle way of hers.

"So, then, I'll see you tomorrow?" I said on impulse, as if we had already discussed this.

"Yes," he replied after a moment. Then he grinned, eyes crinkling up, shaking his head ever so slightly at my quick thinking.

I barely slept that night. As the fan clattered above my bed, its breeze slapping the curtain against the wooden window frame, I lay with my hands under my head wondering, in that way one wonders in the dead of night, if I had imagined the whole thing. It seemed impossible to reconcile the Mili I had known in school, star cricketer, head prefect, with what had happened in that bedroom. Yet this was not his first time. Once he had got past his nerves, there had been no fumbling awkwardness.

15

THE MORNING AFTER SRIYANI'S PARTY, I turned down my grandmother's request to go out with her, claiming I had a headache, and lay in bed reading. Whenever a vehicle came down our road, I lifted my head from the pillow and strained to make out if it was Mili's motorcycle. Finally I heard him pull up outside our house and ring the gate bell. I rushed out of my bedroom and overtook Rosalind, who was making her way across the saleya. "It's for me," I cried, waving her away. When I was on the verandah, I gathered myself together, then sauntered down to the gate.

Mili was seated astride the motorcycle, his grin curiously rueful. The sight of him, so handsome, his eyes crinkled against the glare, caused something to loosen in me, a slipping into pleasure.

"You look like you've been asleep," he said.

I began to smooth down my hair. "No, no, I like it," he said shyly.

"I . . . I was just lying down." Then I added, "You tired me out last night."

He laughed.

"You didn't say when you would come. But I was hoping it would be this morning." I touched his knee briefly.

"Cocky bugger. What if I hadn't come at all?"

"Oh, no, you would have come. After all, you are the great Sex Fiend of Cinnamon Gardens."

He shook his head, grinning, and held out a spare helmet. "Come."

I was expecting we would go to his house in Cinnamon Gardens or to a restaurant, and I was puzzled when we rode outwards from central Colombo past Nugegoda towards Kalubowila. Once we left the older part of the city, the buildings became shabby concrete boxes with narrow windows and flat roofs, the streets winding chaotically, devoid of pavements and trees. Mili turned down a dirt lane and came to a stop at a house that had a boundary wall splotched with green mildew. We went through a rusted takaran gate into a front garden with a few dusty shrubs and a sickly looking bougainvillea growing in it. Mili led me along a path around the side of the house and stopped in front of a door with flaking brown paint. "This is home now, Shivan." He pressed his lips together and shrugged at my astonishment.

The flat was dark and had that fusty smell of clothes folded away while still damp. In the living room were a rattan settee and armchair that had lost their varnish, the cane strips which held the joints together loose and curling. Farther back was a dining table, its glossy maroon veneer chipped. Faded curtains hung in the windows and doorways to two bedrooms.

"Mili?" a querulous voice called out. One of the curtains parted and his mother came out.

The Mrs. Jayasinghe I had seen, at prize-givings and sports meets, had worn expensive organza saris, her hair done by a stylist, face carefully made up. The woman before me was dressed in polyester slacks which were out of fashion and a white cotton blouse slightly yellowed with age and washing. The handbag over her shoulder was expensive but battered around the edges and of another era. There had always been an arrogant bustle to the old Mrs. Jayasinghe, head held high, plump figure a symbol of her wealth and beauty. But now she was thin and she moved slowly.

When Mili introduced me and told her I was from Canada, she said, "How lucky you are to be there, son, and not living in this hell we call a country."

She was going to spend the afternoon with a cousin, and as we were chatting about my life in Canada, a taxi honked outside the gate. She nodded to me, kissed her son on the cheek and left, walking in that way my mother did, parcelling out her energy as if she were sick.

Once she was gone, Mili, stating the obvious, said, "My pater and mater are separated." He put his helmet down on the dining table. "And you know how Sri Lanka is. Unless you have a lot of money, court cases are out of the question." He shrugged. "The kind of lawyer we could afford would have no chance against my pater's Cinnamon Gardens lawyer. So now my pater lives in our old house with his mistress and we live here. He gives my mater a small allowance, but this is as far as we can get with it and my salary."

While Mili spoke he went about the room, putting his bag down, looking through the mail. He was trying to appear nonchalant, but I could see that he was desperately ashamed of this place.

"Ah, Mili."

He turned to me with a crooked smile and I put my arms around him. He rested his chin against my shoulder, running his fingers up and down my back in an absent-minded manner. Soon the movement of his hands became more purposeful.

We took our time undressing each other as we lay face to face on his bed, stopping to gaze and touch and run our tongues over every part that came exposed. I could feel Mili's muscles slide under his skin as he moved. The hair on his chest, arms and legs was fine and very black against his lighter skin. His cock was pulsing against the white fabric of his briefs, and when I drew his underpants down, his erection slipped sideways across the V of his groin, the shaft a smooth satiny brown, the head a dark purple. The baby powder, which he used to absorb the sweat in his groin and underarms, gave him a familiar musky smell. We spent long periods just kissing and holding each other, then we would resume making love again.

Those early weeks with Mili were glorious and we saw each other every evening. When my grandmother found out he was the son of Tudor Jayasinghe, she was delighted I had a friend from such a prestigious family. She urged him to treat our house as if it were his, saying she was happy he was looking out for her grandson and that I had been thoroughly bored in the company of "two old women." On her instruction, Rosalind began to set an extra place for Mili at dinner. Afterwards, I would sit with him on the verandah and listen to the crickets and birds while he smoked. When we talked about our school days or Mili told me what had happened to the boys in our class and various teachers, I would think of all the Canadian men I'd had affairs with and the strain of having to explain myself and Sri Lanka to them. With Mili it felt so peaceful, this shared history, this elliptical way of talking, because we both understood the same world and its idioms. Mili was always delighted with my quips and sarcasm and he would encourage me by protesting, "that's too far, Shivan, that's too far," then laughing as I continued to skewer some boy or teacher or a person we were observing on the street.

Mili's social world consisted of three couples he worked with at Kantha, and I soon got to know them well. Dharshini was second-in-command under Sriyani, and her husband, Jagath, looked after the organization's finances. They came from upper-class Kandyan Sinhalese families and had that slow ease born from generations of wealth. Though their salary was paltry, they lived in a nice Cinnamon Gardens house that was Dharshini's dowry. Dilan and Avanthi were from the US and spoke with American accents, having lived there since childhood. They had met at the University of Chicago, where they were both doing their Ph.D. theses on Sri Lanka's ethnic problem. They were intense in that way of returning expatriates, anxious to assimilate into Sri Lankan culture.

The last couple was Ranjini and Sri, the man with the bushy beard who had hung around us at the party. Their relationship had been forbidden by Ranjini's parents because Sri was Tamil. She had acquiesced to parental pressure and was betrothed to a distant cousin. Yet she and Sri kept their love affair going in secret. The others were constantly urging Ranjini to assert herself, teasing her about working in human rights and not standing up for its principles in her private life. She was good natured about this, letting out little squeals of laughter and wiping tears of mirth with a frilly-edged handkerchief. Her time in jail—where she would still have been but for the intervention of Sriyani's husband, who had high-level connections in the government—gave her hallowed status among her colleagues. Also, her demure manner was an advantage with village women, who opened up to her in a way they didn't to others.

Ranjini regarded me as a younger brother and called me Shivan-malli. I would often find her watching me, head to one side, eyes merry with some knowledge. She did not speak English fluently and would ask me the meaning of a word or if she had said something correctly. She would unconsciously take my hand as we talked, in the way Sri Lankan girls did with each other.

Mili's friends treated me as one of his school chums visiting from abroad. I was sure they never suspected Mili—cricket captain, motorbike fanatic—of being gay. But then, there was his ongoing single state. Since they never questioned this or tried to set him up with a woman friend, I formed the theory that to them Mili was so hardily male he could not fit into the domestic routine of women or bend to the softness of loving one. I felt the other men greatly admired him for not succumbing to domesticity.

The bars and restaurants we went to with Mili's friends were bare-walled rooms that looked like canteens, with metal chairs and tables and fluorescent lighting; not the opulent hotel lobbies our former classmates frequented. We would spend entire Saturdays and Sundays at the cabanas on Mount Lavinia beach, sending one of the cabana boys for kotthu rotis and hoppers from the local Muslim restaurant or a trishaw driver to The Great Wall for Chinese food.

One weekend at Mount Lavinia, Ranjini and I went in search of the pineapple vendor who patrolled the beach. As we walked along the water's edge to keep our feet cool from the burning sand, we fell into talking about Buddhist stories. I had told her earlier that my grandmother often used to narrate them to me. Ranjini, having studied Buddhist literature, knew many more tales than I did. "But have you heard the Rupananda story, Shivan-malli?" she asked, and when I shook my head she told the story of how Lord Buddha had created a phantom, a very beautiful sixteen-year-old girl, to teach his vain cousin Rupananda a lesson on beauty. The phantom was visible only to Rupananda, who saw it when she came to hear her cousin preach. She fell immediately in love and could not stop gazing at the phantom's beauty, consumed with desire for this girl. The next day, she rushed back to see the object of her love. But this time the phantom appeared as a twenty-five-year-old, and Rupananda felt her love diminish a little. Still, she returned again and again, and on each successive visit Lord Buddha aged the phantom to a middle-aged woman, an old woman, and finally into a sick crone who fell dead at his feet and began to decay and suppurate, worms crawling out of her body. Rupananda was cured of her attachment to her beauty. She cut her hair, removed all her lovely garments and put on the robes of a nun.

"It is a good story, no, Shivan-malli?" Ranjini said, smiling at me sweetly, yet holding my gaze. "Yes-yes, I knew you would especially like that story." I nodded, looking towards the horizon to hide my consternation. She had guessed we were lovers. I was sure Ranjini, like my grandmother, had rendered an altered version of the original, to get her point across.

The most splendid time of Mili's and my first weeks together was a visit to Sriyani's beach house.

The bungalow was on the south coast, and Sriyani, ever the communist man's daughter, lent it to anyone who asked. The house had verandahs all around, and airy rooms that were sparse but tastefully furnished, concrete beds and divans built into the floor and painted white, their mattress covers and cushions an aquamarine-and-emerald stripe. From the front verandah the garden sloped down to the sand and turquoise sea glittering with shards of light, a mist trembling where the waves crashed against the beach. The bungalow was in a grove of coconut trees that kept the building cool and shady. The rustle of palm fronds, as they bowed and reared in the wind, was like the sound of a second sea. An amiable old man named Piyasena served as cook, cleaner and watchman. He had a family in the village nearby and was pleased when Sriyani had guests because he could return home for the night and not guard the place.

The sea was a little rough, but Mili and I went in, as far as we dared, and spent the morning in the water. When we came back to the bungalow, lunch was laid out—nutty brown rice, fresh fried fish, huge prawns in a red coconut curry and local village vegetables like batu, pathola and kathurumurunga.

After we had eaten, the man left, saying he would be back to cook dinner. We locked the gate, raced each other to the bedroom and made love, chuckling as we pulled each other's clothes off as if this was a gleeful, forbidden treat, tasting the sea salt on each other's skins. Once we had slept, we made love again more languorously under the mosquito net, the smell of salt mingled now with our dried sweat.

In the evening, we told Piyasena not to wait and serve us, that we would wash up after we had eaten. We sat on the front verandah in planter's chairs, our feet up on the leg rests, sarongs wound tight around our shins, sipping beer. The sun was setting in that rapid way it does in the tropics, going under the horizon suddenly, with a burst of pink, orange and purple. The sea changed to bottle green, glowing as if light pulsed upwards from the seabed. Looking over at Mili, I longed to slip into his chair and hold him, yet the ache of his distance filled me with pleasure.

Those early weeks were magical, but the impossibility of our love was already between us. When Mili visited my grandmother's house in the evening, there was often an unspoken sexual frustration between us. Sometimes I would invite him to my room and we would kiss, but always with an eye on the curtain in the doorway, our bodies barely brushing. As in a lot of Sri Lankan homes, we left our doors open for ventilation. Shutting mine would raise questions. As time passed, Mili had less to say as we sat on the verandah. He would often stare out at the garden, smoking. Or he would speak moodily about the rising violence of the JVP in the south, that more and more bodies were being found by the main roads, some killed by the government, some by the JVP. The thing he dwelt on most was the recent murder of a prominent human rights lawyer who was falsely arrested by the police for the death of the actor-turned-politician Vijaya Kumaratunga. A government press release had claimed the lawyer was a high-ranking member of the JVP and responsible for this assassination. He had died in a Colombo hospital, the post-mortem revealing that his body bore more than a hundred wounds and that his death had been caused by bludgeoning with a blunt instrument. "The cord is getting tighter and tighter, Shivan," he would say, "tighter and tighter." While I believed that this rising violence truly troubled him, at the same time, I felt he sensed my dislike for talking about such things as they spoilt our time together, and he was doing it to thwart and irritate me.

He would never tell me about the other men he had been with and where he had met them. For some reason, I was frightened to inquire directly and tried to probe by asking how he had figured out I was gay. He always laughed in reply, and when pressed would say, "I just knew, I just knew." There was something about the way he said this that put up a barrier. Driven by my greed for him, I would push, saying jokingly, "You must be a truly experienced bugger to know just like that, ah?" or, "Yes, yes, I am not surprised you could tell. I bet you used to zip around Colombo on your motorbike, servicing all and sundry, didn't you?" He continued to evade with laughter and grins. If I got too persistent, he would change the subject or look at his watch and declare, "Look at the time! My mater will begin to worry."

Once, I asked him about that encounter between us at the American Center, if he'd invited me to his home hoping we would have sex.

"Of course not," he replied, grinning teasingly. "I asked you back so we could look at Cinnamon Gardens' titties through my binoculars. Remember, I am the Sex Fiend of Cinnamon Gardens."

I punched him lightly in the side. "But would you have made love to me?" I persisted.

"Would you have?" he countered, an edge to his voice.

"Yes, of course."

"Rubbish."

"I would have. The moment we got to your room."

Mili shrugged and lit a cigarette.

After he left, I would often curse myself for having driven him away and vow that the next time I would not ask about his sexual past. But the need to know would writhe in me until I found myself blurting out some question. Then once again we would be sparring and dodging, our tone light to hide the darker currents below.

16

One morning my grandmother paid me a visit while I was putting away some clothes Rosalind had washed, ironed, folded and left on my desk. She sat on my bed and watched as I went about the task. "Don't think I, too, have not been sad, Puthey, at how little time is left." She nodded at my surprise. I hadn't realized she'd noticed my recent melancholy. There was only one week left to my holiday.

"Puthey, why don't you stay on?"

"Forever?" I blushed at my involuntary reply.

She gave me a keen look. "Well, just a few months. It would mean so much to me."

"But Aacho, what about my getting a job? I have a student loan to pay."

"How much?"

I told her, and she snorted. "That is all? I can easily pay it off."

"You can?"

"Of course, from my London account."

I thought of Mili and the way he would press his lips together in suppressed delight when he came to visit in the evening and found me waiting on the verandah, as if I was the thing he had been contemplating all day; thought of the slow comfort of my days here, getting up late, having a leisurely breakfast, a nap after lunch, no scramble to find work and pay my loan, no evenings in that basement with its musty smell, fake wood veneer and lumpy mattress.

"So, Puthey?"

"I can't take money from you, Aacho."

"Why not?" she cried indignantly. "You are my grandson. Who else is the money for?"

Then a thought struck me. "What about Amma and Renu?"

She gave me a sharp look, taking in my dismay. "This doesn't concern anybody else."

"Aacho, it does. They are my mother and sister. They need to at least be asked."

This was the first time I had raised my mother and sister with her. From the few comments she had made and her look of distaste when a letter came for me from Canada, I knew she was not interested in mending the breach with her daughter. I remained silent on the subject of my mother as well, telling myself I should not reveal anything about her plight which would allow my grandmother to gloat at her mistakes and failures.

My grandmother straightened the pleats of her sari. "Very well, you must call your mother and ask her permission." A coy, almost sly, expression came over her face. "But you do want to stay, don't you?"

"Yes, yes, of course."

She clapped her hands. "Good!" She called Rosalind to tell her the news and the ayah wept predictable tears of joy.

I felt I had been bested in some way I could not explain.

In the last week, Mili and I had become more distant, hardly speaking as we sipped beers on my front verandah, drifting apart when swimming at Mount Lavinia. Yet we spent all our free time together. We never mentioned the dwindling days, but his friends would bring it up, saying they had got so used to having me around and would miss me. When they said these things, Mili and I would not look at each other, but later we would embrace fiercely in my bedroom or be reckless and kiss outside our gate at night.

I waited until after dinner when we were seated on the verandah to announce my news. Mili was silent after I told him, legs stretched out and crossed at the ankles. A man selling lottery tickets passed by on a bicycle, calling out the dates and prizes into a cheap microphone he held in one hand, his voice chirping hoarsely, like a frog in the grass.

"Mili?" I could not see his face in the shadows.

He straightened up in his chair. "That's great, Shivan."

"You don't sound happy about it."

"No, no, I'm really happy."

"You're not." I went to sit on the balustrade, looking out at the garden. He came to stand behind me, running a finger up my back. "It's just that, you know, you must go back to Canada at some point."

"Only temporarily. I want to return for good, like a lot of people do."

"But things are getting worse here, don't you see? Sri Lanka is really heading into a time that will make the '83 riots seem like nothing. It's going to be a bloodbath here, what with the Indians, the Tigers and the JVP all increasing their violence, all vying for power. The bodies on the sides of roads, floating down rivers, on the beach, keep increasing. If the JVP succeed in gaining control of the country, we English-speaking Cinnamon Gardens types are finished. They'll hang us from trees. Sri Lanka could end up like Pol Pot's Cambodia. And don't forget you're Tamil. They despise the Tamils. Then there is the murder of that lawyer, the ridiculous way the government is still trying to tarnish his name by accusing him of murdering Vijaya Kumaratunga. It's a frightening time.

"What about us, Shivan?" he continued into my silence, dropping his voice to a murmur. "You know the rules here. We can't set up house like people do in Canada. Always and eternally we will be two bachelors living with our mother and grandmother. I accept the situation because I have no choice. But are you willing to?"

"You think I haven't considered that?" I demanded in a fierce whisper. "Don't patronize me. Yes, I am willing to make that compromise."

"But Shivan," Mili said in a low voice, holding out his hands in appeal, "to always live with your grandmother? To rarely sleep with me?"

"Here I am, doing this so we can be together, and this is how you treat me? With all these silly objections?"

My voice was trembling with anger, but he must have thought I was close to tears, because he touched my hand, saying, "Shh, shh." After a glance around, he drew me back against his chest. "I'm sorry, I'm a terrible bugger." He kissed the back of my neck, then released me. "I . . . I love you, Shivan, I know I do, and I have never said that to anyone else."

"I love you too," I replied, my voice husky from having to hold back my emotions and speak softly. "I have been with so many men and never felt this. I want it, Mili, I want it no matter what."

I led him to my bedroom, closed the door and locked it. I did not care anymore. With our shirts on, our pants around our knees, we made love as best we could, Mili's body trembling, half with desire, half with fear.

The next evening, when my grandmother was at the temple, I called my mother. As I waited for the operator to put the trunk call through, I was nervous. Soon after arriving, I had called to leave a message that I had arrived safely, timing it for mid-morning when everyone would be out of the house. Since then, I had written a brief aerogram with little bits of bland news, leaving out all the interesting developments during my visit.

My mother answered, and instead of returning my greeting, said, "Son, are you alright? Has something happened?"

"No, Amma," I replied impatiently. "Not at all."

I heard my sister's voice in the background, and my mother said, "Yes, he's calling from Sri Lanka."

"So, you're sure everything is alright?" my mother repeated, and now I heard the receiver click as Renu picked up the extension.

"Yes, Amma."

"Good," she said doubtfully.

"Why are you calling, then, Shivan?" Renu demanded. "It's just barely seven thirty in the morning here."

"I'm having a wonderful time, Renu. I'm so happy, you know."

"You are?" my mother asked.

"Yes, and guess what, Amma?" I feigned excitement. "I'm going to stay for the summer."

My mother was silent. "But you can't, Shivan, the ticket . . ."

"I can extend it for three months."

"But . . . but what about a job, you have to pay your loan."

"Aacho will pay it from her London account."

"No," my mother said firmly, "no, I want you to come back. Shivan, you must return."

"What for?"

"Your life is here."

"No it isn't. I hate my life there. I don't want to come back at all, really, but I will before my ticket expires. Then I . . . I'm seriously thinking of returning to live here."

"Shivan, are you mad?" Renu said after a moment of silence on the other end. "Are you blind to what is going on in that country? You are a Tamil, have you forgotten that?"

"Only in name."

"What do you mean?"

"I speak Sinhalese, I eat Sinhalese food, I live in a Sinhalese house. If I change my name, I will be Sinhalese."

"Change your name to what?"

"Ariyasinghe, what else?"

I could hear one of them breathing fiercely on the phone. "Let me speak to your aachi," my mother demanded.

"She's gone to the temple. There is no need for you to talk to her. And no, she has not influenced me. I am a grown man. I have come to this decision on my own."

"Shivan," my mother cried, "you come back next week, you hear?"

"No, Amma, I will not."

"You must, I insist."

"Amma, I'll write soon." And with that I put down the phone.

I went to sit on the verandah, hands clasped as I leaned forward, gazing out at the garden. The thought of what awaited me in Canada—my basement, the scramble for money, my mother's depression—sickened me. I should have felt gladness and relief for this extended reprieve from all that, but instead I felt threatened by my Canadian life, as if even at this remove it had the power to destroy my current happiness.

How quickly things progressed from there. A few days later, I was awakened in the early hours by Rosalind, saying, "Baba, come, your aachi is not well."

I tied my sarong and followed her to my grandmother's room.

She was lying in bed, forearm over eyes.

"Aacho?" I went and sat by her.

"Ah, Puthey," she said faintly. "I'm fine. Just a little weak today, it will pass."

"I'll call the doctor."

"No, no." She lowered her arm. "I am just coming down with a cold."

Rosalind and I had a whispered discussion in the saleya. I telephoned Dr. Navaratnam, our family physician, and also Sunil Maama for good measure.

When I led them into my grandmother's room, she looked cross. "Now, what is this?" she said to me. "For nothing you are wasting Dr. Navaratnam's time." She glared at her cousin. "You better not bill me for this visit, Sunil."

"Of course not, Daya." Sunil Maama laughed nervously.

"Let's see, let's see, Mrs. Ariyasinghe," Dr. Navaratnam said with a little smile. She took out a blood-pressure meter from her black Gladstone bag and checked my grandmother's pressure. "Hmm, seems normal." She gave my grandmother a thorough examination, then declared, "Nothing really wrong. Might be the flu."

My grandmother glowered at me in triumph. "Ah, see, you have wasted everybody's time."

"Now, come, Aacho, I did the right thing," I scolded. "You really aren't that careful with yourself. If you don't watch out, you'll end up having another stroke."

She rolled her eyes at the doctor. "My grandson is far too worried about my health." Yet she was delighted at this public display of my concern. She lay back against her pillow with a moan. "Aiyo! Now what am I going to do about today? I have to visit a property and collect the rent."

Sunil Maama offered to go, but my grandmother shook her head and covered her eyes with her forearm again.

The doctor packed her bag with an amused smile. I could feel the expectation swell in the room. "Of course, Aacho, I'll do it," I blurted out.

She sighed and lowered her forearm. "See, Dr. Navaratnam, what a blessing my grandson is in my old age. Like rain soaking a parched land."

"You are very lucky, Mrs. Ariyasinghe," the doctor replied dryly.

I had to collect rent at the row house in Pettah from which my grandmother had ejected that woman Siriyawathy and her boy all those years ago. The roof was missing even more tiles and had rusting takaran patches all over it, like sores on a beggar's back, the verandah pillars swollen and warped, the paint blistering. As I went up the front steps, they listed beneath my weight. Boards in the verandah floor had rotted away, the jagged gaps revealing muddy ground a few feet below.

The tenant was two months in arrears. I knocked and, when no one came, went to the front window and peered through the chinks of the wooden shutters. Bloodshot eyes stared back at me.

"What do you want?" a man demanded.

"Hello, I'm here to collect the rent."

"You are who?"

"Mrs. Ariyasinghe's grandson."

He continued to scrutinize me, and I frowned proprietarily at the gaps in the verandah floor as if they were his fault.

After some time, the tenant turned away from the window. Bolts grated back and he stepped out, shutting the door behind him. He wore only a pair of frayed shorts that looked grease-stained like he had been under a car, pot belly hanging over the waistband. His hands were enormous, tufts of hair on knuckles. An old wound on his forehead was shaped like a gecko. "What is it you want again?" he asked, as if he had not heard me correctly before, arms folded over broad chest.

"The rent." Then I added, "You're in arrears, my grandmother says. Two months."

He was chewing a wad of bulath leaves, his mouth red from it. He spat out a stream of juice, which just missed my feet. "Tell your grandmother I don't have the money. I can't pay her."

He grinned at my stupefaction and stepped closer. "You're a fine boy. From Cinnamon Gardens, aren't you? Beautiful face like a girl's, soft hands like a girl's."

"Look, I just want to get the rent." A heat throbbed in my head. "Why don't you pay for one month."

"I don't have the money for one month. I don't have any money at all."

"Then . . . then you must leave. You must vacate the premises."

He whistled. "Big talk, nah? From a boy with such pretty hands and face." He stepped even closer. I could smell his stale sweat and sour, leafy breath. "Get inside and I'll fuck you for the rent.

"Yes," he said with an amused grunt at my gasp, "I'll fuck you good for the rent."

"Look, are you . . . are you going to pay the rent or not? I don't have all day for this."

"Ado, ponnaya, you got too much wax in your ears? I just told you I don't have the money."

I shoved the receipt book in my bag, hands shaking. "Well, you must pay the rent. Or you must leave." I turned away with chin tilted up. "I will tell my grandmother of all this."

When I reached the car, he yelled in a falsetto for the whole street to hear, "Aney, look, a ponnaya!"

As we drove away, I longed to lean my head back against the seat and shut my eyes, but the driver was looking at me in the rear-view mirror and I pretended to stare nonchalantly out the window. "Ponnaya" was used frequently as an insult and I did not think the man thought I was actually gay. He had just wanted to emasculate me.

In my bathroom, I splashed my face with cold water, then rinsed my mouth, spitting vigorously to expel the taint of that man, his sneer, his smell of sweat and bulath. "That thuppai pariah," I whispered as I dried my face, looking at my image in the mirror. Yet I was impotent against him, and this only increased my anger.

My grandmother was not in her bedroom. I found Rosalind in the kitchen, and she informed me that the Loku Nona had suddenly felt better, called a taxi and gone on an errand. The ayah's eyes were wide with concern for me. Our driver was seated on a stool at the back of the kitchen, bent over a newspaper, frowning. Their worry about my encounter with the tenant only increased my humiliation.

I went back to the saleya and roamed about, stopping to look out of various windows. My grandmother would be home soon; it was nearly lunch time. What would she do? The moment I posed the question, the answer was clear. "Soma," I called to the driver as I strode towards the kitchen. "Soma!

"Come, we have to do an errand," I said urgently as I came back out onto the back verandah. I ignored the look of alarm that passed between him and Rosalind.

In her letters, my grandmother had told me about the renovations to Chandralal's home, but I was still taken aback when I saw it. There was a high boundary wall topped with rolls of barbed wire. A security guard, gun slung over his shoulder, opened the gate. He glared at me inquiringly but then, recognizing my grandmother's car, he smiled with genuine friendliness and ushered me in. The old house had been replaced by a two-storey mansion, the properties on either side annexed to accommodate this expansion. The only part of the old home that remained was the marble fountain, plastic flamingos and penguins still around it, like petitioners gathered outside a seigniorial manor.

The security guard escorted me up the front path and rang the doorbell. A flustered servant answered. The guard told her I was the Ariyasinghe Nona's grandson and she beckoned me cordially into the living room, then went to get her master. I sat on a plush red velvet sofa which gave off a smell of mouldy animal fur in this tropical heat. The décor suggested simultaneously a colonial smoking room and a Victorian lady's parlour. The ornate teak furniture had leopard-skin-pattern upholstery and there were antlers and even a stuffed sambar head mounted on the wall. An elephant-foot wastepaper basket sat in a corner. Yet all the armchairs and sofas had dainty antimacassars on them. Ruffled and frilled lace curtains hung in the windows and the china cabinets were crammed with porcelain bric-a-brac.

Chandralal came out immediately from what must have been his study clutching papers and a pen, reading glasses perched on his nose. "Baba . . . your aachi?"

I stood up. "No, no, Chandralal." I patted his arm awkwardly, moved by his fear. "There is nothing wrong with her."

Bafflement twitched across his forehead. "Then, baba?" He removed his glasses and put his papers and pen on the coffee table.

I could not speak for a moment and he gestured for me to be seated.

"I am having a problem with a tenant, Chandralal, and I need your help."

"Of course, baba." He gave me a keen look and sat down across from me.

"It's the Pettah property."

I told my story hesitantly, but then, seeing his surprise and anger at the tenant's behaviour, my own anger returned. "Can you believe, Chandralal, that pariah dog actually spat at my feet? And he had the insolence to call me a ponnaya."

He shook his head in wonder at this insult and leaned back in his chair.

"Yes, Chandralal, this man, who has crawled out of some sewer, had the gall to insult my manhood, yelling for the whole street to hear."

"The whole street, baba? What a disgrace. How can you ever return there again?"

He held his glasses up to the light, examining the lenses. He was waiting for me. "So, Chandralal, I need you to—"

He lifted his hand as if to stop me saying something I might regret. "It is done, baba." He stood up. "My blood boils to think of that wild dog talking to our baba in such a way." He gestured towards me with open palms. "Why, I have known you since you were a little boy, nah? I think of you like a son." Then, perhaps feeling that was too much, he added, "Like a little cousin-brother. And to think that spawn of a sperm-eating whore—" He broke off and shook his head again in wonder. He patted my back. "Now, you go home. I will deal with this."

Chandralal escorted me to the car. As we walked down the front path, I complimented him on his renovations, saying they were even more elegant than my grandmother had described. He blushed and said he was grateful they met my approval. I was someone who had, no doubt, seen much fine architecture in Canada.

When we parted, he shook my hand instead of bowing his head, as he usually did.

On the drive back to my grandmother's house, I began to question what I had set in motion, telling myself that I was now in Chandralal's debt. Still I pushed this reasoning away, because a greater conviction was taking hold of me—by going to him I had set myself free. What, exactly, I meant by this I could not say, except it was like the time I had gone to the Canadian High Commission to get that immigration form.

When I got home, my grandmother was having her afternoon nap. The events of the day had exhausted me. I fell asleep after lunch and woke up only when Rosalind nudged my shoulder. The Loku Nona wanted to speak with me. The ayah's lips were thin with worry; she wanted to offer advice but was holding back. I went to quickly wash my face and comb my hair.

When I entered my grandmother's bedroom, I found Chandralal standing by the window, legs apart, hands behind his back, face lit with satisfaction, as if he had brought us a gift. My grandmother was beaming too. "Look at him, Chandralal, truly a man, truly a man."

"What pride you must have in him, madam!"

I blushed, not out of delight but unease, pressing back against the doorpost.

"Puthey, I am very proud of you." My grandmother held out her hand. I went and took it. "Now, I hope you aren't questioning if you did the right thing." She pulled me down next to her. "I wanted to give that pariah dog one more chance and was hoping he might respond better to someone gentle and diplomatic like you. But it was a waste of time. Being kind to that man is like pouring honey into a pot that contains feces."

"I also hope you are not regretting your decision to see me, baba," Chandralal added. "You did the only thing you could have. This is not Canada. Over there, people are civilized and understand the meaning of paying their debt and observing the law. Unfortunately, the majority of our people are just animals. In Sri Lanka, it's always like two dogs fighting in the street. One must triumph. So better you than the other person, I always say."

"That is what I say too, Chandralal!" my grandmother exclaimed. "It is a lesson I have been trying to teach this boy, who unfortunately has a gentle spirit. But I see I underestimated him. He is really my grandson." She squeezed my arm and I felt throttled by her gesture.

Chandralal wanted me to look at the Pettah property. We drove through Colombo at a terrific speed, the driver blaring his horn to clear the road, forcing cars to the side. Chandralal kept up a steady patter about how Sri Lanka was going to be the next Singapore; how the government was opening up even more garment factories and free trade zones, building even more new roads; how the famous village reawakening scheme was going to bring prosperity to the outlying districts of Sri Lanka. I nodded and feigned interest, but all the time I felt giddy. Occasionally I added a comment to his monologue, and each time I did he pronounced some compliment, like, "I would never have guessed you were so astute, baba! But it doesn't surprise me. You are, after all, madam's grandson."

When we got to the property, one of Chandralal's golayas was standing guard by the broken door. Chandralal led me through the rooms, with which he seemed very familiar, pointing out what damage had been done and waiting patiently while I wrote it all down in an exercise book so I could tell my grandmother later. The inside of the house had deteriorated just as badly as the outside. Plaster had come down in places, exposing the red brick beneath, leaks from the roof had left a web of marks on one wall like inflamed varicose veins. Taps in the kitchen and bathroom were rusty and dripping, streaks of green fungus on the shower walls below the leaks. The tiny backyard was jammed with the detritus of previous tenants.

All the furniture in the house had been removed and stacked on the verandah, to be sold in the next few days, as it was when Siriyawathy was evicted. Still, there were remnants of the man's life in the empty rooms—a spilled canister of rose talcum powder, a bottle of women's Kohinoor shampoo, a broken toy cricket bat, scattered crayons and a pink hair ribbon. The man had a wife and children. "He gave me no choice," I said to myself, lips set grimly. "What choice did I have?" If he had offered to pay one month's rent, even half a month's rent, if he had not insulted me, none of this would have happened.

When we finally left, Chandralal eyed the broken door. "What shall we do here, baba?"

"Let's get a new door, Chandralal. I am sick of this old one. Also, we must get this place fixed up. Then we can attract a better type of tenant."

"Very good, baba." He smacked his hands together in admiration, giving me a keen look. I was taking a decision without consulting my grandmother. "This very evening, I will send a baas to look around and give you an estimate." He patted me on the back and beamed. "See now, baba, you know what you are doing. Your aachi has taught you well. You mustn't let a few pariah dogs put you off."

"Thank you, Chandralal. You have been a great support to me."

"Your grandmother believed in me when no one else did, baba. I have come to my current good fortune because of her. I will never forget that. She treated me like a proper human being."

He was silent for a moment, glancing ruefully around the neighbourhood. "You know, baba, my father was a mere gardener in a Cinnamon Gardens house. He was there through two generations, and all the family, even the young children, referred to him as '*oomba*.'" He raised his eyebrows, and I nodded to say I understood the casual insult of that feudal term. "They didn't mean anything bad, baba, it was just the way they spoke. That's how we were to them. Little better than animals." He jutted out his jaw, lost in contemplation. "They used to call me 'moon-face.'" I frowned, not sure I had heard the English words correctly. "Yes, baba, 'moon-face.' Of course I didn't speak English at the time and it took me a while to realize they were talking about my pockmarked skin." He smiled wryly. "After that, I swore my children would never witness their father being humiliated. And no Cinnamon Gardens person would ever humiliate my girls."

When we were back in his Pajero, he turned to me with a shy smile. "Baba, my wife is very keen to meet you, and my daughters, too. I have told them you live in Canada. Will you come and have tea with us now?"

"Yes," I said, surprised at this invitation. "I would be happy to meet them."

At his home, Chandralal ushered me to the velvet sofa. Soon his wife appeared wearing a freshly laundered light-blue cotton Kandyan sari, bringing with her a gust of lavender perfume. She was a plump, pretty woman with a milk-tea complexion, her well-oiled jet-black hair coiled in a bun at the nape of her neck. She greeted me in the traditional way, palms pressed together, her smile shy and jolly.

Looking at me with a smile, she began to question Chandralal about my life in Sinhala.

"Why are you asking me, woman?" he exclaimed jovially. "Ask the young sir, he speaks Sinhala just like us."

"Aah." She put out her tongue in embarrassment, then gave me an apologetic smile. She asked what I had studied in university. When I told her English literature, she drew in her breath. Such fluency in English raised me greatly in her estimation. I liked her. She was not at all the strident, over-dressed, over-made-up wife I had expected; not one of those women strained from the anxiety of social climbing.

Chandralal asked where their daughters were, and his wife called in the direction of a curtained doorway, "Come, come!"

The girls emerged promptly with trays, one carrying cakes, patties and rolls from Green Cabin, the other bringing cups of tea. They had their mother's complexion and plump prettiness, and wore jeans, T-shirts and sandals, just like women from our social class. Their hair was short, cut in the latest style.

They placed the trays on the coffee table and sat on a settee next to mine. After an awkward pause, Chandralal gestured to them and said teasingly, "Now talk, will you. I'm not paying all these high fees at the Colombo International School so you can sit here like billas."

The girls asked me in fluent English about Canada. Soon we were chatting in a fairly easy way about North American life. They would both be going to America for university, once they finished their A-levels, and wanted to know what universities I might suggest and what life they could expect there. Chandralal and his wife looked on with pleasure. After a while, his wife brought me a trophy the older daughter had won in tennis and a certificate the younger had got in piano. There was a shy hopefulness in her smile as she presented them to me, and I took in, as if seeing them for the first time, the trays the girls had carried out, having waited for their cue to appear. All these arrangements for tea had been made even before I was asked, so sure was Chandralal that I would accept his invitation. Then the parents had sat so that the only place for their daughters was next to me. I pretended to admire the trophy and certificate, but I wanted desperately to leave.

When I got home, my grandmother was seated on the verandah, and she called out with a teasing smile, "Was the tea pleasant?"

I frowned at her suspiciously as I came up the steps. "How did you know?"

"Chandralal asked my permission before you left."

"I see." There was a pitcher of water and glasses on the verandah table and I poured myself some.

"And the daughters? Were you surprised they were just like our Cinnamon Gardens girls with their tennis and piano?" My grandmother threw back her head and laughed. "Yes-yes, how all those British things go on. But that is how people like Chandralal rise up, nah, Puthey, teaching their children tennis, piano, elocution. And fortuitous marriages into good but impoverished families."

I gave her a narrowed look and she chuckled. "Don't worry, I'm not marrying you off to one of *his* daughters. We certainly don't need their money."

Yet I felt a strategic marriage was precisely what Chandralal had in mind.

"Puthey." My grandmother patted the low stool next to her chair. I sat down by her feet. "As you know, I am on the board of trustees at our local temple. I have been thinking for some time I would like to build a new bana maduwa. Our one is so old, and the roof is leaking. Other Colombo temples have such lovely bana maduwas. I want to build one in the old Kandyan style with a pagoda roof and carved wooden pillars. But this requires time and money. While I have money, my time is running out. I must collect as much merit as possible to ensure a better future life." She played with her glasses for a moment. "I was wondering if you could look after my properties. This is good training, nah? After all, they will be yours sooner than you expect, and I want you to be ready for them."

I had anticipated this, and had already assumed some of the responsibility by telling Chandralal we must get the Pettah property fixed up.

"Aacho, I will do it, but on my terms." I stood up. "If I am going to run your properties, I want to run them the way I wish."

She waited for me to continue.

I leant on the balustrade, looking down at her. "To start with, that Pettah property must be repaired."

"What for?" she cried. "I am going to run it into the ground and then sell off the land."

"No, Aacho, I don't want that. In fact, Chandralal is going to send a baas to give me an estimate. That verandah is dangerous. Someone could seriously hurt themselves."

Her lips thinned, but I pushed on. "Even if I have to rent that property a little cheaper, I want the right kind of tenant."

"Cheaper? Why should you rent it cheaper? After fixing it up, you should charge more."

"And I will. All I'm saying is, I would prefer to go cheaper and get someone who will actually pay the rent rather than have another tenant like that man."

She shrugged, not pleased at all.

"Aacho?"

"Yes-yes, very well." She sighed. "You are in charge now. I am just a feeble old woman."

I felt a thrill at her submission. But riding tight behind my jubilation was unease.

I called Mili and suggested a sunset swim at Mount Lavinia. When he came to pick me up, I couldn't meet his eyes. As I got on the motorcycle, I made a joke about my tight jeans ripping and my voice cracked.

The beach was crowded with strolling families. Lovers sat on rocks behind umbrellas, vendors walked up and down carrying basins of pineapple slices, mango achcharu and gal siyambala in newspaper cones. A group of Muslim women shrieked and darted back and forth at the water's edge like terns, colourful saris raised around their shins, palus slipping off heads.

My grandmother had also agreed to give me access to her accounts, and feeling well-heeled I insisted on paying for our loungers, then ordered beers and some snacks, tipping the cabana boy generously. "Gosh," Mili said, "did you win the lottery or rob a bank?"

I smiled as I put away my wallet, still not able to tell him what had happened with the tenant, or that I was taking over my grandmother's properties.

We left our clothes with the cabana owner and ran down to the water. Once I was in deep enough, I dove under with a shout and felt the events of the day wash off me.

Later, when we were sipping beer, I said, "Mili, why don't you ask Sriyani about the beach house."

"Yes, a very good idea."

We grinned at each other over the rims of our glasses. I was craving the freedom to hold him and talk, lying face to face, our naked limbs tangled; longing to sleep curled up against his back.

17

I MET WITH A BAAS ABOUT THE PETTAH PROPERTY a few days later and got an estimate from him. When I showed the quote to Chandralal, he shook his head, amused. "These baases are ungrateful dogs. Here I am, giving this rabid monkey work, but he cannot return that favour with honesty. I will have a little talk with that buffalo."

"No, Chandralal, I will speak with him."

He gave me an appraising look. "Very well, baba." Then he showed me where I was being overcharged and told me what the prices ought to be. He also prepared me for the justifications the baas would give, and how to counter them.

I asked the baas to meet me at the Pettah property, then purposely arrived half an hour late. When my car pulled up, he rose from the verandah steps, dusting his sarong and smiling. I did not return his smile but pretended to busy myself with something in the car before I got out.

"I thought I'd left your estimate at home," I said as I came up to him, "but I did bring it. Come," I beckoned him to follow.

I led the baas into the house and stopped at the first item on the list of repairs, a room whose walls needed replastering once the brick had been repointed. We had talked about this repair the day before, but I got him to explain again what he planned to do. Then, my lower lip stuck out, legs apart, non-existent belly pushed forward, I declared, "Yes, but this price is not correct. It doesn't even make sense."

"I would not offer such a low price to anyone else, mahattaya," he cried. "This is a favour to Chandralal."

"Chandralal might not see it as a favour," I snorted.

I suggested, as I had seen my grandmother do, an absurdly low price. He countered with another price, and we bargained until settling on an agreeable cost. I was nervous he would see through my facade of shrewd bargainer, but he seemed fooled by it. As we made our way through the house, I grew into my new persona.

In the end, I did not get everything I wanted, or even the price my grandmother or Chandralal might have got. But I did bring down the cost considerably, and this left me feeling triumphant.

When we sat down for lunch that day, I told my grandmother I had received an estimate for repairs on the Pettah property, met with the baas that morning and got him to lower his price.

"But I should have come with you," she cried.

"No need for that, Aacho. Chandralal looked over the estimate and gave me advice."

"It is my property. You shouldn't have done that."

"The bana maduwa is already too much work for you, Aacho. I don't want you overdoing it."

She glared at me, but when I held her gaze, eyebrows raised, she turned away and washed her hands in the bowl Rosalind was offering. "I hope you know what you are doing."

"You have trained me well, Aacho," I said teasingly. "All those years of taking me to properties. You knew what you were doing then, nah?"

She smiled despite herself. "Yes, they were nice times. It was a good thing I did teach you. Still, Puthey, I want to see the estimate after lunch."

I made a noncommittal sound.

She did not ask again for the estimate, probably distracted by the preparations to construct the bana maduwa, which were more exhausting than she had anticipated. I was concerned by the oily glaze of sweat on her face when she came home from attending to this matter. Yet her fatigue also gave me a jubilant sense of my own health and strength as a young man.

I had experienced the worst with that man at the Pettah property. Many of the other tenants complained and had little goodwill towards me, the grandson of a landlady they despised, but no one was aggressive. I began to take happy satisfaction in having a tap or roof repaired without being cheated by a baas, feel a sense of ownership as I supervised the replacement of a gutter or the re-cementing of steps or a verandah floor. I had the charm and diplomacy my grandmother lacked. Tenants were soon pleased that I arrived promptly to fix a problem, asking for me now when they called our house, plying me with tea when I collected the rent.

I visited Sunil Maama frequently at his office. Sitting beside him as we went through a complicated legal document, I felt gratified I understood its meaning and was able to ask relevant questions and make suggestions. Sunil Maama complimented me lavishly, no doubt relieved to not be dealing with my grandmother. Running her business began to give me a feeling of manhood, which I realized I had been denied in Canada because of my race.

My life intersected frequently with Chandralal's because of construction on the Wellawatte property. The building was to be a three-storey low rise, each floor having four apartments. We met often at the site to see how things were progressing, to deal with disputes and absences among the workmen. In all this, Chandralal took the lead. He put his hand on my shoulder in a fatherly manner as he explained an aspect of building or pointed out a mistake in construction. When he saw I was quick to learn, that I could spot a problem or query a decision that seemed wrong, he was delighted. We had to be vigilant. Contractors were constantly trying to cheat us and had many ingenious scams we had to watch out for. One of them was trying to pass off sea sand in place of river sand for mixing concrete. The former, which was easier to get and cheaper, would cause walls and floors to sweat and rapidly deteriorate because of the salt it contained. Chandralal and I would check every consignment. The best cement and metal bars came from the government corporations and bore the stamp of "Sanstha." We would frequently examine the shipments for the stamp. Another swindle was using unseasoned, unsmoked wood which would be attacked by termites in the years to come. Getting smoked wood was so important that Chandralal appointed his most trusted golaya to take the unseasoned wood to Jafferjees, have all the wood smoked and see it safely delivered back to our construction site. But, by far the greatest scam was ordering too many bags of cement and selling off the excess. In order to prevent this financial loss, Chandralal had all the bags numbered and then would insist he or one of his golayas see all the used bags.

The construction progressed at a surprisingly fast rate thanks to Chandralal's influence. Permits and inspections were passed quickly, water, electricity and sewage connected in record time through contacts in various city departments. The chief baases were afraid of him and kept their workers busy and disciplined.

I felt an increasing gratitude towards Chandralal. He had come to my rescue with the man at the Pettah property and done so diplomatically, not tarnishing my masculinity. We both knew that without him I could never get these flats built. I would be cheated by the baases and blocked at the government offices, not knowing who to bribe. He never even hinted at how unequal my contribution was.

Occasionally he brought one of his daughters. Under Chandralal's smiling eyes, I would, out of nervousness and some helpless desire to please him, become charming and attentive, asking them about their lives, offering advice on living in the West and even making them laugh with some droll sarcastic comment. Then later, on my way home, I would berate myself for being such a fool and vow to be more reserved next time. Yet having become friendly, I could not retreat without giving offence, and was forced to be equally friendly and charming the next time we met.

Within a month of taking over my grandmother's duties, I became aware, while looking at legal paperwork for the enterprise, that Chandralal was co-owner of the flats. When I saw this, I realized I had not asked myself what his stake was in the development, having vaguely assumed my grandmother was paying him a fee and he was being extra helpful out of fondness for her. Sunil Maama, who had shown me the papers, saw my consternation and a secretive, distressed look crossed his face.

I queried my grandmother about the co-ownership when were sitting on the verandah that evening.

"Ah, Puthey, why are you surprised?" she asked mildly. "Did you honestly think an old woman like me could undertake such an arduous concern?"

I took a sip of my beer, not knowing what to say.

"I consider myself lucky to have a partner like Chandralal. Do you know how dishonest the average person is here? Chandralal will not cheat me, even though it would be easy for him to do so."

She was waiting for my agreement, and I nodded. This man, who was a thug and perhaps even a criminal, had a genuine love for my grandmother, and his loyalty now extended to me, her grandson. Men like Chandralal needed sentimental outlets to lavish kindness on. By doing so, they believed themselves to be good.

I had to visit the flats the next morning. Chandralal was there, and though he greeted me civilly, he looked grim with fury. The risers on the staircase to the first floor were not uniform and it was too late to fix this error, as the concrete had already been poured into the wooden formwork. Some of the steps would always be slightly higher than the others. The carpenter who made the formwork was summoned and he stood in front of us, hands pressed together before him as if handcuffed while Chandralal yelled at him, his eyes bulging with anger, double chin bloated like a toad's. Watching his rage and the baas's terror, a memory bloomed.

Sunil Maama was not expecting me. When I walked in he saw the disquiet on my face and stood up alarmed.

"Come, come, putha, sit." He gestured to a chair.

I shook my head and went to stand at the window, where I stared out onto an alley. "Sunil Maama, how is it that the house in Wellawatte was the only one left standing on the street? It was Tamil owned, after all."

Sunil Maama sat down slowly in his chair. "I don't know, putha."

"You do, and so do I. Really, I've known all along, if I think about it. I've just not admitted it to myself." I turned to him. "Chandralal and Aachi made a deal with that family, didn't they? Protection from the mob for a cheap price on the house. When he came by our house that first morning of the riots, it's what they were discussing on the verandah. Keeping an eye out for a Tamil family who needed protection."

Sunil Maama fiddled with the lid of his fountain pen.

"I wonder how many other Tamils Chandralal made that bargain with."

Sunil Maama licked his lips. "Shivan, putha, you must not judge your grandmother too harshly."

"But it's a terrible thing, a terrible thing."

He took out a handkerchief and mopped his brow. "Don't, Shivan. Just leave it alone. It's too late to do anything now." He frowned at me, pleading. "If she finds out I told you . . . Your aachi is my biggest client, one of the few who has stuck with me. I'm not very good anymore at this law work. The rules, the country, have changed too much. It's no longer really a gentleman's profession."

As I walked towards the door, he called after me, "And he, that man, you must not cross him."

All the way home, I stared out numbly at the passing world. I simply did not know what I was going to do next. When the car stopped in the carport, I sat lost in thought, then went up the steps and into the saleya, my footsteps clacking heavily against the cement floor. I could hear my grandmother hobbling about her room, the tip-tap of her stick. I started towards my bedroom, then went to hers instead.

She was standing before her bed, contemplating a document laid out on it. "Ah, Puthey, come and see the plans for my bana maduwa. It's going to be magnificent." I went to stand by her and she squeezed my arm with excitement and affection.

"It's wonderful, Aacho," I said after a moment.

There was nothing I could do. By bringing up the Wellawatte property with her, what would I gain? And the moment I asked myself that question, I saw all that would be lost by doing so.

The next time I met Chandralal was at the Wellawatte property a few weeks later. He was waiting by his Pajero, and as I got out of my car he came forward grinning. "Baba, we have the shuttering to the first floor in place!" He slapped my shoulder. "Come, come, you must see the view." He ushered me towards the entrance as if I were an important guest, unaware of the dark mood that had come over me on the way here, a mood grown blacker at the sight of him, his hand on my shoulder a dead weight.

When we were on the wooden platform over which the concrete of the first floor would be poured, I was astonished at the vista before me. We were already higher than the surrounding houses and had an uninterrupted view of the sea, ships passing on the horizon. It was cooler up here, a breeze coming up from the water with a tang of salt, the tops of coconut trees fanning gently in the wind.

"Baba, I have been thinking about something." He came to stand by me. "Perhaps we should turn the third floor into one big flat. You know, 'penthouse suite,' as they call it in English. After all," he looked at me with a little smile, "you will not live with your grandmother always, nah? One day you will want to get married and start your own family. It is becoming fashionable now to live in flats like this, above the dirt and heat and diesel fumes of Colombo."

"I don't know." I turned away and pretended to stare at the view, bothered by this allusion to marriage. "I'm not sure it's the best idea in terms of profitability."

The architect had come up and Chandralal went to talk with him. I looked at the view again and found myself thinking of Mili and me living even higher up than this, waking together to this view, the privacy of being far above prying eyes.

"What do you think, baba?" Chandralal asked, rubbing his hands with boyish enthusiasm as he came back to me. "Changed your mind? A 'penthouse suite'?"

"Yes," I replied, "why not?"

"We must tell your grandmother." He winked. "She complained to me, the other day. You are not keeping her fully informed."

"No, let it be, Chandralal. She doesn't need to know everything." I had already decided to have Sunil Maama arrange the legal papers to make this suite mine.

He laughed and gently punched my arm.

As we went downstairs, he walked ahead with the architect and I followed. "What has been done cannot be reversed," I said to myself, flicking a hand across my face as if to remove a cobweb.

One of my greatest delights was to buy Mili an occasional shirt or a book I had seen him looking through with longing. When I presented the gift, he would always say, "Come on, Shivan, I'm not some desperately poor bugger."

"Oh, don't be so proud, Mili." I would hug him, or squeeze his knee. "It's only given with love."

He would acknowledge this with a wry smile, then say lightly, "But it's not really your money."

"It might not be mine in name yet, but I bloody well work hard to keep things going."

His smile would grow stubborn. He never wore the shirts I gave him unless I pestered and pouted, and then only if his friends were not around.

When I had told Mili about taking over my grandmother's properties, explaining she was not well and wanted to build a bana maduwa as her last great act of merit, he had accepted my explanation impassively. When I pushed him to acknowledge my sacrifice he'd murmured, "Yes, yes, you are a good grandson, Shivan. She is truly lucky to have you."

With my newfound wealth I liked to treat us to dinner and drinks at the various five-star hotels around Colombo. It was always a struggle to get Mili to come, and sometimes I had to settle for the places he and his friends frequented.

We ran into his father one evening in the lobby of the Galadari Hotel. He was having a drink with his mistress, the former film star. There was a moment of awkward staring, then Mili turned away. In the same instant, Mr. Jayasinghe raised his hand in greeting and beckoned him. Mili sighed. He strolled over, hands in pockets.

I had not met the mistress but had seen all her films. In her forties now, she was still beautiful, turned out in a diaphanous white organza sari with magenta border. Her hip-length plait glistened, studded with araliya flowers.

Mili ignored her even though she gave him a willing smile. He introduced me to his father, saying I was visiting from Canada.

"Ah, how nice to see you, son," his father said enthusiastically, as if we had met before.

"It's very nice to meet you, too, uncle," I said, thrilled to be in the presence of such a powerful man and to be able to call him "uncle," this familiarity reflecting we were social equals. He introduced me to his mistresses and I blushed as I shook her hand. "I am such a fan of yours. I love all your films."

Her laugh was a tinkle. "And which one is your favourite?"

"Oh, that is a hard choice." Ignoring Mili's brooding presence next to me, I recounted the first time I had seen her, when I was eight years old. Rosalind had taken us to the cinema, and I had been enchanted by the singing and dancing, her marvellous saris and bell-bottom pantsuits.

Tudor Jayasinghe tried to appear interested in my story, his smile tight, eyes slipping to Mili. The moment I was done, he asked, "How is your mother?"

Mili glared at him, then looked away.

"And your human rights work?"

He continued to stare across the lobby, face immobile.

Tudor Jayasinghe sighed. "When are you going to give up this nonsense and let me send you abroad to university? Or at least come and work in my firm."

"You know my answer to that," Mili said, and walked away with a quick frown for me to follow.

"It was a pleasure to meet you, uncle."

"You too, son," he said, gazing after Mili as he shook my hand.

His mistress offered her hand, and I held it briefly in both of mine. "My family will be so envious I met you."

"And what will your report be?" she asked, with that imperious coquetry of the star.

"That you are still as beautiful as ever."

She let out a peal of laughter and clasped her hands together. Then she smacked Mr. Jayasinghe on the knee to distract him from his son. "My, Tudor, darling, you must ask this boy to come and have dinner sometime."

He shook my hand again, forgetting he had just done so.

I found Mili slouched in a chair by the pool. A waiter came up, and knowing what Mili liked I ordered two Lion Lagers.

"Is everything alright?" I finally asked.

"Why did you fawn over that bitch?"

"Well, I love her movies. She's one of our greatest stars."

"You should have ignored her."

"But that would have been impolite."

"But that would have been impolite," he echoed with a mocking whine. "You know what your problem is, Shivan? You love all this glamour and sucking up to people who you think are dazzling, but who are really vile. It's disgusting to watch you."

"Mili, you're being ridiculous," I snapped. "Don't take out your anger at your father on me."

After a moment he sighed, reached across the table and pressed my arm. "Sorry, I'm an awful bugger. It's just seeing that bastard with his whore . . ."

As he sipped his beer, I watched him curiously. I had assumed his father would not pay for his studies abroad, and I'd admired Mili's dignity in accepting this misfortune. But his decision was aimed at thwarting Mr. Jayasinghe's ambitions for him, even though it meant giving up his aspiration to study international relations abroad.

I had got to know Mili's mother, Charlotte, well. She was grateful Mili was invited so often to my house and reciprocated by having me to Sunday lunch every week. She was an excellent cook and made the old Burgher foods, like lamprais and bolo fiado, which I praised lavishly. She would often say to her son, "Now, see, Mili, what a polite boy Shivan is," as if he was not. I often came in my grandmother's car and after lunch would take Mrs. Jayasinghe shopping or to visit relatives.

A few days after I had met Tudor Jayasinghe, Mili's mother and I were in the car together when she said, "I understand you bumped into my husband."

I nodded, taken aback Mili had mentioned it, given the mistress was there.

She smiled faintly. "It was my husband who told me. He called this morning." Seeing my surprise, she added, "Tudor and I have been married twenty-six years. We raised Mili together. You can't just erase all that time, no matter how much you might want to. That woman knows it, which is why she persuaded Tudor to put me out on the street. It eats away at her that I won't give him a divorce.

"The thing is, son," she said, changing the subject to relieve me of my discomfort, "you are a good influence on Mili. I have noticed how happy he is since you returned. Tudor also knows the effect you are having on our son. We both feel it's not right for Mili to give up his education because I have been cast off. I've begged Mili to take up his father's offer and go to university, or at minimum work in his firm. Human rights work pays so poorly and is very risky. I worry so much about him, given all the madness that is happening right now, the dangers to anyone who speaks up. I wish you could persuade him to give it up."

I leaned towards her confidentially. "I am very glad you brought this up, aunty. Perhaps I could persuade Mili to come and study in Toronto. After all, since I am there, it might be an incentive."

"Ah, son," she pressed my arm, "if you could only persuade him. My husband and I would be eternally grateful."

I assured her that I would speak to him the next time I had the chance.

Yet before I could follow up on my promise, the world around us suddenly fell apart.

18

THE FOLLOWING WEEK, Mili was supposed to come for dinner one evening but did not show up. I waited on the verandah an hour, then telephoned his home. Mrs. Jayasinghe told me he had been held up at the office, but when I called there the line was constantly busy. I could not keep Rosalind waiting any longer, so I ate with a book propped in front of me. My gaze kept wandering towards the verandah, as if I expected Mili to materialize there.

The phone rang just as I was finishing my meal, and I rushed to get it.

"Shivan," Mili said curtly, "something has happened. I'm not coming tonight."

"What is it?" I heard raised voices in the background. "Where are you?"

"At the office. I have to be careful what I say."

No matter how much I pressed him, he would not tell me any more. The phone, he said, could be tapped.

After he abruptly got off the line, I went to sit on the verandah. Despite what Mili had said, I was still hoping he would come over and tell me what had happened. Finally, Rosalind began to lock up the house, and I went to bed so she could too.

I lay with hands under my neck, staring at the fan's shifting patterns on the ceiling. A few hours later I was woken up by a soft knocking at my window. Mili stood outside, his face obscured by the dark.

I let myself carefully out a side door, then we walked in silence along the driveway and stopped under the canopy of an araliya tree a good distance from the house. His eyes were jaundiced in the moonlight. He put his arms around me, his body shaking as I held him. Finally he pulled away and lit a cigarette with unsteady hands. After he had taken a few puffs, exhaling deeply, he told me what had happened.

That afternoon, Ranjini had gone home for lunch but not returned to the office. Finally Sri got worried and had one of the secretaries at Kantha call Ranjini's house. Her mother answered and said she'd assumed Ranjini had eaten at work or gone out with her colleagues. A quiet dread gripped the office. Sriyani left in her car, taking the route Ranjini usually walked home to see if there'd been an accident along the way. Mili and Sri set out on his motorcycle along an alternate route. Someone called the hospitals to find out if she had been admitted.

Then just before the end of the work day, they received a call from a Catholic priest in Negombo. One of his parishioners, a fisherman, had found Ranjini's body on the beach and brought her purse to him.

I stared at Mili, unable to comprehend his words for a moment. "Are you . . . are they sure it's her?"

He nodded. "The priest found some business cards in her purse and contacted Kantha, suspecting she had been killed because of her work."

After that, the police had moved rapidly. They claimed she was raped and strangled; they knew of her relationship with Sri. He was taken into custody and charged with killing his girlfriend in a fit of jealousy when he found out she was betrothed to her cousin.

"But it doesn't make sense, Mili," I whispered. "Why Ranjini?"

"Isn't it obvious," he said with irritation. "An example had to be made of someone, and she already had a record with the Special Task Force. Her death is another warning to all of us in human rights. To stop sniffing around."

The shadows around us seemed to swell, as if a more potent darkness was pouring into them. Some rodent rustled in the bushes nearby.

"I must go," Mili said.

"Please, you have to give up this work, you have to stop."

He did not appear to hear me. As he started down the driveway I made to go after him. Not glancing back, he signalled me to stay where I was. Mili disappeared into the shadows and then, as if emerging out of water, hauled himself up the moonlit gate and, careful to avoid the spikes, dropped down the other side.

I barely slept that night and was exhausted by the morning. We were at breakfast when my grandmother peered at her newspaper and gave a small surprised sound. "Look at this," she said to Rosalind, who was placing a glass of thambili before her. "See what happens when you disobey your family."

Rosalind glanced at the paper. "What does it say, Loku Nona?"

"Evidently, this girl was promised to her cousin but having an affair with some Tamil man. When the lover found out about the betrothal, he killed and violated her. Can you imagine? What a state of affairs!"

I picked up a piece of toast, then put it down.

"Aiyo, Loku Nona, what is wrong with the young today?"

My grandmother thrust the article at me. "See, Shivan, see what this girl has come to."

Ranjini's bruised and bloated face was like one of those lacquered exorcism masks, eyes bulging, mouth grotesquely misaligned because of a broken jaw, hair a snarl of river snakes.

"Well, she deserved it," my grandmother declared. "This is what happens when you lose your virtue and carry on like a vesi."

The bile rose swiftly in me. I pushed back my chair and ran from the table, hand over mouth. I fell to my knees in the bathroom, lifted up the toilet seat just in time and vomited into the commode.

When my stomach had stopped heaving, I sat back on my haunches, breathing harshly.

"Shivan, Puthey, did you eat something bad?" My grandmother hovered in the doorway, our ayah behind her. "Aiyo, I hope you're not coming down with dysentery. Shall I get Rosalind to mix some lime juice and salt to settle your stomach?"

"Leave me alone," I yelled at her, "just leave me the hell alone." Feeling another wave of nausea rising up, I shoved the door shut in her astounded face and threw up again.

I had to go out that morning to see about our Nugegoda property.

The tenant, Miss Balasuriya, was a retired teacher who had taken the bungalow before the steep rise in inflation, and before Nugegoda became a desirable place to live. Because of rent control, my grandmother could not get market value. Whenever she visited, the two women had a row, my grandmother claiming she was being robbed blind, Miss Balasuriya accusing her landlady of not doing repairs in the hope she would be forced to leave. This, unfortunately, was true. The roof leaked, the floor was pitted and needed a new coat of cement, the toilet was broken and a bucket of water had to be used to flush it. The night before my visit, a beam in the roof that was already cracked had given way. A shower of tiles and dirt had tumbled into the living room, leaving a gaping hole.

All my charm and diplomacy had not softened Miss Balasuriya, a brittle stick of a woman with a lean, sour face and eyes that were permanent slits of dissatisfaction. When I arrived, she rushed out onto the front stoop screaming, "Do you think I am an animal? Is this the Dehiwala zoo? How can a human being live here?"

Usually I would have given her a placating smile and said some soothing words, but today I pushed past and went into the living room. She followed, and as I stood gazing at the broken roof she continued her tirade, calling me a vulture, a hooligan, a slum landlord. Finally I rounded on her and yelled, "Why don't you shut up, you dried old spinster?"

She was shocked, then rallied herself. "Ah-ah, but look at the way you speak to me. I am a teacher, I am respectable. Who are you? The grandson of a woman who is no better than a Mutwal fishwife."

"If you don't like it here, go and find another home."

"That will never happen. You will have to drag me kicking and screaming from this house."

"That can be arranged, you know."

"You wouldn't dare."

"Really? All I have to do is give the word to our man."

"You think this is some banana republic, some Soviet dictatorship? That there is no rule of law in this country?"

"There isn't," I cried, my voice splintering, "there isn't a rule of law." I laughed. "You claim to be an educated woman, but have you no eyes to see what is going on? Do you think you are living in the old Sri Lanka? That country is no more. This is a banana republic, this is a dictatorship!"

She was gaping at me. I turned away embarrassed and walked towards the front door. Miss Balasuriya followed. As I went down the steps she asked in a tired voice, "So, will you have the problem fixed?"

"Yes," I said without looking around. "I'll send a roof-baas this afternoon."

As the car took me home, we passed a school where the kindergarten was getting out. Little children in frilly dresses and brightly coloured shorts, handkerchiefs pinned to shirt and blouse fronts, stood with their parents at the bus stop or crowded around an Alerics ice cream cart. In the playground, their delighted shrieks trailed them like ribbons as they chased each other.

The world out there seemed so untroubled, but how swiftly it had changed for me. And yet, remembering the 1983 riots, I was not surprised. Things *did* change swiftly in this country.

"Mahattaya, are you alright?"

The driver was frowning at me in the rear-view mirror. Without realizing it, I had been thumping my head against the window frame.

I found my grandmother and Rosalind in her bedroom going through saris in the almirah, picking out ones for the temple poor.

"Ah, did everything go well with that Balasuriya woman?" my grandmother asked, not looking at me. She was annoyed at my earlier rudeness.

"A roof beam has broken in the living room. There is a hole."

"Good! Let's see how long she lasts now, that blood-sucking leech."

"Actually, I'm going to ask a baas to fix it."

"Why would you do that? This is a perfect opportunity to get rid of that woman. She can't last there now."

"She's not an animal, you know." My anger was returning. "She has been a loyal tenant all these years and deserves to be treated better. After all, she is a lady, a teacher."

My grandmother pressed her lips together. She was going to say something, but I continued, unable to stop myself. "And that girl who was killed, the one in the newspaper, her name is Ranjini. I knew her. And she's not a vesi," I added, seeing their shocked looks. "She was not killed by her boyfriend. She's a human rights worker who had become a nuisance to the government."

My grandmother took out a sari and passed it to Rosalind, her hands trembling. "She's a friend of yours?"

"Actually, she's a friend of Mili's, a colleague." Now I was wishing I had kept my mouth shut.

"But how can that be? The papers didn't mention anything about human rights. Why would they print a lie?" She held on to the bedpost. "This woman,

Ranjini, you said she was a colleague of the Jayasinghe boy? But what is the son of Tudor Jayasinghe doing at this organization? Isn't he just back from university abroad? Isn't he working for his father?"

I played with the bunch of keys I was carrying. I'd kept Mili's work from her so far, knowing she would disapprove. "He works for the human rights organization run by Sriyani Karunaratne."

"Are you involved with this group?"

"No."

"Good. Please, Puthey," her voice cracked with worry, "don't get involved with those people."

"Those people are my friends," I said quietly. "I liked Ranjini so much, and she liked me too. She used to call me Shivan-malli."

My grandmother gave me a keen look, which I held until she dropped her gaze and returned to sorting saris, her hands still shaking.

"And I am involved, because I care a lot for Mili."

She didn't appear to hear me, frowning as if lost in thought.

Mili did not phone the next day, nor return my call. I decided to give him some time to himself and hoped that he would miss me. A part of me was relieved at this break. I was frightened to face him, already sensing what this murder had done to our happiness.

In the days that followed, the government-controlled newspapers reported on Ranjini's funeral. There was a photograph of her mother, hair let loose to signify her grief, shrieking her anguish to the skies as other weeping women kept her from collapsing. There was also a photograph of the intended bridegroom standing soberly by the grave.

My grandmother was observing me closely, and I avoided being alone with her. Rosalind had stopped putting out an extra place setting at dinner, on her instructions I was sure.

I had nothing to do with my evenings now but sit on the verandah reading a novel. My grandmother gave up going to bed early, so great was her worry. She took to sitting at the other end of the verandah with Rosalind. The ayah massaged her mistress's feet and they talked about temple affairs—the drunkenness of the podi hamuduruwo, the pettiness and in-fighting on the various committees. Often I would find my eyes had drifted to the front gate and I was staring broodingly at it. Then I would catch myself and return to my book, aware the women had fallen silent and were watching me.

The strain of my grandmother's worry finally made her speak to me one afternoon at lunch.

"I know you are fond of that Jayasinghe boy, Puthey," she said, as Rosalind served us, "but it is a good thing he has not been coming by. You have to be careful." She made to put her hand on my arm, then stopped herself when she saw my expression. "These are difficult times for our government, what with those pariah Tamil Tigers in the north, the Indians trying to take over our country and now the JVP gaining support in the south. The government has to take a firm hand, otherwise our country will fall apart. And all these busybodies going around criticizing the government and shaming us in front of Western countries, they're all naive and foolish. Traitors, nah, showing us in a bad light to Europeans and—" She caught herself, and this time she did pat my arm. "I am glad you and that Jayasinghe boy are not friends anymore."

"We are still friends." My voice rang brokenly. "Mili is my best friend, one of the people I love most in the world."

"No, Shivan, no, you must cease contact with him. I insist."

"I'm sorry, but I won't do that. I will not let Mili down when he needs me most."

She leaned back in her chair, gazing at me sideways, head cocked and nostrils flared to some dawning knowledge. Then she got up and left the table, lips set in a thin line.

"Friends are people who stand by each other in hard times, Aacho," I called after her, my pain making me reckless, uncaring of what she felt or surmised. "No, I will not let Mili down in his moment of need."

My declaration made me decide to go and see Mili that evening. We had been apart four days. It was too long.

When I arrived at his home, a Mercedes-Benz was parked outside. Though the windows were tinted, I could see Tudor Jayasinghe's mistress in the back.

Mili's parents were seated on the sofa talking in low voices, and they stood up in surprise when I entered the flat.

"Ah, son, how nice to see you." His father shook my hand.

"Shivan!" Mrs. Jayasinghe came and took me by the elbow. "Aiyo, son, I am so glad you are here. Can you please help us? It's Mili—I'm at my wits' end."

"Talk to him, make him see sense," Tudor Jayasinghe urged.

Mrs. Jayasinghe guided me to a chair by the sofa, then husband and wife sat again, leaning forward.

"He has been in there for the last few days and barely comes out," she continued. "Since yesterday he hasn't had a thing to eat. Aiyo, I don't know what to do. I have knocked and knocked on the door, but he just won't let me in. He won't even answer. Get him to come out, Shivan. He'll listen to you."

"I'll try, aunty," I said in a low voice, "but perhaps it's best if you both left for a few hours."

"Yes, yes, good idea, son." His father stood up.

Mrs. Jayasinghe got her purse and flicked a comb through her hair. She made up a tray for Mili of crackers, cheese and thambili. All this while, her husband waited by the door, and when she was ready she asked caustically, "Why are you still here, Tudor?"

"But don't you want a lift?"

"Get in your car with that woman? You must be mad. I'll take a trishaw to my cousin's." She swept by him and went out.

"Shivan," he whispered before he left, "Mili must give up this work. I could not bear to lose him. He needs to get out of the country. Charlotte was telling me about your idea of university in Toronto. I would happily pay all his expenses. Please convince him to apply."

In the disarray of these last few days I had forgotten the idea. But the thought of Mili safe in Toronto softened a brittle tightness in my ribs I had not even been aware of.

Once they had left, I called out, "They're gone."

I heard the bed creak, the shuffle of his slippers. Mili unlocked his door and pushed aside the curtain in the doorway. He was wearing a crumpled sarong and singlet. His beard had grown out in irregular tufts.

"Ah, Mili." I took him in my arms. His hair smelt of slightly rancid Brylcreem. He waited motionless until I let him go, then sat at the table and began to eat and drink what his mother had put out, chewing in that deliberate, slightly disgusted way of an invalid. I sat across from him, worried at how he had changed, at his indifference to me, yet also aware, after this short absence, of that settled feeling I always had in his presence.

"They wouldn't let us go to her funeral, Shivan, can you believe it? Ranjini's parents forbade us because we abetted her affair with Sri." He dragged the back of his hand along his beard in a curve from one sideburn to the other, something so poignant and vulnerable and childlike in this gesture. "And what did my mater and pater ask you to tell me, ah?

"Come on, Shivan," he pressed, when I tried to look innocent, "I could hear you all koosoo-koosoo-fying."

"They want you to give up this human rights work and go to university."

He gave a small "hah," then lit a cigarette. He looked at me under lowered eyelids. "And you agree with them?"

"Mili, for God's sake, don't put it like that." My fear made me exasperated. "Your parents and I, we love you, we're frightened. We don't want you to end up dead on a beach like Ranjini. I couldn't bear it," I added beseechingly, but he seemed unmoved by my personal appeal.

"To give up now would be exactly what this government wants. I won't be a coward."

"It's not a question of bloody cowardliness. It's about prudence. I have talked to your parents about university in Canada. Your father is willing to pay for the whole thing. Think about it, we could live together and be happy. The University of Toronto has an excellent international development program. With that degree, you could come back and work for the UN or even open your own NGO." I sensed him weakening and pressed forward. "Mili, this rebellion against your father has to stop. Even your mother is against your—"

He was staring at me in shock. "I didn't know you saw my work as merely rebellion."

"But you're not being sensible, you're not. I'm just frightened for you and—"

"Don't think I haven't noticed how you've changed since taking up your grandmother's work, strutting around like a big mahattaya. The Cinnamon Gardens tone you use with waiters, even your driver, it's disgusting. The way you flash your money around, paying for things, buttering up my mother with your car."

Now it was my turn to stare at him in shock.

"And I suppose you want me to be like you. Work at my pater's firm, help exploit those women in his garment factories. You're so impressed by my pater's good-old-chap manners, calling you son and everything. But does he give a damn about those poor women? That stingy bastard makes so much money off them and he can't buy a fucking bus to transport them to their boarding houses after a late shift. So they have to walk in the dark and be harassed by men. But I suppose you think that's alright, don't you, Shivan? What about your grandmother's business? Don't tell me it's all clean and above board. You can't get rich by being honest and ethical." He was shouting now.

I stood up, my chair grating back across the floor. "I'm not going to listen to you when you're being irrational and cruel."

"Then get out. Go, because you can't bear to face the truth."

"I've done nothing wrong. Nothing! You're such a self-involved arsehole. Hasn't it struck you that I, too, might be mourning Ranjini?"

"Go fuck yourself."

He went into his room and slammed the door. I was stunned. I had been certain he would ultimately capitulate, as he always did with me. I waited, hoping he would come out. But he didn't, and finally I left.

I did not hear from Mili for the next few days and I could not bring myself to call him or go to his place. I was frightened by his contempt for me.

My grandmother continued to watch me suspiciously, but I was too involved in my own predicament to pay her much attention. I stayed away from the house as much as possible, not having the energy for a confrontation—as there certainly would be—if she tried again to make me break with Mili.

A few days later, Sriyani hosted a small gathering for her workers to celebrate Ranjini's life and offer some consolation for being barred from the funeral. Her assistant called and invited me, too. The thought of meeting Mili was frightening, yet I could not miss the opportunity to see if he had relented at all. As the driver took me to Cinnamon Gardens, the nervousness I had suppressed all day flooded in, giving me a sudden headache.

Sriyani was at her usual place on the verandah greeting guests. Her husband was not present, probably away on business. When I got to her, she said, "Ah, Shivan, welcome," then turned quickly to greet someone else. I did not know if she was just upset or distracted, but there seemed a new reserve in her manner.

Mili was seated in the sunken mada midula with the other workers from Kantha. He glanced in my direction as I walked towards them, then continued chatting with a fellow guest. The others called out greetings when I reached the steps.

Mili spun around to face me. "Ah, machan! Here you are!"

The hearty "machan" put an immediate barrier between us. He tried to rise, but stumbled and fell against the pillows. The others laughed.

"What, Mili, drunk already?" Dharshini said, giving him a playful rap on the head.

He grinned sloppily.

I walked down the steps with a tight smile and then stood, not knowing where to sit. Mili gestured in a loose way to a gap between him and another worker on the floor. "Come, come, machan."

There wasn't much space and we were pressed close, the wet heat of his body against mine, his musky smell of baby powder and sweat strong. I felt a great longing push up in me, which turned to misery at the alienation between us.

"We haven't seen you in a while," said Avanthi, the student from America. The others nodded in agreement.

I gave them a diffident smile. "I've been a bit busy with my grandmother, helping her out."

"You're really great, machan," Mili cried. "I mean, you're so good to your grandmother."

I held his gaze to see if he was being conciliatory, but he smiled back in a hard, bright way.

The others resumed their conversation about the cricket matches to be played in Colombo between India, Pakistan and Sri Lanka. There was some change in their faces I could not name, except to say it was like a shifting of bones, a new spareness. The only one who seemed untouched by the tragedy was Sriyani, who came to join her guests and sat in a planter's chair with that serene, distant smile.

I soon realized that with the exception of Sriyani they were all quite drunk. When they picked up glasses, alcohol sloshed on the floor. Their laughter was slightly hysterical, bodies leaning into each other for support; cashews and peanuts missed mouths and fell unnoticed in laps. The discussion about cricket was becoming heated, workers sparring over whether Sri Lanka's captain was the man to lead the team, or if that position should go to their star bowler.

My misery was suddenly unbearable. I excused myself and went upstairs to use the toilet. When I came out, Mili was leaning against the wall, gazing at his feet. A sconce cast a glow on his shoulders, hands and silky hair, as if he were lit from within. He started to cry, his shoulders convulsing. I went to touch him, but he moved away with a hiss, as if my hand would burn.

After a while, he shrugged and gave a bitter smile. "The whole world has gone mad. There is nothing to believe in anymore."

"There is us."

He grimaced wryly and walked past me. Yet when he got to the stairs, he glanced back at me with a timid look, which gave me the courage to go, the next evening, to his home.

Charlotte Jayasinghe welcomed me. Mili would soon be back, she said. She seemed calm in some new way, her face scrubbed of makeup, hair pulled back tight in a rubber band. Once she had got me a glass of lime cordial, she said, "Mili and I had a long talk this morning about his job at Kantha. He really believes in this work, you know, he really loves our country and wants the best for it. I am frightened for my son, but also very proud of him. I won't stand in his way."

We heard Mili's motorcycle at the gate. Mrs. Jayasinghe shrugged and smiled to convey she had said all she wanted to.

When Mili came in and saw me, he stood tapping his helmet against his thigh, then said with a dry smile, "Ah, Shivan." He came and sat across from me, "So-so, what is new?" He was reserved, but there was again that timid look in his eyes.

"Mili," I said, longing to have him just to myself, "would you like to go out for dinner? I have this urge for thosai."

"Very good, now you accept, Mili." Mrs. Jayasinghe pulled his ear tenderly. "Mustn't take yourself so seriously, nah?"

He grinned boyishly at her, extending his warmth to me, then went to get the spare helmet.

She mouthed "thank you," and added softly, "He needs some cheering up, he really does."

"Ah-ah," Mili called out playfully, "what is this koosoo-koosoo-fying again?"

The restaurant, Shanthi Vihar, was a plain dining hall painted pink, with old wooden tables and metal chairs. It served Tamil vegetarian food and was famous for its thosais, idli and vadais. We went to an air-conditioned inner room with booths, where one paid more for the food. Once we had ordered, Mili pressed his knees against mine under the table. "I have been thinking about you all day and was actually going to call and visit this evening. You are right, Shivan. There is us. And what we have will bring me back to happiness."

"So everything is okay? You have forgiven me?"

"There is nothing to forgive. You were only thinking of me. I didn't mean any of those things I said, about you changing and all that."

"But I have, Mili, I have changed. You were right to point it out."

"Ah, no, Shivan, don't take that seriously."

I wanted this to be a new start for us, without any secrets, so I told him about the Tamil house in Wellawatte and how I'd had that man and his family evicted from the Pettah property. As I spoke, his frown deepened.

"So now do you despise me?" I asked, wretched at the image of myself before me.

"No." But seeing I was still worried, he squeezed my knee under the table. "It's not that." After a moment he asked, "And what is the name of her thug again?"

"Chandralal. Mili?"

"It's nothing."

"Please, you have to tell me."

Our food had arrived and we waited until the server left.

Mili broke off a piece of thosai and dipped it in the sambar. "He is known as the Kotahena mudalali. Very close to the government. If the prime minister requires a crowd at one of his political gatherings, this mudalali provides it."

"What else?"

"You mean human rights? We have not been able to pin anything on him yet. Shivan," he nudged my elbow, seeing I was unnerved, "this is not your problem. And, really, look at my pater. You think he doesn't line the pockets of our politicians? You think he doesn't have thugs who keep the unions away and prevent anyone from politicizing his workers? I know he does, because the people at Kantha have had problems when trying to talk with the workers."

He tapped my plate. I had not touched the thosai. "But the thing is, he is my pater and he does love me a lot. My mater has been trying to make me understand this for a long time, and I think I'm finally ready to accept him. I don't want his money or his job, but I won't hate him anymore. And you, too, you must not hate your grandmother. Eat!" he commanded.

Later, when we had finished and were waiting for the dishes to be cleared, Mili said, "There is something I should have told you a long time ago. I used to be involved with a German man named Otto, who worked for the Goethe Institute here. Our relationship ended a year ago, when he was transferred to another country."

I nodded, then reminded him that I had seen this Otto, a young man with pale skin and hair, when the Kantha workers had picked up Renu for her goodbye party. Mili had been in his car.

He reached over and pressed my hand briefly. "I don't want things to ever be bad again between us. After all that has happened, I could not bear for us to be parted."

A few days later, Sriyani called to say she wanted to have a "little chat." I was to meet her for cocktails at the Galle Face Hotel that evening.

She was seated on the terrace that gave out onto the beach and rose to greet me, pleasant and calm. After we ordered shandies, she told me in a bemused tone that Sri was now being held under the Prevention of Terrorism Act. He was Tamil, so that was enough for them to suspect him of being a terrorist. The lawyer she had hired did not know what to do next. I tried to seem interested, but grew increasingly nervous as I waited for her to broach the real subject of our "chat."

Finally the drinks arrived. Once the waiter had left, Sriyani spoke. "I have known about you and Mili for a little while now, Shivan." She shrugged to say it wasn't so difficult to figure out, then helped herself to some chili cashews. "I am most concerned, to be honest, for Mili. When push comes to shove, you can get on a plane and go back to Canada, or seek the protection of your embassy. Mili doesn't have those safeguards. And so you must think carefully about what you are doing." She dusted the salt and chili powder off her hands. "You know there is still a law here, nah? Ten years in jail, not just for getting caught in the act, but for actually being so inclined."

I took a gulp of my shandy.

"Of course, we are not some fundamentalist Muslim country. You know our people. Live and let live, most of the time. But the law is still there, and these laws are kept on the statute books because they are very helpful to governments. They can be used most effectively to shut someone up who is being a nuisance. To put them away for a while, or at least give them a jolly good scare." She peered at me as if my face were in shadows. "And Mili, along with everyone in my office, everyone in human rights really, has become a bloody nuisance to the government. This regime has plans afoot to deal with the JVP situation in a brutal way, which means they don't want us sniffing around making a fuss about murders and disappearances. Poor old Sri Lanka is heading still further into the Kali Yuga."

"But Sriyani," I said, desperate to neutralize her concern, "how would anyone figure out Mili is, you know, gay? We have been discreet," I continued, clinging to this argument. "Why, his friends think I am just his chum visiting from abroad, nothing else."

She smiled and held out her hands, examining her nails. "The son of Tudor Jayasinghe befriends a German man, a teacher at the Goethe Institute. They are seen shopping at the market, driving around in his car, going on holidays." She nodded, seeing my dismay. "Of course his friends at Kantha know. But they don't acknowledge it, which is what Sri Lankans do. And Mili can't accept that anyone knows, because, really, the shame and embarrassment of it would be too much for him. He has to be blind out of necessity. In fact," she added, "I am sure the whole of Cinnamon Gardens knows he is so inclined. With the exception of his parents, who also have to be blind to it. And it is Cinnamon Gardens that runs this country.

"The thing is, Shivan, I can't talk to Mili about this. You must make the right choice."

I frowned. Then her meaning came to me. "You want me to give Mili up?"

She leaned forward, chin cupped in hand, and gazed hard at the sea as if she had seen something out there. Then she sat back in her chair. "I cannot make that decision. You must do the right thing."

"Yes, but really you're saying I must give him up."

"I'm not saying anything of—"

"Then why would you tell me all this? What if I can't give him up, Sriyani? What if I love him? But I suppose, since we are two men, such love could not have much depth."

Sriyani flinched.

"Did you tell Ranjini and Sri to give each other up?"

"That was different."

"I know exactly what the difference was."

She took a long sip of her shandy, then looked out at the sea again with that little smile on her face. "And yes," she said, changing the subject, "this tapping of my phone is bloody annoying. So clumsily done, really. I can actually hear the clicking when I make or receive a call." She raised her eyebrows at me. "But I think I'm meant to hear it, don't you?"

I looked away at the kites wheeling and dipping above Galle Face Green. "I will not give him up. I could not bear it, I simply could not."

"No," she cocked her head, "I don't suppose you could." She touched my arm. "Just be careful, Shivan, please."

I nodded, even as I felt that all the happiness in my life was bleeding away.

19

I WAITED UNTIL I GOT HOME FROM MY ERRANDS the next afternoon to talk with my grandmother. I found her at one of the almirahs in her bedroom, looking through a drawer. "Ah, Puthey." Seeing my determined expression, she became still.

"Aacho, I know you and Chandralal got that Tamil family's house by offering them protection."

Her cane, which was against the almirah, clattered to the ground. I picked it up and handed it to her. She hobbled over to the dressing table stool, sat down slowly, then looked at me in the mirror. "Sunil told you."

"No. Let's just say I found out."

"That Jayasinghe boy has been filling your mind with poison against me, hasn't he? No doubt against Chandralal, too, because of his reputation." She was scrutinizing me in the mirror, taking in the unyielding look on my face. She was frightened, and her fear gave me further courage.

"Mili is a good person. Much better than either of us. Despite all the avenues open to him, he has chosen to do the work he does. Out of love for this country."

My grandmother picked up a tin of talcum powder, then put it down. "Do you know what happened to Tamils who could not get to refugee camps before curfew started? That family had three teenage daughters. The mob would have turned those girls into soiled goods, then murdered them." She gestured to me in appeal. "Chandralal saved them from all that. He put his reputation, his golayas, his own life, at stake. What is that compared to a cheaper house price? They were grateful to him, don't you see? Now look at that family. They have a new life in Australia, a better life than here. Those three girls are probably all in university and will be prime candidates in the bridal market. They will be able—"

"Stop talking nonsense, Aacho. That family is probably very poor. You have no idea how those people exist in the West, the jobs they do to survive, the cramped apartments they live in, the daily contempt of white people." I stood by the dressing table. "We have to remedy this. Somehow, we must find out where they are living and compensate them. Offer the balance of what the house is worth."

My grandmother's face grew red. "You want me to hand out my hard-earned money to those people?" She laughed in disbelief. "Are you mad? We gave them a fair deal, we gave them their lives."

"You're such fine people. You and Chandralal will surely be reborn in Thusitha heaven for your goodness."

"How dare you mock me." She picked up a pen and flung it at me, grazing my shoulder.

I reached in my trouser pocket and took out the ring of keys she had given me when I assumed control of her properties. I held it out to her. "I don't want to be soiled by what you have done. If you won't compensate that family, you can take over running the properties again."

"But my work for the temple! I have to build that bana maduwa. Will you send me to my death without enough merit for a good rebirth?"

"No matter how many bana maduwas you build, do you think you'll even be reborn as a human being?"

"Shivan," she whispered in shock.

"You'll be lucky if you're born as a cat or a dog," I continued, unable to stop myself. "Most likely you and your Chandralal will be worms or insects for eternity."

"How could you curse me like this?" Her voice was hoarse with disbelief.

I put the keys down on the dressing table and walked out.

When I got to my room, I sat on the bed, my breath shallow. Yet I was determined to stick by my decision. I had before me Mili's great goodness. I was humbled he had chosen me to love. I wanted desperately to be worthy of him.

What I had not taken into account was that my grandmother, seated in her bedroom, was terrified she might be losing me. She had lived for so long with the burden of unhappiness, she could not bear to be cast back to her lonely state again.

That evening I was seated on the front verandah alone, trying to read but finding it impossible to concentrate, when a horn sounded at our gate. Rosalind came out the front door and, after giving me a quick look, went down the steps.

I closed my book and waited. As an SUV sped up our front driveway, my grandmother hobbled out onto the verandah. The Pajero stopped under the carport. Chandralal jumped out and came up the steps towards my grandmother. Then, pretending to notice me at the other end of the verandah, he cried, "Ah, but here is our baba!" He opened his arms and grinned with pleasure.

I got up and strolled towards the front door, passing him as if he were invisible. My grandmother was standing in the doorway, and when I brushed past I glared at her for dragging this thug into our quarrel.

"See, Chandralal," I heard her say querulously. "Look at what has come over him. My beloved grandson. Why would he behave like this?"

Chandralal murmured soothingly in reply.

After dinner, I took my plate to the kitchen. Rosalind was seated on a stool reading a newspaper. She folded it away and followed me as I went to wash my hands at the sink.

"Baba," she said, handing me a kitchen towel, "it's time you returned to Canada. Only bad will come from your staying."

I waited for her to continue, but she looked away, face numb with worry. "You must go, baba, you must."

I handed her the kitchen towel and muttered, "One can't just change plane tickets like that, Rosalind."

Mili and I met the next day for lunch. My grandmother had not spoken to me that morning, and had passed me in the hallway with her face averted. I did not mention our quarrel to Mili, nor how she had tried to draw Chandralal into our dispute. I wanted to prevent ugliness from leaching into the part of my life that was good.

My chaos of emotions made me impatient for Mili's caress and I could sense he too was frustrated by our limitations. When we had finished our meal and were standing outside the restaurant, I said, "I suppose your mother is at home."

He nodded and grimaced.

"I don't know how I can bear another day not being with you."

Mili examined me curiously. My plea had come out more desperate than I intended.

"There is a place . . ." He shook his head.

"Yes?"

"No, forget I mentioned it."

"Mili!"

"This house, for people like us. I've never been there, but my friend, Otto, used to point it out when we went swimming at Mount Lavinia. Tourists use it, so he heard through other German expats."

"Let's go there, Mili, let's go."

"It's sure to be a real thrada place, Shivan."

"We can always leave if we don't like it."

"It would be unworthy of you, of us. I wish I hadn't even brought it up."

"Unworthy? Why? For God's sake, don't you want to be with me? Don't you want to hold me anymore?"

"Ah, Shivan, don't say that."

"Let's go." Seeing he was still hesitant, I added, "You're not pulling away from me again, are you? I really couldn't bear that, Mili, I couldn't bear it if you hurt me again."

After a moment he nodded and sighed.

The three-storey house was a thin tower on such a small plot of land that the outer wall of the house also served as the boundary wall. Its slimness gave the building a curiously long-necked fragility that was enforced by the absence of windows overlooking the street. Mili said that the place belonged to a German man. Since foreigners could not buy property in Sri Lanka, the house was owned by his boyfriend, a former beach boy. It was used by other beach boys who needed a place to bring foreign clients.

Mili stayed on his motorcycle, keeping the engine running. I rang the front door bell, then raised my eyebrows at him. He reluctantly went to park nearby. As he came back, hands shoved in pockets, he glanced up and down the street as if nervous someone we knew might see us.

A peephole slid open in the door and a young man stared out at us. "Yes?" he asked rudely in Sinhala.

"We want to take a room for a few hours."

There was stentorian breathing on the other side and it took me a moment to realize he was accompanied by a dog. "This guest house is only for foreigners."

"I am a foreigner," I said, switching to English. I took out my Canadian citizenship card and he looked at it carefully.

There was much moving of bolts and chains, then he opened the door. He led us down a short dark corridor without saying a word, the pariah dog nudged up against his side. We emerged into a shady courtyard that was neat and clean, magenta bougainvillea growing up the white walls. Foreign men, their skins the colour of overripe papaw, sat at tables with boys, some of whom looked like teenagers, dressed alike in tank tops and jeans, with tight coral necklaces around their necks. The other guests examined us, but we avoided meeting anyone's gaze.

Our host, who had not given his name, led us up some narrow stairs to a room with a double bed neatly made up with clean sheets. There was a mirror on the opposite wall and a side table with a gurulettuva filled with water. He stated his price and I paid him. When he had counted out the notes, he said sternly, "I need the room in two hours. When you are done, please remove the sheets and put them in there." He gestured towards a wicker laundry basket.

Then we were alone. Mili and I stared at each other as if neither knew what to do. "This is quite a place," I said.

Mili grinned. "Yes, a bloody whorehouse."

I put my arms around him and pressed my crotch into his. "And here we are, a couple of whores."

He brushed his hand across my forehead, then gently kissed my eyes, cheeks, nose and throat before slipping his tongue into my mouth.

After we had made love, Mili propped himself up against the headboard and I sat between his legs, leaning back against his chest as he smoked, his breath tickling the top of my ears. "I have a little surprise for you," he said after a while. "I asked Sriyani for the beach house."

"She said yes?" I asked, half turning.

"Of course. Why not?" He gave me a puzzled look.

I pressed back against him and squeezed his knee. "No reason. That's great. How nice of Sriyani. When do we leave?"

"Tomorrow, after work. I have asked for a few days off. I need time to think." He grinned teasingly at my inquiring look. He was not going to share his thoughts with me yet.

We spent the rest of the day together, having tea at the Mount Lavinia Hotel and a beer at our regular beach cabana. By the time Mili dropped me off at my grandmother's house, the last red glow in the sky was purpling, shadows moving swiftly over everything. I was reluctant to let him go, dreading the tense silence between my grandmother and me.

After he left, I opened the gate wearily and started to make my way up the driveway. Rosalind rose from a bench in the garden and gestured for me to stop.

"Baba," she whispered as she came up to me, "please, don't go inside." She shook her head. "You cannot go inside."

"Why Rosalind?" I gripped her elbow. "What has happened?"

She began to cry, wiping her face on the edge of her sarong. "It pains me too much to say it."

I walked rapidly up the driveway, the skitter and crunch of gravel loud in the still evening. The verandah was deserted, and when I entered the saleya it was dark. I started towards my room. A lamp was switched on and I turned to find my grandmother seated in an armchair, hands folded in her lap, face stony.

"So, you're back." There was something very tired in her voice.

"I've been out." I swallowed hard. "Out with Mili."

"Yes, I know." She closed her eyes for a moment. "I know exactly where you have been. Chandralal had you followed by one of his golayas."

She nodded at my shocked expression, then her face flooded with anguish. "That Jayasinghe boy, taking my obedient, innocent grandson and changing him into this grotesque . . ." She made a disgusted sound. "I cannot even say the word." She leaned forward in her chair. "How could you be so gullible, Puthey? How could you let yourself be led into such corruption?"

"Mili didn't corrupt me." I laughed briefly, still stunned. "I'm like this. It is my nature."

My grandmother shook her head. "Nonsense, nonsense. The Jayasinghe boy has bad blood. Though the father's side is good, the mother is a Burgher, it's all that vile European blood. You are my grandson, you cannot be that way." Yet there was a helpless plea in her denial.

"It's not Mili or his blood. I live like this in Canada."

She struggled to her feet. "You are saying such a horrible thing to mock and punish me. All you want to do is break the heart of an old woman who has been nothing but good to you."

"You call the way you have treated me good?" My head was flooding now with a white heat at the thought of her asking that thug to spy on me, to violate Mili and my privacy. "Do you know how much I hated those afternoons in your room as a child? Do you know how much I hated going around with you on all your errands, looking at those thuppai properties? Do you think I did any of it out of love? You must be mad. I don't love you. I have never loved you."

My grandmother let out a cry. "Your mind is clouded, ruined by that Jayasinghe boy."

"No, Aacho, I don't love you," I continued in an awful, reasonable tone. "I have never loved you."

She hobbled away in the direction of her bedroom, but I went after her, still speaking in that sensible, wounding tone. "If I had not bent to you, we would have been thrown out onto the street, or so I thought as a child. And you knew I was thinking like that and took advantage of my innocence. You used my fear to get me where you wanted me to be."

"Stop yourself before you say anything you cannot take back," she cried, turning to me. "Don't do what your mother did, I beg you."

"Whatever my mother did, you drove her to do it."

She gave me a haunted, helpless look, then went into her bedroom.

The house felt stifling. I could not bear to be there anymore. I went out to the garden and paced the dark lawn, the dew-heavy grass *hush-hush*ing beneath my feet. I was planning my next moves with a steadiness that surprised me, the steadiness that comes when you finally speak a truth. "How easy it was, how easy," I said to myself with wonder as I picked up an araliya flower that had fallen on the lawn and looked at the brown stains where its petals had been crushed.

I would tell Mili everything at the beach house. Then, when we returned from our holiday, I would ask Sriyani to take me in for a while, explaining why. I was also going to urge Mili again to study in Canada. Some shift was happening in him and I hoped to influence that change. If he still refused, then I would stay on in Colombo. I had not given up my Sri Lankan citizenship and could find work here. With my foreign education, my family name, my facility in English, I had plenty of options.

20

MILI AND I WERE TO LEAVE THE NEXT EVENING after he finished work. Our plan was to stay four days, taking in the weekend.

The morning felt long without any work to do. I tried reading but it was impossible to concentrate. I would not venture into the saleya. Every time my grandmother's footsteps came towards my room, I felt that hot white anger flooding me, then relief when she passed on in another direction. While I exulted in this newfound cruelty towards her, at the same time I was frightened by it.

Finally my grandmother summoned Rosalind and informed her she had some errands to run and would be back for a late lunch. I made sure to have my meal early, then visited a bookstore in the afternoon and had a long tea at one of the hotels. I returned home in the early evening when I knew she would be visiting the temple. I had already packed and hidden the knapsack under my bed. I sat down to write my grandmother a letter in Sinhala.

Dear Aachi,
I have gone away for a few days with Mili to plan what we will do next. When I return, I am going to ask Mrs. Karunaratne if I can move in with her for a little while. She is generous, always giving out rooms to people in need, as I am now. Beyond that, I don't know what I will do. My days in Sri Lanka might be over—and you have yourself to blame for this.

With loving respect,
Shivan

When I heard Mili's motorcycle at the gate, I put the note on the dining table and ran down to the front gate.

I was panting when I got outside and Mili squinted at me quizzically. "Are you alright?"

I nodded, slipped the knapsack around my shoulders and put on the spare helmet.

We rode south through Colombo and soon left its urban sprawl behind. The motorway was open to the sea on one side. I held Mili close, enjoying the speed of the motorcycle beneath us, its power, feeling the slip and slide of his cotton shirt against his ribs as he shifted with the curve of the road. The cool ocean air smelt of freshly grated coconut.

It was dark when we got to the beach house. Piyasena came rushing to open the gate, smiling shyly in welcome. Our dinner was ready and suddenly we were starving. Piyasena had made crab curry, and when I expressed my delight he said he remembered how much I had liked it the last time.

Later, after Piyasena left, we sat on the front verandah sipping beer, listening to the ocean thunder against the beach. Nothing was visible beyond the light by the back gate, but then the moon rose and the sand began to glimmer like some awakening scaly beast. We went down to the beach, let our sarongs fall around our ankles and ran naked into the waves. Because of the currents at night, we stayed close to the shore, crouching in the water, our knees and thighs grazing the bottom when we swam. Mili drew me to him and we made love in the water.

As we floated in the waves afterwards, I told Mili all that had happened with my grandmother. And though it frightened me to tell him our relationship was no longer a secret, I felt the lightening of my burden. We were now in this together. When I finished, Mili turned and struck for the shore. I gave him some time, then followed. He was slipping on his sarong when I reached him, tying its ends into a knot at his waist. I sat on the sand by him, still naked, and lightly touched his calf. "There is nowhere to run, Mili. What has happened cannot be changed. You might as well sit down by me so we can talk."

After a moment, he lowered himself to the sand, and I could see in the moonlight that his eyes were lustrous with alarm.

"I am going to visit Sriyani when I return," I said, "tell her everything and ask if I can stay with her a little while." I shifted so my shoulder was touching his.

"Sriyani knows too?"

"She put two and two together." I spared him her opinion that everyone knew about him.

"But you know, Mili, my days in Sri Lanka might be numbered. I might have to return to Canada. And I wish you would consider coming too, sometime soon."

Mili played with a shell, some emotion working in his face. "Yes."

"Yes?"

He smiled ruefully and moved a strand of wet hair from my forehead. "Going abroad to study is something I wanted to think about this weekend."

Then he told me that a few days ago Sriyani had called her workers together and advised them to secure visas to whatever country they could get. They might have to leave suddenly if things got very bad, as they probably would. If the government did not make their lives hard, the JVP would, as it began to clamp down on all dissenters. Even she was thinking of taking up a fellowship at a university in England, one she had been offered before but turned down. If their long-term goal was to do some good in their country, then they had to accept that certain short-term battles must be lost.

Mili had talked with Sriyani privately to see what she thought of his applying to universities abroad. She had urged him to do so; a degree would be useful when he returned. She was getting old. New leaders would be needed.

"Did she mention what university she might do her fellowship at?" I asked.

"No," Mili replied, surprised by the question.

Sriyani, I was sure, had no plans to leave. She was not going to abandon Sri Lanka and her cause. Yet she was giving the others a way out, and I could already see who would choose what. Dilan and Avanthi would return to America; Jagath and Dharshini would stay on, their ties too strong. Mili had been on the fence, but our relationship no longer being secret had pushed him towards leaving.

I had been imagining the joy, the relief, I would feel if Mili agreed to my plan. But now what welled up was a great sadness. For Sri Lanka was changing rapidly and soon I would not know it anymore. Mili leaned over and lightly brushed his lips against mine, as if he sensed my sadness and shared it. We slept that night curled up together, each sighing in protest if the other pulled away.

We talked more about our plans in the next two days, and a quiet optimism came to us. We allowed ourselves to drift into the somnolence of a beach holiday, the rhythm of the waves rocking us into torpor.

On our third morning we slept in later than usual. Finally Mili nudged me, whispering it was getting late and Piyasena must be making our breakfast.

When we came out on the verandah, however, the table was not laid. I went to the kitchen. Piyasena was not there. "Strange," Mili said. "I wonder if he got delayed."

I went through the kitchen cupboards and found a jar of Nescafé. Mili discovered the bread and cut some slices. When he took them out to the verandah, I leaned against the counter, eyes closed, an inexplicable fear thumping at the base of my throat.

Mili returned to the kitchen and I quickly turned away to pour boiling water into cups and stir in the instant coffee. I was being ridiculous, I told myself. Everything was fine.

"I wish I knew where he lived," Mili said as we washed the dishes after eating. "I would go see."

"Maybe he had some family emergency."

"But what shall we do about lunch?"

"Just . . . let's give it some time. We can always go to a hotel."

Mili peered at me. "Are you okay?"

"Yes," I nodded vigorously. "Of course."

It would soon be too hot for swimming. We changed and went down to the sea. As we swam, I scanned the beach. I wanted to share this unease with Mili but felt articulating my fears would bring them to life.

A group of men approached in the distance, their forms wavering behind a shimmering curtain of heat. I felt a throb of fear. But they were just fishermen. They waved as they passed by, and I waved back, feeling foolish.

Piyasena had not turned up by lunch, and since we were too hot and tired for a trip into town, we dug around the fridge and found some cheese and Elephant House ham, which we had with the remaining bread.

That afternoon Mili fell asleep immediately, but I lay there, the heavy stickiness of his thigh over mine, listening to the sigh of his breath. After a while, the *thump-thump* of the ceiling fan wore down my vigilance and I closed my eyes.

A clicking sound awakened me. Mili had rolled over to the other side of the bed, snoring lightly. I raised my head from the pillow. Someone was fiddling with the latch at the gate.

I slid into my slippers and crept out of the room. As I walked along the side verandah, I could see a man's bare feet under the takaran-covered gate. He heard me approaching down the driveway and stopped trying to undo the latch.

"Who is it?"

"Ah, mahattaya, Piyasena, your man, sent me. He is detained. His wife is sick."

"Oh," I said with relief, "we were wondering what had happened." I lifted the latch and pulled the gate back, enough for him to enter.

The man was in his twenties, with the stringy muscled body of a fisherman, dressed in sarong and banyan. He smiled at me. "Are you the mahattaya from Canada?"

I nodded and waited for him to come in. But he stood there smiling, and it took me a moment to realize he was holding a knife inches from my stomach. Its dark blade glinted along the edge where the sun caught it. I let out a grunt of surprise. "Shh, mahattaya," he said, then gave a low whistle. Some men materialized from behind a clump of trees on the other side of the road. They were carrying heavy gnarled sticks and the short axes used for splitting coconuts. They, too, were dressed in banyans, sarongs hiked and tied above knees, prepared for a demanding task. One of them had a small black gun that looked curiously harmless, like a plastic water pistol. He wore bright blue pleated pants and a garishly pink flowered shirt and appeared to be the leader. He signalled for the men to cross the road.

My aggressor had also turned his head to watch them, and in that instant I shoved him away, leapt back and slammed the gate shut. He cried out, threw himself against it and managed to slip his arm through. I leaned my weight into the gate, his arm waving about like a tentacle, the other men shouting encouragement at him as they rushed over. His fingers brushed my face, my chest, and then he got me by the shirt. With a ripping sound, he pulled me to him, gripping my neckline so tight, the material burnt along my collarbone and I gasped. In that instant, the man pushed against the gate, I fell back and they charged in.

The man with the knife locked my arms in a hold from behind, hand over my mouth. He pressed the blade against my neck and my entire world was reduced to that cool, sharp point, my skin fragile as tissue paper. "Our quarrel is not with you, mahattaya," he panted in my ear. "Please don't struggle. Our instructions are not to hurt you."

I jerked in shock, understanding who had sent them. The man held me even tighter. His breath had the leafy tang of bulath and he smelt of dried, salted fish.

The men had shut the gate and were darting towards the house, crouched low, their feet a muffled thudding on the sand. I began to struggle, no longer caring about the knife. "Please, mahattaya," the man said, and now he actually moved the knife away, afraid to hurt me, "please do not make this difficult."

I broke from him, his nails scraping a jagged seam across my arm, and I ran towards the house.

The other men had already entered, and I heard Mili's shout of surprise. There was a scuffle, something fell over, the ringing of brass hitting the cement floor. I raced through the house to the bedroom, shoving the door so hard it crashed into the wall. The men turned, startled. As if time had stopped, I took in Mili, half lifted off the floor, arms held splayed by two thugs, another bent to grasp his legs which were out before him, his heels digging down to find some purchase on the polished floor. His shorts had slipped down, revealing his lean hipbones.

"Shivan, get away, get away."

Mili kicked out and the men came into action. They tried to subdue his limbs, one of them yelling to the man who had the knife, "Grab his legs, you ponnaya. Don't stand there." The man gripped Mili's ankles but he kicked him backwards.

"Let him go," I cried. "I know who sent you. It was Chandralal."

Mili started at the name, and in that instant the men took advantage of his surprise and secured their hold. He gave in, limp in their arms.

All this time, the leader had been standing to one side, watching. He gripped his pistol tightly, yet his tongue moved casually in his cheek, making a sucking sound as he tried to dislodge some food from his teeth.

"I will talk to Chandralal," I said to him. "Let my friend go."

The leader made a prolonged "ttttch," through his teeth. "I don't know who you are talking about. I know no Chandralal."

"Mili, don't worry." I went to him. "I'll put a stop to this."

"Shivan, what has your grandmother done?" he whispered, his voice cracking with terror.

There was a wound on his head and the blood was beginning to pulse up, matting his hair. "Mili, I'll take care of this."

The leader gestured with his gun and the men began to drag Mili towards the door. I slammed the door shut and stood against it. "Let me talk to Chandralal first."

The leader pointed to two of the men who were holding Mili and they came towards me. "You don't understand what you've taken on, who you're dealing with," I cried.

One of the men pressed his forearm around my neck and I could feel my windpipe harden as I tried to draw a breath. They half lifted, half dragged me across the room and threw me face-first on the bed. The force of it sent a pain fanning out from my nose and across my eye sockets. The rubbery, musty smell of the mattress choked me, yet I struggled, for the men were dragging Mili from the room. He was crying out in protest, his heels squelching along the floor. His cries grew fainter as they pulled him out of the house. Once they were on the verandah, they found some way to silence him. All I heard was the thud of the men's feet in the sand and the *hoop-hoop-hoop* of a dove. The gate clanged shut, a vehicle started up and I finally went limp.

The men let me go. I turned over, my breath harsh, and gaped pleadingly at the leader. He studied me for a long moment. "We're just poor people following the instructions of the rich, you understand?"

"Where are you taking him? What are you going to do with him?"

"So be very careful what you do next." Seeing my incomprehension, he added, "This is not abroad, there is no point going to the police. That will only jeopardize your friend further." He sat on the edge of the bed and I could smell his cheap flowery cologne, the coconut oil in his hair. "If you want my advice, here it is. Soon, a bus to Colombo will pass in front of the gate. I'll have one of my men flag it down and put you on it. When you get to Colombo, talk to the people who you think are responsible for this. Agreed?"

"Please don't hurt him."

He stood up and checked his pistol to make sure the safety catch was on, a strand of his oily hair falling over his forehead. He slipped the gun into his waistband, nodded for the man with the knife to wait with me and sauntered towards the door. After a short while, I heard the vehicle outside pull away. By now I was shivering. Without even really knowing what I was about, I began to pack my bag. The man gave me a sympathetic look. He picked up one of Mili's shirts and started to fold it. "No, leave that," I yelled. In my distress I was possessed by the hope that if I left Mili's things as they were he would return for them.

When I was done, the man carried my bag out to the road. "You stand in the shade inside, mahattaya. I'll let you know when the bus arrives." He gave me a worried look. "And try to stop shaking. It will not do for people to ask questions."

I waited on the side verandah, trying to control my breathing. I was so cold now, the flesh on my upper arms was puckered. I knew I had to calm myself. The leader was right. There was no point in going to the police or anyone else. The person I had to talk to was my grandmother. Images of Mili's terror and pain pushed forward, but I held them away. I needed to be as clear as I could. The bus stopped outside. I walked slowly down the driveway, no longer trembling.

Before I went out the gate, I glanced at the beach house. The palm fronds brushed the red tiled roof as they swayed in the breeze. Beyond the back garden, the sand glowed and the sea was brilliant. A gull wheeled and soared over the waves like a white kite.

21

During the two-hour journey to Colombo, I considered my options. My first instinct was to tell Sriyani everything. But if I did she would raise the alarm, and this would force Chandralal to protect himself at Mili's expense—though what he might do, I would not allow myself to contemplate. I also had to keep my rage contained and play the contrite, docile grandson. I recoiled from the idea but placated myself with images of Mili and me walking the sunny autumn streets of Toronto, the little apartment we would get above some store that would have the cosy, woody, fusty smell of radiator heat. All the while, thoughts of what was being done to him kept bellying forward, like wind pushing against a flimsy sail.

When I was finally at my grandmother's gate, my hand shook as I lifted the latch, a great sob tightening my chest. I pulled at the straps of my knapsack as if steadying myself, then went up the driveway.

My grandmother had heard me enter the compound, and when I came into the saleya she was seated in a chair pretending to read the newspaper with a severe expression. She was frightened—not for Mili, because she trusted Chandralal, but at the enormous gamble she had taken. This abduction could shake her grandson to his senses or cause him to break from her completely.

"Aacho." I sat next to her on a stool, putting my knapsack by my feet, revolted by the pious look on her face. "Get them to let him go."

She folded her paper. I took her hand and stroked it. "Aacho, I was wrong, and I'm very sorry for all the hurt I have caused you. I'm ready to give him up. I'll never see him again. Just tell Chandralal to release Mili, to not hurt him."

She patted my hand and I could see her relief that the gamble had paid off. "Ah, Puthey, nothing bad will come to that boy. I just wanted him given a good scare, to stop him corrupting you."

"But those men, they had axes and a gun. They're not Chandralal's regulars. I know all his golayas."

She tried to look amused at my concern. "Nonsense, they will only rough him up a bit. Nothing worse than a schoolboy fight." Yet I could see she was beginning to have doubts.

I stood up. "I must go and see Chandralal."

"There is no need to bother him." My grandmother flapped her newspaper open. "Everything is alright, Puthey."

I shook my head and walked towards the kitchen to get our driver.

"Don't make a nuisance of yourself, Puthey, and disturb Chandralal on a Saturday evening."

Rosalind had been standing outside the back door on the verandah, and when I came out she grasped my arm, forcing me to stop. "Baba, please don't get involved any further."

"But Rosalind, what can I do? I am involved. His life is in danger."

She shook her head in distress but let go of me.

As the car took me to Kotahena, I reviewed what I would do. I still felt it was a bad idea to tell Sriyani, but I would use her and Tudor Jayasinghe's renown to make Chandralal release Mili. I would assure him that if he let Mili go we would not report the abduction, as it would compromise my grandmother. Part of me watched this cool planning with wonder.

When the car stopped in front of Chandralal's house, I sat, hands in my lap, palms pressed together as if in prayer, bilious at the thought of having to be meek and diplomatic. I got out and knocked on the gate. A peephole slid open and the security guard glared out. "Ah, mahattaya!"

He opened the gate beaming, escorted me up the driveway, rang the bell and told a surprised servant to get Chandralal. Then he bowed and returned to the gate. How incongruous his respect was, given the begging mission I had come on.

I sat on that red velvet sofa with its stink of animal fur and gazed at the glass-fronted cabinets filled with his wife's bric-a-brac. The porcelain crinoline ladies, cavorting horses, European peasants, Japanese dolls in silk kimonos, Wedgwood bowls, platters and tea set were the same sort of trappings my grandmother and ladies of her social stature amassed.

After some time, Chandralal came out wearing a sarong and buttoning up his dress shirt. "Ah, baba," he gave me a keen look, "what a pleasant surprise, what an honour. Wait, let me ask my wife to bring you a drink."

"No, no."

He lowered himself languorously into a chair across from me as if settling in for a long, relaxed chat.

"Chandralal, I want you to release my friend. He has done nothing wrong. My grandmother has completely misunderstood our friendship and has assumed all the wrong things about it."

"What has she assumed, baba?" he asked mildly.

I dropped my eyes under his gaze. "Vile, untrue things. She is just jealous of any friendship I have. Even when I was a child, she did not like my mother spending time with me and tried—"

"Your grandmother is a good woman," Chandralal interrupted gently. "She is renowned for her pious deeds. Look at this bana maduwa she is building."

"I have promised my grandmother I will no longer see him. Within a year, I will get married," I found myself adding. "It will be entirely her choice whom I marry, Chandralal. Also, I am guaranteeing you that my friend will not speak of this abduction. Neither he nor I would want to see an old woman suffer. You know, Chandralal, I could go to Sriyani Karunaratne, who runs the human rights organization where my friend works. Do you know who my friend is? He is the son of Tudor Jayasinghe."

"But what will you tell these people, baba? Particularly Mr. Jayasinghe? He will surely want to know the reason for your grandmother's anger against his son? And if he wants some action taken, won't he have to tell his friends in the police or army about her reasons too? They will want to know."

Chandralal turned from me to his wife, who came in bearing a tray with glasses of lime soda and a bowl of fried del chips, "Ah! Here are some refreshments."

As I took the glass he held out I understood I was at his mercy. I had to do as he wished if I wanted to protect Mili. So I forced myself to eat their chips, drink their lime soda and chat to his wife, all to show Chandralal I was obedient.

Later, as he walked me down the driveway, I made one last attempt to assert myself. "The leader of those men you sent advised me not to inform the police. I have followed his advice, Chandralal. I am keeping up my part of the bargain. You must keep up yours, Chandralal."

"Ah, baba, you worry too much."

"So, it's a promise, you will release him?"

He clapped me on the shoulder. "You are like a son to me, baba. Would I do anything that would cause you true distress?"

"Thank you, Chandralal." I grasped his hand and shook it. "Thank you."

My grandmother was waiting for me on the verandah. "So," she said, as I came up the front steps, "it was just as I said. No harm will come to that Jayasinghe boy."

I collapsed into a chair and leaned my head back, eyes closed.

"And what did Chandralal say?"

"He will not do anything that would cause me true distress." My voice trembled with weariness.

"There, Puthey! It will all be resolved by tonight. That Jayasinghe boy will be home safe and sound."

I turned towards her as a thought struck me. "How did you know where we went?"

"I called Mrs. Karunaratne's assistant and got the address. After all, you went there before, no?" She gave me an indulgent smile that faded into a defeated grimace under my glare.

I was revolted by the sight of her, yet straining not to show it, reminding myself over and over of that apartment in Toronto, how wonderful it would be to wake every morning with Mili, how he would gently cuff my chin before he got out of bed, just as he had at the beach house.

My grandmother retired for the night, but I stayed on the verandah, eyes riveted on the gate, as if longing hard enough would bring Mili on his motorcycle to stop outside. I thought again of going to Sriyani, but after seeing Chandralal I knew it would be a misstep. I clung to how he had said I was like a son and he would never cause me true distress; reminded myself of his affection for my grandmother, for me, his loving indulgence towards his daughters, his jolly wife.

Rosalind started to close up the house and I went to bed after instructing her not to padlock the gate in case the Jayasinghe Mahattaya came by. I did not change into my sarong but lay down as I was. The events of the day had exhausted me.

I was woken just before dawn by the faint clang of the gate being opened. A vehicle came slowly up our front driveway, the gentle grumble of tires crushing gravel. It passed my window and stopped under the carport. I heard the clunk of one of the vehicle's doors, Rosalind hurrying across the saleya, her murmur of greeting. Chandralal replied gruffly and their footsteps clipped towards my grandmother's room. I sat up in my bed, clutching the edge of the mattress. I heard the lilting of their voices and then my grandmother letting out a choked gurgle. I rushed to the saleya. Chandralal was coming out of my grandmother's bedroom. Our eyes met and I saw he was frightened. He strode on towards the front door.

I found my grandmother lying with her arm across her eyes.

"Aacho?"

She lowered her arm and her gaping horror made me fall to my knees by her bed.

"Puthey, those men . . . they did not know to be careful with that boy. One of them struck him. He fell and hit his temple against the corner of a table and . . ." She began to cry.

I grasped her hand. "What are you saying, Aacho?"

"In the middle of the night, they took the body and released it beyond the reef so it will not float back to land."

I got up and hurried towards the door as if I had somewhere urgent to go.

"Aiyo! See what that boy has brought on us. He was a curse from the moment he walked into this house."

I made it to the verandah before I had to sit down in a planter's chair. Rosalind came and squatted by me. "Baba, do nothing, do nothing. Our Loku Nona is involved in a murder now. How can she spend the rest of her life in prison?"

Before I could respond, the phone rang. Rosalind frowned. "Should I get it, baba?" I stared as if not understanding her question. She went to answer, then returned. "It's the Karunaratne Nona."

A panic took hold of me. "Tell her I'm not here," I whispered. Rosalind continued to stand there uncertainly and I finally got up and went to the phone.

"Shivan," Sriyani said abruptly. "I am coming to see you."

"No, no, I . . . I'll come to you."

"You will come right away, won't you?"

"Yes." I licked my lips. "Yes now."

I put down the receiver.

My grandmother had come out of her room. "Who was that, Puthey?" she asked cautiously.

I shook my head in dismissal and went towards the front door.

"Aney, Puthey, tell me, will you? Tell me."

The driver was standing ready by the car, having been woken by the commotion and guessing his services would be needed.

There was a Sunday calm all around as we drove along Bullers Road to Cinnamon Gardens, the sun rising. Early devotees were entering a temple, summoned by the bell's dolorous clang and chanting of the monks. The women wore white saris, the men white pants and shirts. They carried shallow round coconut-frond baskets, overflowing with araliya and jasmine. How disconnected this serenity was from me; and yet this very disjunction made my present anguish all the more real.

I was terrified at having to tell Sriyani what had happened to Mili. "Ah, no," I whispered, shaking my head. For I could hear her crying out that we could have saved him if only I had told her what I knew.

The driver let out a low exclamation."We are being followed, mahattaya."

A man on a red scooter was tailgating us. He wore a black helmet, only his eyes visible. When he saw me staring, he raised his hand briefly in acknowledgement. I wanted to sink into my seat, but a modicum of pride made me sit straight and stare ahead.

While we waited for Sriyani's gate to be opened, Chandralal's man parked across the road and took off his helmet. I had seen him before on various occasions. He smiled in a friendly, deferential way. I looked away.

It was Piyasena, from the beach house, who let us in. His left arm was in a sling. A dark bruise bloomed on one side of his face like a purple hibiscus. I stared at him in horror as we drove past, and he held my gaze with miserable anger.

Sriyani and her husband were on the verandah, faces set, as if prepared for bad news. "I'm being followed," I said, as I went up the steps, "I'm being followed."

"Are you sure?" Sriyani asked.

"Yes, yes, it's his man, Chandralal's man. I know him. He's probably the one who followed us when we went to Mount Lavinia and—"

"Shivan, Shivan." Sriyani grabbed me by the shoulders.

"He needs a cup of tea," her husband said.

There was already a tray with cups and teapot in the living room. Sriyani sat on the couch and I collapsed into an easy chair. Her husband stood a little distance away, watching. She had lost her usual composure, features gaunt with worry. Her hand shook as she poured me some tea.

She waited for me to have a few sips, then took a deep breath and let it out in a stuttering sigh. "I dread to ask, but I must. Where is Mili? Is he alive, do you know?"

I began to cry. Sriyani leaned forwards and shook my knee. "Shivan, gather yourself together. Every minute makes the difference between Mili being alive or not."

I put my head in my hands, hardly able to breathe between sobs.

"Stop!" Sriyani pulled my hands away from my face. "Stop crying or I will give you a slap."

I forced my sobs down, chest aching.

"That's better now," she said gently.

I told her of Chandralal's visit that morning, the news he had brought. Once I began, I could not stop talking, spilling out the story of how my grandmother had discovered our relationship, how she had called on Chandralal to intervene. By the time I finished, Sriyani was bent forward, fingers pressed into temples. Her husband had gone to stand at a window to hide his shock.

"I should have come to you right away. I should have taken my grandmother's discovery of us more seriously. I, more than anyone, should have known what she was capable of. By my stupidity I killed him. You warned me, Sriyani. Why didn't I listen?"

"Shh, Shivan." She pressed my shoulder.

In the stillness I could hear a flock of babblers in the garden, the hiss of frying in the kitchen.

Sriyani turned to her husband. "What are we to do, Priya?"

"Well, Sriyani, you know what you always say."

"Protect the innocent and vulnerable first." She sat back, hands cupping her neck, gazing at the ceiling.

"Yes, that's right." Then he added, "Piyasena."

"And Mili's parents." She continued to address the ceiling. "It would kill them to be confronted with their son's true nature."

"We cannot bring Mili back. Nor do we have proof to back up any accusations."

Sriyani hunched forward, her hands clasped, jaw pushed out. She looked so sad and tired. "We shall say that Mili was spending some time at our bungalow alone. He went for a late-night swim and currents . . ." She rubbed her forehead. "I'll make some calls. Let friends at newspapers know about this accidental drowning.

"Priya, can you call the police station in Bentota and report Mili's disappearance? I don't have the strength for that. All you have to say is he might have drowned. They will understand, and the rest will flow smoothly." She smiled bitterly. "Yes, our state machinery is a well oiled one when it comes to these obfuscations. We received it well oiled already from the British."

Sriyani started to walk towards her study, then stopped and stared speculatively at me, as if she had forgotten I was there. "You must get your grandmother to tell Chandralal our decision. You also need to leave." Just in case I misunderstood, she added, "Leave for Canada." She squinted at me. "You will leave, won't you, Shivan?"

"Yes," I whispered, "yes."

"And I don't blame you for anything. You loved our Mili and perhaps that made you a little blind, but so were Ranjini and Sri. You could not have known it would come to this. If you don't mind me saying, you misjudged this country, because you are now foreign to it. You wanted poor old Sri Lanka to love and accept the person you became in Canada. But it cannot. That does not make you responsible for Mili's death."

On the way home, our car was stopped at a checkpoint that had sprung up on Bullers Road. Two soldiers carrying machine guns came along either side and peered at us. They got the driver to open the trunk, rifled through it, then pointed to the side of the road, where we were to wait. The president was passing.

We parked under a banyan tree and soon were joined by other motorists, cyclists and pedestrians. Half an hour later, we heard horns and the revving of motorcycle engines, as if a parade were drawing near. Soon the cavalcade came into view, swinging around the Kannatha roundabout. Four motorcycles roared past us, followed by five limousines with tinted windows, followed by army Jeeps blasting their horns, crammed with soldiers at the ready with guns. I glanced at the people around me, who stared with resignation at the passing vehicles. Chandralal's man was parked a little distance away, sharing a cigarette with one of the soldiers.

By the time I got home, my body felt clammy, teeth rattling against each other. In a fevered state I hurried to my room, pulled out my suitcase and began to throw things into it. Then a weakness overtook me and I curled up in bed, facing the wall, shaking with cold. I heard the clack of my grandmother's stick as she made her way across the saleya and came to stand in my doorway.

"Sriyani Karunaratne wanted me to give you a message," I said, still facing the wall. "Tell Chandralal the story is Mili drowned. He went for a midnight swim alone and never came back." When my grandmother did not reply, I said, "Do you understand? Now go tell him."

"Are you ill, Puthey?"

"I don't know." I left my bed and went to gaze out the window, hands in my armpits for warmth.

"I'll tell Rosalind to get you a Disprin." She let out a cry. "But what is this?"

Even though I was turned away, I knew she was referring to my suitcase.

"I have to leave for Canada." I continued to look out at the side garden, where the gardener had left some saplings in tin cans to sun on the path. "It's what your man, your thug, wants. I have no choice in the matter."

"No, Chandralal would never harm my grandson. He would never do that."

"He is having me followed again. And this time, the man does not even pretend to be discreet. It is clearly a message."

"I will go and speak to Chandralal. He would never harm my grandson."

"Are you blind? I am already harmed." I opened my arms. "Look, look, I am damaged. And you have done this to me."

"Ah, Puthey, don't say that," she said, her voice cracking. "You're speaking in anger."

"Remember how you said our Sinhalese ended up eating themselves by causing the riots? Now you have eaten yourself. Through your stupidity and evil, you have lost the thing you value most." I went back to packing my suitcase, folding my clothes neatly so they would all fit. After a moment she left, and I heard her hobbling towards the front door, calling for the driver.

Rosalind brought me a Disprin, put her hand on my forehead and declared I did have a fever. Once she had persuaded me to lie down, she drew the curtains and left. In the gloom, the sight of my desk, my almirah, my bookshelf, caused a vertigo in me. I closed my eyes and soon the nausea subsided. I fell asleep for a couple of hours and then the ayah woke me to drink some chicken broth. Afterwards I felt well enough to do something I had planned since coming back from Sriyani's. I went into the saleya, found the phone book and began to call hotels to see if they had a room—not the five-star ones, but simpler, cheaper places. Surprisingly, they were full. There was a meeting of South Asian leaders in Colombo, and as part of the conference cricket matches were being played between India, Pakistan and Sri Lanka. This had brought a lot of people from outstation into Colombo, one of the clerks informed me.

I was still calling hotels when the car returned. I put down the phone and watched from the saleya as it pulled into the carport. My grandmother got out with difficulty. She signalled impatiently for the driver to give her his arm. Leaning on him, she stumped up the steps. When she came inside and saw me, she was still for a moment, gaping as she caught her breath. Then she hobbled over, pinched with exhaustion, face streaked where she had wiped the perspiration.

"He would not see me," she whispered in disbelief. "I sat for two hours in his living room, on that awful velvet sofa, but no one came out to me. I was not even offered a glass of water."

She craved some comfort, but I turned away and dialled the next hotel in the phone book. "Yes," I said, when the reception clerk came on the line, "I am looking for a room in your hotel." I heard my grandmother exclaim and I turned more fully from her. "Preferably tonight. But I'm willing to wait, if I have to, until tomorrow." The clerk went to check.

"Please." My grandmother put her hand on my arm. "Don't go."

I shrugged her away.

The clerk came back to say they did have a room available, starting tomorrow, late afternoon.

"Yes, I'll take it. Make the reservation for three days to start."

I put the phone down and went back to my room without a glance at my grandmother.

22

THE NEXT DAY OUR NEWSPAPER, which was government owned, carried the story of Mili's death on its second page. There were quotes from fishermen confirming strong currents that night; also a quote from the "grieving father" on what a decent, intelligent son Mili had been. "A star has gone out in the firmament of our brilliant youth," Tudor Jayasinghe was reported as saying. There was no mention of the parents' separation, of the mistress. Mrs. Jayasinghe was, according to the father, "too indisposed with sorrow for commentary." There would be no funeral until the body was found. The article spoke of his father's accomplishments and family lineage, then went on to list Mili's achievements in school with no mention of his work at Kantha. The piece continued to another page, and turning to it I found a photograph of Mili from when he was a teenager, wearing our school tie and blazer, holding aloft a cricket trophy won under his captainship, grinning in that old, easy way.

I had taken the newspaper to my room and read it seated on my bed. When I was done, I leaned back against the wall and stared at the shifting pattern of sunlight on the curtains as they swelled and crumpled in the breeze. I felt nothing because it was too soon for feelings. I tore the article out of the paper and folded it away in my knapsack.

That morning, I visited the Air Lanka office. They had space on a flight in five days, but I would have an eighteen-hour wait in London for my connection.

I went to tell Rosalind of my departure. The ayah was pounding dry chilies, and she leaned against the mol gaha and listened to me with great sadness. "Ah, baba, I shall miss you so much. You will never come back, I know that."

"I want you to tell her."

The ayah squared her shoulders. "No, baba, it is your duty to do so." And to make her point, she turned her back on me and continued with the pounding.

My grandmother had stayed in bed and not gone on her usual morning errand. She lowered her forearm from over her eyes when I entered.

"I have only come to tell you that I leave in five days. It would be rude not to inform you, since I have enjoyed your hospitality these past months."

She struggled into a sitting position. "Puthey, you don't have to go. Please, everything is alright now, everything has returned to normal."

"Normal?" I said bitterly.

After lunch I was seated on the verandah, waiting for the hours to pass so I could go to the hotel, when an SUV stopped outside the house. One of Chandralal's golayas opened our gate and the Pajero sped up the driveway. Even before it had come to a complete stop in the carport behind my grandmother's Bentley, Chandralal jumped out. "Ah, baba, here you are!" he cried, as if he had not seen me in a long time.

He strutted up the steps in great spirits. "What's this I hear, baba? Your aachi telephoned to say you were leaving on my account?"

His swaggering buoyancy caused that hot whiteness to bloom in my head. "Yes," I leaned back in my chair, "isn't that what is expected of me?"

"Ah, no, baba, you must stay." He smiled down at me. "Stay and let your aachi finish her bana maduwa." He sat across from me, uninvited.

I pulled away into a corner of my chair as if to avoid pollution, not taking my gaze off him. "Why? What good will any of that do? A bana maduwa cannot erase a murder. In fact, as you well know, Chandralal, everyone must pay for what he does. It is the law of karma. There is no escape from our evil deeds. We pay in this life or the next one."

He laughed, disconcerted. Then, leaning in to me, he asked, "But, baba, do you not know the story of Siri Sangha Bo?" He proceeded to tell me the tale of Prince Siri Sangha Bo, who refused to become a king because the actions required of a ruler, either in war or in sentencing criminals to death, were ruinous to a person's chance of a good future birth. A delegation of Buddhist monks finally changed his mind by describing how a leech, when it came into contact with a woman's breast, gave pain, whereas an infant suckling on a breast produced pleasure. In the same way, an ignorant, vacillating king earned nothing but demerit for his future life whereas a wise and composed king gained merit. Siri Sangha Bo, convinced, assumed the throne but was unable to perform the necessary harsh actions and his kingdom was plagued with crime. Eventually he had to renounce his title and retreat to the forest, where he became an ascetic.

As Chandralal spoke, I saw for the first time the madness in his eyes. This man believed that though his deeds were harsh they were for the greater benefit of others too ignorant to know what was best for themselves.

"And see, baba, because of me, everything is alright now, nah? Everything is back to normal."

"But the man I was in love with has been killed."

He gaped at my admission of love. I had truly shaken his composure and left him speechless.

"Ah, Chandralal!" My grandmother hobbled out onto the verandah pretending surprise at his arrival, though I was sure she had been standing in the saleya, listening.

He sprang to his feet.

"How kind of you to come and see me." She held out her hand and he took it in both of his, bowing.

"Kind, madam? If anyone has been kind, it is you to me."

"No, no, Chandralal, whatever generosity I have showed, you have repaid it manyfold. If anyone is in debt, it is I."

"Ah, madam, I am so sorry about yesterday. I had no idea you came to visit. I was very upset when my security man told me you had sat in my living room for two hours and no one even brought you a cup of tea." His voice grew resonant with anger. "I scolded my servants for such rudeness. What pariah dogs they are! Even my wife, I was furious at her. What can I do, madam? Despite all my efforts, she is a crude village woman. You cannot make gold from brass, you cannot."

My grandmother and I looked at him askance. Chandralal collected himself, then inclined his head towards her. "I should go, madam."

"What, already? But you just got here. Please stay, Chandralal, you must let me give you a cup of tea. After all—"

"No, no, madam," he said impatiently, "I must go."

I saw he could no longer stand to be around her. Unlike everyone else in his life, she had been unafraid of him until now, and her lack of fear made him feel a good person. It was the reason he'd had such affection for her. Now she did fear him, and he could not bear her new wheedling tone. I was not sure if she understood his change towards her or not.

That afternoon, when my grandmother was asleep, I left her house. Rosalind waited with me on the verandah for my taxi. As the car pulled up the driveway we watched it transfixed, as if we had never seen a taxi before. When it stopped at the carport, behind my grandmother's Bentley, I picked up my bags and nodded to Rosalind.

"Will I see you before you leave, baba?"

"Yes. We won't say goodbye yet." Then I went down the steps and got in the car. As the taxi drove away, I did not glance back at my grandmother's house.

In the days that followed, I spent most of my time in my hotel room. Mili's death seemed a remote event and sometimes I would forget he was dead. I'd be passing time in a bookstore and see a new Robert Ludlum or Jeffrey Archer novel and think I ought to get it for Mili; or I'd wake in the morning and wonder if Mili might be able to steal away from the office for lunch today. I would remember something I wanted to tell him, then realize I could not do that anymore. Whenever I slipped up like this, I felt no pain or grief, just an emptiness that both surrounded me and was inside me, as if I were encased in a casket of thick silence; as if I were silence itself.

This emptiness grew more profound when late one night I received a call from my mother and sister.

"Son," my mother said, her voice resonant with worry, "we have heard." I did not ask who had told her. It might have been Rosalind, Sunil Maama or even Sriyani.

"Shivan," Renu said on the extension, "I am so glad you are coming back."

I felt no surprise, no longing, no gladness to hear their familiar voices. Their words simply reverberated in the emptiness.

"I am fine."

"Son, how can you be fine?"

"No . . . not fine. I suppose just numb."

"Ah." My mother sighed to say she understood that feeling well.

Sriyani somehow found out where I was. She sent her driver with a note inviting me to stay with her. She had not come herself, wanting, I supposed, to remove any obligation I might feel at her kindness, to give me the freedom to decide what I wanted. By sending the driver, she was letting me know she was there if I needed her.

Two days before I left, Sriyani's assistant called to inform me that people were gathering at Charlotte Jayasinghe's home the next afternoon to offer their condolences. Mr. Jayasinghe had, evidently, wanted the event at their Cinnamon Gardens home but, with the mistress living there, his wife had refused. I felt panic at the thought of going, and yet I could not stop myself, like a thief drawn to the site of his crime.

The street was lined with cars, some of them very expensive. As I went around the side of the house, I could hear the murmur of many voices, like the amplified humming of bees around a hive. The area outside the annex was crowded, people packed together in groups so tight it was impossible to tell who belonged to what social circle. A servant woman was struggling to thread her way among the mourners with a tray of passion fruit cordial, the glasses sweating in the afternoon sun. At the far end of the side garden, among a grove of banana trees, were some folding metal chairs. This was the only shady spot and it was occupied by Cinnamon Gardens dowagers who were relatives or friends. Also seated were the wives of various ministers, come in lieu of their husbands and largely ignored by the dowagers. There were a lot of pot-bellied business men and heads of corporations who were friends of Mili's father and had probably gone to school with him. Lalith Athulathmudali, a senior cabinet minister and close family friend, was leaving as I arrived, escorted by armed body guards. I was made to stand aside by the soldiers until he had passed.

The workers from Kantha were gathered together, and when I came up to them they shook my hand soberly. "It is good to see you, Shivan," Dharshini said, and the others nodded in agreement.

They were talking about Mili. "But why would he go to Sriyani's on his own like that?" Jagath said.

"You know he was very upset by Ranjini's death," Avanthi replied. "Perhaps he needed some time to recover."

"What has Sriyani said, though?" Dilan asked.

"Not much," said Dharshini. "Just that Mili asked to use the beach house."

They began to talk about various incidents from the time they had known Mili. I nodded and smiled, trying to appear interested, yet all the while suffocating under my secret knowledge and wishing I had not come. At one point, Dharshini turned to me. "But you must also have some wonderful memories from your school days, nah, Shivan? I hear Mili was a real rioter then." There was something too light in her tone.

The others all turned to me, smiling in a fixed way. "Tell us some of those stories," Jagath said in that same light, careful way.

They were trying to draw me in without acknowledging the nature of my relationship with Mili. "Yes," I said with a thin harsh smile, "lots of memories." I was furious at them for failing even to hint that my suffering might be keener for having been in love with him. As soon as I could I walked away.

A group of boys from our old school stopped me and shook my hand, expressing their sadness at Mili's death, reminiscing about "the good old days." Some of them had grown portly already, their faces jowly, even though we were just twenty-three. They spoke in that ringing way of young men who are moving into their years of power and privilege. I stood among them dumbly, then excused myself and went to pay my condolences to Mili's parents before I left.

This home, which I had come to know so well, seemed a foreign place because of all the strangers pressed together inside, shuffling sideways to get in or out and pass each other. Charlotte Jayasinghe was seated on the sofa, a dull, distant look on her face, hands folded in her lap, palms turned upwards. Tudor Jayasinghe stood by the sofa and a line had formed to shake the parents' hands. Sriyani was a little ahead. Once she paid her respects and turned to leave, she saw me. I could not stop myself from looking away. She patted my shoulder as she passed and I nodded, frightened I would start crying if I met her gaze.

Soon it was my turn before the Jayasinghes. "Ah, son," Mili's father said, as I proffered my hand silently, "how good of you to come." When I offered my hand to his mother, she looked up blankly as if she did not know me and murmured, "Thank you for coming."

As I moved around the sofa, I saw that the curtain to Mili's room had been drawn back. There was the bed we had made love in, there his motorcycle helmets on the side table. One of them probably still smelt of my hair gel and cologne. People bumped into me as they passed, and finally I tore my eyes away from these last vestiges of Mili and left.

The evening before my departure, I returned to my grandmother's house to get a few things I had left behind. I called Rosalind to tell her I would come when my grandmother was at the temple. A taxi dropped me outside the house. I did not ring the bell or open the gate, feeling I had lost some right to do so. Like my mother all those years ago, I waited until Rosalind came around the side of the house, saw me and made her way down the driveway. She walked in a cautious manner, as if she were nervous of me and doubted my sanity. When she let me in, her eyes scoured my face to see how I was and what had changed in the last few days. She reached silently for the empty knapsack on my shoulder, but I would not let her carry it.

When I reached the carport and saw my grandmother seated on the verandah, I understood Rosalind's nervousness. The ayah had informed her of my visit. Rather than rage, I felt sadness well up at the sight of her, a barbed thing swelling my throat. I nodded in greeting, my lips pressed together. Then I went past her into the house.

I was on my knees in front of the bed, examining the items I'd left behind and now laid out on my coverlet, when my grandmother came to stand in the doorway. I glanced at her, then started to stuff my possessions into my knapsack. I could hear Rosalind watering the plants outside my window, the scouring sound of the hose dragging in the gravel. Sinhala film music drifted in from another house, a koel trilled dramatically in the mango tree. The sun had set and dusk was spreading rapidly across my room.

"I don't have a choice, you understand." I turned away to take my travel alarm and stuff it in my knapsack. "I must go."

"But why must you go? Chandralal has guaranteed your safety."

"It's not about his guaranteeing anything. It would be intolerable to stay. In the last few days, I have become a stranger in this country. And you have made this happen. You have made me hate my country. Everything is ruined now, everything is ruined for me here."

"If you leave, you will never return," she said with a quiet certainty.

I glanced at her, and for a moment I was moved by her desolation.

I continued to pack and she continued to stand there. It was nearly too dark to see what I was doing, but I did not want to turn on a light, I did not want to see in her face the tearing of the last threads between us.

But my grandmother was not willing to give up that easily. When the silence had grown heavy, she began to speak. "That man, Charles, my cousin, whom everyone said I loved, whom everyone said I compromised myself with, the story was not like that at all."

Then she told me the secret that had contorted her life.

23

"I WANT YOU TO UNDERSTAND WHAT HAPPENED, SHIVAN," my grandmother said, as she came to sit on my bed in the darkening room. "And why I was so helpless to do anything about it." Her voice throbbed with appeal, a modern day Scheherazade who hoped telling her story would keep at bay the death my departure would bring. And her desperation brought a great clarity about herself—that lucidity we always seem to find when at the end of our rope.

So my grandmother, gesticulating with her hands as if I was a child again and she hoped to win me over with a tale, brought alive that vast family compound of her youth, perched on top of a hill overlooking the sea: red-roofed bungalows around a common paved courtyard, each with its carved teak verandah posts; coconut-frond mats on cool polished floors where the women sat to sew or pick stones out of rice or crochet the famous Galle lace. She described, with a swell of longing in her voice, that large, fat clan of aunts and married cousins, her beloved soft-spoken mother, all led by the matriarch, Thushara Nanda; the way those women travelled in a group, their parasols flapping in the sea breeze, half-moons of perspiration in the armpits of their white lace-edged blouses, brightly coloured sarongs wrapping ample hips.

The men were away working mostly as civil servants, except for my great-grandfather, who ran a thriving dry goods and hardware store in the town of Galle. The boys were in boarding schools. So my grandmother, Daya, enjoyed great freedom in this world ruled by women. Her wildness was encouraged by the aunts, who dared her to climb the roof and walk along its ridge, or sent her up a mango tree to throw down ripe fruit to them, which they caught in woven baskets. Then there were those nights in the hot season, when my grandmother would creep out of her house, go down the winding path to the main road and across to the beach. There, she would strip off her nightgown and swim to the reef in her underwear, then squat on the honeycomb of coral shelf to examine shells, or stare at the blinking lights on the horizon, arms dangling between her legs, swayed by the waves breaking around her, as she dreamed of where the passing steamers were going.

Into this world Charles arrived from abroad, hungry for happiness, for belonging. One morning, the women had gone to Galle on a shopping expedition, and they returned in their bullock carts to find a young man seated on a bench in the courtyard. His clothes immediately gave him away as a foreigner. Instead of the light-coloured linen or cotton coats their men wore over sarongs or pants, he was dressed in a double-breasted brown pin-stripe suit with padded shoulders. His tie had broad maroon and blue stripes and he wore a matching handkerchief in his breast pocket. He clutched a fedora in his hand. As the carts came to a halt in the courtyard, he rose slowly from the bench, squinting up at the women, fingers plucking nervously at his hatband.

Thushara Nanda descended first from the cart. She asked the man who he was. "I'm sorry," he replied in a crisp British accent, "I don't speak Sinhala."

My grandmother and her cousins, who had been educated to some extent in English, glanced at each other.

"I am your nephew, Charles," he said, speaking slowly and loudly. "I am the son of your sister, Visaka."

Hearing her name, the women let out little cries of wonder, "Visaka Nangi" passing among them like a breeze. Their sister had married into a Colombo family, and a year later died giving birth. Her husband, fulfilling a lifelong dream, had taken his infant son to England. That was the last they had heard of Charles, though my grandmother and her cousins were aware he existed. As if to confirm his lineage, Charles reached in his jacket pocket and produced a slightly faded and creased photograph of his mother. Everyone crowded around to look at it. Some of the aunts began the ritual sniffling and weeping for a sister they had mostly forgotten.

My grandmother, under the guise of examining the photograph, drew near to take a closer look at this cousin. He was petite and fine-boned, wrists no wider than her own. His face was long, delicate and clean shaven, unlike the men in their family, who sported bristling moustaches and goatees. This hairlessness made him look vulnerable and feminine. His most distinguishing feature was his eyes—large and slightly protruding, the yellow irises and black pupils like a cat's. He had noticed her staring and smiled hesitantly. She glanced away.

A nervous jocularity had spread among the older women and they began to push various younger married nieces and daughters forward, saying, "Come-come, all those English classes and English convent school. Speak to the young man." The women resisted, making a pretence of modesty. My grandmother, embarrassed by their silliness, blurted out in English, "You are coming directly-directly from England?"

He leant forward eagerly towards her, "Yes, that is right. I came last week."

Her aunts and mother made little discreet noises to warn my grandmother. It was improper for an unmarried woman to address a strange man, even though he was her cousin. "And . . . and why are you coming now to Ceylon?" she continued, ignoring them, drawn by his beautiful, strange eyes.

"I want to meet my family and get to know them. I want to know who I am, where I come from." Defensiveness had crept into his voice; an edge of rawness, some wild sadness. The women saw this and their faces turned neutral and guarded.

My grandmother knew Charles would never get what he wanted. He had been away too long to establish the connection he sought. He should not even stay amongst these women.

My great-grandfather was sent for. Thushara Nanda and my great-grandmother wanted him to take Charles back to Galle, but my great-grandfather pointed out he slept on a cot in the rear of the shop. It was not a place for a young gentleman. They were stuck with him. Asking a guest to leave flouted conventions of hospitality; doing so brought serious consequences in a future birth.

In the weeks that passed, Charles became a disconcerting presence in their lives. He seemed to spend a lot of time sleeping in the men's quarters of Thushara Nanda's house, where he was billeted. When he was awake he would sit sprawled out on the verandah, his moody gaze following the women as they came and went in the courtyard. He was always polite when addressed, standing up respectfully. Yet he was stiff and shy around them, and because they did not speak the same language the women could not communicate much with him. When he occasionally went down to the beach and swam, a flutter of relief would pass among them at his temporary absence.

"Like a peréthaya," Thushara Nanda would later declare of Charles, "come to haunt us with his silent, starving presence." That was how they would speak of him later in their hatred.

My grandmother was the only one who felt sorry for him, and he must have sensed this, because he watched her attentively whenever she passed. If she caught his eye, he would smile and sit up, nodding in a friendly manner. Finally, one day, he asked where she was going with the basket under her arm and if he might come along. My grandmother assented. Rosalind was with her and would be chaperone.

They had hardly spoken to each other before and walked apart towards the vegetable garden. My grandmother finally asked shyly, "England is very nice?"

"Oh, yes," he declared, "it's the best place on earth." Seeing she was ready to be impressed by this mythical place studied in school, he began to tell her about the marvels of London and how he had seen the king, and about the wonders of the 1938 Empire Exhibition that he had seen in Scotland last year.

Of course, when they returned from the garden, both her mother and Thushara Nanda had a talk with my grandmother. She argued back, telling them they were being rude and unkind to their visitor. Charles was a nephew. This inhospitality was a shame to their dead sister's memory. Did Charles hear the argument and understand its meaning, even though he did not speak Sinhala? Or did he just sense the tension between the older women and his cousin? He began to waylay my grandmother as she passed, asking questions about the village and the world around them. He went with her and Rosalind about their tasks, rolling up his sleeves to dig the ground so they could retrieve yams, going up a tree to throw fruit down to them, carrying their heavy baskets. In the evenings, he began to drop by her house to talk about England, to show her picture postcards he had brought of London.

Did my grandmother fall in love with him? In recounting her story, she claimed all she felt was sorry for him. "I was stupid, Shivan, just stupid. I should have been more careful and listened to my mother and aunts. I should not have ignored that craving in him to belong."

In the midst of all the tension his presence brought, my grandmother kept up her nightly swims to the reef. It was as if the hand of karma guided her down to the beach at night as the moon grew increasingly full, her near-nakedness more and more visible.

One afternoon, my grandmother returned from an errand with Charles and Rosalind to find a gentleman in his forties having tea with the older women on Thushara Nanda's verandah. The buttons of his white linen coat strained against his rotundity, his cheeks flushed from the heat, round glasses perched on the edge of his nose. His bald head was shiny with sweat, a raw rim where his solar topee had sat, the hat now on the table before him.

Something had changed in Daya's aunts and mother. They were looking at their nephew with sympathy and curiosity.

Charles's face reddened. He took off his fedora and held it to his stomach like a shield.

This gentleman, Mr. Ariyasinghe, addressed Charles in a mild tone that was slightly jocular to hide his discomfort. "It's nice to find you hale and hearty, young man. Your father's relatives in Colombo were wondering what had happened to their nephew. They wish you back with them."

Charles flicked his hat against his stomach and scowled into the distance, ignoring my grandmother's surprise at these other relatives he had not mentioned.

"It has been delightful having young Charles," Thushara Nanda said, beaming at Mr. Ariyasinghe, who was cousin to Charles's father. "But we must not take your foreign relative over in this way. It is important he spends some time with his paternal family as well." The other women nodded, trying to hide their relief behind pious expressions.

Later that evening, Rosalind, who had heard from other servants, told my grandmother the reason Charles had left England. According to Mr. Ariyasinghe, Charles had been in love with an English woman who had led him on to amuse her friends, all of them entertained by the temerity of this dark colonial. Finally, there had been a public humiliation at a dance.

Mr. Ariyasinghe, a judge on circuit, would pick Charles up in a week on his way back to Colombo. The older women became very hospitable and gracious towards Charles. But he grew increasingly sullen and dismissive of their cordiality, guessing they were sorry for him but also relieved he was going. My grandmother would find her cousin sitting in a secluded corner of the garden, lips twitching as if carrying on a conversation with himself, or pacing the road that led to the family compound. She wanted to express her sympathy, to promise she would write to him, but there was a wild speculation when he looked at her that warned her to stay away.

A few nights after Mr. Ariyasinghe's visit, Daya returned from the reef to find her cousin waiting on the beach. She let out a small cry and clutched at her wet underwear to cover as much of her body as she could. "I . . . I'm sorry." He backed away. "I didn't mean to offend you." He turned to give her privacy. My grandmother grabbed her nightgown off the rock where she had left it and wriggled into it.

"Cousin Charles," she said softly, struggling to communicate in a language that was not her own, "you are not being seen here with me. It will only bring trouble for a young girl seen such with a man."

"Daya, Daya," he whispered, coming to her, taking her cold wet hands in his, "I love you, and I want to marry you."

"Ah, no, Cousin Charles." She gently pulled her hands away. "That is not to be. I am not feeling for that."

"Do you not love me?" he demanded tearfully.

"But you are not loving me," she said, and touched his arm out of sympathy. "You are wanting to belong and be like us. But marrying will not make it so. Only, it will make you unhappy, living-living with country folk. You will be missing your other life soon and then hating your wife."

"No! I will not miss that other life. I am nothing there, nothing."

My grandmother made her way up the beach, lurching as her feet sank into the sand. She was afraid of his appeal, afraid of her sympathy. But also, perhaps, afraid she did love him and that such love would only lead to misery.

Charles must have sensed her feelings, because he followed, importuning her all the way up the steep road, my grandmother saying, "No, no, it is not to be." When they were at the gate to the compound, he grabbed her shoulders and tried to kiss her. For a moment their lips met, then she broke away with a cry. The dogs in the compound heard her distress. They began to bark, the alarm spreading from dog to dog on each verandah. Lights in the houses flickered on as lamps were lit; the alarmed voices of her relatives and their servants warbled as they struggled out of sleep. My grandmother lifted the hem of her nightgown and darted towards her house, hoping to slip in through the back before she was discovered. Charles hurried after her.

They made it only as far as the middle of the courtyard before the women charged out, some with rifles, others holding up lamps, accompanied by male servants with sticks and scythes. Thushara Nanda had a torch. Its beam swept the courtyard and caught my grandmother and Charles. The long sigh of waves against the shore could be heard in the silence. Her nightgown was torn at the neckline, she realized, from the brief scuffle with Charles.

The women converged from all directions until they were a circle around Charles and Daya. Her mother, her aunts, her cousins, were ghostly in the lamplight. Charles pushed past the women with a cry of despair and ran to his room. My grandmother was left alone, the women staring at her as if she were a stranger. "Amma," she whispered, and held out her hands. But she might as well have been invisible to her mother. She turned to her aunts and cousins. Some averted their faces, others backed away.

Rosalind came forward and put her arms around my grandmother, who had begun to shake, her breath stuttering. It was the ayah who led her mistress to their house, the other women following behind in silence as if trailing a hearse, my great-grandmother weeping softly.

After that my grandmother became a spectral thing who stayed in her room or the back garden of her parents' house. She was their only child, and they alternately wept and railed at her. "No one would listen to me, Shivan. No one would let me tell my story. It did not matter. The damage had been done. Because, by the next morning, our servants had spread the word throughout the village. The marriage prospects of my unmarried cousins were in jeopardy."

So my grandmother lived like this, in seclusion. Sometimes she would stare at herself in the mirror feeling as if she had been hollowed out, no longer a young woman but a ghost.

Then about four months after Charles had left, Mr. Ariyasinghe came to call on the family. The story of what happened had somehow reached their family in Colombo. He did not mention what version they had heard, and referred to the whole thing diplomatically as "that regrettable incident." He told my great-grandparents that after Charles's humiliation in England he'd had "difficulties" involving unsavoury new friends and opiate addiction. "This is not a young man in charge of all his faculties," Mr. Ariyasinghe said, wiping his glasses and speaking in his measured, kindly way, as if in court. It was clear he felt Charles was more to blame than Daya.

"What good does telling us this achieve?" my great-grandfather asked bitterly.

Mr. Ariyasinghe nodded. "Yes, of course," he said evenly. From where he sat on the verandah, he was the only one who could see my grandmother standing inside by the threshold of the front door. Half glancing at the parents, half glancing at her, he informed my great-grandfather that he was a childless widower and would be "honoured and delighted" to marry his daughter. My great-grandfather did not ask if he wanted to see his future bride, nor even what her expectations might be.

"He was a good, kind husband, Shivan," my grandmother said to me. "He never treated me as if I were soiled. Yet he never asked what happened. In our time, those were not things people discussed, not even husbands and wives. And living each day with that unspoken thing, the daily knowledge that to my family and the world I was guilty of something I did not do, corroded me. And so I was never happy; that is, until you came into my life. When I looked up and saw you standing in my room, sniffling, my heart broke with happiness. You were like rain soaking a parched land."

She had finished her story and was waiting now for my judgment. I could not bear to look at her. By offering this secret she was hoping to tie us close again. But all I wanted was to be free of the suffocating weight of our past together.

"Why are you telling me all this now?" I asked harshly. "It's too late. Nothing you can do or say will fix what has happened."

"Ah, Puthey," she said softly, holding out her hands to me, palms cupped as if to receive a gift.

I could feel my throat constricting. To escape her, I had to deliver a fatal blow. "There is something you should know, something I have been meaning to tell you." I turned to her with a thin smile. "It wasn't Amma's idea we go to Canada. It was mine." She dropped her hands in shock. "It was me, Aacho, who went to the Canadian embassy and got that form. I begged and pleaded until Amma gave in and filled it out."

She searched my face in the hope I was lying, but I held her gaze. An ancient tired expression came over her. She stood up and hobbled towards the door. She held on to the door jamb for a moment to steady herself, then continued out to the saleya.

Another of my grandmother's stories, "The Demoness Kali," begins with this line: *As a forest fire raging out of control only stops when it reaches a lake or river, so hatred and vengeance can only be quenched by the waters of compassion.*

In the household of a rich merchant, the senior wife, who is barren, discovers one day that the junior wife is pregnant. Overcome with jealousy and fear for her status, she poisons the junior wife, killing the unborn child in the process. In her death throes, the junior wife makes a fervent wish for her next birth, "May I be reborn to devour your children," thus unleashing a bad karma that follows the two women through many lives. They are reincarnated as cat and hen, tigress and doe, the two women taking turns as aggressor, the stronger animal consuming the weaker one's offspring each time, the distraught mother making a fervent wish to be reborn to devour the other's young. Finally, after many life cycles, the senior wife is born as a noblewoman and the junior wife as the Demoness Kali. In disguise, Kali insinuates herself into the household of the noble-woman and twice eats her children, gobbling them up like plates of rice. The noblewoman gives birth again, and one day she is bathing in a river near the Devram Vehera monastery when she sees the demoness approaching without her disguise. She snatches up her child, who is sleeping on the riverbank, and flees. Kali gives chase, and since she has supernatural power she soon catches up, just as they reach the gates of the monastery. The demoness grabs on to the edge of her victim's sari, but the noblewoman rips herself away and rushes inside the gates with her baby. The demoness cannot follow, because the god Saman guards the entrance and will not let her pass.

In the monastery a great throng is gathered in the audience hall, because the Lord Buddha is giving a sermon. The noblewoman pushes her way through the crowd, and interrupting the Tathagata shouts, "Lord, you alone can save my child." She lays him at the Buddha's feet. The Tathagata sends a monk to fetch the demoness, and when she is before him he asks the cause of her anger.

She tells him of their previous rebirths. The Lord Buddha says to her, "Listen, demoness, if your body is unclean with spit and phlegm and snot, can you use more spit and phlegm and snot to clean it? In the same way, you cannot use vengeance to cleanse a past wrong. No, it is only the waters of compassion that can cleanse your past enmities."

The Lord Buddha instructs the noblewoman to place her child in the arms of the demoness. She refuses at first, but then finds the enormous faith to pick up her boy and put him in the hands of her enemy. The demoness hugs and caresses the child as if he is her own, rocking him in her arms. She begins to weep thinking of the two children she has already eaten. "My lord," she cries to the Buddha, "how shall I live now?"

The Tathagata preaches the Dhamma to her and she enters the first stage of enlightenment, becoming a stream-enterer. He instructs the noblewoman to take the demoness home with her. "Give her the first serving of whatever you make and look after her well."

The story doesn't end there, for denouements are often long in Buddhist stories and are, in fact, the point of the tale: Actions are easy to perform, but working off the karmic effects of those actions takes a long time.

So the noblewoman invites Kali into her home and places her in the rafters. But when the noblewoman pounds rice with her long wooden pestle, the top keeps hitting the demoness in the eye. "Oh, sister, I am in pain, this resting place brings no comfort. Move me somewhere else," she cries. The noble-woman carries the demoness and places her in a corner of the room where the pestles are kept, but every time a pestle is thrown into the corner it strikes her on the head. "Oh, sister, I am in pain, this resting place brings no comfort. Move me somewhere else," the demoness cries again. The noblewoman moves the demoness to the end of the hall where the water barrels stand, but when little boys rinse their mouths from the barrels, they spit dirty water on the demoness's head. She is moved to the hearth, but the dogs huddle there, leaving dirty fur and ticks on her body; she is moved to a corner by the eaves, but little boys urinate and defecate around her, fouling the air she breathes; she is put in the village compound by the garbage heap, but villagers empty their refuse on her head; she is placed at the entrance to the village, but little boys practise with their bows and arrows there, using her as a target.

Finally, the noblewoman takes the demoness from the village and places her under a tree at a spot that is between the village, where everyday life happens, and the forest, where the ascetics live. Here, she finally finds rest. The village prospers from her knowledge and advice about when to cultivate grains and when there will be rains. Through her good deeds, over time, the demoness changes into Bhadra Kali, Goddess Kali, the merciful.

PART FOUR

24

THE GARBAGE BAGS STAND READY IN THE HALLWAY. My mother's kitchen is bare of all food, her draining rack so swarmed with empty spice bottles and Tupperware containers some must dry upside down on the counter. They drip in the exhausted way of leaves after a storm.

I have gone further than my mother asked, have taken out each shelf in the fridge and scrubbed it, removed food spills in the freezer with boiling water. I've also moved the fridge, swept and mopped up years of dirt and dried-up old bits of food underneath, then done the same for the stove. I have taken apart each element and made sure there are no scraps below it, made sure not a crumb remains on any cupboard shelf. It is long work, removing all traces of food from a kitchen.

I see from the microwave clock that it is now two in the morning and so eleven in Vancouver. If I am going to telephone Michael, I must do it now, as he will soon go to bed. I have been avoiding this call, pretending not to notice the passing of time.

I dial our number from the kitchen phone, but when it starts to ring I slam the receiver down. Lowering myself shakily onto the stool by the phone, I lean my head back against the wall, waiting for my breath to calm.

Michael, before he left for work this morning, was oddly distant, not meeting my eye as he rushed about the apartment. He looked gaunt and severe with his wet curls flattened against his skull and glistening. As he slapped bread onto the cutting board in the kitchen, spread mustard, scrambled through the fridge for deli meat, he kept up a steady murmur of endearment towards his kitten, who had got onto the counter to watch, this hum of affection tightening to a snap if she tried to sniff his sandwich. I sat on the couch pretending to read the newspaper, my fear draining the words of their meaning. After a time of sweetness between us, he had fallen back into his grim mood. Finally, there was the roar of his blow dryer, then his verbena cologne opening like a flower in our apartment. He put on his coat and tied his scarf, and I went to stand by the door. Only when he had scooped up his keys from the hall table did he meet my gaze. "Well," he said, with a curiously wry expression, "be safe in Sri Lanka." He gripped the side of my neck with one hand, drew me forward for a quick kiss, then left.

I followed him out, bewildered by this goodbye, and watched from our apartment doorway as he waited for the elevator. He kept his face averted so I couldn't read his mood, couldn't tell if he was angry again. After a moment, he let out a strangled sob. "Michael," I cried and started forward. The elevator door opened. He lifted his hand, holding me off as he disappeared inside.

In our goodbye, we made no arrangement to talk, and seated by the phone now, arms folded, I understand that if I don't telephone him he won't call me. After tapping my fingers against my elbows for a moment, I pick up the receiver and thump in the numbers.

"Did you just ring?" he asks, when he comes on the line.

"Yes, but I got cut off."

"Huh, strange. And how are you?"

"Drunk."

In the silence that swells between us, I can hear the scratched notes of Noriko Awaya, the old Japanese queen of the blues, for whom Michael has a fondness. "How come?"

"I don't know, Michael. I'm just drunk, you know. D-R-U-N-K."

He doesn't respond to my irritation but asks in a pleasant tone, "How is your mother?"

I tell him she is fine and, to keep the silence from separating us again, describe all the changes to the house, how the old carpeting on the ground floor has been replaced by hardwood flooring, how the kitchen and hallway are newly tiled and the kitchen cupboards fitted with new doors. I am in the middle of my narrative when his breath changes rhythm.

"Michael?"

He begins to cry freely.

"Michael, what's wrong? What is happening?"

"I don't know, I don't know. I . . . I started this morning and can't stop. They sent me home from work . . . I was useless."

"But why? Are you so sad I'm going? It's only three weeks."

"No, no, it's not that."

"Then what?"

"I said I don't know."

I want to ask, as I've wanted to ask so many times in the last few days, "Are you planning to leave me? Don't you love me anymore?" But this is not the right time.

He calms down and blows his nose. "Look, it's getting late. I have to work tomorrow."

"I can't let you go when you're like this."

"Well, what do you want to do about it, Shivan? There is nothing to be done. I'm just crying. Is it really that surprising, given all the shit in our lives?"

"I will really miss you," I say, humbled, frightened. "It feels like I'm going for much longer than just three weeks."

"The time will pass."

I want to hear that he will miss me, too, that the three weeks will seem longer for him as well. But he says "Love you" and rings off.

I stand by the phone, knowing he will not call me back yet paralyzed by hope, knowing also that this crying all day is just another form of anger, even if Michael doesn't know it. Finally, I tug at the cuffs of my sweater, then go to get my jacket as I need a walk. All the plastic bags full of old clothes and food have to be taken down to the garbage hut. Once I pull on my jacket, I fumble with the zipper because my hands are cold. A chill has spread its way to my bones in the last hours, my muscles involuntarily stiffened to prevent heat escaping. There is nothing I can do about this coldness, though I have tried holding my fingers above an element on the cooker. I reach in from the hallway and pluck the garbage-hut key from a hook by the telephone. Then, clutching two bags in each hand, I stumble out the door. A thin film of ice has formed on the walkway. It rustles under my feet.

"Michael, Michael," I silently beg as I stagger towards the garbage hut, "where are we these days? Why are we caught in this strange tussle?"

❦

My flight back from Sri Lanka, that summer of 1988, arrived in Toronto just past sunset. I had an aisle seat, so couldn't see our descent over the city. I did not particularly care and kept my eyes closed, feeling that awful dullness which sets in once the sharp shock of a tragedy is past and you are confronted with the mundane day to day in which you must participate, dragging along your heavy pain. The thought of getting off the plane, going through immigration, finding my bags, seemed impossibly exhausting.

The wheels touched the tarmac and the plane shuddered. We hurtled forward at a fierce speed, then the aircraft slowed to an amble and stopped. The seat belt sign pinged off, there was a scramble to retrieve bags and jostle into line, then an interminable wait until the doors opened. I remained seated through all this, eyes still closed. Once the plane emptied, I took down my knapsack.

The grey corridor along which I walked was glass on one side, giving a view of the runway. Beyond it, the airport scrubland had that late-summer bedraggled look, the brown grass heaving and settling as planes came and went as if fur on the rump of some sleeping beast.

When I came out the sliding doors into the arrivals lounge, Renu and my mother were waiting. There was a stillness to them, as if prepared for the worst.

"Ah, son." My mother took my face in her hands. "You look so tired. Your eyes, they're so old." Her own eyes glistened as she drew me close and held me fiercely. "You're trembling," she said after a moment.

"Am I?" I asked into her shoulder.

Renu gave me a quick angular embrace and a fervent look. Then she grabbed my cart and wheeled it towards the elevator. My mother took my arm and we followed. When we were out in the parking lot, she pointed at a rather worn-looking red Honda Civic. "We bought a second-hand car."

Once on the highway, my mother driving, I leant back in my seat and stared out at the relentless ranks of squat grey buildings, their ugliness only emphasized by large, colourful billboards on their gravelled roofs. Grass growing in the highway medians accentuated the filthy rails and ponderous pocked overpasses. I gazed at the other motorists, jarred by the fact that they were mostly white. Soon, the effort of just looking was too much and I closed my eyes.

When we turned into Melsetter Boulevard and pulled up in our driveway, I said to myself, I am home, but no feeling arose in me.

"Shivan?" my mother said, after she got out.

I did not move. My sister opened the trunk and began to take the bags out. "No, Renu, no." Summoning up a burst of energy, I struggled out of the car, seized the bags from her and lumbered up the driveway, ignoring my family's warnings not to strain myself.

I had to wait for one of them to unlock the door, then I lurched down our hallway and dropped the bags by the dining table.

"You must be starving, Shivan," my mother said. "Why don't you have a quick shower and I'll feed you."

"No, Amma, they gave us a meal before we landed."

"Are you sure?"

"Yes, I am, thank you," I replied formally, suddenly nervous to look at them, nervous at what they might secretly think of my role in Mili's death. "It's late," I added, even though it was only nine o'clock. "You both have things to do tomorrow. I . . . I think I'll just have a shower and go to bed." I reached for my bags. Again my sister came forward to help, again I shooed her away. "I'm alright from here, thank you."

My mother signalled Renu to let me manage. "Well, if you get hungry during the night, there is milk and cereal, or crackers and cheese. Also lots of Sri Lankan leftovers, though I suppose you are tired of that food."

"Thank you." I stumbled with my suitcases to the basement door.

"Son."

I turned to my mother.

"If you need anything, wake us, okay?"

"Yes, Shivan," Renu added, "don't suffer in silence."

I nodded, then went down to my bedroom.

At the bottom of the stairs, I stood in the darkness, bags leaning against my legs like dogs sticking close to their master for comfort. I was afraid to turn on the light, as if something precious would vanish the moment I did. "This is silly," I muttered, and fumbled for the switch.

The basement flooded with fluorescent light, and there they were, my mattress with its scratchy brown-and-white comforter, my wobbly table teetering with old textbooks, the mossy-green tub chairs cratered with cigarette burns, that odour of damp carpet. I caught my fractured reflection in the mirrored squares and suddenly felt very tired. I lay on my bed for a while, then got undressed and took a shower. When it came time to use the scented aloe soap and citrus shampoo, I hesitated for a moment, feeling I was washing away the smell of Sri Lanka.

By the time I had bathed and changed into a sarong, the footsteps above had ceased, my family gone upstairs to their bedrooms. A stifling quiet was all about me, like smoke. I went to stand at the window and look out through its bars at the back garden. I could hear water rushing in the gully, muted male laughter and the throb of music from down there. On the other side of the channel, the apartment buildings loomed; trees at the edge of a dark forest.

I awoke at four in the morning, jetlagged, and lay in the dark, watching the dawn light gradually brighten my window, then fell back asleep and rose late.

When I came upstairs, my mother was cooking our Saturday dinner, something she always did in the morning before going to the doughnut shop. Renu had gone for her weekend shift at the shelter. "Ah, how did you sleep?" my mother cried. "Do you want a coffee? Some cereal? Can I make you bacon and eggs?" She was frightened to be left alone with me, frightened she would fail me if I broke down. We had become that estranged over the years.

"No, no, Amma," I smiled to reassure her. "I can manage."

Once I had eaten my breakfast, taken a shower and changed, I sat in a tub chair not knowing what to do with myself. Finally, I went upstairs again. My mother was rushing about the kitchen, checking pots, chopping garlic. I watched her from the doorway for a while, then offered help. She assigned me to cut up the brinjals and we worked in silence. After a while, she clicked her tongue in annoyance, "*Ttttch*, I don't have enough oil for frying."

I volunteered to get some from the Bridlewood Mall.

As I walked through our neighbourhood, I felt separate from everything, encased in my shell of stillness. The low-income housing complex had even more detritus on the sidewalks—a ripped car seat, a mangled doll, a hamburger squashed underfoot. An old black woman knelt in one of the minuscule front gardens tending her flowers; in another, a white man, wearing a singlet and red-striped pyjamas, sprawled in a lawn chair, glaring ahead, beer in hand; two women in hijabs chatted in a doorway while their little girls played hopscotch on the pavement. At a dumpster, squirrels and pigeons were feasting on the contents of a ripped garbage bag, grey chicken skins baking in the sun.

When I neared the Bridlewood Mall, my energy ran out. I could not bear to enter the building. Instead, I went to the pioneer cemetery in the corner of the parking lot and sat on a bench. As always, it was tranquil there. The surrounding trees still had their summer foliage, which gave the place an even greater feeling of being cut off from the world. I leaned forward, staring at the graves without seeing them. "I cannot bear it here," I whispered. Rising in me was a great longing to be back in Sri Lanka and also, paradoxically, a revulsion against being there. These two irreconcilable feelings pressed tight against each other.

The Monday after I returned, I went downtown to see if I could get any shifts at my old bookstore. The owner was pleased to see me, even though I had only informed him by mail of my extended stay in Sri Lanka. He did not have any vacancies. Walking farther along Queen Street, I saw a new store had sprung up that sold remaindered books. The tables and even the floor were cluttered with crooked piles of books; unvarnished shelves with protruding bolts and screws suggested a temporariness and haste. There was a Help Wanted sign by the cash register. The manager was behind the counter, and he warned me the store would be closing in a couple of months. He then offered me the job and I accepted. I would start the next day.

In the weeks that followed, I drifted through neighbourhoods during my lunch break and after my shift, wandering down to the lake, up to Rosedale, west as far as the Mental Health Centre and east as far as the Don River. I had no destination in mind, just trudged along, hands in pockets, staring at the ground.

Summer was in its last mad whirl, the Queen Street sidewalks crowded. Pavement stalls sold colourful Indian block-print skirts, Chinese paper and bamboo ornaments, silver bracelets and necklaces from Mexico. Already, the first knitted caps and scarves were beginning to make their appearance. There was a busker on every corner. Music students played violins and saxophones, swaying with self-importance; old men eked out melodies on accordions and mouth organs, their sad strains overpowered by the strident rhythms of seasoned buskers on guitars, banjos and ukuleles who would outlast young and old once the weather turned. Fire eaters and jugglers in medieval costumes performed to admiring crowds, a tarot card reader told fortunes in a parking lot under a gaily striped umbrella. On restaurant patios, revellers laughed and called to each other, couples kissed as if they were alone. The air was redolent with grilling hotdogs, sizzling fries and car fumes. I walked through all this encased in my still shell.

When I got home in the evening, I'd be so exhausted I would go to bed and not come up for dinner. My mother tried a few times to rouse me, but I glared and turned over on my side. Eventually, she left me alone. On her last attempt, I caught a wry grimace of empathy as she went upstairs. My sister was hovering at the top step as if fearing contagion. "Tell him he has to eat," she insisted in a high tone of annoyance, but my mother replied, "I'll leave food in the fridge. He can have some later." This was intended for me to hear. She understood my need to eat alone.

Late at night, I would pace my basement, stopping to stare out the window, my mind frantic as it reconstructed various paths I might have taken that would have saved Mili. If only I had listened to Sriyani; if only I hadn't pushed Mili to visit that house in Mount Lavinia; if only I had taken my grandmother's anger and disgust at Mili more seriously. I should not have agreed to leave the bungalow once those thugs had taken him, I should have phoned Sriyani right away instead of wasting time coming back to Colombo. I should not have trusted Chandralal's assurances. And always, always, my thoughts returned to the terror in Mili's face just before they dragged him away, his heels resisting against the cement floor. What did those men say to him? They must have told him he was to be taught a lesson for corrupting me, insulted him, called him a ponnaya. Did he hate me then? Did he curse me for putting my happiness before his safety? I would sit on the edge of my mattress, head in hands, unable to prevent myself from imagining the impact of their fists on his body, his face.

I had told my grandmother that, through her selfishness, she had lost the thing she valued most. But I was no different. By placing my happiness first, I, too, had destroyed the thing I cherished.

Once my mother said to me, as I was putting on my coat for work, "I just pray the resilience of youth will help you recover." She leaned against the wall and studied her feet. "Would you consider seeing a counsellor? Renu says the . . . the gay community centre downtown might have a list."

I was surprised at this, but then my anger surged forward. "What do they know about Sri Lanka, or what I've been through? It's all theory to them."

My mother nodded to say she understood. "I'm trying, Shivan," she said softly. "I really am." For a moment it seemed she wanted to say something more, but whatever it was, she couldn't bring herself to utter it and turned away.

A few weeks after I returned to Toronto, Renu left for Cornell. I had hardly seen her since I came back. She kept away from home with the excuse that friends were demanding her time and she had so much to arrange before her departure. When my sister finally stood in the hallway with her suitcases, waiting for our mother to come down, her eyes flitted about as if she found herself encumbered with an unruly class and was trying to keep track of her charges. She kept taking out her ticket and passport, frowning at them as if she didn't know what they were. Renu dreaded being tainted by her family's tragedies, and these last moments in our house were excruciating.

In those final weeks of summer, the September evenings were as hot as the days even though the sun was now setting earlier and earlier. Asters and goldenrod offered up their last flowers along highways and roads, then began to shrivel and brown, a new sparseness coming to the world, nature drawing itself in for the approaching onslaught.

And then in October, two months after I had returned, a letter arrived from Sriyani. When I opened it, an obituary for Mili fell into my lap. Mr. and Mrs. Jayasinghe had eventually given up hope his body might be found and held a memorial service. In the photo above the obituary, Mili was dressed again in our school blazer and tie and looked straight at the camera, his face blurred because of the cheap print. There was a note with the cutting: "I thought you might like to see this. Very sad. Would you like to write to his mother?" The accompanying address was for Mili's old home in Cinnamon Gardens, and below Sriyani had added, "The only good thing to come out of Mili's death is that his mother is back in her proper home. I doubt the father has given up his mistress, but it seems their common loss has brought them together. I might be coming your way one of these days. Sriyani."

This was her way of saying she had not forgotten me, that she hoped I was healing. I wanted to honour her gesture, but I couldn't write to Charlotte

Jayasinghe, even though I sat down a few times that evening to try.

The next day, during my lunch break, I was walking along Queen Street when I saw a man on the other side who I thought, for an instant, was Mili, with a milk tea complexion, glossy black hair, his same elegant, loping stride. Some urge told me I must follow him, so I crossed over and trailed the man. He entered a comic store. I went in after him and stood at a rack close by so I could see his face. He had a rather bulbous nose and a small moustache, and I was disappointed. I had been hoping he would be a replica of Mili, or at least a close approximation. When he left the store, however, I shadowed him up McCaul Street to the Art Gallery of Ontario. He sat on the base of the Henry Moore sculpture in front of the gallery and read a *Now* magazine while I hung back by the entrance steps and watched him. He was soon joined by a woman. They kissed and went in together. I thought to follow, but having to pay admission brought me to my senses.

I walked back to my job, an exhilaration taking hold of me that I didn't understand. Around me the trees were beginning to bristle with red leaves, and a breeze with a hint of chill blew up from the lake.

The bookstore closed. I joined a temp agency and, in late October, was posted to an insurance company for a three-month assignment, the only man in its filing department. The supervisor was white, the other workers middle-aged immigrant women from India, China, Iran and the Philippines. Our manager was obsessed with getting her nose fixed, though I could see nothing wrong with it. She also desperately wanted to adopt a baby from China and was indignant that the authorities questioned her suitability. The other women listened to her, cooing in sympathy, taking her hand and stroking it. They brought her sweets and cakes. I wondered if her petty dramas provided distraction from the anxieties of their own lives.

I began a sexual relationship with a man I met on the elevator. His name was Paul, and he was good-looking in an insipid way, with white-blond hair and skin that reddened when touched. He'd graduated from the University of Toronto with a degree in Russian and recently spent time in Moscow. He had a boyfriend there named Yuri and was saving enough money to return and spend a year with him. Paul had an apartment close by, and we went there once or twice a week on our lunch hour. There was a framed photograph of

Yuri on the dresser. He was also pale and blond, but with heavy features and a thick neck. While we got dressed after making love, Paul would talk soulfully about his Russian boyfriend, how he was counting the days to their reunion. I felt a hot prickle of anguish, like panic, as I listened to him speak of Yuri. For I, too, should have been dreaming of returning to Sri Lanka and Mili this fall, or counting the days until he joined me here.

Within a month of her departure, Renu was threatening to return, writing that she was homesick for Canada. My mother replied with sympathetic but firm letters warning her not to give up the wonderful opportunity luck and talent had put in her lap. When my mother told me about this, I wondered if she understood that Renu had no intention of returning. Her declarations of homesickness were motivated by pity and guilt, meant to console us for being stuck here. I missed my sister's fiery presence around the house, the whirlwind of her comings and goings, her certainty.

Then she phoned one day towards the end of November. "Have you heard, Shivan?" she cried, when I came on the line. "Sriyani is coming to Toronto. She has been invited by the University of Toronto and Amnesty International to speak on the situation in Sri Lanka."

I was too taken aback to answer, recalling now that Sriyani had said she might be coming my way.

"So, are you going to go?"

"I . . . I don't know."

"*Ttttch*, Shivan, don't be such a billa. You must go."

The university hall was crowded, a subdued hum of expectant chatter giving gravitas to the event. Most of the audience was Sri Lankan, though there was a scattering of white students—the kind who wore handmade toques, scarves and peasant blouses from South America and were earnestly interested in uplifting the "Third World."

The more affluent, integrated immigrants from Colombo sat in clusters near the front and spoke to each other in English. The men wore sweaters, ties, dress pants and sports jackets. A group of middle-aged ladies smiled and conversed with each other in an easy, familiar way, their hair backcombed, their blouses formal with shoulder pads and bows at the throat. I suspected they were Sriyani's school friends, or were related to her. A large number of

Jaffna Tamil men sat closer to the back, distinguishable because they spoke to each other in Tamil, were poorly dressed and wore unfashionably thick moustaches. There was also a contingent of South Asian students in the first rows who were probably members of the university's Sri Lankan Association. Looking at them, I felt how much older I had suddenly become.

The back doors opened and Sriyani entered with a white woman who was her host. A ripple of silence followed them as they made their way down to the lecture pit. I watched her draw near to my row and felt a swell of longing for the smell and humid heat of Sri Lanka, for Mili, for the life I'd had there. Sriyani wore a heavy coat, which made her look frail and lost. Yet once the host had taken her jacket, I saw she was wearing her usual Barbara Sansoni shirt and slacks as if in defiance of the cold weather. And as she shuffled her papers on the lectern, then squared her shoulders, she became even more the poised woman I knew. While the host introduced her, she looked around the room with that distant smile of hers, transferring it to the host when the words of welcome were done.

At first, Sriyani's talk described nothing so different from what I had already heard discussed by the workers at Kantha—abuses by the Special Task Force, the Prevention of Terrorism Act, the atrocities committed by the Tigers. But then she mentioned a new development I hadn't known about, having avoided any news of Sri Lanka. The conflict between the Tamil Tigers and the Indian Peace Keeping Force had reached a decisive point a month earlier in what was being called the Jaffna University Helidrop—an operation launched by the Indians to disarm the Tigers and secure Jaffna town. The guerilla leadership had been using a Jaffna University building as their tactical headquarters, and the plan was to drop three waves of Indian troops by helicopter on the university football ground and capture them. The Tigers, however, had pierced Indian military intelligence, and the operation ended with nearly all the Indian troops massacred. Sriyani saw this battle as the beginning of the end for the Indians in Sri Lanka. Neither the Tamils nor the Sinhalese wanted this force that acted increasingly like an occupying army.

Sriyani spent the latter part of her lecture talking about the growing violence in the south, where the JVP were tightening their stranglehold. In early September, they had called a country-wide curfew, and the entire population had observed it, even in Colombo. Not a shop, not even a pharmacy, had dared stay open, and there had been no vehicles on the roads. People were scared even to turn on their radios and televisions, frightened of being punished for not taking the curfew seriously. The insurgents were also beginning to attack members of the intelligentsia they considered traitors—left-leaning academics, human rights workers, reporters and artists who questioned their movement. In response to all this, the government had invoked emergency laws and killed many young people. The government had also increased its attempts to stifle dissent through censorship of the press and threats to human rights groups.

As Sriyani catalogued the atrocities committed in our country, I felt doors shutting inside me until I was in that numb, quiet place I retreated to so often. The only emotion I felt was homesickness, evoked by her accent, which had not flattened out like mine to accommodate being here.

When she finished speaking, only the students clapped. Then the discussion was opened to questions from the floor. A Tamil Catholic priest in a cassock leapt up. He treated the room to a harangue on all the wrongs done to the Tamil people and insisted Sriyani call the Tigers freedom fighters, not terrorists. On behalf of the Tamil people, he demanded an apology from her. She listened to him impassively, nodding. When he was done, she defined a terrorist organization according to the UN charter and said that by using child soldiers and targeting civilians, the Tigers fitted the definition. As she spoke, an angry murmur went through the Tamil sections of the room.

Next she was attacked from the Sinhalese side. A man in a suit and tie got up to say she was a traitor to Sri Lanka and that the government had the right to defend its sovereignty in the Tamil north. He demanded to know why she was sympathetic to the JVP and asked if she wanted Sri Lanka to descend into a Cambodia. She replied that she did not support the JVP but felt their grievances were real and should not be ignored. Government tyranny was not the way to fight insurgent tyranny.

Sriyani had mentioned she was here to raise funds for sewing machines so that women affected by the war could be self-employed. A white woman stood up to take issue with this, asking Sriyani if she was not perpetuating gender stereotypes by giving the women sewing machines. Sriyani struggled to hide her surprise and amusement. She answered simply, "Who are we,

Western feminists, to tell these women what they should or should not want."

When the lecture was over, the host invited everyone to a reception at Massey College, across the road. I had come not knowing if I would speak to Sriyani, but now I couldn't leave without making contact. She was surrounded by the Sri Lankan students, yet as I rose to put on my jacket, thinking I would get a word with her at the reception, Sriyani saw me and gestured that I was to remain in my seat. She said something to her host. The woman came and ushered me to an abandoned classroom.

I leaned against a desk, arms folded tight to hide the trembling in my hands. Soon the host brought Sriyani, then discreetly shut the door and left us alone.

She examined me, legs slightly apart, hands behind back, smiling in her inscrutable way. "Shivan, it is good to see you. I was hoping you would come."

I grinned and blushed, tears pricking the corners of my eyes. It was as if Canada had fallen away and I was back home. She gave me a quick hug, patted my shoulder, then stepped back. "But, my, you look older, nah? Is it your hair? Are you growing it out?"

"Um, yes." I could not stop smiling. "And how are you, Sriyani?"

She made a sideways nodding gesture. "What can I say, trudging along, trudging along." Then she asked rather urgently, "Was my accent clear, did people understand?"

"It was very clear."

"Good, that's good." She gave me a knowing look. "So, when are we going to see you again?"

"Back in Sri Lanka?"

"Yes, of course. What did you think?"

I blushed again.

"Now, despite everything going on there, you must return, nah? After all, your poor grandmother, her second stroke . . ." She trailed off as I stared at her in shock. "Oh, dear, but I thought you knew, Shivan."

"I didn't."

"Hmm. Well, I visited her after hearing the news."

"What happened? How is she, Sriyani?"

"Still fiery as a chili. But with this second stroke her left hand is useless. And of course the old servant woman really cannot manage. She told me your grandmother will not abide attendants and nurses in her house for fear of being robbed by them. The garden is a mess because she had a fight with the gardener last month. And I must say, the house looks ramshackle without a coat of whitewash."

Sriyani did not look at me while she spoke. She had known I was unaware of this stroke.

There was a soft knock and the host put her head in, wincing apologetically. "We should really go to the reception, Sriyani."

"Ah, yes, of course. Are you coming, Shivan?"

"I don't know."

"Well, hope I see you soon. It's time to come back." Smiling at me, she made a gesture of farewell that I will always remember, clicking her heels together, a small ironic salute. Then she was gone.

When I came outside, the world had transformed around me. Snow lay over the pavements in swirls and crescents, like fine sea sand washed by a wave. There was a hushed stillness, the cars and pedestrians seeming to hold themselves poised. Then the wind came down the street, picking up snow in a roaring cloud before it.

The next morning, I waited until my mother left for work at the law firm. Then I informed the filing department I would be late, and telephoned my grandmother.

Rosalind answered. When she heard my voice, she let out a little cry. "Babba," she whispered, "is that really you?"

"Yes, Rosalind it is me."

"Ah, baba." She began to weep.

My grandmother called out, asking who it was, but our ayah was too choked to answer. The clack of her walking stick echoed as she drew near. She picked up the receiver. "Who is this telephoning me?"

That old sadness rose in my throat. "Aacho," I whispered, "it's me, Shivan."

She was silent, her breath harsh across the line.

"I . . . I heard you had another stroke."

"Ah, is that why you called? Hoping I am going to die soon and you will inherit my fortune?"

"No, Aacho, no."

"Don't bother. I am giving everything to the temple."

"Why didn't you let us know you were ill?"

"Why should I, after the way you betrayed me?"

"Aacho!"

"Do you know how hard it has been for me, struggling along on my own, having to construct that bana maduwa and look after my properties? That is why I have ended up this way. It is you who has caused this stroke."

"Aacho, please, I beg you, stop."

"Now you feel guilty, nah? But it's too late for that. What use is your guilt? It's like rain falling outside a water barrel. My left hand is useless, useless! Through your selfishness, you have deprived me of my hand."

"Aacho, I . . . I'll come and see you. I'll return. For a little while at least."

"I don't need you anymore. I wish I had never taken you into my house. You have brought me nothing but misfortune." She slammed the phone down.

I went and curled up on my bed, stunned by her hatred.

When I arrived at the office later that morning and took up my work, I was thankful to lose myself in the monotonous search for documents along rows and rows of metal file shelves.

I was supposed to meet Paul on my lunch break, but instead went to a park across the road and sat down on a bench, my bagged sandwich next to me. The weather had taken an unexpected turn, and it felt more like the first day of spring than late November. A mild breeze came up from Lake Ontario, bringing an odour like fresh fish on a market stall. The last of the green grass was holding out in places against the surrounding brownness, and a few purple asters bloomed improbably beneath my bench.

Somewhere between that telephone call to my grandmother and sitting in this park, I seemed to have arrived at a decision. I had to leave Toronto.

When I finally set out in the direction of work, my step was lighter.

I considered Montreal briefly, but settled on Vancouver because it looked nothing like Toronto. There would be no reminders of my previous life, which was what I needed. Just as I had arrived at this decision to leave in some intuitive way, I also understood I would not tell my mother. I simply could not bear another parting.

Since Renu had left, my mother and I had fallen into an evening routine of dinner on the sofa as we watched *Jeopardy.* The show had no appeal to me, but my mother was gripped by it and often announced the answers or berated the contestants for being stupid. The evening before my departure, one of the categories was Broadway Melodies. I was good at this, and my mother knew nothing about the subject. When she got the first question wrong, I offered the correct answer. She pretended to be unsurprised at my participation, and when the next question came up she said, "Carol Channing's signature song? Now, who on earth is she?" I gave the answer, and we fell into a light patter of question-and-answer, even as my mind was churning with the secret I was keeping from her.

My flight was on Saturday afternoon, a plan I had made so I could leave our home while my mother was working at the doughnut shop.

I arrived in Vancouver that evening, just as the sun was going down between the mountains.

25

THE BOTTLE OF SCOTCH IS ON THE COUNTER where my mother left it. As I move about her kitchen once again, wiping and putting way the washed containers, I stare at it with longing. After I am done clearing the draining rack, I get the mop and bucket along with the detergents my mother carries around in a plastic basket. She has not kept up the house because she knows David will arrange for his cleaning woman to come by after the fumigation. Yet I have decided to go through and clean, unable to bear being idle.

In the powder room, I catch my reflection in the mirror and lean forward to look closer. Though I am not gaunt like my mother was during those early years in Canada, there is some inner hollowness to my face that reminds me of her then, scooped out by the memory of her mistakes. I sprinkle Comet in the sink and begin to scrub with a plastic scouring pad, pondering what she told me recently of her reaction to my departure and all the changes that came so swiftly after in her life. I've thought about her story often since I made this decision to return, imagining how she felt and thought, picturing moments, expanding scenes she only mentioned briefly, filling in things she did not touch on but which I knew had to be part of her journey, inventing and elaborating the story, like my grandmother with her Buddhist tales.

That evening of my departure, after my mother eventually did arrive home, she mistook my farewell letter for a piece of old mail left on the kitchen table and went about her usual routine of having a shower then dishing out food she had prepared earlier. She assumed I had gone out for the evening the way I used to, and was in the middle of her meal, seated in front of the television, when she felt a strange absence in the house. As she would later tell me, it felt like a piece of furniture had been taken away. She went down to my room and found the bed neatly made but then noticed my open closet, a jangle of bare hangers on the rail. Recalling the envelope on the kitchen table, she bounded upstairs and tore it open, hands trembling.

Dear Amma,
Life has become unbearable for me in Toronto and I have moved to Vancouver. I will contact you once I have a phone number. Don't worry about me. You must also know Aachi is ill again. Please phone Sunil Maama about this.

Your loving son,
Shivan

My mother sat down on the low stool by the telephone, letter trailing from her hand and brushing the floor. Through the thin kitchen wall, she could hear a child crying, the shimmering notes of what was probably Chinese opera. A couple passed on the street, talking in some African language. She went to the window and watched them, marvelling that the woman wore only a long cotton tunic under her winter coat, stockinged feet in slippers. They disappeared from view, and in the silence left behind, the house pressed in on her.

My mother, Hema, got her coat, slipped on boots and went through the patio doors into her back garden. She walked purposefully out the gate, stood at the edge of the gully and looked down at the water, not knowing why she had come here with such intent. Unsure what she must do next, she sat on the grass, its frosted spikes scratching at her coat and track pants. Clasping her knees, she stared across at the apartment towers, thinking of all the families in there, all the immigrant women with their impossible lives.

An old feeling of defeat dripped through her, bringing with it the memory of those nights after she failed her exams when she sat in bed, knees clasped, helpless to reverse her mistakes, frantic at her failure. She had not thought of her husband in a long time, but now recalled how she had found him dead in his office. And she wept a little to remember him lying there, like a child fallen asleep at a school desk, head turned sideways on folded arms, cheek pressed against wrist, his mouth pushed open in a cherubic pout, long eyelashes shadowing his cheekbones. She wept to think how she had failed him, and herself, because, if she could not love him, at least she might have been grateful for his devotion.

My mother didn't phone Renu to report my departure. Shame kept her from doing so. She believed she had failed both her children and that this failure had become permanent. It was like that old Sinhala saying: rice, once cooked, cannot revert to its former raw state. Her failure had made her incapable of offering her son sufficient help, and so he had fled to the other side of the country to escape what she knew was inescapable.

A few days later, she came home to find a message from me on the machine saying I had got a room at the YMCA. I had not left a phone number. A rage took hold of her at my lack of caring or awareness that she might be suffering too. Yet she listened to the message so many times the cassette ribbon wore thin and my voice became garbled.

At the doughnut shop the next weekend, her boss set my mother to clean up the "community board." This cork panel on which people could post notices was one of the owner's projects to make the café a "community space"—an aspiration she then undermined by directing workers to keep up a brisk turnover of tables, to clean the floor beneath dawdling customers, to whisk away cups and plates as soon as they were empty.

My mother had decluttered the board before without giving the notices much thought. But now, as she pulled them off, she found herself mindful of their contents—beloved lost dogs and cats; mattresses, cars, even pots and pans for sale; English, math and science tuition from people with only foreign qualifications; offers to cook and clean and babysit. As she peeled back these layers of appeals, she found herself thinking how much sadness and need there was in the world and how much a part of that she was. Then, towards the bottom, she came to a pamphlet with the image of a woman facing a turbulent sea. Above this was the title "Why We Suffer and How to End Our Pain." It was a brochure for a Buddhist meditation centre. Turning it over, she saw from the little map on the back that it was in her neighbourhood.

The centre turned out to be in a detached town house, about fifteen minutes' walk from where my mother lived. The ground floor had been opened up into a meeting hall, a dais at the front with a dark purple cushion on it. The room was already quite full, the majority of people white. Rows of chairs were lined up before the platform. Keeping her gaze down, my mother hastily took a place at the back. After staring at her hands for a while, she looked around. Along the back of the dais were elevated altars with statues of bodhisattvas and what looked like bottles of juice as offerings before them. She was peering between people's heads to get a better look at the statues when a man, who had taken the seat next to her, whispered, "Yes, it's most confusing, isn't it?"

Her neighbour was in his fifties, short and stocky, with thinning sandy hair that fell over his forehead. "Just like the Catholic saints of my childhood." He leaned back, hands placed self-importantly on his thighs. "Let me explain them to you. That one over there is the goddess Tara." He expounded on the goddess, then went on to describe the rest of the pantheon, my mother nodding awkwardly, wishing he hadn't singled her out in this way.

"And how did you hear about the centre?" he asked, the moment he was finished this explanation.

"The notice board where I work," my mother replied, in a cold but polite tone. She was by now irritated at being patronized by this white man with his lordly manner.

"And where is it you work?"

"The Bridlewood Mall," my mother said warily.

"Ah, I'm often in there. My daughter requires a lot of work on her teeth at the moment, so I take her to a dentist in the mall and wander around while I'm waiting. Where exactly do you work?"

She told him the name of the doughnut shop, feeling somewhat reassured he had a daughter. Also, she had noticed the wedding band on his finger.

"Well, I must pop by and say hello when I'm next in the mall."

He told my mother about the centre's philosophy, which was based on the teachings of a Tibetan lama—"our guru," he said, indicating a large framed photograph of an emaciated monk on an easel beside the dais. His officious manner and way of constantly checking in with her, eyebrows raised, forced my mother to keep his gaze, nodding. Her irritation climbed a level.

He had just started to expound on a charity the centre ran in India when a plump bhikshuni hurried into the room, head down, as if on some embarrassing mission. She mounted the dais, sat cross-legged on the cushion, settled her robes, took a sip from her glass, then surveyed the room with a surprised smile, as if the audience had suddenly materialized before her. An acolyte, who had followed, rang a little bell, and a silence that was intense, like the aftermath of a loud bang, settled over the room. The congregation gathered themselves into positions of meditation, hands cupped in laps, palms open, shoulders shaken and squared, spines settled in. My mother's neighbour gave her a nod of encouragement, and she took up a similar position and closed her eyes, glad to shut him out.

She tried to concentrate on her breathing, but soon the irritation this man had kindled flared through her with a greater intensity. Out of rebellion and spite, she opened her eyes, glanced at her neighbour, and despised the smug look on his face, the sweat that beaded his forehead. Typical white man, she thought with bitterness, so brash and cocky, always thinking they were better than anyone else. It wasn't enough she had to put up with their nonsense at work, now she had to deal with them on her off time too. The nerve, thinking she didn't know the first thing about Buddhism. She was from a Buddhist country! She looked around at the other people, and their meek expressions disgusted her. They looked like cud-chewing cows. Slights she had experienced in Canada, her anger at me, her humiliations at the law firm where she worked, the indignities she faced at the doughnut shop, fed into her anger at this man and the congregation, sweeping her up in a spiral of rage. Wisps of past wrongs, half thoughts, all those retorts she wished she had uttered but been too abashed to express, spun her faster and faster. By the time the bell finally tinkled, my mother was exhausted.

The sermon that day was on something called "The Four Limitless Qualities: Loving-Kindness, Compassion, Joyfulness and Equanimity." The bhikshuni went on to talk about the enemies of these qualities: attachment and hatred being the enemies of loving-kindness; pity, foolish compassion and cruelty the enemies of compassion; overstimulation and jealousy the enemies of joyfulness; indifference and self-righteous bigotry the enemies of equanimity. The measured tone of the bhikshuni tightened my mother's anger until she wanted to get up and yell at the woman to speak with greater animation.

Once the sermon was over, the acolyte tinkled her bell to announce a tea break, after which the bhikshuni would take questions. My mother stood up, grabbed her coat from the chair back and shoved her arms into the sleeves.

"But you're leaving already?" her neighbour asked.

His gaping disappointment nearly choked her. "I have to pick up a child," she murmured, and with a tight smile she wrestled her way past the people in her row towards the door.

Soon she had left the centre behind. As she bustled along a quiet street, coat pulled tight about her, arms crossed, feeling humiliated as if she had made a public spectacle of herself, she silently cried, "Why did I submit to such foolishness?" But then, as she neared her house, she found herself chuckling at how over-the-top her anger was, how completely out of proportion to anything that had been done to her at the Buddhist centre. "Oh, Hema," she laughed, "you fool, you poor fool." And somehow her words, her laughter, momentarily released the distress she had been suffering since my departure.

I had by now taken a sublet I found advertised in the *Georgia Straight.* A few days after I moved into the apartment, I called home during the day while my mother was at work and left my phone number on the machine. She rang that evening. When I answered, she was silent for a moment. "Shivan, this is Amma. How are you?" Her flat tone surprised me. I had expected some harsh accusation, or at least a note of anxiety in her greeting.

"I am fine, thank you."

"Good, that is good to hear. Have you found any employment?"

"Yes. Temporary work at an office."

"Good, that is good."

Then we were silent again.

When my mother spoke next, her voice was resonant with emotion. "Shivan, do you think I didn't know about all those afternoons you had to endure, sitting in your aachi's room? Son, do you actually think I didn't know about them? But what could I do? I was so helpless. After that one time I opposed her, I knew she would throw us out if I did it again. You think I didn't agonize that I sacrificed you so we could live there? I hated myself for it, but what choice did I have, Shivan, what choice?"

"I don't care about the past," I replied, my voice hushed and cold. "Let me get on with my life. I don't want this rehashing."

"Yes, yes," my mother said hastily, taken aback at her outpouring, "let's not dwell on all that. Tell me, is it much warmer there than here? Do the trees still have leaves?"

After my mother got off the phone, she heated a can of tomato soup, peeled back the cover of a sardine tin and put slices of white bread in the toaster. This was how she ate now, having given up any proper cooking after my departure. She sat at the dining table turned sideways in her seat as if perched at a food court counter. "Enough, enough," she murmured to herself as she slurped soup with a new charge of energy. But enough of *what* she could not name, until she was at the kitchen sink, washing up. She'd had enough of the past's grip on her. It was time to take her failures and bend them to something better. She would return to Sri Lanka and her mother. It was the only path that would save her son.

The flight my mother, Hema, took to Sri Lanka a week later arrived, like most international flights do, in the early hours before dawn. On the way into Colombo, the taxi driver complained about how difficult it was to get petrol now that the JVP had called for a work stoppage at the refinery, which none of the workers dared disobey. People had to line up for hours to get fuel, paying exorbitant prices. The poor suffered most, struggling to find kerosene for cooking and lamps. There were food shortages, and shops had to close for weeks when ordered. The intent of the JVP, whom the driver referred to by their popular name, "the little government," was to make it so difficult for the poor they would rise up in revolt against the ruling classes.

Halfway to Colombo, they saw flashing red lights ahead on the dark road. A policeman waved his torch for them to stop and soldiers materialized out of the gloom and surrounded the car. The officer indicated for my mother and the driver to lower their windows. As he checked her ID, my mother asked what had happened. The JVP had cut down a tree so it fell across the road, bringing down a power pylon and transformer with it. They could wait until it was cleared or take an alternative route. The officer did not grill my mother, despite her Tamil surname. There were greater threats at the moment than the Tigers. "You have returned to Sri Lanka at a bad time, madam," he told her, as he handed back the ID. "These dogs are ruining our country. They are punishing and killing our families and friends because we are in the security forces. But for every one of us or our kin that die, we will take twenty of them."

By the time she arrived at her mother's home, the sky had lightened and a mist was lifting off the road. The garden walls were slick with dew, the gate dripping. She stood outside without ringing the bell, sure her mother did not know of this visit and was probably still asleep. Rosalind had been awaiting her arrival on the verandah. As the ayah lumbered towards the gate, followed by a grandnephew who had come recently to help, my mother found herself thinking of the last time she had stood at this gate eighteen years ago, newly widowed, not knowing how she was to make a life for herself or her children, the future massive and swollen in its impossibility. All she had been able to do was move in a bewildered fumbling fashion to the next thing, and then the next thing.

Rosalind limped because of a recent back problem and the short walk tired her. She stood panting at the gate. As the grandnephew undid the padlock and drew back the bolts, the two women did not take their eyes off each other. Yet when the gate was no longer between them, they did not embrace. The grandnephew, Saman, took the suitcases and my mother and Rosalind followed him. As they went up the driveway, she marvelled at the knee-length grass, the blotched decay of flowers and browning leaves, the hedge tangled with creepers, the flower beds choked with a bilious green weed, the stone bench layered with slime.

"But how did it get so ragged?" she murmured in awe. "Is it not possible to hire a new gardener?"

"No one will come for the money Loku Nona will offer, baba."

They were at the house now and, because my grandmother was asleep, went around the side. My mother, as if walking among the ruins of a great civilization, took in the walls discoloured with mould and dirt, the cracks and holes in the kabook that would have to be repaired before the next rains, the rotting eaves and missing roof tiles.

The kitchen, at least, had been kept up, and Rosalind's herbs were healthy in their pots. When my mother was on the back verandah, she said to her ayah, "She doesn't know I've come?"

Rosalind nodded.

Taking off her shoes, my mother entered the house.

Though the saleya was dim in the morning light, she could see a brownish-green mould in a corner of the ceiling, its tentacles reaching in all directions. One of the doorway curtains was ripped, a windowpane cracked. The dilapidation outside had built up a great weight in her and now these final mortifications of her old home overwhelmed my mother. The task before her seemed impossible. She longed for Toronto, her little house, her sparse routine. "The next thing, Hema," she murmured to herself, "do the next thing, and then the next thing."

She went to her mother's room and stood outside it, the ceiling fan fluttering the doorway curtain against her shins. She nudged the drapes and stepped inside.

Her mother slept on her back, head turned towards the door, breath coming in quivering rasps, stirring the grey wisps plastered to her cheeks. With her loose hair about the pillow, she looked both girlish and ancient at the same time.

My mother's intent stare pierced my grandmother's sleep. She opened her eyes, contemplated her daughter, seemed to accept her presence as if part of a dream and turned away.

"Amma, it is I."

After a moment, my grandmother rolled over slowly, gazed at her, then closed her eyes, lips pressed together. She was still for a very long time. Finally, she sighed with a great tiredness and searched her daughter's face for some answer. Whatever she found did not bring her comfort. "Where is that Rosalind with my bed-tea?" She spoke as if she needed the fortification, the calmness, of her ritual, before facing this new ordeal. She reached for a bell by the bed and rang it. This bell was new; she had always counted on the strength of her voice to summon the ayah in the past. The bell was also a dismissal of her daughter.

As my mother left the room, my grandmother reached over and turned on the radio. The gentle drone of monks chanting pirith followed my mother as she crossed the saleya. When she was in her old room, she sat on the bed, mouth agape with exhaustion. Finally she leaned forward, chin cupped in hand.

"I'm sorry, baba," said Rosalind, who had followed her into the room after giving my grandmother her tea.

"Well, it's only the first day. She will adjust to my being here."

Rosalind did not reply. For the first time in all the years my mother had known her, there was bitterness in the ayah's face, and she was disheartened by this lack of comfort from the woman who had always bolstered her. Perhaps what she wished for was unattainable. Her failure with her mother had endured for too long, as it had with her children. To reverse it now was likely impossible.

"What a terrible country we live in, baba," Rosalind said into their silence. "A country that gobbles up its own young." And now she told my mother that recently, in Ratnapura, her ancestral town, three university students, suspected of being JVP activists, had been picked up at a bus stop by security men under directions from the provincial chief minister. The security men, along with the minister's son, had taken the students to an estate, cut off their genitals, broken their hands and feet, then burnt them. A post-mortem revealed that nails had been driven into their heads while they were still alive. This was why her grandnephew had been sent here, so he would be safe from such things.

"He is a bright student, in his first year of university," Rosalind added, nodding to acknowledge my mother's horror, "but it's too dangerous, baba, too dangerous. Better to be uneducated than dead." She sighed. "This movement is supposed to benefit us poor, but as always, we pay the price."

Later that day, while my mother sat on the back verandah eating lunch, her old ayah told her all she knew and had surmised about what happened during my last visit. She referred to my homosexuality as "the baba's strangeness."

When Rosalind was done, my mother asked, "Does *that one* come around anymore?" She used the derogatory "*araya*" to refer to him, and Rosalind knew exactly who she meant.

"No, *he* seems to have disappeared from our lives." She used the even more derogatory "*oong*."

"What about the flats?"

The ayah shrugged. "You must ask your Sunil Maama."

When my mother met with her uncle that afternoon in his office, she listened, her face neutral, as he told her that keeping up my grandmother's properties was occupying too much of his time, and that my grandmother had become almost impossible to deal with.

"Then we must start to sell them."

Sunil Maama laughed briefly in disbelief. "Daya will never allow that."

My mother shrugged. "She must. She will." She stretched out her arms and examined her hands. "And what about the flats? We need to ask that thug of hers if he will buy us out. Shall I go and see him?"

For a moment Sunil Maama was silent looking out the window, waiting for the weight of all that had happened to settle. "There is no need, Hema. I will deal with it. But you will not get Daya to agree."

In the car going home, anger bloomed within my mother, fuelled by her impotence to change anything. By the time she got home, she was electric with rage and stormed across the saleya to her mother's room. She pulled back the curtain and went inside. My grandmother was propped up in bed, reading.

My mother stood at the foot of the bed and gripped the rail. "I have been to see Sunil Maama. You must start to divest yourself of your properties. All of it must go. Particularly the flats. I have told him to contact *that one* and sell our share."

My grandmother examined her, that appraisal again. "Sunil does not have the power to do that. Neither do you."

"Then you must give it to me. I want, I demand, power of attorney."

My grandmother made a *humph* of dismissal at this ridiculous request. She went back to her reading, and now my mother saw what she was studying: one of those pious Buddhist tracts that temples sold.

To turn each page, my grandmother had to lay the booklet on her lap, flip the page with her good hand, then pick up the volume again. She noticed my mother was watching this and said, even as she kept her eyes on the page, "What ill luck you and your children have brought me. I wish I had never let you into my life." When my mother did not reply, she tossed down the tract, not caring if she lost her place, and thrust out her left arm, hand stiff like a claw. "You cannot do anything that will reverse this," she cried, her voice cracking. "I am only sixty-five and already a cripple. Tell me, what can you do that will give me back the use of my beloved hand?"

My mother gazed at that discarded Buddhist booklet. It, more than anything, symbolized the terrible place her mother was in. She backed out the room and quietly drew the curtain into place.

If my mother had been her old self, she might have given up now, accepted that this return had been in vain, that its central mission to save her son would never succeed, because my grandmother was so wounded she would never admit she had done wrong. But Canada had wrenched some new self out of my mother. She could not name this change, but she could see dimly its markers—those awful early temporary jobs, her attempted suicide, the years of rage, her children's departures, even the visit to that centre and her recent simpler diet.

That evening, my mother went into the garden. Rosalind's grandnephew followed, bewildered at the sight of this nona dressed in track pants and the gardener's old wellingtons, hoe in gloved hand. Rosalind came to watch, too. My mother crouched down and began to tear at the bile-green weeds that choked the flower beds. Saman stood leaning on a spade, gawping at her, until Rosalind gently smacked the side of his head. "Bolo, what is wrong with you? Can't you see our nona is working?"

Soon, between them, they had ripped out all the weeds. My mother set Saman to cut the grass, but seeing how inexpertly he wielded the scythe, she said to Rosalind, "Find me a gardener, any gardener, and I will pay the price he asks."

In the cool hours of the next morning, my mother returned to her flower beds, helped by Saman and a new itinerant gardener who did many homes on the street. She gave herself over to the task with gratitude, lost herself in uncovering the old beds, nursing back the flowers. At one point, drawn by a sense of being watched, she looked towards the front verandah. After staring into its dimness, she made out my grandmother seated in her old planter's chair. My mother returned to her work elated. "I am carried along," she murmured joyfully, "just carried along."

After lunch that day, she went to her mother's doorway, stood before the curtain and called out, "Amma?"

"Yes?" my grandmother answered peevishly.

She was lying down and struggled to sit up as her daughter entered, but she could not support herself and collapsed back on the pillow. My mother went to the bed without calling for Rosalind or Saman, who usually propped her up. "Now, let us try again, Amma," she murmured. She slipped her hands under my grandmother's arms and dragged her up into a sitting position. The effort caused both women to pant, and once my grandmother was settled, they stared at each other, breathing raggedly.

My mother went to stand at the foot of the bed, then changed her mind and sat beside her.

"Amma . . ." She made to take my grandmother's hand, and there was a jumble of gestures as my grandmother offered it and my mother withdrew her own hastily, feeling she had gone too far. "Amma," she continued, resting her hand inches from her mother's on the coverlet, "I want to ask your old baas and his golayas to come and fix the ceiling, the roof and the outside walls."

My grandmother's knee twitched in surprise. "You will not know how to deal with them. I must come or they will take advantage of you."

"Don't worry, Amma." My mother took her hand. "Aren't I your daughter? Haven't I learnt a thing or two?"

"Well," she said crossly, even as she hesitantly squeezed her daughter's hand, "don't agree to a price immediately, they will try to cheat you."

My mother arranged for the men to come, then told my grandmother the cost. "Aiyo, you are bankrupting me," she cried, shaking her head. Yet my mother could tell she had got a fair enough price from those baases.

While the men worked, my grandmother stayed in her room, and if my mother looked in, she shut her eyes and pretended to be asleep.

The workers were done in a few days, and when they needed to be paid, my mother went to see her mother. "If you cannot afford it, Amma, I will settle the bill myself," she said, as she sat beside her.

"Why can't I afford it?" my grandmother demanded with the weariness of someone speaking to the stupid. "Do you think I have frittered away my fortune in the last few months?"

Because my mother knew how much it would please her, she asked the baases to come and get the money from their old patron. They stood at the foot of the bed, and my grandmother hectored them about cheating her daughter. Did they think, now she was sick, they could take advantage and ruin her financially?

They had worked for my grandmother for a long time and were used to her ways, so they took this dressing-down with equanimity. Besides, she always paid them immediately, which was not often their experience. They were moved to see her state and thanked her gently when at last she thrust the money at them.

After they left, my grandmother said, as if her daughter had fallen short, "But there is still so much to do. And you are only here for a few more days."

My mother smiled. "Yes, Amma, there is a lot to do. But I can't get everything done on this one trip. Things will have to wait until I come back."

"Problems don't wait like that," my grandmother grumbled, trying to hide her relief that my mother planned to return. "Everything just falls to pieces in this hot, damp weather. See what just a few months of neglect has done to the house."

And so in this way, my mother took over running the house. She got the inside and outside painted, the caned seats on various chairs redone. She went out to my grandmother's properties and inspected them, taking along the same baas to each one so they could catalogue all the work that needed doing. She would not, however, visit the flats to inspect their progress. An accidental meeting with Chandralal would lead to a confrontation, and her rage would fracture all she was working towards for her son.

The day before her departure, my mother, Hema, said to her mother, as they had their breakfast together in her bedroom, "Amma, I would like you to dress nicely tomorrow morning. I want to take your photograph on the verandah before I go."

"But why do you want a photograph, duva?" my grandmother complained. "Take any old one of me out of an album. I don't wish to be remembered as I am now."

My mother didn't say anything. She spread butter and Marmite on a piece of toast from the tray in her lap. This was the moment she had been building towards since she took over fixing the house. "Please just oblige me, Amma," she said softly. "It is one mother asking another for a favour."

My grandmother stared at her and there was a struggle in her face. Then she plucked at the ribbon on the yoke of her nightdress, no longer meeting her daughter's gaze. "I wish that Jayasinghe boy had never come into our lives, otherwise none of this would have happened. From the day he entered our house he brought with him his bad karma, and it ruined our lives. There is nothing to be done about all that now. It is the workings of fate."

My mother put her head in her hands.

"But no matter bad karma. I know now that I brought some very good karma from a previous life to this one. Yes-yes, I must have done something of great merit in a past existence to get a daughter like you, duva. Like rain soaking a parched land you are to me, like rain on parched land."

My grandmother's voice rang poignantly hollow to my mother, these words poor compensation for what their speaker could not find in herself to do. My mother finished buttering the toast and held it out, her hand shaking. My grandmother took it.

Each day after breakfast, a Buddhist monk came to spend time with my grandmother, explaining the pious tracts he brought and chanting some pirith—this rare privilege of a private daily visit granted because she was giving her fortune to his temple.

That morning, as my mother sat in the saleya and listened to the murmur of the monk, she thought of how my grandmother became wretched and desperate if he missed a visit, thought also of the tracts my grandmother pored over, underlining sentences sharply, like a student anxiously memorizing for an all-important exam; she never missed a radio broadcast of pirith or bana. All these thoughts filled my mother with pity.

When it was finally time to leave the next day, she knelt in front of my grandmother's chair and, in the traditional way, touched her feet.

My grandmother drew her daughter up and took her face in trembling hands. "Rattaram duva, the house will be bereft without you. Promise me you will return soon."

"I will, Amma, I will." She placed her hands over her mother's, then sat back. They gazed at each other for a long while, both aware that, despite the promise, this might be the last time they met.

My mother stumbled to her feet and nodded for Saman to load the bags into the car, no longer able to look at my grandmother. When the car pulled away, she did glance back, but my grandmother had been swallowed in the shadows of the verandah.

Before she left for Sri Lanka, my mother had called to tell me she was going. The resonance in her voice when she said "I must do my duty" made it clear she thought I should go with her.

I knew the date of her return and that she arrived in the early afternoon. I was expecting her to call the same evening, and so I waited with dread for some verdict I could not name.

She didn't call that evening, or in the days that followed, and I found it difficult to concentrate at work. I drifted through my routines as if suffering from a low fever, unable to call her because of my anxiety and some misplaced sense of pride.

When she did eventually telephone one evening, I rushed to pick up the receiver, sure it had to be her.

"Shivan," she said after a moment, "it is your mother."

"Ah, Amma, did you just get back?"

Her silence made it clear she had seen through my charade. "How have you been, son?"

"Excellent. So much has happened while you were away. Guess what? I've got an eight-month clerical contract with the University of British Columbia which could turn into full-time work. The woman I've replaced might not come back after maternity leave."

I went on to extol the campus's beauty, then told her about my lunchtime routine of going for a stroll on the beach. I could feel myself growing further and further from my words, as if caught in a withdrawing tide. At last I became silent.

"Son, she is not well, not well at all."

"I see."

"Oh, Shivan, I don't know what to say to you, son, I really don't."

"Well, what do you want to say?" My voice was hard with fear.

"I hoped . . . I really hoped this illness had softened her, that she would admit to her error, that she would allow you back in her life. Then you could forgive and move on."

"Did you really think she was capable of that? Why on earth would you think that?"

"I tried so hard, Shivan, to please her, to love her, in the hope that would soften her. I don't understand, I don't at all. How can she call me rattaram duva but not allow you back into her life?"

"Rattaram duva? Gosh, how wonderful for you. You sacrificed me all those years ago to live in her house. Now you've sacrificed me again and made up with her. Once more, you have gained something at my expense."

"Shivan, don't say that." My mother was sobbing now. "Don't say that, son."

"It's true, it's true. I don't want to hear anything further about her. If you ever speak of her again, that will be the last time we talk. I'll cut you out, I swear."

I slammed down the phone, twitching with anger, but also heady with relief. My grandmother would never admit she was wrong, so I was free of her. I had no choice but to go forward with my life.

About a week after I spoke to my mother, I went for one of my lunchtime strolls down to Wreck Beach by the university. My walk took me behind the Museum of Anthropology. There were a few totem poles in the museum grounds, and near them I saw some ritual in progress and stopped to watch. A circle of white, mostly middle-aged, men and women swayed to the beat of a drum, arms held aloft, chanting in some language that could as easily have been Gaelic as Native. It was a healing ceremony, and the drummer was leading. She slowed her beat and instructed the participants to each place an object that symbolized heaviness in his or her life on a mat in the centre, then choose an item discarded by someone else. This chosen object, cleansed of its past heaviness, would represent a new beginning. As the participants converged on the mat, the drummer beckoned me to join them. I shook my head shyly and moved on.

Wreck Beach was one of the few beaches in Canada where nudity was legal. Even in winter, when there was a warmish sunny day, diehard nudists camped out in little nooks created by the massive logs and rocks that offered shelter from the wind—nooks they staked out with boom boxes, blankets, coolers, Thermoses and garishly flowered sippy cups to conceal alcohol. Each nook had its reflector, positioned to shine the sun onto naked bodies tanned the colour of blood oranges. Today was grey and the beach was deserted, but some nudists had left objects in their nooks as territorial gestures, and as I passed along, I found myself considering them—a worn pair of Hawaiian rubber slippers, a rolled-up tattered mat, a circle of troll dolls half buried in the sand. One nudist had made an installation, and I stopped to look at it. The artist had glued pieces of coloured glass, worn a smoky smoothness by the sea, onto a rock. Washed-up bottles had been inserted upside down in a semicircle before the rock, like candles at an altar. I looked both ways along the beach, then took out my wallet and withdrew a hundred-rupee note that had been folded small in one of the inner pockets. I pulled a bottle from the sand, slid the note in carefully so it expanded and was clearly visible, then stuck the bottle back in its hole. I pried off a prominent piece of coloured glass, creating a gap in the design. Scrambling out of the nook, I continued on my way.

I did not go back to the beach again until a sunny day had passed and the weather was grey and drizzly once more. The artist had understood my gesture. He or she had taken the hundred-rupee note and left the gap unfilled.

I walked away elated. But by late afternoon what I can only describe as a great inner parchedness took hold of me. It lasted a few days, then lifted.

During the evenings now, my mother wandered aimlessly about the house, unable to settle on anything. She wanted desperately to hear her mother's voice but would not call, because it was a betrayal of me. She also felt guilty because she had gone to gain my freedom but secured her own instead. Finally she settled for writing an aerogram to Sri Lanka.

On her first Saturday back, my mother was at the doughnut shop, absorbed in punching in a customer's order, when someone across the counter declared, "Why, you're still working here!" The man from the Buddhist Centre was grinning at her, head waggling side to side like a schoolboy contemplating some mischief.

It was soon time for my mother's break. She joined him in a far corner of the café, bringing along a doughnut and coffee for him, insisting employees were allowed this free privilege when he tried to pay.

He glanced skeptically at her sour boss, then thanked her. "I realized the other day, that I was holding forth so much I forgot to introduce myself."

They exchanged names. My mother liked that David was aware he'd been "holding forth."

"I'm so pleased you're still here," David said, smiling shyly. "Where have you been? I've come by a few times."

She told him she had gone to visit her "estranged" mother. He did not ask the reason for the estrangement but nodded sympathetically. "My wife was Cambodian, and she had family back home, though we were never able to trace them because of all the killings there." He told her more about his wife—how she had come here as a refugee in the early seventies; how he'd met her while teaching English to foreigners; a little about their life together. He was talking about her in the past tense, all the while unconsciously twisting his wedding band. Seeing my mother had noticed this, he paused, clasped his hands together tightly and told her his wife had died five years ago from cancer, leaving him with a son and daughter.

As my mother listened to the warble of sadness in his voice, she wondered how she had failed to notice the sorrow behind this man's forward manner.

David changed the subject, asking how long she had worked at the doughnut shop. When she told him it had been almost two years, he shook his head. "But that's far too long. You should be looking for a better job than this. The economy is doing well. I'm sure you could find something." His voice took on an evangelical tone as he began to hold forth on how she shouldn't be discouraged by the barriers she faced as an immigrant woman and settle for so little. He worked at a vocational college now and knew a lot about job placement. He would be very happy to look over her resumé, help her shape it, and show her some innovative ways of looking for employment.

He had assumed this was her full time job, and my mother let him go on, amused. He reminded her of that know-it-all Sri Lankan folk character Mahadana Muttha, who always got things wrong. The thought made her want to giggle like a schoolgirl, and she saw now that David was attractive, with a square jaw, fine sandy hair, strong forearms. There was something endearing about the earnest triangle of wrinkles between his brows as he "held forth."

26

IN THE DOORWAY OF MY MOTHER'S BEDROOM I take a long sip from the glass of Scotch I have not been able to resist pouring myself, the basket of cleaning equipment by my feet. On a high semicircular table beside the door is a photograph of her "guru," an emaciated Tibetan monk with a shaven head, seated cross-legged, one hand raised in benediction. To either side of him are statues of bodhisattvas from the Tibetan pantheon. There are flowers in a bowl before the shrine, a red, flame-shaped bulb in lieu of the traditional oil lamp.

My mother's fervency about her new faith can be excessive, her self-righteous quoting from the *Guide to the Bodhisattva's Way of Life* irritating, yet I am envious of her. This new spirituality has provided her a way to step beyond her history, to see her life clearly, with all its problems and mistakes.

I sit on my mother's bed for a while, fingering the pages of one of her Buddhist books, then get up and begin to dust. As I gently lift things on the altar and place them back, I find myself thinking of my grandmother's story of the hawk pursued by other hawks, how it finally lets go of the meat in its talons and flies away, bloodied and starving, but free of the thing that caused it so much suffering.

I moved to Vancouver in December 1988, and it was three and a half years later, in the summer of 1992, that I met Michael at a party in Kitsilano. The host, Bill, was a man in his fifties whom I had got to know when I was transferred to the President's Office, a prestigious promotion, that marked me out as a rising star in the university's bureaucracy. He often came by and perched on my desk for a chat, eyeing me merrily with frank interest, or leant in close from behind when giving instructions on a document he'd placed before me, his smell of cologne mingling with the faint odour of clove cigarettes on his beard and moustache, his belly tight like a drum against my back. He adopted a girlfriend-ish manner when talking to me, his high silly laugh sounding like he was faking amusement. Though I was not attracted to him, I could see he might be appealing to other men his age. He had a nice boyish smile and, despite the belly, was well built. He "pumped out" (as he put it) at the gym.

I was aware he had a boyfriend through other workers in the office, though he never mentioned this to me. Then one day the woman at the desk next to mine told me she had run into them at the Granville Island Public Market and, much to her surprise, the lover was in his twenties and "gorgeous." This surprised me, too, and suddenly Bill took on an aura of interest. I wondered if I was missing something about him, some quality of attractiveness that had escaped me. I became more tolerant of his advances, and when he asked me to a dinner party, I accepted, curious to meet the boyfriend and understand Bill's allure.

He lived in an art deco apartment building just off West 4th Avenue. When I came up the cobbled path, I saw a man of about my age seated on a second-floor balcony reading a book, head bent over the pages, bare feet propped against the railing. As I passed under the balcony, I looked up, wondering if this was the lover, and glimpsed a tangle of black curls, silky tanned arms, thighs that turned a paler colour beneath his white shorts.

Bill welcomed me into the apartment with a crushing embrace, his smell of clove cigarettes now mixed with roasted garlic and tomato sauce. "Ah, my dear, you're the final guest to arrive."

There were two middle-aged men on the sofa who I surmised were a couple because they wore matching hoop earrings, jeans, and white T-shirts under leather vests. An obese woman in a lilac cotton peasant dress sat to one side of them in an armchair. She had greyish-blond hair down to her waist and copper bangles embellished with multicoloured beads.

Bill introduced these three as very old friends, telling me that the woman, Moon, and he had been in grade school together when she was just plain old

Mary (which made her shake silently with mirth). Their pleasant greeting gave me no indication whether Bill had spoken of me before.

All the while, I was aware of the boyfriend on the balcony, who appeared not to notice or care that the guests had arrived. Seeing my glances, Bill called out with a proprietary smirk, "Michael, visitors are here."

Michael gave a little smile and raised his hand, but he kept his eyes on the page until he had read as far as he wanted. Then he snapped the book shut, slipped on his loafers and stood up. In his white, cuffed shorts and lavender dress shirt—its sleeves rolled up above the elbows, collar pushed back—he looked, I imagined, like someone on a yacht. As he strolled into the apartment, I tried not to stare at his rumple of curls, aquamarine eyes, angular features and lips whose colour spread beyond their borders, like a stain of pomegranate juice.

The others seemed to know him well, because they greeted him with lazy familiarity, not getting off their seats. He saluted them playfully, then turned to me. As we exchanged names and greetings, I was aware we were under scrutiny, as if Bill had arranged this meeting to entertain his friends.

I noted the book Michael was reading and said, stuttering, "Oh . . . um, *Clear Light of Day*, my sister has that. I've read it. I liked it."

"She's an author my mother loves," he replied, turning the book over and looking at its cover. "So I thought I would give her a try."

Anita Desai was not the sort of writer one might find easily in a bookstore. I knew this from working in one and browsing through many. I wanted to ask how Michael's mother had discovered the writer, but instead nodded stiffly and accepted the glass of wine Bill was holding out to me with a smirk that said, Yes, you have undervalued my charms.

Now I was sure I had been invited to learn this lesson and that the other guests were in on the plan. I glanced at Michael, but his remote smile conveyed nothing. With a polite nod to me, he went to put his book away in the bedroom and emerged sometime later, curls slightly damp.

The evening progressed in the way these parties always did for me, with white people talking while I remained silent, my fixed smile gradually dissolving as I drank more, my laugh increasingly hectic. Michael moved with graceful ease among the guests, sitting for a time between the couple on the sofa then sprawling over the arm of the woman's chair, hand resting on her shoulder. They treated him with fondness, as they would a nephew, and he took their attention with what I felt was the entitlement of the beautiful.

At one point I went to get some wine from the galley kitchen, and Michael sauntered in and stood by the fridge, right foot perched on left like a stork, hands jammed in pockets, his neck strained back as if to look over a fence, something diffident in his posture. He said nothing for a moment, observing me with a restrained smile. Then we both spoke at once.

"Bill tells me you work—"

"How come your mother—"

We each gestured for the other to speak, and I said, "How does your mother know of Anita Desai?"

He shrugged and smiled. "Some small bookstore in Kitsilano . . . you know, for people who consider their tastes to be above the plebeian readers." He said this fondly, as if he found his mother's snobbishness endearing. "Besides, Desai isn't nobody. She's been nominated for the Booker a couple of times."

"Indeed," I said, nodding vigorously. After the silence came between us again, I asked, "What were you going to say?"

"Oh, just that I might be starting work at the university too. I've applied for a job." Then, seeing what I was surmising, he added defensively, "And no, it's not Bill's influence. A completely different department."

"Of course, of course," I said quickly.

Then we were grinning at each other, as if our exchange had been funny.

"Well, if you do get this job, one of the perks is the long lunch break. Enough time to get down to Wreck Beach and ogle the nudists."

"I don't need the lunch break for that. I occasionally go down there anyway." He waited for his meaning to sink in and caught the quick flit of my eyes as I mentally undressed him. Then he let out a throttled laugh, head thrown back as if struggling to release the mirth from his throat.

In an instant Bill was in the kitchen. He gave us both a sharp look. I blushed from being caught out and Michael smirked. "Young men," Bill cried waspishly, "away with you. I must begin *le dîner.*"

After that, though Michael and I did not talk again that evening, I was aware some connection had formed between us, that we were oddly on the same side against the other guests.

About a month later, the phone rang one evening, and when I picked it up a man asked for Shivan Rassiah. His accent was Canadian, and yet, remarkably, he pronounced my name correctly.

"Who is this?" I demanded.

"It's Michael," he said, as if surprised I had not figured it out.

I was silent, then I blurted, "How did you . . .?"

"My contacts at the university."

"Oh," I said, and then "oh" again, puzzled that Bill had provided my phone number, given his apparent jealousy over our conversation in the kitchen.

"No, no," he replied with a chortle. "The dean of arts. My mother. She's had this secretary for years, Anjula Wickramatunga. Sri Lankan," he added, not realizing I could figure this out from her surname. "I just asked her to inquire around. You're the sole Sri Lankan guy working in the President's Office. Then I looked you up in the directory. There is only one of you in Vancouver, by the way."

"My goodness, I'm unique," I quipped to hide my astonishment. "Well, you're quite the detective," I added, wanting confirmation of his interest. "That's a lot of trouble to take."

"It was worth the effort," he said quietly. "How about dinner? Would you like to come on Friday?" There was a sheepish lilt to his voice.

"Yes, sure. Where?"

"Well, Madam Dean and Mr. Dean are away for a few days and I have their well-appointed home in Point Grey to housesit. Wanna come over?" He gave me the address. Before he got off the phone, he said, "By the way, Bill and I are no longer an item. That ended a couple of days after the party."

"Ah," I replied. Now I understood why Bill had seemed curiously subdued in the last month, not coming by my desk to chat and flirt in his old way.

Michael's family home was so charming, I stood for a while on the pavement outside to admire it. A two-storey house with a broadness that hinted at spacious rooms, it nonetheless had a cottage-like charm because of its greyish-blue clapboard siding, multicoloured stained-glass windows and steeply sloping slate roof with wide eaves. The fence on both sides of the house was long, and like many fences in this moist city, its slats had the water-logged blackness of driftwood. A green creeper spilled wildly over the top, pink flowers in the tangled tendrils.

Michael had left the front door open, screen closed. I rang the bell and watched him come towards me down the gloom of a hallway, emerging into light on the other side of the door. As he let me in, he smiled, lips pressed together. "Ah," I said and gestured at his Sri Lankan batik shirt, unmistakable in its gaudy colours and border of trumpeting elephants, "a gift from Anjula Wickramatunga, worn in my honour?"

He laughed in that nerdy way of his, and I was pleased my humour worked with him. His laugh made his beauty less intimidating.

Michael gestured for me to go past him into the hall, then turned on a light. As I offered him my bottle of wine, I took in the polished oak floors and the expensive-looking kilim beneath our feet. Beside the antique hall-stand stood a tall wooden African carving of an antelope, graceful and stylized in the way a tourist trinket would not be. As we passed two doorways on our left, Michael waved his arm, saying, "living room, dining room," drawling out the vowels to show he was being dismissive of the expensive Persian rugs, the comfortable sofas and armchairs, the Arts and Crafts dining set, the silver coffee and tea services, the walls lined with books that looked well read because of the way they were crammed in, spines faded and loose.

The hallway ended at an enormous kitchen with an island in the middle, expanses of quartersawn oak floor between it and the surrounding cabinets, which were of a light-coloured wood and made in the Shaker style. The countertops were black slate, the appliances stainless steel. At one end of the room, a bay window looked out over the extensive garden. Michael had been preparing dinner, and he went back to it. An Indian meal, I could tell from the smell and spice containers on the counter. Unlike my mother's old jam and pickle bottles with their faded and peeling labels, Michael's little glass jars had black lids with spice names stencilled on them. They had magnetic bottoms, and after he had used one, he would stick it back on a stainless steel panel so its name faced out front. I watched him for a short while as he pretended to be absorbed in his task, bending periodically over a cookbook, elbow on counter, hand cupping chin. He was trying to make me comfortable by keeping at his task. There was an assured grace in this gesture; it was how the family made guests feel at home. Taking my cue from him, I drifted over to the bay window, knelt on a distressed red leather seat in the alcove and looked into the garden with its massive ferns and hostas, purple-flowered thyme growing in the gaps of the cobblestone patio.

I noticed the bookshelves on either side of the window and called back to Michael, "Someone in your family must really like poetry."

"Mr. Dean's," he called back. "He's a poet, a published one." I turned to him in surprise, and he nodded as if confirming gossip about someone we both knew. "One of those West Coast types. The poetry's all about driftwood logs, kelp and the sea. Oh, and of course the working man." He grimaced. "Don't be fooled by all this. Madam Dean and Mr. Dean are old hippies. Michael is my middle name, which fortunately my grandparents insisted on. Guess what my first name is."

I drifted back, stood close to him and shrugged as one might with an intimate, a boyfriend.

"Breeze." He started to laugh, but seeing I was looking at him solemnly, he stopped, mouth slightly open, then leaned in and kissed me dryly on the lips.

"I like that," I said, reaching out to grip his bicep as he pulled away.

"What?" he asked, hoarsely.

"That you make all the first moves."

"Others don't?"

I shook my head slowly, not taking my eyes off his.

"Huh," he said, as if surprised other admirers could have been so apathetic about trying to win me. He returned to chopping tomatoes. The rapping sound of knife on cutting board reverberated between us.

"Waiting . . ." I said, grinning.

He threw down the knife with a huff of amusement, washed and wiped his hands, then came to me.

"Ah-ah." I gestured at his stained apron.

He shook his head to say I was incorrigible, shucked the apron off, then moved in again, his knees against mine. He took my face in his hands and looked at me solemnly, then kissed me, his hands sliding back to caress my ears.

We made love in Michael's bedroom, which was the same blue as the house's exterior, accented with darker blue baseboards. The bed had a coral duvet; the walls were covered with framed Japanese film posters. I'm not sure why I thought he would be an awkward lover, but he moved up and down my body with fluidity and grace. He kissed without fully opening his mouth, taking my tongue between his teeth and biting on it gently, this refusal to grant me entry increasing my desire. There was a slight roughness to him, his hands and teeth leaving marks on my skin, which added a charge to our lovemaking.

And yet, aroused as I was, a familiar despair soon materialized, as it did whenever I made love now. It was not a particular memory of Mili, but rather an inner hollowness into which I sank, then surfaced, again and again; and in those moments of surfacing, the colour of Michael's skin, the part of his body I was running my tongue or hand over, was crushingly alien.

When we were done, I lay on my back with Michael's head against my chest and looked out the window, a great sob welling up in me. I kept it down by clenching my fists. "I am starving," I finally said, after I had gained enough control of my voice. Michael raised his head to kiss me before getting out of bed. I wanted to keep lying there, to have some time to myself, and he must have sensed this, because he drew the duvet up to my chin and whispered, "No need to hurry down, hey?"

Once he was gone, I waited for my despair to propel me out of bed, make me scramble into my clothes, go downstairs and offer some brusque excuse about why I had to leave. Instead, to my surprise, the despair began to subside, becoming muted, it seemed, by the peaceful colours of this bedroom, the blue-haloed mountains through its window. When I went down to dinner, however, I saw it was really Michael who had subdued my desolation. There was a graceful ease in his relations with others, the same ease I had seen with the guests at Bill's party. Loving or liking someone, thinking well of someone, came effortlessly to him. He felt no anxious need to amuse or entertain me or keep up the conversation, and this made me relax too. During my years in Vancouver, I had never stayed over at a lover's place. Michael seemed to assume I was going to, and I found myself slipping into his assumption without protest.

This ease of being with Michael continued over the weekend. On our first morning together, after we had been out for a walk and returned, Michael picked up a translated Japanese novel called *Kitchen*, which he had left face-down on the hallstand, and became instantly absorbed, right foot balanced on left ankle, not ignoring me but somehow encompassing my presence in his absorption. I went to the washroom and came back to find him in the living room sprawled across an armchair, lost in the book. He finished his paragraph, marked the page, looked up at me as I stood over him, and asked mildly, "What would you like to do?" as if we were an old married couple. We ended up reading for an hour, me pretending to be engrossed in a book but looking over at Michael from time to time, filled with wonder at this new tranquility I felt. For lunch, Michael dug around in the fridge and produced olives and cheese, then made a salad of tomato, basil and bocconcini drizzled with balsamic vinegar. I had not yet heard of cheeses like bocconcini, nor tasted balsamic vinegar, and was surprised at how much better these olives were compared to the brine-soaked ones I had eaten from a bottle.

That evening, after we had gone for a swim on Jericho Beach and were on our way home, Michael took me to an expensive grocery store nearby, on 4th Avenue. "What do you want to eat?" he asked.

I was taken aback, having assumed he'd come with a recipe in mind. "Mussels," I declared to test him, smiling wickedly. He winked, nodded and moved quickly about the store, picking various items and holding them up with a grin to say he was meeting the challenge. That night, we had seafood pasta in a white wine sauce, and it was delicious.

The next day, we came back from an afternoon movie to find his parents' car in the driveway. "Ah," Michael said with satisfaction as he took my hand, "Madam Dean and Mr. Dean are home." He quickened his pace as if he couldn't wait to present me. His confidence lessened my nervousness.

Suitcases crowded the hall and we heard someone moving around upstairs.

"Michael?" A woman's voice fluted down.

"Yes, Hilda, 'tis I. Where's Robert?" I gave him a sharp look, and he smiled, enjoying my surprise that he called his parents by their first names.

There was a flurry of footsteps across the floorboards above, then his mother came lightly down the stairs. Hilda was a tall, slim woman with greying hair cut in a bob, her light cotton dress showing off tanned limbs. With her narrow chest, small breasts, long neck and sinuous legs, she looked like an ex-ballerina, an effect enhanced by her flat satin slippers. She gave me a friendly nod and kissed Michael in a formal way, cheek brushing cheek.

"It's very nice to meet you, Shivan." She shook my hand without waiting for an introduction, seeming genuinely happy to meet me. Though soft spoken, there was a focus and confidence in her bearing and I imagined she could be formidable without ever raising her voice. "Did you boys have a nice weekend here?"

I nodded, a little embarrassed that she presumed so blithely I'd slept over in their home.

"Ah, kiddo," a man called out from the kitchen end of the hallway, and Robert came towards us. Michael had got his looks from his father, who, even in his late fifties, was handsome, his soft greying curls and round tortoiseshell glasses giving him a boyish look.

Michael's parents had brought a chicken pie, and they invited me to join them for an early supper before going. By now I was at ease with them; like Michael, they made no extra fuss to please me and went about their tasks as if I were an old friend. While Robert tossed a salad and Hilda opened a bottle of wine, Michael set places at the kitchen island, where I was perched on a stool, telling Hilda about the goings-on in the President's Office, pleased that she was so impressed at my rapid rise in the university. Michael kept smiling and nodding, and at first I thought he was trying to reassure me, but then I realized he wanted confirmation that his parents were splendid, that I admired them as much as he did. Earlier, I hadn't known how to take his "Madam Dean and Mr. Dean," unsure if it was boasting. But now I saw the nicknames were just an ironic way to hide his genuine admiration for Hilda's achievements.

Once we were all seated, Robert asked me, "Now, how did the two of you meet?"

"At . . . at the home of someone I work with." I glanced quickly towards Michael, unsure what his parents knew.

"Bill," Michael added.

"Oh, goodness, Bill," his mother murmured and shook her head. "I'm very glad that is over. I can't believe I introduced the two of you."

Michael grinned at me. "Bill used to work under Hilda in the dean's office."

This was the first time Bill had come up, and I held Michael's gaze for a moment. He looked away easily, as if he had nothing more to communicate on the subject.

"I certainly would not have introduced you if I'd known what would happen," Hilda continued.

"Don't worry, *mother*," Michael said with a laugh, and touched her wrist, "I am over my old-man phase."

"You and your phases and passions, kiddo." Robert aimed a fork at Michael as if it were a gun.

Michael's parents elaborated on his "phases and passions," how he had sported a white umbrella in all weathers when he was ten, attempted to master Sanskrit at sixteen, taken up Irish dancing because of a boyfriend, even going to university in Dublin for a year because of him. I also learnt that for the longest time Michael had been interested in Japanese culture and had studied the language at university. "A Japanophile," his parents kept calling him.

Michael enjoyed his parents' teasing, shaking his head at me as if disavowing what they said.

When we parted that evening, I proposed he come over to my apartment for dinner the next night. "After all," I said, gesturing to my too-large T-shirt and rolled-up jeans, "I have to return these to you."

He took me by the elbow, kissed me chastely on the cheek and whispered, "Thank you for a really nice time." Then he added, "About Bill. I didn't bring him up over the weekend because I didn't want his ghost hanging around and spoiling our time together. You work with him, after all . . . and, well, he's a nice guy. I genuinely liked him, but nothing more. I was clear with him about that. Not in love, you understand. Not bowled over."

He looked hard at me to say that I, however, bowled him over.

As the bus took me home from Point Grey to Vancouver's Downtown Eastside, where I was subletting an apartment, the neighbourhoods grew treeless and shabby. I felt all the goodness of the weekend leaking out of me, and by the time I arrived at my apartment, the feelings of despair and grief and rage that periodically engulfed me had come back with renewed vigour. Driven by a familiar compulsion, I kicked off my shoes, went into the bedroom, knelt before the dresser and pulled open the bottom drawer. At the back was a faded biscuit tin in which I kept important documents. From a white envelope, whose aging paper had browned in concentric rings, as if successive teacups had been placed on it, I drew out the newspaper article that had appeared after Mili's abduction, along with the obituary Sriyani had sent. Spreading them out on the carpet, I stared at the faded images: Mili holding aloft a cricket trophy, grinning in his easy, confident way; Mili dressed in our school blazer and tie, looking sombrely at the camera. I sat back on my haunches, eyes closed, wretched.

I didn't sleep much that night. When Michael arrived at my apartment the next evening, I held him fiercely, then pushed him up against the hallway wall and kissed him, pulling at his shirt buttons. "Whoa," he said, laughing but disconcerted, "doesn't a person even get to take his shoes off?"

"We'll deal with the shoes later." I pressed my mouth against his.

After we made love, the restlessness was still with me. When we were done dinner, I suggested a stroll along the beach; walking until exhausted might numb my agitation. Michael had been looking at me quizzically all evening, sensing my distraction, and now I felt him watching me as he struggled to keep up with my brisk pace. Finally, he touched my arm to stop me.

"Everything alright?" He cocked his head.

I was still for a long moment, then blurted out, "I'm sorry, Michael. I haven't told you the whole story of my life . . . I . . . You see, I don't know how much you understand about Sri Lanka, it's recent history. The horror of it." Then I told Michael about the 1983 riots, brushing over my family's personal experience by saying, "We were lucky because Sinhala friends hid us." I described instead, to an aghast Michael, what had happened to Tamil people, my voice ringing with the real anger I felt towards my country and all that had occurred to me there, but also hoping that the tide of my angry words would carry me to a place where I was able to tell the full truth. It didn't. Instead, I found myself telling him of my mother's unhappiness and widowhood in Sri Lanka, implying it carried the same social taboo as in India, saying that she had struggled in relative poverty to raise us, and that this had soured her. I relayed all this in terse sentences. Then, in greater detail, I elaborated on my mother's attempted suicide, her rages at me and my sister, what she had said when I told her I was gay.

I spoke rapidly, my words carrying me breathless, beyond thought, beyond conscience, desperate to share my unhappiness with Michael in the only way I seemed able, drawing comfort from his sympathy, from the way he took my hand and pressed it as we walked along. My bewilderment at my failure turned to rage as I spoke of my mother, so that when I ended my story at last, I cried to him, "Can you imagine, Michael, she said she would rather have aborted me, rather strangled me at birth, than have a gay son? Can you imagine a mother saying something so awful, a mother being such a bitch?"

By the time I finished, we were seated on a promontory, waves crashing close to our feet.

"Well, I do attract them," Michael said with a rueful laugh. "That old boyfriend I followed to Dublin spent his teenage years in foster care. I suppose it's because I come from a stable home." He said this reflectively, but I detected the faintest trace of smugness in his voice.

"So, you don't mind, then, that I'm fucked up?"

He put his arm around my shoulder. "I'm afraid it's too late to mind." He gave me that same hard look he had used to say he was bowled over by me. "You were right to choose Vancouver, Shivan, to make a life for yourself away from all that pain. And I'm glad you did, because now, see, I have you."

"I . . . I don't want you to think my mother is some truly horrid person," I said, wanting to distance myself now from my impulsive confession. "She has come around to accepting who I am."

"No, no, Shivan," he assured me, "she's just human."

After that, Michael and I spent every evening together, and within a month I moved into his apartment on Harwood Street. I came with nothing but my clothing and a few books. Even after three and a half years in Vancouver, I had still been subletting, the very thought of buying furniture, pots, pans, plates, cutlery seeming an impossible task.

Michael had bought his apartment the previous year with a down payment from his parents. It was a one-bedroom in an older block. I knew his parents could have afforded one of the fancier condos being built on the peninsula's other side, overlooking the harbour. This, however, was what they were willing to give their son, and such moderation pointed to the soundness of their family relations. Michael's furniture was what he called "basement rejects," pieces that had, over the years, fallen obsolete at his parents' house. The couch and wing chairs were slightly worn around the arms, the upholstery a bit faded, but they were firm and comfortable; the rugs on the floors, though frayed, were subdued Persian ones that spoke of expense.

Michael loved to browse through antique stores and flea markets, and we often went to them on weekends. He would excitedly examine a piece of china or a painting which he felt was a steal, then later move the picture or antique plate to various places around our apartment before deciding on the perfect spot. Watching him, I would be filled with awe and gratitude, as if he spoke a foreign language that allowed him to navigate me through an alien land.

I had never been with a man long enough to know what happened once the initial edge of physical passion wore off, and I was surprised, then delighted, to experience how that sharpness of early desire softened and spread its goodness through every part of our lives so that I floated through the routine of my days in a warm haze of well-being.

Except when it was raining, we had our morning coffees out on the balcony, bundled up in blankets, a heater pumping away as we shared the *Globe and Mail*, trying to trick each other into taking the sports or business sections. This joke, which would have grown tedious between strangers or friends, was fondly amusing to us, because it was part of our history of intimacy, each repetition, like all rituals, deepening our life together. As I sipped my coffee in its Thermos mug, I marvelled at English Bay, with its ships drifting along the horizon, the view always a reminder of my good fortune. Then there was our commute to the university, where Michael now worked too, as a secretary in the English department. I always waited for that moment when the bus crossed the Burrard Bridge, craning to look at the glittering sea below, sunlight trembling on passing sails. Soon our bus left downtown behind and passed along 4th Avenue, through the neighbourhoods of Kitsilano and Point Grey with their expensive grocery stores, restaurants and clothing shops. I would occasionally glimpse down one of the streets off the avenue, the lovely bungalows with their emerald lawns inlaid with the dew-glistened gems of abandoned toys. In the last stretch of our journey, we were in the Pacific Spirit Regional Park, a mist hanging over the cedars and firs, the bus speeding towards the university at the edge of the Pacific Ocean.

Michael would join me on my occasional lunch-hour visits to Wreck Beach, and we'd stroll along, chuckling at the nicknames we invented for those hardy regulars who lay around naked in all seasons—Our Lady of the Pacific, Knotty Beard, Blond Rasta, Mouldy Bo Derek—names that were added to the private language that existed only between us.

In the evening, we often stopped off at Safeway on Davie Street to get groceries, nudging each other at the old queens who lined up for the cashier we had nicknamed Jail Bait, a blond boy with tanned skin and sun-whitened hair who kept his shirt open to belly button, smooth torso on display, his lips twisted with casual disdain. Then there was the solitude of our apartment, that sense of being in the centre of our life together after a day of administering to demanding faculty and students. Sounds and smells from the apartments around us formed a comforting cocoon in which we passed our evenings: the muted cadence of harp music from the French couple on one side; rolling and thumping in the kitchen of our neighbour on the other side, the smell of the baking bread she made to earn a little extra money seeping through our wall; the lilting calls of children racing each other down the corridor.

Whenever I had to go away for a conference, I missed Michael in bed, the day's last sleepy words between us. On the flight or bus home, I'd think of some joke or anecdote that would amuse him, just for the pleasure of seeing Michael laugh in his nerdy way. And this quirk, which many might consider the least attractive trait about him, made me lightheaded with affection because it was uniquely his.

Two years passed in this way, and still I dreamt periodically of Mili. I would run into him on the street in Vancouver or Toronto—a Mili now grown slightly jowly and paunchy, like so many Sri Lankan men in their late twenties. Our conversations in my dreams were friendly but stilted in that way of old school friends who had lost touch. I was aware, as we chatted, that there had been some embarrassing or hostile incident between us in school. I couldn't, however, remember its particulars, and the thought that he might be recalling it as we chatted made me self-conscious and eager to be on my way.

After waking from these dreams, my old restlessness would take hold of me, making it difficult to get through a day, and causing me to feel distracted and irritated by Michael's presence. I felt guilty because his little annoying habits, his tiny failures, made him less than Mili. I was aware this comparison was unfair, but had no control over the feeling, and this only increased my distress.

My brooding and inaccessibility made Michael anxious. His smile would grow fixed, and his voice would take on a tight politeness when he addressed me. The tension would boil over into an argument sparked by one of us over something minor. We would follow each other from room to room, quarrelling, refusing to give in, sulking, even as we went through the rituals and tasks that bonded us. Eventually, one or both of us would capitulate and a renewed sweetness flooded our lives.

But for me an invisible residue remained. These quarrels were a warning that our relationship might not withstand the entry of my past into it; that Michael might not be able to tolerate knowing about my dreams of Mili.

In the years that passed, my mother and I developed the habit of speaking about once a month. Our conversations were pleasant but careful because of the subject we were avoiding. To hide her unease, she adopted a brisk tone, as if she could only speak for a short time and had somewhere to go, even though it was generally she who telephoned me. She had told me about David, and I wasn't surprised when, about a year after her first visit to Sri Lanka, my mother informed me they were not merely friends anymore, saying, to hide her embarrassment, "Oh, he was making such a nuisance of himself, I finally gave in to his badgering and agreed." She often spoke of David in this way, as a sort of loveable nuisance, calling him Mahadana Muttha. Yet I could tell she loved him, and if she thought she had gone too far in belittling him, she would say, "But he is a good man. Very kind to me. I am lucky, son. Yes, very lucky." I knew, through my sister, that David wanted to marry my mother and have her move into his house, but my mother preferred her independence, preferred, as my sister said, "to live in sin with a white man." My mother and David were deeply involved in the Buddhist centre's activities, organizing retreats and fundraisers, providing refreshments during the breaks.

About a year after that first visit to Sri Lanka, my mother also started a part-time degree in history at York University. She would tell me in detail about the courses she was taking, the books she was reading, complaining that young people these days were "catatonically stupid," smug because she was top of her class and enjoyed besting the younger students.

Very soon into our relationship, Michael had an opportunity to talk with my mother. He answered the phone one day when I was out. My mother, who knew about Michael by then, was gracious, saying she was happy to speak to him at last, inquiring about his job at the university and saying she looked forward to meeting him one day. "She's very nice," Michael said, once he had relayed all this to me. This little statement set me off. "Of course she's 'nice,'" I cried, "She's a well-bred woman who knows to be polite with strangers. And, anyway, I never painted her as a demon."

"Whoa, Shivan, I'm not taking her side against you."

I glared at him to say that was exactly my accusation, and stomped away.

After that, if he happened to answer the phone first while I was home, he would spend a few moments chatting politely before passing the receiver, his tone slightly formal because he did not want me to think he was on my mother's side. She always mailed him tea when she returned from her now-regular visits to Sri Lanka. The first time the tea arrived, he asked if I even knew she had gone back. "Why would I care who comes and goes from that hellhole," I retorted, in a way that warned him I did not want to discuss her trip any further. The truth was, I couldn't have discussed her trips. Whenever she left for Sri Lanka, my mother, still afraid of losing me, would call my office early in the morning before I got to work and leave a message to say she was going. After she returned, she would telephone so I knew she was back, but never speak about the trip.

I talked to my sister too, about once a month. I would tell her about my work and my life with Michael, and she told me how her Ph.D. was progressing, her conflicts with other grad students and what she called "Ivy League racism." Sometimes she would make me laugh with her descriptions of homecoming, the vapid sorority types and jocks in the first-year courses she taught, the appalling ignorance of young Americans when it came to the world. Her favourite new term was "blond," which she used for anything or anyone stupid. Renu and Michael got on well, and if he picked up before I did, or I was out, Renu would make him chuckle with her descriptions of "American insanity" at the university—always a good way, as my sister knew, to charm a Canadian.

Though my conversations with Renu were easier than with my mother, she, too, understood she must keep silent about my grandmother. Despite her earlier impulse to escape our family and Canada, she now often went to Toronto, and my mother also frequently took the bus to Ithaca and spent weekends with her daughter. Renu's recountings of their visits, of her little squabbles with my mother, her growing relationship with David, were not meant as an accusation against me, and yet we both knew that it was my estrangement from them that had curiously drawn mother and daughter closer together. After I spoke to either of them, I was often gloomy and a feeling from my adolescence would surface—that their progress had been won at my cost, that I was stranded, watching my sister and mother in all their happiness moving farther and farther from me.

It is interesting to think now that Michael accepted without much argument these boundaries of silence around my family; interesting to note that, after the one time I told him of my past, he never questioned me more about it. Terms like "your mother's issues," or "1983," became a shorthand between us for that history, and he explored no further. I think he understood, without daring to articulate it to himself, that to press for more information, to look more keenly at my odd family relations, would be to confront the disparities in my story—and that the truth, once revealed, would take us where, in the end, it did.

27

My sister's room, which I have finished dusting and tidying, has its old furniture still in place. Many of her books are on the shelves, her white duvet, with its whimsical pattern of rainbows and sunbursts, still on her bed. In the closet she has left some summer clothes. A new robe and pyjamas hang from a hook, new Bata slippers sit by her bed, a jar filled with American coins waits on the desk. When I leave, I stop to gaze across the landing at what will be my grandmother's bedroom, recalling how my mother, the first time she took me around the house to show off the renovations, hurried ahead and closed that door.

As I start downstairs to continue my cleaning, a line from the blind monk Chakkupala's tale is with me: *Like a leopard stalking its prey through tall grass, a man's past life pursues him, waiting for the right moment to pounce.*

Just last year, in the summer of 1994, only weeks after Michael and I celebrated our second anniversary together, my mother called to announce that she and Renu were coming to Vancouver. Simon Fraser University was having a conference on gender, race and migration in late July, and at the last minute Renu had decided to attend. "It's been so long since we've seen each other, Shivan," my mother said briskly into my stunned silence. "Nearly six years, can you imagine? I feel responsible, I should have come and visited a long time ago. Michael is so important to you, and I have never even met him. Yes, yes, it's good we come." When my silence continued, she gave me the dates of their arrival and departure. They would be staying a week. There was a defensive, injured tone in her vigour, as if she was aware she was imposing but determined to do so anyway. "Are you writing down what I'm saying?" she demanded.

I reached obediently for a pad and pen. "What was your flight again?"

She repeated the information, then said, "Can you accommodate us? If not, we can get a room on campus. Renu has looked into it. But we're quite happy to sleep on a pull-out couch, or even the floor if you have sleeping bags."

There was another significant pause. She was waiting for my invitation. "Of course," I blurted, "yes, you can stay with us."

"Thank you, son," she said, her voice softening.

She moved on, tone brisk again, to tell me about a recent retreat she and David had attended in Northern Ontario. As she prattled on about all they had done, the people she had met, the stunning vistas of lake and forest, I could feel my suspicion growing. This visit was prompted by something else; the symposium was merely an excuse.

After she finished telling me about the retreat, my mother hurried on to the latest news about Renu. She was in the process of completing her Ph.D. and would soon be applying for academic jobs. My mother had been to see her the previous week and complained that Renu was "in a constant snit," stressed by having to finish her doctorate. "And she eats rubbish, Shivan, utter rubbish. You should see her refrigerator, not a vegetable or salad leaf in it. If I didn't visit and cook up meals and freeze them, she would vanish into thin air or get scurvy.

"But, aiyo, where did the time get to?" my mother finally cried, as if I had kept her. "David will be around in a couple of hours, and I still haven't baked the cookies for today's meditation class. Goodbye, goodbye."

Once I put down the phone, I went to stand on our balcony, still stunned by the news. Elbows resting on the railing, I gazed out unseeing. After a few minutes, I returned to the living room and began to walk among its furniture, picking up objects and putting them down. It was impossible to imagine my mother and sister here, seated on the sofa, eating at the dining table with our plates and cutlery; impossible to imagine taking them around Vancouver, past the familiar markers of my new life.

I was still wandering the apartment when Michael got back.

"Hello," I called out, stopping abruptly by the coffee table, arms by my sides as if caught doing something illicit. He gave me a curious look, put his grocery bags on the floor and went to remove his light summer jacket and shoes. I followed.

"My mother and sister are coming to visit."

He turned around startled. Frowning at me, he continued to slip off his jacket. "When?"

"Late July. My sister wants to attend a conference at Simon Fraser's downtown campus. She decided at the last minute. They will be staying here. Is that okay?"

He nodded, then asked again, "When do they arrive?"

"Late July," I repeated. "So, is it really okay I invited them to stay, Michael? I sort of couldn't avoid it. My mother asked."

"Of course, Shivan." He kissed me briefly on the lips. "Why are you even asking permission? This is your home too. I'll look forward to having them."

I trailed after him as he went to the kitchen with the groceries.

As we put things away, Michael glanced at me a few times, but I would not meet his eye. I knew I was being ungracious, given his generous response, so after a while I said, with a long sigh, "It's so typical of Renu to decide like this at the last minute. Anyway, it's time they came, I guess. I haven't seen them in nearly six years, for goodness sake."

"Well," he said carefully, "I did suggest you go to Ithaca for your sister's graduation when she got her master's, and then to Toronto."

"Yes, yes, I know." I grinned at him. "You are so wise. I should call *you* Mahadana Muttha."

He did not respond to my attempt at humour. "I think my parents have an air mattress. We must get it."

"Great! That will do fine for them."

He gave me a mildly amused look. "Not for them, idiot, for us. You can't ask your mother and sister to sleep on the living room floor." Then, as the thought struck him, "Jesus, we must get new sheets, and some guest towels too."

"Michael," I laughed, "take it easy. They don't get here for a month."

As he made dinner later that evening, I could tell from the gentle clicks of spoons in pans that Michael was not himself. I went to check on him under the pretext of getting some water. He gave me a perplexed, beseeching look to say he wanted to know what I was thinking, how I was feeling about this reunion. But I just opened the fridge and leaned inside to get the water jug, frowning as if preoccupied.

Even though I tried hard to conceal my growing disquiet, it was obvious to Michael. We knew each other too well by now.

One evening, on the bus ride back from work, when it was our custom to catch up on the day, he took out a book of crosswords he carried around and began to fill in a puzzle.

After a moment of surprise, I realized he was sulking. I peered over his shoulder, anxious to get him out of his mood. "*Groom.* Hmm." I counted the boxes. "Five letters. Ah, yes, *preen.*" He folded his lips with martyred patience, but wrote the word down.

"*Wrath.*" I thought for a moment and then declared, "*Ire,*" nudging him playfully to say I knew he was irritable.

"Shivan," he said quietly, and moved the book so I could not see the page.

"Fine," I muttered, took out a novel and pretended to be absorbed, glancing over occasionally to see if he was still sulking.

By the time we were preparing dinner, Michael was willing himself out of his bad mood, straining to be in good humour. I was desperate to please him and so took over most of the cooking, even doing the washing up, which I hated.

My anxiety finally drove me to call Renu.

After we greeted each other, we were silent. Then she said, "So, you've heard about us coming."

"Yes."

"Well, it was last-minute. My supervisor pressured me. I'm almost done this wretched Ph.D. and I need to build my resumé and schmooze. It improves my chances in the cattle fair of academic employment."

I believed Renu, yet her slightly hangdog tone confirmed for me that the conference was also a convenient pretext for their visit. She must have sensed this, because she added sheepishly, "Amma was also keen we seize the moment. A good excuse to come. Though," she added hastily, "of course, we don't need an excuse to see you."

"Of course."

I could tell she was waiting for my prompt, and I knew that if I asked, she would tell me the real reason for this visit. But now that the opportunity was there, I could not bring myself to take it. Six years of not talking about anything intimate had created an impossible distance between us. Our mutual dismay at this separation was palpable in the silence.

Finally, she blurted out, "I'm not sure if you know, Shivan, but Aachi had another stroke a few months ago. That is why Amma went to visit so suddenly in May."

"I . . . I didn't know."

"It's just one of many. The doctors say this is the way it's going to be from now on, until a massive stroke ends it all."

"I didn't know," I repeated and sat down on the bed.

"You never ask," my sister said gently. "If you asked, we would tell you."

"Yes, I understand. Thank you," I replied formally, then changed the subject.

Once I got off the phone, I leaned forward, hands clasped, unable to move under the weight of desolation. When Michael came home, he found me still sitting there. "Bad news?" he asked anxiously.

I shook my head. "Just chatted with my sister." I gave him a wry look. "I wish they weren't coming, I really do. Why do they have to come now, after all these years?"

"I know." He sat beside me and squeezed my hand to acknowledge that he, too, was nervous. After a moment, he gently pushed me back on the bed, and there we lay, chests rising and falling against each other, listening to the poignant chug of a motorboat out in the bay.

In the days that followed, my apprehension grew, fuelled by the certainty that my family's visit had everything to do with my grandmother. I could not figure out what else besides the stroke they were coming to tell me, but clearly the news was so important they had to convey it in person. Sometimes, on the commute to or from work, I would catch my reflection in the bus window and realize my tongue was pressed against the inside of my cheek as if I were trying not to cry.

Michael became increasingly tense because of my distance, and our mutual anxiety reached a peak the weekend before my family came.

That Sunday morning, when we went to get the air mattress from Michael's parents, we arrived to find a note on their hall table saying they had gone shopping. They would return, no doubt, with great amounts of cheese, pâtés, pickles, olives and expensive bread, which they always declared impossible to finish and sent home with us. As I removed my shoes, I could smell saffron bread, a recipe from Robert's Cornish ancestors, which he knew I liked and baked often for me.

Michael went to the basement for the mattress and sent me upstairs to borrow guest towels and sheets, having lost interest in shopping for new ones. They were kept in his old room, and when I entered, I was stopped for a moment by the sight of the sun slanting across the bed where Michael and I had first made love. I took out the linens from a drawer, put them on a chair and went to stand at the window, looking out at the mountains. Despite all the good that had happened in my life during the last two years, I found I was comparing that first time here to the first weekend Mili and I spent at Sriyani's beach house. I had been so uncomplicatedly happy then, without the shadow of tragedy that trailed me now.

Michael had come to stand silently in the doorway, and when I turned to pick up the linen, he saw my wretchedness.

"What were you thinking about?"

"Our first weekend here," I blurted.

His face froze, then he turned and left. "Michael," I called, and went after him. He paused on the staircase, not looking back. "What's wrong? I didn't say anything wrong. It was a lovely memory."

Before he could respond, we heard a key in the door and his parents' voices. They came in and found us like that.

"Ah, boys," Hilda said, with a quick glance at her husband. She slipped off her shoes.

"Look, kids!" Robert held up two grocery bags. "Food, tons of food."

Michael bounded down the stairs, brushed past his parents and went to the kitchen.

When I reached the hall, I said, "The house smells amazing, Robert. Thanks for making your saffron bread."

"Oh, you're welcome, you're welcome." He gave me one of the grocery bags to alleviate my awkwardness.

When we entered the kitchen, Michael was kneeling on the floor, pumping up the mattress to check for leaks. By the time it had been inspected, he had recovered enough to put on a show of good humour and join in talk about my family's visit and our plans for them.

I had expected Michael to bring up the incident later, that we would have one of our cathartic fights, following each about the apartment, bringing up past grievances, flinging around the word "always" even as we prepared dinner. But he did not refer to it at all and instead, like me, maintained a distracted air as we went about fixing dinner. I could sense he wanted the catharsis as much as I did, but could not bring himself to fight and was bewildered by this new barrier between us.

In those last days before my mother's and sister's arrival, this separation between us remained so that by the time we stood in the airport lounge, waiting for my family, we were strained with each other.

Soon, my mother and sister came through the sliding doors.

"Amma, Renu," I called, and moved forward to meet them.

They saw me, nodded, and started to come down the ramp. We walked parallel to each other but separated by the ramp bars, the two of them paying close attention to their trolleys, not looking at me. My mother's face had filled out and her hips were rounder. She had grown her hair and styled it in waves to her shoulders. The increasing greyness contrasted well with her caramel complexion, giving both hair and skin a glow. Though Renu was still skinny, her face too had filled out, softening her severity and giving her a curiously dreamy, bemused look. She had cut her hair into a puffy bob that bounced as she walked along.

When we met at the bottom of the ramp, we stood, looking at each other, nervous and unsure. But then all the years of our life together gathered and took on weight so that, when my mother leaned forward to kiss my cheeks, it felt as if a much shorter time of separation had passed. She held me for a long moment before she pulled back. Her eyes were luminous. "Ah, son, it is good to see you."

Renu gave me her usual angular embrace, patted my back and declared, "Seems like the Vancouver air agrees with you. You're looking very well. Do I see the beginning of love handles?"

I laughed and pulled my shirt tight around my waist. "Only very small ones."

Michael had joined us, and I made the introductions. He shook my mother's hand. "It's nice to thank you in person for your tea. I can never get anything as good here. My parents are envious." His tone was formal, the words prepared in advance.

"But I wish I'd known! I would have sent you more, Michael," my mother cried. "Honestly, Shivan, why didn't you tell me Michael's parents liked our tea? I would have got them some, too."

This admonishment established her role as my mother and eased her shyness with Michael. I grinned sheepishly, playing the recalcitrant son.

As Renu shook Michael's hand, she said, "I see you're the gentleman responsible for my brother's love handles. Good going."

Michael nodded, amused.

"It's nice to finally put a face to the voice," my mother said, and Renu added, "Yes, and a very pretty face, too, if I may say so. What are you doing with a train wreck like my brother?"

Michael blushed and laughed. He took one of the trolleys and I grabbed the other, and we led the way out of the building. As we walked along, I noticed a large cooler under the suitcase on my cart.

"What on earth is this?" I asked.

My mother and sister chuckled.

"It was Amma's idea."

"No it wasn't," my mother retorted with mock crossness. "You're an equal partner in crime."

"Sri Lankan food," Renu announced to Michael. "We went a bit overboard, as you can tell."

"You should have seen the look our ticketing agent gave us when she checked the luggage," my mother added with a laugh.

I laughed too. "You both are incorrigible."

"Great," Michael enthused, "I love spicy food."

"And I'm a lousy cook. Poor Michael."

"Yes, you are lousy," he replied fondly, then nodded to my family. "Thank you, it's very kind and generous of you."

By the time we got to his parents' car, borrowed for the occasion, we were all slightly exhausted from the conviviality.

To keep the silence at bay on our drive, my sister complained about her bus ride from Ithaca to Toronto. "Oh, it was intolerable," she said. "An obese American sat next to me, and I got squished against the window. But, so, what's new? It's impossible to escape them on any bus journey. And then there are those agents of Canadian imperialism at the border. They're so blond. Always treating me as if I'm illegal."

"They have to be vigilant," my mother said, giving Michael and me a nod as if we were on her side. "Otherwise Canada would be flooded with migrants from Mexico and everywhere else."

"So?" My sister spread her arms. "Let this place be flooded. It's the price we must pay for exploiting the rest of the world."

"Anyway, it's your fault," my mother said, tapping me on the shoulder. "Look at her shoes, will you?" I turned and took in Renu's scuffed footwear. "Doesn't she look like a real refugee, Michael?" my mother said, drawing him in. Michael tried to subtly observe Renu in the rear-view mirror. He smiled noncommittally, unsure if she was trying to put him at ease or a real quarrel was brewing. "I've told her and told her to get Canadian citizenship and a passport."

"Never, never." Renu shook her head vigorously.

"Then you must suffer the consequences," my mother declared.

Unlike Michael, I could clearly see that no real rancour existed between them. There was also a new wryness in my sister's declarations, an acceptance that her political positions were radical and she no longer expected everyone to adopt them.

That evening, we decided that for dinner we would have the lamprais my mother had brought. Michael showed her around the kitchen then kept a discreet distance, staying nearby if she needed him. While my mother steamed the four rice and curry portions, each wrapped in its banana leaf, Renu and I caught up on the balcony. Michael came out to join us between laying the table and helping my mother put away the rest of the food she'd brought in the fridge and freezer.

Two extra people in our small apartment demanded an alertness that kept Michael and me occupied. After we had settled them in and eaten dinner, we took our guests for a late-evening stroll along the beach, made sure they had everything for the night, then inflated our mattress, glad to be so busy. At last, my mother and sister were in bed and the apartment grew quiet. There were a few last creaks from the bed in our room, the sound of someone switching off a light. Michael lay on our air mattress with his hands under his head, gazing up at the ceiling. His silence and the dark now pressed in on me. I propped myself up on an elbow and looked down at him.

"Your family, they're very nice," he whispered, but his face was pensive.

"Charming but fucked up." I placed a hand on his stomach. "Thank you for making them feel so much at home. I really appreciate it, Michael."

He nodded, then turned away to face the balcony door. Beyond it we could see the faint twinkle of ships along the horizon. I pressed hard into him, putting my arms around from behind, and he grasped my hands fiercely and pulled me tight.

My family had come on a Friday and so the weekend was taken up with sightseeing. We went on Saturday to the Museum of Anthropology, which gave me a chance to take them through UBC and show off my office which was in the oldest building on campus, explaining to my impressed family how the 1920s building was in the "collegiate Gothic" style. On Sunday we went to Galiano Island for a picnic. All of this kept us busy, and it was only at night that Michael and I were alone. His mood would turn pensive then, as if he had been holding in his melancholy all day and it flooded him in the dark. I would lie next to him, concerned about his mood but too overwhelmed by my own worries to address his emotions.

On Monday, Renu's conference started and Michael went back to work. I took my mother to the Capilano Park, as Michael had told her about the ancient Douglas firs and she was keen to see them. On the way there, my mother chatted about her life in Toronto and described a trip she and David had made to McGill University in Montreal, where his son was in third year. She did not get involved in his children's lives—"I've raised two of my own, that's more than enough, thank you"—but had gone, nonetheless, to help the son find new accommodation, as he was not happy in his current digs. My mother also told me about her new friendships among fellow students at York. Some of them were older single women with whom she went for dinners and films, but she also had a coterie of young friends—mostly children of immigrants who saw her as a liberated woman, since dating a white man was more than many of them would have dared. Though she pretended to find their image of her droll, I could tell she enjoyed acting as a mentor and advisor. Her hectic chatter filled me with dread. This was our first time alone without Michael, and I could sense we were heading for that conversation she had come all this way to have.

Finally, we were in the park, and my mother grew silent as we followed the wooden boardwalk from fir to fir and stared up at the massive trees, many of which were hundreds of years old. We soon came to a fir that had stairs leading up its side to a deck built into the trunk. A sign at the bottom told us we could get a "squirrel's view" over the landscape. By the time we reached the deck, my mother was panting, and she sat down on a bench to recover her breath.

I was reading an interpretive sign about the surrounding scenery when my mother declared, "Shivan, I am so pleased to see you have a happy life here." She patted the bench, but I leant back against the deck rail, arms folded. "I think you are healed enough to begin some reconciliation with Aachi. It's important you do so. She won't live forever."

I went back to studying the sign, lightheaded with relief. So this was the reason for her visit, not something unimaginably terrible.

"Has she accepted responsibility for what happened?"

"Whether she accepts responsibility or not isn't the issue. The issue is—"

"Only time will heal what happened, and as you see, it is already doing that." I held out my arms to show proof.

"Time isn't enough, you must also forgive."

"How can you forgive someone who hasn't taken responsibility for their actions?"

"You start by forgiving yourself, that's where you start."

"What should I forgive myself for? Did I kill Mili? Did I? Is that what you think?"

"I want you to know," my mother continued, ignoring my anger, "that your aachi gave me power of attorney and I sold our share in those flats to that wretched thug of hers. I am looking for the Tamil family who lived there to give them their proper dues, and I have a lead in Australia. Aachi, of course, doesn't know this."

"It doesn't fix what happened." I went to the top of the stairs. "Nothing can fix that, nothing can reverse her actions. It's too late to make any—"

"No, no, enough of your anger." She stood up. "I won't pander to it anymore."

I started to go down the steps and she yelled at me in that old way of hers. "Come back here. I haven't finished with you."

I stopped and turned in surprise.

My mother ran a hand over her forehead and gave a frustrated gasp. Then she straightened the shoulders of her blouse and smoothed down the front of her trousers. "The thing is, son," she said quietly, "the thing is, you need to consider letting Aachi into your life again, because she is coming back into it." She grimaced at my questioning look. "Perhaps I should have told you this before. I applied last year to bring her over to Canada."

I was silent, waiting for some emotion to well up in me, but instead it seemed as if a void had opened within.

"The application has to be considered by the Immigration Appeal Division, because Amma is too old and ill to be a productive member of society. Anyway, our lawyer tells us we should hear back soon, and it looks promising."

"I wish you hadn't come here."

She leaned over the interpretive sign, pretending to read it. When she had gained control of herself, she turned back to me. "And I am guessing that Michael doesn't know anything about what happened, probably doesn't even know you have a grandmother. You have kept it all from that poor man."

I fiddled in my pockets as if looking for something.

She sat down and clasped her hands, staring at me. "It's not fair, Shivan. He deserves better."

"Just keep out of my relationship," I snarled.

"We should have stayed on campus," she said wretchedly.

"You should have. Instead of which you've come and shat all over my happiness. Yes, *shat*," I cried, at my mother's shock. "I was happy. Why did you have to come and ruin everything? Haven't you done enough damage to my life?"

Emotions struggled with each other across my mother's face, then it became impassive. She stood up. "Let's go on and do the suspension bridge."

I followed her down the steps, frightened and furious.

We spent the rest of our day visiting the Vancouver Museum and then seeing a film, avoiding further intimate conversation. When we got back to the apartment, Michael and Renu had already returned and were seated on the sofa looking at albums from Michael's time in Dublin. He came to greet us at the door. "Did you have a nice day, Hema? Were the firs impressive?"

"Yes-yes, they were wonderful." She touched his elbow. "Thank you, Michael, for everything you have done to make this visit so pleasant."

He laughed, taken aback by the fervency of her gratitude. "It's a pleasure, Hema."

"You're a good man, son." She kissed him on the cheek and went to her bedroom.

Michael frowned at me and I shrugged. "What happened?" he whispered.

"Why should anything happen?"

Ignoring Renu's appraising stare, I turned away to take off my shoes, fumbling with the laces. I went into the washroom, locked the door and sat on the closed toilet seat, leaning back against the cistern. "How dare she," I whispered, "how dare she."

I heard my mother come out of the bedroom and go towards the kitchen. We were having more Sri Lankan food that night, and Michael offered to help. "No, son," she replied, "I can manage. All I need is that steamer again."

There was a clatter of pots as Michael moved things around in the cupboard. "Hema," he said, "I ran into my mother today, and she would love to meet you."

"Oh, how nice, Michael. But your mother is a very busy person and I don't want to inconvenience her."

"No inconvenience at all."

"Well, then, we must try and arrange it."

Yet I knew that my mother would avoid meeting his parents.

I splashed my face and dried off, then stood with hands pressed on the edge of the sink, staring at myself until I felt ready to go out. I could have joined Michael and Renu on the sofa, where he had returned to show my sister more photos. Instead, I went to the kitchen, determined to wrest back my home, which my family had transformed into a perilous place.

My mother had laid out various plastic containers on the table, lids open. "Oh, very nice," I said, not looking at her as I examined the dishes. "Shrimp curry, ala thel dala, kiri hodi and coconut sambol." She ignored me and went about the kitchen, stern and harried, putting batches of string hoppers in the steamer.

"I can't believe you took such trouble for us, Amma. Polos cutlets! I haven't had them in years."

She grunted in reply.

I began to take down serving dishes and empty curries into them.

Something about our exchange, the clatter of dishes, alerted Michael, because he came to hover in the doorway.

"Shivan," my mother said, "leave it. I would like to manage on my own." I continued with my task and she added in Sinhalese, "I make a meal and bring it across the country, and all you do is irritate me. Is that my reward?"

I slammed down my spoon. "Have you no manners? Talking Sinhala in front of Michael. You're so rude."

"I'm sorry, Michael—" my mother began to apologize, but I interrupted her.

"See, Michael? Do you see now what we had to put up with? This is how she drove me all the way across the country and her daughter to the US."

My mother turned off the burner. She removed her apron and laid it on the counter. Then, she left the kitchen. After a moment, the bedroom door clicked shut. By now, Renu had also come to the kitchen doorway, frowning at me questioningly. I avoided her gaze and bustled around, putting food into dishes.

Michael grabbed my arm as I passed him and indicated sternly towards the bedroom. "Shivan, talk to her." He would not release me, and I didn't struggle, because now I felt weak with fear. In exposing our conflict, I had alerted Michael to the fact that there was something he was not privy to. I went to apologize, desperate to have normalcy restored.

My mother was sitting on the bed. She got up, blew her nose, placed her carry-on bag on the duvet and began to pack some of the things she had bought at the museum. "What a lovely apartment you have, Shivan. How did you come to afford it?"

"A . . . a down payment from Michael's parents."

"Some people have all the luck," she said mildly. "Canadians like Michael and his parents are blessed to have lived without seeing their world erupting around them. It is our good fortune if we can tie our lives to theirs, as you have been able to, Shivan. It is something to value." She gave me a beseeching look. I dropped my gaze, and she went back to her task. "You can go. I will be out soon."

Michael was heating the food, and Renu was on the balcony, pretending to be absorbed in the street life below. I took placemats and serviettes from the buffet and laid the table, aware Michael was watching me. When I came into the kitchen to get plates and cutlery, he said in a sad, defeated way, "Shivan, what happened when you were out today?"

"Nothing, nothing." I took down plates with a furious clatter.

My mother came out of the bedroom only when Renu went to tell her the meal was ready and we were waiting for her. She smiled at us politely as she sat down, eyes veined from crying. "I'm sorry, Michael, all this has made you uncomfortable in your own home."

"No need to apologize, Hema." He passed her the string hoppers. "Would you like some wine?"

"Yes, that would be very nice, thank you, son."

The way my mother called Michael "son" made me want to cry.

Later that night, when we were alone on our air mattress, I dreaded that Michael would probe further, but instead he grasped my chin, searched my face, then let me go. He turned on his side, legs drawn up to stomach, hands under one cheek, looking out at the night. I closed my eyes, vertiginous.

After that, my mother and I spent our remaining days like two strangers finding themselves thrown together in a foreign land and deciding to make the best of it. Renu stayed away in the evenings, as she had done all our years in Canada, socializing with colleagues. I could tell from her hard, bright manner with me that my mother had shared our conversation in the park. She too was uneasy being in our apartment and enjoying my partner's hospitality.

Michael began to come back later from work. Once, he called to say he had to dine at his parents'; a forgotten commitment, an old family friend visiting from England. At night, when we were alone, he would reply tersely when I asked about his day. Before he kissed me goodnight, he would examine me sternly, and my eyes slid away, unable to return his gaze. I knew he was waiting until my family left before confronting me. Yet instead of fear at the prospect, all I felt was numbness, as if everything was out of my control and I could only watch as events unfolded.

My mother and sister were to leave on Sunday afternoon. After their bags were packed and by the door, they still had a couple of hours before the airport bus. My mother asked me to walk her down to English Bay for one last look at the ocean.

We were silent all the way there, and she rested her hand on my elbow as if needing support. When we were on the beach, she let go and we walked in tandem, a little apart. Finally, she overtook me and blocked my path.

"The reason you haven't told Michael about the past is because you want to put all that behind and start a new life. He is that new life. So, Michael will forgive you."

I scuffed the toe of my shoe against a log.

She shook my elbow. "What you went through was terrible, Shivan. Anyone will understand you didn't want to revisit it. Anyone will understand."

I moved away, not daring to look at her, for I didn't want to see the desperation in her face.

Yet my mother wouldn't give up so easily on me. She went to sit on a nearby log, hands clasped in front of her, waiting, and when I came at last and sat by her, she said, quoting the *Guide to the Bodhisattva's Way of Life*, "When the mind burns with anger, immediately cast aside those angry thoughts or they will spread the way an unchecked fire travels from house to house."

And so she told me the story of her early life and mistakes, then told me how it had been for her in the months after I left for Vancouver; how, during her trip back to Sri Lanka, she had learnt to love and forgive my grandmother, despite her faults and failures. By offering me her stories I could tell she was hoping I would start to forgive, and not let acrimony ruin my life as it had hers; hoping also that opening her secrets to me would give me courage to do the same with Michael. But I could only listen dully, overwhelmed, carried along as if caught in a current out at sea.

Before my mother boarded the airport bus, she took my face in her hands. "Son, you are to me like rain soaking a parched land." I knew that by redeeming this expression of love from its history, she was trying to put me on the path to doing the right thing.

28

I HAVE COME OUT TO THE GARDEN AGAIN, come past the back gate to stand at the edge of the gully. The water below has taken on an infinite depth, as if it, rather than the sky, will catch the first light of morning, dawn blooming from within. In the apartment towers across the way, lights are switching on like fireflies in the dark. I glance at my watch. Three thirty. The night workers have returned. I think about the smell of them, like dusty cardboard boxes, in that bus I'd sometimes take home after the bars downtown had closed, their odour of defeat and resignation.

As I gaze at the apartment buildings, a dark flotilla out at sea, the line from one of my grandmother's stories is with me again: "They stand at crossroads or even outside the walls of their own homes, these silent peréthayas. They are standing at their own gates, wanting to be let in."

After the airport bus that took my mother and sister away had rounded the corner, Michael and I stood gazing into the absence it had left behind. The familiar landmarks around me, the other apartment buildings I passed every day, the concrete planters, the fire hydrant, seemed to have swelled with some greater physicality. We returned to the apartment and, avoiding looking at each other, went about restoring it to ourselves: we deflated the mattress, changed the bed linen, cleaned the washroom and kitchen, vacuumed and dusted, as if to get rid of my family's presence.

I was in the middle of my final task, watering the living room plants, when I heard the closet door open and turned to find Michael putting on his shoes. "We need something for dinner," he said, busy with the laces.

"Shall I come with you?"

He gave me a haunted look and left.

When Michael didn't return after forty-five minutes, I went out on the balcony and looked up the street, craning my neck every time I thought a person might be him. But he had gone for a long walk, and when he returned, he came in at the back of our building. I did not hear him enter the apartment, but at some point I glanced inside and saw him through the glass door, seated on the sofa, watching me, feet cocked on the coffee table, hands clasped between his thighs.

I took my time shutting the balcony door, then stood against it.

He closed his eyes. "Shivan, if you love me, if you value the life we have built together, I beg you to tell me the truth. The truth that you have, I know now, hidden from me for as long as we've known each other." It had taken all his courage to ask this, and he kept his eyes closed, as if fearful his gaze would weaken my own resolve.

But I did not need courage. I was at the end of my rope, and there was nowhere to go except to the truth or its alternative, the end of our relationship.

I walked past him and went into the bedroom. When I unfolded Mili's obituary, the brittle paper cracked. I laid the article gently on our bed and gazed at Mili's smudged image for a long moment, as if bidding it goodbye. "Michael," I called.

When he appeared in the doorway, he was prepared for the worst, his face impassive. He glanced at the newspaper clipping, then leaned against the doorpost as if needing to keep a distance from it.

"This is someone I loved. Very much. An old school friend. But there is more. Much more."

And so, palm resting on the obituary as if taking an oath, I told Michael my story in a last attempt to keep at bay the death of all that was good in my life.

At some point, Michael came and sat on the other side of the bed, half turned from me, leaning forward with fingers knotted as he gazed ahead.

When I was done, he put his head in his hands. "How awful, how awful."

I was frightened by the hollow anguish in his voice.

He stood up. "Thank you for telling me all this."

"Michael, I beg you, let's start again."

He folded the duvet, put it on a chair, then began to get ready for bed, taking off his clothes, putting on his boxer shorts and T-shirt. After a while I did the same, both of us following the ritual that had been ours for two years. As always, Michael used the washroom first to brush his teeth, and while he did so, I, as always, filled two glasses with water and put them on our bedside tables.

Once we were in bed, the lights off, Michael said, as he turned away on his side, "I wish you hadn't told me. I wish I hadn't asked. Perhaps I didn't need to know."

"No, you had to know."

"So I can find out the last two years of my life was a mirage?"

"Ah, don't say that, Michael. It wasn't a mirage, we love each other."

He pushed the top sheet aside and sat on the edge of the bed. Then he gathered his pillows, his water glass, and left. I listened, frightened and helpless, as he prepared the living room couch, going to the linen closet for a spare blanket.

For the first time, we slept apart in our home.

In the days that followed, Michael did not ask further about my past, and I knew better than to bring it up. During the nights, when he thought I was asleep, he would steal out of bed and go into the living room. Soon I would hear the careful tearing sound of Kleenex being pulled from a box.

Some days after I told Michael about Mili, his mother came to the President's Office. I had by now received another promotion that came with its own office, and I saw her from my desk, making her way down the second-floor corridor towards me, walking in her light, brisk way, linen jacket flapping gently against silk bodice. I stood up when she reached my office and she smiled, pausing outside the door. "Shivan, an office of your own. Certainly moving up the ranks, I'm glad to see."

I smiled uneasily and beckoned her to enter. She shut the door and sat across from me, palms together as if in prayer, jewelled rings glistening. "Michael has missed two afternoons of work."

I raised my eyebrows, and she lifted hers back to say we both knew this was serious.

"The chair of the English department told me. He's an old friend. I confronted Michael this morning. All he will divulge is that he goes to Wreck Beach to walk. Claustrophobia."

"Thank you for informing me, Hilda," I said after a moment.

"But, Shivan," she leaned forward and patted my desk, "why is Michael in trouble? Are you two having difficulties? I noticed he seemed out of sorts when he visited recently."

I fiddled with the stapler on my desk.

She stood. "I won't interfere any further, but you must promise to take care of him. He is our son. Please fix the problem between you. Robert and I would be happy to pay for counselling, anything. We care about you, too, and want you in our life."

"Yes, I know," I said, grateful she had come to see me. "I will take care of him."

Hilda lifted her hand briefly at the doorway as if she wanted to say something more. But then, with a slight shake of her head, she walked away down the corridor.

That evening, as we rode the bus home in silence, I kept glancing at Michael, searching for signs of panic and claustrophobia. We got off on Davie Street and walked down to Harwood. When we were at the corner, I said, "Let's go to the beach."

I nodded firmly at his surprise, lifted the bag off his shoulder, slung it over mine and went ahead, afraid he would refuse. After a while, he followed.

We reached English Bay, and I sat on the log that was our usual place to watch sunsets. He perched by me.

"Your mother paid me a visit today."

He nodded to say he had figured that out.

"What is going on, Michael?"

He cupped his chin and gazed out at the sea.

"You can't screw up like this. Apart from everything else, it puts your mother in an awkward position when the department chair is a family friend."

He nodded again to say he would not miss further work, then took back his bag. "I bought some parmesan cheese this morning. It needs to go in the fridge."

"You've been walking around all day with parmesan cheese in your bag?" I laughed. "It's probably gone off in this heat. Why didn't you wait to buy it after work?"

He did not appear to hear me and strolled back up the beach.

A few evenings later, Michael had a department event after work and was due home late. When I arrived at our apartment, I switched on the light in the hallway, put away my bag, took off my shoes and looked through the mail I had picked up downstairs. As I opened bills and dropped offers for credit cards, insurance, and theatre subscriptions into a wastepaper basket, an uneasy feeling began to prickle through me, as if there was a presence in the apartment. I ignored the feeling for a while, but when it grew I flung the bills on the hallstand and went through the apartment, turning on lights and checking rooms.

The note on my pillow was weighted down with a celadon porcelain egg that had belonged to Michael's grandmother: "I have taken some leave and gone for a few days to Vancouver Island. If there is an emergency, here is the number in Tofino where I will be staying."

I passed through the next few days living moment to moment, dazed with fear. I wanted to visit Hilda and ask if she knew what Michael had gone to ponder, sure the chair of the English department would have told her he had taken leave. Yet every time I thought I saw her on campus, across the Student Union Building or walking between buildings, panic would peal through me and I'd swerve along another route, breathless.

On the third evening Michael had been away, I came home to find he had already cleared our mailbox. I went up in the elevator, throat swollen with fear.

Even before I reached our apartment, I could smell the stewing curry. I came in and shut the door carefully, then turned and stood against it, as if ready for flight.

Michael was seated on the sofa watching me, head cocked, smiling as if amused at my fear.

"Hi," he said softly but with pleasure, and it was then I noticed how he was sitting, slouched with ankle on knee, so his lap dipped to hold something. He beckoned me forward, and when I reached him I saw the kitten curled up asleep. "Our new baby." He lifted the kitten and it continued to sleep, drooping in a quarter-moon shape from his hand. "Meet Miss Murasaki." He raised his eyebrows, and I nodded to say I remembered she was the author of *The Tale of Genji*, a Japanese book he was fond of. The kitten was a tortoiseshell, an orange splotch on its nose and the most delicate little orange sock on one front paw.

"Take her." He held the kitten out, looking up at me in that same tender way he did on weekend mornings when he stretched his limbs and watched me pull open the curtains before I came to lie on top of him and slip my tongue between his teeth into the wet-moss taste of his mouth. Yet his tenderness frightened me, for it seemed tinged with nostalgia.

"Don't worry about waking her up," he said, still holding out this tangible emblem of some change in him.

I turned away and went to hang my bag in the closet.

Later, when we were at the dining table having dinner, I said, "Did I ever tell you the story Chandralal told when explaining what he had done? The one about Siri Sangha Bo?"

"Chandralal . . ." Michael helped himself to more curry and chapatis, then batted away Miss Murasaki, who was on her hind legs, gazing into the bowl as if the chunks of chicken and vegetables were goldfish. "He's your grandmother's cousin, the lawyer."

"How can you forget, Michael? He's my grandmother's thug."

"Oh, yes, right."

"Mistaking him for poor Sunil Maama."

"It's all these names, it's hard to keep track."

"And yet you can remember the names of characters in Japanese tales."

"That's my interest."

"Look, if you don't want me to talk about my past, if you don't give a damn, just say so and I'll shut up."

"Yes, I want you to shut up." Michael pushed back his chair and stood. "I don't want to fucking know, do you hear me? It's none of my business."

"Michael!"

"You lied to me, you betrayed me, betrayed our love." He picked up his plate, then put it down. "The fact is, you didn't respect me enough to be honest. You had nothing but contempt for me."

"But Michael, I couldn't tell you, don't you understand, I couldn't."

"Why? Did you think lying would make our relationship work?"

I folded and unfolded my napkin.

"Your mother had to come here and prick your conscience before you got off your arse and told me the truth."

"Do you love me, Michael?"

"*Me?* What *me* would I love? I don't know you at all. I have been living with a stranger."

"Michael! How could you say—"

"You brought your grandmother, and your fucking lover into my life, into my apartment. You've soiled it with these people. I don't even know what they look like, and I've been living with them for the past two years."

Michael went into the kitchen and finished his meal leaning against the counter. Miss Murasaki followed him and flicked a plastic wrapper around his feet. He ate furiously, distraught.

Once he was done, Michael rinsed his plate, put it in the dishwasher and came to stand at the head of the table, hands on top of a chair back. "I'm thinking I would like to begin my master's in Asian studies next year," he said, struggling to sound reasonable and pleasant. "I'm going to enrol in fourth-year Japanese. I'll need it. I want to do my thesis on the Heian period and *The Tale of Genji.*"

"It . . . it's a great idea," I replied enthusiastically, wanting to support his decision. "After all," I added, "who knows better than I that you do love all things Asian." It was a line I often used to tease him that I was part of his Asian fetish. But this time my line fell flat; he did not respond with his part of the patter: "But you're the only thing Asian I *lust* for."

Instead, Michael said, "I'll get a student loan to carry me through, as I won't be able to work at the university anymore."

"Look, Michael, I'm earning a fair amount. I can support us both."

"I can't ask that of you, Shivan."

"For fuck's sake, don't be silly. We're a couple. That's what couples do."

He gave me a feeble smile and nodded his thanks.

That night, when we were in bed, Michael pushed himself against my back, slipped his arms around my chest and whispered, "Thank you."

"We love each other," I said, "no need for thanks."

Because I knew he did love me; his love had brought him back. And he was to me like rain soaking a parched land.

Surely this reconciliation should have been a turning point for us. But a few days later, I had one of my dreams about Mili and the old restlessness returned. This time, wanting to be truthful from now on, I told Michael about the dream and its effect on me. But despite this unburdening, my traitorous mind continued on its way, restive and aggrieved, holding up Michael's annoying little habits, his messes, the smell of his dirty clothes in the hamper, as if they were failures. And now, because he knew the reason for my brooding, I was naked and exposed, and this produced a greater irritation than usual, a longing for my old concealment.

Michael tried to be patient, but I could see he found it unbearable to think that, all through our relationship, my moody distance might be because he didn't measure up to Mili. Soon he was accusing me again of being a liar, of soiling his apartment, his life, and I was yelling at him for being insensitive and uncaring. After this quarrel, there was a period of loving amicability and we took a trip to Salt Spring Island courtesy of his parents. Yet a few days after we returned, some minor disagreement set off the accusations again, only to be followed by another respite before the cycle began once more. Time, I kept telling myself when we were in the midst of the bad phases, will cure everything. We would get past this terrible period if we both clung on.

And yet little estrangements crept in to stay. Michael began to swim at the university a few evenings a week; I took on an extra project at work and spent part of several weekends at the office. The hour when we had a drink together before dinner became shorter and shorter until we just had our glass of wine with the meal and gazed at the television or out to English Bay. It was as if the dark tide of the ocean had crept up the seawall and gradually submerged any happiness in our lives.

Then, at the end of January, my mother called me at the office. "Can you talk?" she asked after greeting me.

I got up, shut the door and came back to my desk.

"Son, the Immigration Appeal Division has passed my mother. Her papers will arrive in Colombo by April, then I'm hoping to go wrap things up and bring Amma back."

I leaned forward, my elbow on the table, hand pressed to forehead, waiting to feel some reaction. Instead, as always, a hollowness opened within me.

"Son, are you still there?"

"Yes, I am."

"Did you think she wouldn't pass?" my mother asked gently. "Were you hoping she wouldn't?"

"I . . . I don't know what I was hoping." Burdened as I was with my other problems, I had avoided thinking of this eventuality.

"Why don't you mull on it a while and we can talk further, if you need to. I'm always here for you, son." This was the tender way she spoke to me since her trip to Vancouver, believing I still kept my past hidden from Michael and pitying me.

After I put down the receiver, I swivelled my chair around and stared out at the leafless trees. I went back to work, a taut tiredness draining me, the light seeming too bright.

After some time, I glanced out the window at the Ladner Clock Tower in the distance and wondered if I should ask Michael to meet me for a coffee. I decided against it, unable to deal with whatever reaction he might have.

Rather than get a coffee in the office kitchen, I went down to the street and made my way to the Student Union Building, needing the coldness to pick me up. As I walked along, hands in pockets, shoulders hunched against the wind, I kept saying to myself, "She is coming to Toronto," but this reality would not sink in.

Once I had got my coffee and was strolling back, I found I was thinking of that rainy afternoon in Toronto soon after I heard about my grandmother's first stroke—how I'd stood at the bookstore counter barely able to swallow for the hardness in my throat, understanding I might never again hear her voice calling me "Puthey" in that loving tone, or feel her touch on my arm. I was filled now with that same hard ache of sadness, not for my grandmother, but for my own innocence about what lay ahead that summer in Sri Lanka. I stopped for a moment on the university's main mall amid the chaos of students, recalling the smell of the country when I had got off the plane in Sri Lanka; recalling also how small and frail my grandmother had looked sitting in the airport lounge. I found I was also sad for her. She had waited for me with such hope.

This memory and others followed me throughout the day, and by the end of work I realized I had come to a decision; or rather, it felt like the decision had been with me for some time without my knowing and had gradually sharpened into focus, like those children's paint books where you ran a wet brush over a blank page and the hidden picture slowly came into view. I would go to Sri Lanka with my mother, close up our house and bring my grandmother back.

That evening, I went to join Michael at a party thrown by his instructor in fourth-year Japanese, a Ph.D. student named Satomi Tanaka. They had become good friends over the last semester. She often hosted parties for the master's and Ph.D. students in Asian studies, and he always went early to help prepare food, grateful to be included. I resented and feared this new world Michael had created outside our relationship and generally arrived late, telling myself the parties were dull and that I was always got stuck making stilted conversation with other spouses.

Satomi lived off East Hastings, in a poorer end of town. Her three-storey, red-brick walk-up had a dark maw of a garage on the ground floor. The building's occupants were mostly Filipino and they spent their social time in this garage. Even though it was January, the women, bundled up in old coats, were busy around a barbeque while the men tinkered away at their cars. Their cheap white plastic chairs and table had that ingrained dirtiness of furniture exposed to the winter weather. An odour of car grease and oily fishiness followed me up the stairwell. When I reached the first floor, the corridor reverberated with music from Satomi's apartment and the boom of many voices.

She opened the door and, seeing it was me, pouted teasingly, "Shivan, why you are always so late for my parties?"

I mumbled some excuse and she shook her head, tutting as if I were a favourite wayward nephew. "Michael," she yelled towards the kitchen, taking hold of my arm as if afraid I might bolt.

"What?" he shouted back in the faux-rude manner they used with each other, like a cantankerous married couple.

Satomi's pout grew more pronounced. She shook her head at me to say he was being a naughty boy, then pulled me after her to the kitchen. On the way, various people stopped me to shake hands or pat my back. Michael was leaning over a pot of noodle soup, checking its taste. "Your Shivan is here," Satomi said reprovingly.

"Oh, hi, honey," Michael cried brightly. He kissed me effusively, which always made Satomi beam and was, I felt, the reason he was so affectionate.

I could not figure out what he had told her, because she betrayed nothing. Nonetheless, I resented her for what she might know.

Michael returned to his cooking and waved for me to make myself at home. I went to join the other students in the living room, some cross-legged on rush mats, others on the futon couch and Salvation Army chairs. Their lives were insular, and at parties they mashed over the same tedious subjects. Tonight they were discussing one of the department's secretaries, how she had grown even more erratic now that she was in the middle of a divorce. They had come upon her yelling on the phone at her ex-husband, her lawyer, even a credit agency.

I had heard all this gossip a few times and dropped wearily into a faded armchair by a half-open window.

Their discussion about the secretary grew more animated, and now Michael came out to add his story, also told many times before, of how he had continued to believe the various excuses she gave for her black eyes and bruises. His narration was over-animated, his nerdy laugh more pronounced. It dismayed me to see him so eager to fit in, as did his friendship with Satomi, whose fake, kittenish manner made her, in my estimation, unworthy of him. Their faux-rude manner was, I felt, more an indication of superficiality than any real intimacy. As I watched Michael, I thought how the decision I'd made would save not just me but also him. "Oh, Michael," the students yelled as he finished his story, "so naive and gullible, so sweet."

A breeze from the Pacific Ocean was coming in through the window. In the past I had loved that odour, which reminded me of cool wet seaweed, but now I was impatient with it, eager not to smell it again for a while.

Once we were finally walking to catch our bus on East Hastings, I told Michael the news from my mother but left out my decision to return, as I dreaded his reaction. He gave me a quick glance but said nothing, exhausted and glum as always from his act of good humour.

Later, when we were watching television, which we often did to wind down after a party, he said, gazing at the screen, "Well, I suppose you will be going to Toronto at some point to see your grandmother."

"Yes, I . . . I guess I will. It's a chance to make up with her. I need to do that, Michael. It will be good for me—for us, too."

He rolled his eyes, dismissing its benefits to him.

"My poor mother. I pity her having to close up my grandmother's life over there. Sunil Maama is getting older and anyway isn't very competent. She doesn't know about contracts and repairs the way I do. Then I worry about her Tamil surname. Renu told me she's had frequent difficulties with soldiers at checkpoints. She has no male escort as she goes about the city."

He was scrutinizing my face, and I continued, picking at the cushion in my lap. "My grandmother has already sold our house, but she's kept what is called a life interest. It's hers for as long as she lives in it. Once she goes, it will be destroyed and flats built there. So the furniture has to be sold, an auctioneer hired, Rosalind pensioned off, the— "

"You're thinking of going back."

"I . . . yes, I'm considering it." I shoved the cushion away, realizing I had pulled a long thread out of its embroidery.

Michael switched off the television. After a moment, he rubbed his eyes fiercely, then was still. "Why do you have to go back? All that is past. Put it behind you and move on."

"But you can't just put things like that behind you, Michael. I must come to terms with her, with everything that happened, otherwise I, we, will never move on."

Michael sat back on the sofa, his mouth slightly agape, as if exhausted. "What if she doesn't forgive you?"

"She must, she will."

Yet he saw I had not allowed myself to consider the alternative. "Don't be too sure. She wouldn't even pose for a photograph."

"No, no, she will forgive me."

"But what if she doesn't?" He stood up, strode towards the balcony as if intending to go out, then changed his mind and came to stand behind a wing chair, elbows resting on top. "I am issuing you an ultimatum. If you go and she doesn't forgive you, don't come back to me."

I laughed in disbelief.

"No, I mean it. You take that risk if you go."

"So you really don't want me to visit Sri Lanka?"

"Do whatever you like. But that is my condition. I am sick of taking the consequences of your actions. I don't want you coming back a wreck and burdening me anymore."

"Michael . . ." I got up and went towards him, but he backed away.

"And what does your mother, your sister, think of all this?"

"I haven't told them yet."

"Yes, because they will also tell you this is a foolish idea. To think you can make up with your grandmother and solve everything in three weeks, it's ridiculous. A waste of time and money."

He stormed off to the bedroom, but I did not follow. His doubts and challenges had destabilized me.

The next time I was alone, I telephoned my mother and told her my decision, anxious to know her thoughts. She was silent.

"Aren't you happy I want to go back? Isn't this what you've wanted for me?"

"Yes, yes, of course, son."

"You don't sound glad."

"It's just a bit of a shock, as you can imagine. Anyway," she added, "you've called at a slightly bad time. David has just arrived to take me out for dinner."

I wasn't sure I believed this, but I let her off the phone. I lay on the sofa, arms folded tightly to my chest, my unease like the tremor from a distant explosion. "I am trying, trying so hard, and she can't even stand by me," I muttered, angry now at my mother.

Renu called me at the office the next day to find out if the news was true. "Why are you suddenly wanting to go back, Shivan?" she demanded. "What has happened?"

"Nothing."

"You told Michael!" When I didn't respond, she said gently, "Oh, Shivan, I'm so sorry. We had hoped telling him would be the right thing to do. Why hasn't it helped?"

"I don't know, Renu," I replied plaintively, "I don't know."

I shut my office door, then told her everything that had happened and how Michael barely spoke to me since I had suggested returning to Sri Lanka. "Promise you won't tell Amma," I begged. "I don't want her to know."

"No, no," Renu said kindly, "I'll keep your secret."

"But don't you see. This is why I have to go back and set all that right. So things can be good for Michael and me."

"Yes . . . I suppose so."

"Ah, Renu, can't you back me on this? Do you think I want to return? To face her? But I'm trying, I'm trying everything, and no one will support me. Not you, not Amma, not Michael."

"Yes, yes, I'm sorry, Shivan. I do support you, I really do." But I could hear the lack of conviction in her voice.

When I got off the phone, I looked out my window at the students passing below. My sister's skepticism had heightened that tremor of unease. I wanted to be angry at her but couldn't, given her sympathy. "It doesn't matter what anyone thinks," I told myself. "I know what I'm doing is right."

I had expected my mother would call back that day to discuss my plan further, but there was no word from her. Instead, I got to work the next morning to find she had left a message with the number for Suvara Travels in Scarborough and her travel agent's name. "He is expecting you might get in touch, Shivan," she said, then added, "Son, I don't know what is going on in your life and Renu will not tell me. But I suspect all is not well. Anyway, you must decide what is best. I will not interfere and will support whatever decision you make."

Her backing should have quieted that tremor, but it didn't. Instead I felt grim as I telephoned Suvara Travels, as if forcing myself to do an unpleasant task.

When I informed Michael about the ticket, he picked at his fingernails for a moment, then said, "I'm serious about my condition. If you don't reconcile, I don't want you back here."

"I'm trying, Michael," I cried, no longer caring to placate him. "It's not my fault if she rejects me. It's not my fault for trying."

He shrugged, lips pressed together tightly.

"My mother supports me, my sister too. Why can't you? What are you so scared of anyway? You surely don't think I'll end up moving to Toronto to be with her, do you?"

He gave me a troubled look, and I laughed. "You think I'm going to give up all this," I waved my hand to encompass our apartment and English Bay, "for my mother's shitty basement?" I pressed his arm. "And mostly, how could I give you up?" Yet this tenderness did not touch him, and he moved his arm away.

In the weeks that passed, I began to make little preparations towards my trip, buying some shorts and T-shirts at a pre–March break sale, going down to our storage locker to bring up my old suitcases and check their condition. I made sure to inform Michael of all this, to show him my purchases, explain my plans while over there. He reacted stonily, but I told myself he needed to know, ignoring the undertone of aggression in my forcing him to listen to these preparations. He found many excuses to be angry at me, but I did not rise to his goading. I was doing the right thing; this was the way to save us.

During my lunch break now, or sometimes after work, I visited the university library, where I'd discovered they got the Sri Lankan *Daily News*. I knew already that a new government had been elected under Chandrika Kumaratunga, the widow of the assassinated actor turned politician Vijaya Kumaratunga, and that there had been a ceasefire accord between the government and the Tigers. Now I learnt that the accord was already under threat, each side accusing the other of bad faith. With the beginning of a new era, a new government, the papers were full of reflections on the recent bloody past. The JVP, who seemed so indomitable during my summer in Sri Lanka seven years ago, had been obliterated by the government forces. They had lost the sympathy of the poorer classes, who bore the brunt of their killings, curfews and other edicts. They had also made the fatal error of targeting families of policemen and soldiers, thus galvanizing the forces against them. By the time the JVP were destroyed, forty thousand people had been killed, a generation of young men and women decimated by both sides.

The Indian Peace Keeping Force, too, had met an ignoble end, becoming so unpopular that the old government had united with the Tigers to oust them from the country. The Indians had suffered a high number of casualties, but also stood accused of civilian massacres, disappearances and rapes.

Reading all this should have made me anxious about going, but by now I had thrown up such high barricades around myself, I would not let anxiety in. Things were different now, I kept telling myself. This was a new era; there was a new government; Sri Lanka was moving forward.

I didn't share the newspaper stories with Michael as I felt he would use the crumbling ceasefire to erode my confidence. In March, he found out he had been accepted into the master's program, but even this did not lift his spirits. He remained glum, almost indifferent about his acceptance. I interpreted this as one more sign I had to return to Sri Lanka and make peace with the past.

Then, a little over a month ago, Satomi threw another party. I arrived even later than usual, and once I'd said hello to Michael in the kitchen and gone through our pantomime of affection for Satomi, I went to join the other students in her living room.

There was an addition to the evening. A man who sat on the futon sofa between two female grad students, smiling easily as if he had always been part of this group. His lanky thighs were spread, taking up too much couch, and he held a beer between his legs, thumb and middle finger grasping the bottle below its lip, other digits splayed—this arrangement of fingers like the elegant hand gesture of a bharatanatyam dancer. His heavy expensive watch was loose, and its silver strap hung like a bracelet around his wrist. The newcomer's name, I soon learnt, was Oliver, and the students were extra jocular with him, always a sign of deference, I knew, from my years at university. He looked to be in his forties, though his shoulder-length hairstyle was young, with blond streaks and limp curls gelled in half moons over his forehead.

I was alone in the kitchen later, where I often retreated during these events, when Oliver sauntered in and saluted me with his beer. He leaned back against the counter and just looked at me in a friendly way, head nodding as if on a spring. Though he had nice features, he missed being good-looking because of a receding chin. I thought the young hairstyle emphasized his age.

"Are you a visiting scholar?" I finally asked. "Visiting professor?"

"Professor." He continued to nod as if palsied, lips pressed together.

"From where?"

"Columbia. Just here for the semester." Then he arched his back with a little frown and swivelled his hips from side to side, as if he had noticed a crick in his spine. There was something dismissive about this gesture. "You work in the President's Office," he said when done. He was amused at my surprise. "Michael," he said, as if it was obvious. He took a swig from his beer, watch clattering against the bottle. "Yes, my expertise is Heian court literature."

This was the subject of Michael's proposed thesis—popular culture during this period and how it shaped women's education and national identity. "Ah," I said, feeling the need to prove something. "Sei Shōnagon's *Makura no sōshi.*"

Oliver smiled tolerantly at this mention of the famous *Pillow Book*, then stretched again. "Yes, I've fallen into a sort of advisory role with your boyfriend."

As if on cue, Michael appeared in the kitchen. He feigned surprise at seeing us together and went to check on the Japanese version of curry he and Satomi were making. He bent over the large pot, lips pursed as if unsure what was missing, his concentration exaggerated.

"I was just telling Shivan about our mutual interests."

Michael gave Oliver an uncomprehending look that seemed tinged with alarm.

"In Heian court literature." Oliver laughed teasingly, as if he had tricked him in some way.

Michael's features turned cold.

"I was just about to tell your boyfriend of my offer to have you at Columbia, after your first year here."

"Oh," Michael said in an aloof tone, then seeing my look of surprise, he added, "Oliver just mentioned it in passing. I haven't really given it much thought." He shot Oliver an annoyed glance before he smiled at me. "Anyway, it's not like you can leave your job and move to New York."

I smiled back fondly at Michael. "Yes, we're stuck here, unfortunately, my dear." I shifted my smile to Oliver, "Too bad. Columbia and New York would have been lovely."

Oliver grinned and raised his bottle, toasting us as a couple.

When Michael and I were on the bus home, I asked, "So, is Oliver married?"

"Married?" Michael took my hand. "There are no gay marriages in the US, Shivan."

"He's gay?"

"Of course, silly. He screams New York queen from miles away."

I should have been comforted by his dismissal of Oliver, but it only heightened my uneasiness. Michael hadn't held my hand or talked to me in this teasing way for a long time.

A few evenings later, we took the bus to Point Grey for dinner with Michael's parents. He was silent for most of the way, but when we were a couple of stops from getting off, he sucked in his breath as if he had just remembered something he had been meaning to tell me. "Some of us are thinking of going to New York in two weeks. For a conference."

A jangle of shock went through me. "New York?" I blurted. "I've never been there."

"You're welcome to join us, Shivan." He pressed my arm. "I just didn't think you'd have enough vacation days, not with your trip to Sri Lanka."

I dug through my pocket for a Kleenex and blew my nose even though I didn't have to, needing time to collect myself. "Why wouldn't I, Michael?" I snapped. "It's just the beginning of the year. I have tons of vacation days. And I don't go to Sri Lanka for four weeks."

"Then join us by all means. I'll be busy during the day, but we can do fun things at night. Satomi is going too. We were going to share a room, but that can be easily changed."

His wide-eyed insincerity enraged me. "I think I very well might. I work so damn hard, and Sri Lanka is not going to be a picnic."

Michael got up and rang the bell for our stop.

As we walked towards his parents' house, I was fizzing with a manic energy. I wanted to punish him further, and when Robert and Hilda ushered us inside, I cried, "Guess what! We're going to New York in two weeks!"

Their delight pierced Michael.

"Why New York?" Hilda inquired.

I remained silent and Michael was forced to say, "I'm attending a conference. At Columbia."

I gloated at the way he stumbled over the name, at his glum expression as he went through the small amount of mail that still came to him at his parents' and was left out on the hallstand.

"Do you have a guide we could borrow?" I asked.

"Yes, Fodor's. And just keep it." Hilda led the way to the kitchen. "It's from last year. The next time we go, we'll get a new one."

Robert went upstairs to fetch the book. When he returned, he and Hilda sat on either side of Michael and me at the breakfast bar and pointed out all the sights we had to see and ones we must certainly avoid. Michael tried to appear interested, but his parents had picked up on his glumness and exchanged quick worried glances as they talked.

My bitter verve had worn off by the time we left, and I felt wretched with uncertainty as we sat turned slightly away from each other on the bus. I was desperate to know the truth and, the moment we were in our apartment,

I cried, "Michael, are you having an affair with Oliver? I beg you, please tell me the truth."

He had half unbuttoned his coat and now clasped it shut at his chest in a curiously modest gesture. We could hear our neighbour upstairs dragging something across her room. "No," he finally replied. "No, not an affair." He removed his coat, started towards the closet, but then tossed it over the sofa and sat on an armrest, legs stretched out. "Oliver made a sleazy pass the first time he invited me to his office. I let him kiss me. Kissed back, too. But I told him I am with you and love you. Still, it didn't deter him from trying that shit at Satomi's party." He pressed his palms together between his thighs and rubbed them back and forth as if cold.

"And yet you were planning this trip to New York."

"And yet I was planning this trip to New York." Involuntarily, he nodded like Oliver, head as if on a spring.

I went out onto the balcony. The wind was fierce and a mist had made the floor slippery. When I leaned on the top rail, I could feel dampness soaking through my coat and salt from the air forming a sticky mask on my face.

A grim anger was taking hold of me. "I'm trying," I said to myself. "I'm trying everything. I am trying so hard, and this is how he rewards me." Michael did not care that I was suffering, that I was doing everything I could to mend things between us. Angry tears stung my eyes at the thought of him kissing Oliver. I felt pathetic next to Oliver's professorship at an Ivy League university, his older-man's finesse, the sophisticated life I imagined he could offer Michael in New York.

The next day, Michael told me he was not going to the conference after all. For the rest of that week, he came home early every evening and cooked things I liked for dinner. He even turned down a student party. Yet none of this placated the anger I felt or the grimness with which I spoke to him now. I often just glared in response to questions he asked. I needed my rage. It was the only barrier left to throw up between me and the truth: this trip to bring my grandmother back was not going to restore my happiness. And so what occurred next took place because I couldn't face this truth, couldn't accept I had reached the end of the road.

About a week later, while we were washing up after dinner, Michael reminded me that Satomi's birthday was approaching and that he had promised a while ago he would throw a party for her in our apartment the coming Saturday.

"That woman is not entering our home," I declared, holding out a washed pot to him.

He took the pot and dried it. "Satomi has nothing to do with Oliver."

"You think I'm an idiot, that I don't know you told her about Oliver even before you told me? She was going to New York with you and no doubt would have aided and abetted the whole shitty thing."

"That's not fair!"

"She's always disliked me and been jealous of our relationship. I don't want her here."

"Well, I'm having the party. It's my apartment."

"Yes, I know." I gave him an acid look. "I'm merely a tenant here."

"Shivan! Can't we please find some way to be comfortable with each other?"

I turned my shoulder away and continued to wash dishes.

On Saturday morning, Michael informed me nervously we had to visit Granville Island Public Market and get provisions for the party. I looked him over with disdain. "Do you actually think I'm going to help you shop for the party of a friend I despise?"

"Why are you like this?" he begged softly.

"You dare to ask me that, after what you've done? After you were going to fuck that old sleazebag in New York? I told you the truth. Now I'm even going all the way to Sri Lanka so we can be good together. But you don't care. You don't notice what I do. Nothing is good enough for you."

After he left, I went out onto the balcony and watched him walk up Harwood Street. The stoop of his shoulders made me want to cry, yet I couldn't control this urge to punish him. "Enough," I kept saying to myself, "enough, enough."

I went for a walk along the seawall. It was the first really lovely day of spring. The temperature had risen to twenty, and a mild breeze was coming in off the ocean. Soon I had removed my jacket and tied it around my waist, sleeves slapping against my thighs as I strode along. The pathway ahead was crowded with a group of Middle Eastern families. The women pushed strollers, their burkas cracking like sails against their bodies, their unheeded warning cries to children like ululations. The men walked in front, speaking and gesticulating effusively, passing around bags of nuts and sweets with old-fashioned courtesy. A young boy on roller skates was being pulled along by a large out-of-control golden retriever, the boy pitching from side to side, in danger of going over the seawall onto the rocks below. The vendors had come out, and there was the caramelized odour of scorched hot dog buns in the air, the gunshot smell of popcorn.

I walked for three hours, then sat down in the grass among some totem poles to take a break. By now I was sure Michael would be home, and I exulted at him finding me gone without so much as a note left behind. He would have bought fresh bagels, lox and cream cheese for lunch, as we always did at the market. It filled me with vicious pleasure to think of his worry as he sat eating, wondering what had become of me.

Once rested, I continued on, and when I reached the other end of Stanley Park it was early afternoon. I felt like eating Thai food and wandered into a restaurant on Robson Street. While I waited for my meal to arrive, I flipped through a *Georgia Straight* someone had left on the seat across from mine and read the film reviews. There was nothing I wanted to see at the closest multiplex, but I decided to take a bus to Granville Street and go to whichever matinee I arrived in time for. It would be early evening when the movie finished, and by then Michael would be frantic. Yet even the thought of his panic could not sate me. Each thing I did to punish him inflamed my need to punish him further.

I arrived home after the movie and found Satomi's boots by the door, their soft unzipped tops gaping like open mouths. He must have told her I'd refused to host her party; she had probably rushed down to the Granville Island market and shopped with him.

I could hear them moving stealthily about in the kitchen. "Hello," I called out, clearing my throat.

"Shivan," Satomi called back, "come and taste."

When I entered the kitchen, she kissed me gently on the cheek. "Oh, we have been so busy."

Michael gave me a frightened stare then went back to cooking. Satomi held out a rice dish topped with bits of tuna, cucumber, crab and shitake mushrooms. "It's a special dish called *chirashizushi*. It's made for Girls' Day in Japan, so we are making it for my birthday party."

I nodded, lips pressed together, suddenly embarrassed that she must know I didn't want this party.

"Would you like to try?"

"No, but thank you." I left the kitchen and went to my bedroom.

Soon I heard Satomi leave the apartment, promising to be back in an hour. I had showered and dressed by then and was seated on the bed, reading. Michael came in to get ready. He gave me a quick glance, picked out the clothes he needed and went into the washroom. Once he had washed and put on fresh clothes, he came back and dumped the dirty ones in the hamper. "I've asked people to come at seven thirty, so they should start to arrive in half an hour."

I nodded, not looking up from my book. I knew he was waiting for some conversation that might lead to a temporary truce during the party. But my harsh need to punish him had grown monstrous; my anger flamed so high there was no quelling it. Eventually he sighed and went out.

The buzzer rang at seven thirty. It was probably the four students who shared a house near Gastown and were always on time. I soon heard their gabble of greetings and emerged from my seclusion.

"Shivan!" they cried. The men shook my hand, the women hugged me. They had brought gifts for Satomi, and a moment later she walked in and let out a little shriek of pleasure at the presents they thrust at her.

Michael had gone to get drinks, so I collected the guests' coats and went back into the bedroom. I shut the door and sat on our bed, listening to the muffled voices. Finally, I pressed my hands on knees and pushed myself up. It took enormous effort to stand.

The guests were seated on the sofa and chairs and had already begun one of their tedious conversations about department politics. I went to the kitchen, got myself a beer from the fridge, then leaned back against a counter. By staying out of the preparations, I had made myself a stranger in my own apartment. A student drifted in looking for ice, and I got him some. He stood across from me, talking about his problems with Student Services, asking my advice even though I worked in the President's Office. Other students arrived and the man thankfully left to greet the newcomers.

Soon Michael came in to get snacks. When he found me standing against the counter, he said pleasantly, "You should come out and join us." I winced as if at an unpleasant sound. "Shivan," he whispered pleadingly, then sighed and reached for some bowls he had stacked on the counter. He began to fill them with wasabi-coated peas and Japanese crackers.

"Why are you making yourself miserable?" He glanced towards the living room. "It's so unnecessary."

"It's your apartment, your party," I hissed. "I'm simply a tenant, a guest."

Satomi came in to help, saw our standoff and started to back out. I crooked my finger at her. When she was before me, I said softly, "So, you were going to aid and abet my partner in adultery? No doubt you want to pull him down to your level."

"That's enough," Michael said. He thrust the bowls at Satomi and signalled for her to leave. Then he got drinks and followed her out.

A silence had fallen over the party. They had heard our furious murmurs in the kitchen. "Japanese munchies," Satomi cried gaily. The guests cheered and their conversations resumed, over-animated. I continued to stay in the kitchen getting drunk. My presence was painful to Michael and made the guests uncomfortable, but this was my home and I would do in it as I liked.

Michael served dinner as soon as everyone had arrived, clearly wanting the evening to end quickly. As he went about the kitchen getting food ready, he showed no impatience that I was in his way, requesting politely that I move when he needed to get something from behind me. Satomi came to help, her smile strained. They exchanged instructions in sickbed voices.

Finally, Michael announced dinner was served and the guests crowded around our dining table. Now they could see me through the kitchen doorway, leaning against the counter, arms folded, glowering at the cabinets. They helped themselves, glancing timidly in my direction, commenting softly on how appetizing everything looked.

As soon as dinner was over, the students, also wanting the evening to end, presented their gifts to Satomi. She let out little yelps of delight and surprise over the bowls, mugs and books they had bought her.

I was watching all this unnoticed from the kitchen doorway, and once the gift-giving was over, I came into the room. They fell silent. "It's a beautiful night," I said, raising my beer bottle to them, toasting the fine weather. "We should go for a walk."

"Yeah, hey, good idea," someone said, and the rest mumbled politely.

I went out on the balcony and slid the door shut. The babble of voices resumed, higher and louder.

A mild breeze was blowing up from the sea; the temperature was in the mid-teens. As always on these first evenings of spring, the streets were crowded with cars and SUVs pumping out their music, the parking lots full along English Bay. Now I genuinely wanted to be down there and escape this apartment.

I pushed open the balcony door and stumbled inside. "It's fucking gorgeous," I cried. "I'm going down to English Bay."

The guests gawped at me, then glanced at Michael.

"Shivan," he said pleasantly, "come and see the gifts Satomi has got."

I walked over and took a quick contemptuous look. "Very nice. If any of you want to join me, I'm heading down to the beach. I bet it's warm enough to swim."

The guests laughed nervously.

"Come on, you guys, you're the real Canadians, not me. You should be the ones raring to take a spring dip. Let's go down there and join the party instead of sitting around like a bunch of geriatrics." I went to get my coat from the hall closet.

The others watched me, not knowing what to do, glancing occasionally at Michael, who pretended to be absorbed in a book Satomi had received.

"A walk sounds good," he finally said.

The visitors rushed to get their coats off the bed, grateful to be escaping our apartment.

The beach at English Bay was crowed. Families walked along briskly, lovers strolled arm in arm or huddled under blankets behind large logs. An impromptu singalong had started, the participants seated in a circle, a teenage boy with a shaggy beard strumming a guitar, a woman beating a tambourine, a man in blond dreadlocks playing bongos.

One of the students had brought along a joint, so the guests sat in the shelter of an unoccupied log and passed it among them. I wandered towards the shoreline, certain Michael would be watching me in case I might actually go for a swim. Yet when I reached the water's edge, he had his back to me, purposely I felt, and was talking to one of the grad students and her husband. I turned to the water and observed it lapping against the sand. I took off my coat and threw it on the beach, then pulled off my sweater. Now I was wearing only my T-shirt.

"Hey, dude," a jogger said as he passed, "that's crazy. Too cold for a swim, man."

I grinned and raised my hands, like an acrobat garnering applause before a stunt. He shook his head as he continued on. I pulled off the T-shirt.

My naked torso attracted attention. People stopped to stare. "Oh my god," a teenage girl whispered loudly to her friend, "that guy is out of his mind."

I whipped off my belt and flung it in the sand, then unbuttoned my trousers. But before I could slip them off, Michael was before me. "Put on your fucking clothes," he cried, voice cracking with pent-up rage. He grabbed my arm and jerked it away from my pants. "Put your fucking clothes on and stop ruining my life."

Perhaps if he hadn't said those particular words, I might have obeyed. Instead, I wrenched myself out of his grip and stumbled away. Keeping my eyes on him, I slid my trousers down to my ankles and stepped out, now wearing only boxer shorts and socks. His friends had joined him and they crowded around Michael as if he needed protection. "Shivan," Satomi said, stretching out a hand to me, "come, put on clothes."

I backed into the water, smiling grotesquely. Michael started to pull off his shoes and socks.

There was a dip beyond the water's edge, and almost immediately I was waist deep, the waves bumping and nudging me, my socked feet unable to grip the sand. The water's coldness was clenching and squeezing at my knees and thighs. I could feel a cramp coming on. *If you keep going out, it will soon all be over*, a voice in me whispered, and suddenly I was terrified, because I was seduced by this enticement and the oblivion it offered. Michael had seen me stop. He was no longer undressing, but waited in the still, attentive way one waits to reassure a timid animal. I was losing sensation in my legs. If I stayed in the water any longer, I would not be able to move my limbs. I panicked and struggled towards the shore.

"You're shivering," Michael said kindly when I reached him, shaking his head as if what I had done was endearing and amusing. He bent and gathered my clothes, then held out each piece. I put them on, shaking.

Seeing the crisis averted, people continued on their way or went back to what they had been doing. Satomi whispered something to the guests and they drifted up the beach, scattering in different directions to catch buses or find cars.

When we got back to our apartment, Michael ran me a hot bath, then sat on the closed toilet seat, watching me in the tub. I could tell what he longed for, and I longed for it too. I held out my arms. He took off his clothes and crept into my embrace like some bedraggled thing craving shelter.

Yet within a week we were fighting, and the cycle began again.

29

In my mother's living room, the first light of morning creeps under the sheers. Soon, she and David will be here to take me to the airport. Her bags are with mine by the door. I cross the length of the house to stand at the kitchen window and look out at the world revealing itself. The wind has picked up, blowing the accumulated dust of winter before it like a great sweeper. The grey cloud of dirt settles over the first greening grass, the buds of flowers in gardens. A cat lopes across the street, casual yet intent, sits on a stoop and licks itself furiously. A car draws near, starting and stopping in little spurts, and finally I see that it is the newspaper man. When he opens his door to fling a paper expertly at our neighbour's step, a gust of Hindi film music blows out.

I glance at my watch, then wash my Scotch glass and put it away.

In my grandmother's home it will be four in the afternoon now and the heat will have finally begun to relax its grip on the day, the evening unfurling with a sigh, a breeze starting in from the sea, the light suddenly soft and golden across walls. If I was lying on my bed there, I would see through my window the fronds of a stunted coconut tree begin to shake themselves loose and dance, intoxicated. It would be the time for cups of tea. The pastry man would be weaving his way down our street on his bicycle, ringing his bell continuously, a sound like the chirp of a chipmunk. The silver box perched on his rear carrier is filled with long sugar rolls, spicy fish buns, cutlets and patties, cakes with extravagantly pink desiccated-coconut icing. The neighbour a few doors down, a failed concert pianist, has started her daughter practising scales—picked out haltingly, over and over—teacher clapping to keep her pupil on beat, crying out orders as if the two of them are on parade. A perennial game of cricket has begun on the road, played by the sons of boys who played on this same road in my youth, something poignant and lingering about the thwack of bat on ball. Servants are gossiping over fences before starting dinner, snatches of sound from their various radios borne by the wind, making it seem as if a single person is searching the dials of a radio.

Here in Toronto, I have one more task left, and so I get the vacuum cleaner out of the hallway closet. Before I start down to the basement, I set my watch to Sri Lankan time.

I reach the last step and stand in the dark, reluctant to turn on the light, vacuum cleaner nudged up against my leg as if for comfort. I want to remember this room as I lived in it. When I finally do flick the switch, I see I have forgotten to shut the emptied drawers. They hang open like parched tongues. There is nothing of me here now, nothing. I am effaced.

As I start up the vacuum cleaner and slide it around, I am filled with unexpected nostalgia for that time when I returned from Sri Lanka, those nights I paced this room or sat in one of the cigarette-pocked tub chairs, head in hands, recalling Mili and all the possibilities that could have played out, all the things I might have done, all the paths not taken that could have saved him. I would rage then at my grandmother, at that pious look on her face when I begged her to intervene, at her stupid, stubborn belief that things would work out, even after it was clear they were out of control, at her blind faith in Chandralal, not because she thought him good and right-thinking but because this trust suited her.

In my anger, I would sometimes imagine that quiet conversation between them on the verandah the first day of the riots, when they hatched their plan to keep an eye out for a Tamil family in desperate need. I would imagine the pious way Chandralal might have begun, saying something like, "Nona, it is unbelievable what our Sinhala people are doing to their own countrymen. Women and children are being dragged from their beds and burnt, young girls raped. These are our Tamil brothers and sisters."

"How can people hate each other so much, Chandralal?" my grandmother would reply, watching him closely, sensing he had something to reveal.

"It's not just hatred, nona," he would say reluctantly, as if breaking someone's confidence. "Many people have a lot to gain by killing off Tamils and burning their businesses, lots of property to be had." His voice would grow sonorous. "But I will not stand by and let this happen to our Tamil brothers and sisters. Even now, I have told my golayas to help out whomever they can.

Why, some of them are guarding the house of one famous Tamil lawyer. That house will not burn."

My grandmother would understand. "You are doing a good thing, Chandralal. You will be rewarded for this in your future life."

"And then, of course, nona, unscrupulous people will descend like hawks to offer those people nothing for their lands, their shops."

"How terrible, Chandralal, how terrible. One thing I can say for myself is I have always offered a fair price."

"Yes, nona, you are both fair and generous. You will be rewarded, too, in your future life."

And so in this hideous, sanctimonious way, my grandmother would convince herself of the righteousness of her actions, the blamelessness of her dealings, that if anyone had been wronged it was herself, for giving that family a better price than they would have got otherwise.

I know now that part of my anger is because my own blindness mimics hers. That afternoon, when I went to confront my grandmother and discovered her bent over plans for her bana maduwa, I backed away, telling myself there was nothing to be done about that Tamil family. How easily I gave up my scruples for that penthouse apartment where I could live with Mili and wake up next to him in bed every morning. "No, let it be, Chandralal," I said when he wanted to tell my grandmother about the suite. "She doesn't need to know everything." He had laughed and gently punched my arm, both of us complicit in so much more than deceiving her. "What has been done cannot be reversed," I told myself after, brushing a hand across my face as if to remove an inconvenient cobweb.

Michael is wrong when he says my greatest challenge will be to win my grandmother's forgiveness. She will take me back, because I am to her like rain on parched land. The true question is how I will deal with her refusal to admit culpability in Mili's death, her impenetrable self-righteousness. I don't know how I am going to bear it, how I am going to keep loving and caring for her. I fear my failure, my anger.

As I unplug the vacuum and go upstairs, I find I am thinking of my grandmother's cousin Charles, imagining the closed-in, stubborn look on his face, the look of a person driven by blind desperation.

In the living room, I plug the vacuum in again and glance at my watch. It is four thirty in Sri Lanka and the shadows will have lengthened, the light become a deeper golden, everything moving rapidly, as it does in these final hours before sunset. Koels will have begun to call and rattle the branches. The game of cricket will have climbed in intensity, each side intent on winning before dinner, baths and homework, the sound of bat on ball frantic, the patter of feet more rapid, insincere cries of "bowled!" "caught!" "LBW!" "stumped!" immediately contested, voices quarrelsome and querulous. The servant women will have left the fences, and the sounds of cooking will have begun: the thump of pestles in mortars, sharp slice of knives on boards, shattering of coconuts, smoke from frying chilies stinging the eyes. The piano lesson will not be going well, tunes becoming more askew, notes deliberately off key, accompanied by the occasional wail of, "I want to play, I want to play, it's almost night."

My time is dwindling here and, going into the kitchen, I begin to move the vacuum rapidly back and forth, picking up rugs, slapping them into place, shoving aside a stool, a garbage pail, shoe trays in the hallway.

What I recall now is a quarrel Mili and I had over a jean jacket I bought him for a trip to Sriyani and her husband's family tea estate in the hills. When Mili took the jacket out of the bag, he held it away as if it were soiled, his smile lopsided. "Shivan," he said gently, "why did you go to such trouble? I already have a warm coat." He cocked his head at me. "My pater, after all, has that house in Nuwara Eliya. I used to spend my Aprils there."

I glared at him and tried to snatch the jacket back, but he held it out of reach with an easy laugh and said he would accept the gift.

Yet the next day, when the cars carrying Kantha workers arrived to pick me up for the trip, he had made sure to squeeze himself into a vehicle where there was no extra room. On the journey to the estate, I tried to participate in my companions' singalong to a Tom Jones tape, to laugh at their jokes, but I was seething inside. And when we got out at a higher altitude to look at the view, he, like the other guests, put on a jacket, but not the one I'd bought him.

When we reached the bungalow, Sriyani and her husband were already there to greet us. She had arranged for Mili and me to share a room, and the moment we were alone I rounded on him, whispering fiercely, "You're so ungrateful, so stupidly proud. It is love that made me buy that jacket for you, not pity. And you reward me with this coldness?"

He stood there, hands hanging by his sides, helpless, caught, as I continued to berate him, telling him how I had sacrificed my life in Canada to be with him, that he didn't seem to appreciate all I was doing for him, that despite having so much work, running around all day in the heat attending to my grandmother's affairs, I had made a special trip to numerous stores before I found him a nice jacket. "Well," I asked, when I was finally finished, "do you have nothing to say?"

He shook his head and kissed me briefly, not meeting my eyes. Then he opened his suitcase and exchanged his old jacket for the one I'd bought.

The memory makes me shudder. I am filled with repulsion at myself for the relentless way I went at him, for my blindness to the fact that everyone had picked up on our discord, my failure to understand that wearing the jacket in front of his friends, who complimented him and asked where he'd got it, was an acknowledgement of our relationship.

And suddenly I picture Mili as if he were alive today, taking his place among all the changes happening this moment in Sri Lanka; imagine him on his way home from work, weaving through the rush-hour traffic on his motorcycle, taking the shortcut that goes by the canal, past a Buddhist temple. Mili now returned from studies abroad, having capitulated after Ranjini's death and left the country. Not, however, to Canada, because in this imagining he has never met me. As he weaves his way home, the sea breeze in his hair, he is excited at the new freedoms and possibilities in the changing Sri Lanka, where, despite the current failure of the ceasefire accord, he and others like him will be able to do much good work under the new president. There he rides, back on Galle Road, past the Tamil shops and vegetarian restaurants, the sari shops and Muslim jewellers, Mili grown slightly jowly and paunchy with contentment, as he is in my dreams. It fills me with such pain but also such ridiculous joy to think of him living thus.

It is now five in the evening in Sri Lanka. The crows will have started to return to the neighbourhood trees, the bats to drift out across the city. The piano lesson will have ended and the game of cricket fallen apart in a fight, both sides swearing never to play each other again, though they will reassemble tomorrow to pick new teams, some of today's enemies ending up on the same side. Cars, motorcycles and taxis will start to bring workers home, the sound of impatient horns blaring on the main road and the revving of engines drifting faintly into my grandmother's home. Upstairs now with my vacuum cleaner, I glance at my mother's alarm clock on her bedside table. It is seven thirty, and even though I know it's only four thirty in Vancouver, I imagine Michael waking up as if it is later in the morning there; I recall how he always kisses me briefly before stumbling out of bed to switch on the kettle he filled the night before, then uses the washroom before calling out "alright" to tell me it is mine.

As I work the vacuum cleaner through my mother's and sister's rooms, I am thinking of those early days of our love, how we went to antique stores and flea markets on the weekends to look for things to make our own, how Michael would move an object from place to place in our apartment—"auditioning" it, I teased him. It has been quite a while since we went to those stores, quite a while since Michael brought anything of beauty into our apartment.

The last time was six months ago. One evening, I came into our bedroom to find him, with arms crossed, frowning at the wall, the look on his face as if he had smelt something putrid. "This wallpaper is awful," he declared. "I can't believe we've lived with it for this long."

I examined the wallpaper, not understanding his objection, having always liked its white background and restful pastel flowers. When I told him this, he waved his hand dismissively. "We need something less Edwardian, more mid-century modern."

In the days that followed, he spent hours agonizing over samples, pasting them to the walls in different places, along with paint samples for the trim. They flapped in the breeze and often ended up on the floor, where they stuck to our feet. Finally, he picked a pattern that reminded me of a Miro painting, a white background with whimsical geometric objects done in pen and ink and touched with turquoise. That Saturday, when I left to do the shopping, he looked grim in his overalls, curls tucked severely under a painter's cap. I returned to find he was not home but had left a note. He'd changed his mind and gone to see Satomi for lunch, as it was a nice sunny day. He would save the wallpapering for a rainy one.

The weekends passed, most of them rainy now, and the rolls continued to sit in a corner of our bedroom, piled there along with pasting brushes, a trough for soaking the wallpaper, large tubs of paste, a cutting guide, trimming knife, plumb line and bob, long-bladed scissors, wallpaper scraper, seam roller, and sponge. The one time I asked about his progress, Michael's face purpled with rage and he berated me for taking him for granted, listed all the improvements he had brought to the apartment and demanded to know which were mine. If I was so keen to see the paper hung, I was welcome to go ahead and do it. So the pile continued to sit in a corner, and now, added to its clutter, was that sheen objects take on when they are the repository of conflict.

The reason Michael cannot finish that task is because all those changes and beauty he brought to our life were driven by his broad flowing love towards me. He gave me all of himself, but a part of me, as he now knows, has always been absent from him. He resents my past, resents this trip, because he understands that a piece of me will always belong to my past, where he has no place. This disparity between what we can offer each other is intolerable for him, unacceptable, and that broad flowing has choked, backing up and polluting itself.

When I think now of Michael going through his morning routine without me, I know beyond doubt that, even if he cannot admit it to himself, he is relieved I am not there. I imagine him in his day without me, taking the bus across the Burrard Bridge, the sails of yachts trembling below in the sunlight, past the emerald lawns of Kitsilano and Point Grey, and out, out to the edge of the ferocious Pacific Ocean. And I imagine him, in the coming weekend, going to that cluttered corner of our bedroom and falling to his knees, wisps of curls escaping from beneath his painter's cap. He unfurls the lovely wallpaper to examine its beauty before he begins the task before him.

I am done all my chores and the vacuum cleaner is back in the hallway closet. The kitchen looks so immaculate, so sterile, it is as if people no longer live here. Not a salt shaker on the counter, not a box of cereal or cookies in the cupboards, not a plate or a glass in the draining rack. In the living room, the *TV Guide* no longer lies splayed on the coffee table, the paper rack is empty. The TV and VCR remotes are carefully lined up beside the television. It looks like the house of someone who has died, displayed for sale. I move towards the stairs, finally ready to enter my grandmother's room. As I go up, one hand clutches the banister, the other rests on my right knee, as if I need help to raise my leg at each step. What I am thinking of now is that naked peréthi, how, despite knowing better, she would be driven by hunger to reach for the delicious array of dishes at her table—and I can imagine my grandmother's voice telling that story.

"Ah, Puthey, three times a day, three times, her servants would lay that table. They were peréthayas as well, because of past crimes, reborn as slaves and faceless, as if a wall of flesh had grown over their features, just little holes for breathing, nothing else. These wraiths would drift in three times a day to lay that table, which stretched the length of the room and was covered in an immaculate white cloth. And three times a day the peréthi's agony would rise to new heights as she walked around the table and looked at the saffron-infused rice cooked in a rich lamb's broth; vegetables steamed with a paste of almonds and cashews; chunks of mutton and chicken covered in a golden butter sauce; cauliflower cooked in a gravy made from crushed pomegranate seeds; a dish of fresh leaves from a magical plant found only in the Himalayas that when eaten released an inner coolness throughout the day. Then there were the desserts. A creamy curd with pistachios and steamed lemon rind cut into diamond shapes; semolina with honey, cardamom seeds and anise, made into balls and fried; carrot halva with poppy seeds.

"And as the peréthi walked around the table, her hunger would grow, until finally she would reach for one of the dishes with a cry of anguish and like a savage cram her mouth, hoping that just once the curse would be lifted, that just for one minute she might taste the food. But the instant the food was in her mouth, it would turn into the filth of feces and urine. And she would spit out the foulness, maggots wriggling between her teeth.

"And then, Puthey, the nights, oh, how awful those long nights were, for she had to lie on a hard plank of a bed, because, as part of her karma's curse, any cloth, even sheets, even a mattress, would burn her body. She would lie on that bed and look out her window at the moon, imagining all the people of the world, the gods in the heavens, asleep in their luxurious bedding of soft cotton sheets and down-filled mattresses. At midnight, a cold, cold wind would come off the sea, and she would hug her naked body, trembling. Soon the cold would become unbearable, and she would rise and go to an antechamber where garments hung in rows with enough room between them so she could pass without touching the cloth. She would walk up and down, up and down, looking at those fine Benares silks, those shawls and shifts made from the wool of pashmina goats, those cotton gowns so gauzy and light, patterned with tiny flowers and paisleys, those heavier silks woven with real gold thread. And finally her craving for beauty, for warmth, would overcome sense. She would seize a garment and hurriedly slip it on. Now the curse of her karma allowed her a moment in which to feel the soft brush of wool and silk on her skin, this respite of warmth and beauty really a greater punishment when snatched from her. For soon heat rushed through the cloth as if a live thing, and she would hurriedly start to pull the garment off. But every time she touched the cloth her hands would sear. The garment would burn her body like a hot sheet of metal. The peréthi could do nothing but scream until her slaves came to strip her naked again.

"But then, finally, one day, that ship carrying the disciple of our Lord Buddha came drifting, storm-tossed, to her island."

And I imagine my grandmother leaving the story there so I can finish the tale in my head, and winking at me, a child again, seated on that mat in her bedroom.

The memory of my grandmother's voice, her gestures, are with me now as I sit on her new bed and watch the grey light come into this room. I think again of her bedroom in Sri Lanka, its teak four-poster bed with mosquito netting that spills down on all sides; her heavy almirahs that release an odour of camphor and cloves when opened; her art deco ebony vanity table that was her husband's bridal gift and which she keeps polished and oiled; the old chests with their elaborately carved brass handles and locks, their massive oiled keys, each trunk placed, in the traditional way, on a woven red-and-white coconut-frond mat; her lace curtains that rise and fall with a sigh in the sea breeze.

By contrast, this new room is joyless, despite my mother's attempts to make it cheerful—despite the lovely wallpaper with its design of Chinese pagodas and birds of paradise, the goose-down pillows and duvet, the frilly pillowcases, the vase for flowers, the well-padded armchair. For this is the room where my grandmother is coming to die. The metal bed has an adjustable railing that slides up and down so that when she is finally too frail to get around, she can be bathed and given a bedpan. The head of the bed can be raised so the patient might be propped up and fed. A bell hangs from a cord.

Yet I know by now that my grandmother will not use this room, will not die in this country.

This understanding has revealed itself to me not in a flash, but slowly through the course of the night, like the persistent lap of waves that wear down the surface of a rock to reveal the glittering mica beneath. It is my fate to remain in Sri Lanka so she can pass her last years in her own home. It is I who must give up Michael, not he who will leave me; I who must break us out of our cycle of anger, then peace, then anger again. This time, I will save the person I cherish most by giving him up. My past has tainted Michael, changed him from the man who opened his door, his life, to me two years ago, wearing that ridiculous batik shirt to impress. He has become someone he does not recognize. And I, like that naked peréthi, will find release only by offering it to another, by putting another before myself.

In Sri Lanka it will be late evening now, and in my grandmother's house the light will be receding rapidly from the verandah, chased across the garden by shadows. The sky will be burning with oranges and reds and golden yellows. In the kitchen, the grinding of the miris gala and the thump of the pestle and mortar will have grown more hurried. Sinhala film music will drift in from the servants' quarters next door. The last of the commuters will be straggling home and the last crows heading to their banyan trees. The sound of water and children's voices will ring hollow in bathrooms and drift out through windows. Now that she is unable to visit the temple anymore, is my grandmother in bed or seated on the verandah listening to pirith on the radio? Is she chanting along to it?

Soon I will take my place in her world, and there will be little that is joyful about doing so. My days will be as dull as they were before I met Mili—long evenings of sitting at the dining table, eating slowly and reading to make the hours pass. All those people I knew, those actors in the drama of that long-ago summer—I have no idea what has become of them, who among them is alive.

The one person I have scoured the Sri Lankan newspapers to find is Sriyani. Human rights activists are freer to express themselves under this new government, and there are many articles and pronouncements from them, especially since the war recommenced. I search these pieces carefully, but find no trace of her. The JVP, I know, were punitive with left-leaning academics, journalists and politicians they deemed traitors. The communist man's daughter might, I fear, have been on their list of enemies.

The only person I have discovered much about, because any reading of Sri Lankan news brings one ultimately to his name, is Chandralal. He has switched sides and is prominent in the current government, no doubt arriving there by doing the dirty work of the powerful. He is occasionally quoted making pious platitudes about the triumphant destiny of the Sinhala race, making declarations about embracing the Tamil race as part of Mother Lanka. Sahodara, sahodari—brother, sister—he calls them, while at the same time valorizing the war for peace. I shudder to think that I am willingly committing myself to a place where the derangement of a Chandralal is seen as sanity; committing myself to a world of security checks, disappearing Tamils and suicide bombers. I am giving up Michael, our apartment with its sea view, our weekends together, our peaceful evening routine, my prestigious position in the university for the whirlwind of this war. "Turn back, turn back," a voice within me cries. But as in my grandmother's story of King Nandaka, the road behind me has disappeared.

My mother's car is pulling up in the driveway. I get my coat from the closet. As I slip it on, I look at myself in the mirrored doors. I seem bleached out, as if my skin has developed a greyish undertone over the course of the night. But there is also a calm within me now, the inner stillness of someone who has finally given up, who has stopped clinging to the ridiculous notion that he, or any of us really, can avoid our fate. My mind is light, as if released from a sharp and overwhelming pain, and soaring, soaring like that hawk.

"Shivan," my mother calls as she comes through the door. "Shivan."

"I am here, Amma. Yes, I am here." I catch the rictus of terror on my face as I turn from the mirrors. Taking hold of our suitcases, I settle my back into the base of my spine. Then, chin lifted, I pick up the bags and go towards the door, staggering under the heavy load of them.

ACKNOWLEDGEMENTS

My thanks to:

Early readers Anar Ali, Judy Fong Bates, Catherine Bush, Andrew Champion (who suggested giving Hema and Daya their own voices), Tissa and Lilani Jayatilaka, Will Schwalbe.

Ashok Ferry for information on construction Sri Lanka-style. Rishika Williams for some important thoughts on Renu's Canadian life.

I am particularly indebted to Ranjini Obeyesekere for her marvellous translations of Buddhist Stories in the *Jewels of the Doctrine* and *Portraits of Buddhist Women*, and also for her general guidance in terms of Buddhist stories. Without her translations and advice, this book would have taken a very different direction.

A very special thank you to my editor Lynn Henry at Doubleday Canada for all her insights and guidance. Also thanks to the Doubleday team. My agent Bruce Westwood for his support over the years. Somak Ghoshal at Penguin India.

Lovely places where I stayed and wrote: The magical Civitella Ranieri Foundation (particular thanks to Dana Prescott and the rest of the staff there). The equally lovely Green College at UBC (particular thanks to Mark Vassey, the Principal), where I was writer in residence during the editing of this book. Thanks also to Geoffrey Dobbs for three weeks at The Sun House, and the Fundación Valparaiso.

The Canada Council for the Arts, the Ontario Arts Council and the Toronto Arts Council for their generosity and support. Also the University of Guelph where I was writer in residence during the writing of this novel.

The quote from Kalidasa's *Shakuntala* is based on *The Recognition of Sakunatala*, translated by W.J. Johnson (Oxford World Classics). I have changed the translation slightly to reflect more strongly the combination of predestination and free will that is a theme of the play, the Buddhist stories in this novel, and indeed my novel itself. Many thanks to Professor Adheesh Sathaye at the University of British Columbia's Asian Studies Department for affirming that my change does not dishonour the Sanskrit original. The line on page 143 from the story of the Naga King Manikantha and the Hermit, is taken from *Indian Serpent Lore or the Nagas in Hindu Legend and Art* by J. Vogel.

A NOTE ABOUT THE TYPE

The body of *The Hungry Ghosts* has been set in Adobe Garamond. Designed for the Adobe Corporation by Robert Slimbach, the fonts are based on types first cut by Claude Garamond (c.1480–1561). Garamond was a pupil of Geoffrey Tory and is believed to have followed classic Venetian type models, although he did introduce a number of important differences, and it is to him that we owe the letterforms we now know as "old style." Garamond gave his characters a sense of movement and elegance that ultimately won him an international reputation and the patronage of Frances I of France.